MIND GAMES

ARCANE CASEBOOK 4

DAN WILLIS

Print Edition – 2020

Initial Edits by Barbara Davis
Edited by Stephanie Osborn

Cover by Mihaela Voicu

Published by

Dan Willis
Spanish Fork, Utah.

1

SHELL OF THE TORTOISE

Alex Lockerby picked up his kit bag and stepped out of a cab and into the chilly October air. He buttoned the flap across the top of his trench coat and shivered as he pulled his billfold from his pocket.

"Keep the change," he said, passing a fiver to the pockmarked cabbie.

The man thanked him and pulled away from the curb, leaving Alex standing in the center of an upper-middle class neighborhood in the west side mid-ring. Neat houses lined each side of the street with well-kept lawns, picket fences, and flowerbeds that hadn't completely lost the bloom of summer. Indeed, the only things out of place in this idyllic scene were the half-dozen police cars pulled up in front of house number 3476.

The one nearest to the spot where the cabbie had left Alex was the dark green, 1930 Ford coupe belonging to Danny Pak. It gleamed in the morning light, showing off a fresh coat of wax and there wasn't any mud on the fenders. Danny took good care of his baby.

The car had been a gift from his father to celebrate

Danny's graduation from college. Alex felt a momentary pang of jealousy for his friend. For the majority of his life, Alex had never had enough money to afford such a luxury. He could probably buy a car now; there just wasn't any real reason to do so—between the cabs and the crawlers, getting around in New York was pretty easy. And then there was the fact that Danny Pak's father was the head of the Japanese mafia in Manhattan. Alex's father had died a poor runewright when Alex was 15. All things considered, however, Alex wondered if he hadn't gotten the better deal in the end.

A policeman in a heavy blue uniform coat stood at the end of the paved walk that led to the front door of 3476. He had a pug nose and a scar that crossed his left cheek as if he'd been in a knife fight. As Alex approached, his face twisted into a sour expression.

"What are you doing here, scribbler?" he rumbled in a baritone voice.

"Nice to see you too, Wilkins," Alex said. "Why have they got an important guy like you out here?"

Wilkins grinned, showing a row of fairly white teeth.

"I'm here to keep out the riff-raff," he said, putting out a hand to stop Alex from passing.

Alex knew very well that the detectives had a habit of using Wilkins to keep curious onlookers at bay. His scarred face and sour disposition made him the perfect man for that kind of work.

"Sorry to disappoint you," Alex said, stepping around the outstretched hand. "But I've been invited to this party."

A shadow of indecision crossed Wilkins' face as if he were weighing the amount of trouble he might get in if he held up Alex just for the fun of it. He must have judged that it wasn't worth it, because as Alex passed him, he shrugged and jerked his thumb over his shoulder.

"Your boy is in there," he grumbled.

"You mean Detective Pak," Alex said, putting emphasis on the word 'detective.'

"Uh, yeah," the cop said, straightening up.

Most people didn't have a very high opinion of the Japanese, but Danny had proven himself to be a damn good cop. He'd earned the rank of detective and Alex wasn't about to let a slob like Wilkins forget it.

Satisfied, Alex turned toward the house. It was neat and orderly, with blue painted boards and white shutters. The front door was open, and he could see into a small parlor with a kitchen table beyond that. The parlor had a couch and a comfortable and well-used-looking chair around a coffee table with several books and periodicals on it. A liquor cabinet stood against the far wall with a decent selection of bottles lined up neatly inside. An end table next to the chair had a book with a bookmark sticking out of it and the remains of a cigar in an ash tray. Everything appeared neat, clean, and orderly.

Everything except the body on the floor.

He was an older man, maybe in his forties or early fifties, with dark hair going gray at the temples. He wore a smoking jacket that reminded Alex of the one Iggy wore, over a white shirt and black trousers, with shiny black shoes. He lay on his back near the opening to the kitchen at the back of the little house and his face bore a look of shock and surprise as he stared sightlessly up at the ceiling.

"Good, you made it," Danny Pak said, coming into the parlor from the kitchen as Alex reached the front door. He had just passed his thirtieth birthday but still looked as much like a college kid as ever. His face was long, with sharp cheekbones, almond shaped eyes, and an infectious smile. As usual, his gold detective shield was clipped to the breast pocket of his dark gray suit coat and he carried a flip notebook in his hand.

"So this is the guy we've been waiting on?" a second man said, moving into the parlor behind Danny. He was short and plump with reddish-brown hair and a freckled nose in the middle of his wide, pale face. Like Danny, he wore a gold detective shield on his suit coat.

"Detective Leonard O'Rourke," Danny said, indicating the pale man. "Meet Alex Lockerby, Private Detective."

O'Rourke pulled an exasperated face, but then nodded in Alex's direction.

"Leonard O'Rourke?" Alex said, raising an eyebrow.

"It's short for Leonardo," O'Rourke said. "My mother's Italian. Now can we get on with this?"

"Leonard here is a newly promoted detective," Danny said with an exasperated eye roll. "I'm supposed to be showing him the ropes."

Alex ran his gaze over the young detective again. He clearly thought Danny was wasting their time; his face was a mask of arrogance and disdain.

Probably doesn't think much of Asians, he thought.

"What's the trouble?" Alex said, turning to Danny.

"Meet Henry Scutter," Danny said, nodding to the corpse. "He's the junior manager at West Side Bank. Late last night someone shot him."

"And stole his cash," O'Rourke added, as if that statement explained everything.

"So you're thinking a simple robbery," Alex said, nodding as if he agreed.

"It's obvious," the young detective said. "The city's full of desperate people. Seems like every week there's a new Hooverville springing up in a vacant lot."

As the economic depression stretched into its second decade, cities like New York were fast becoming camps of desperate men and women. Dubbed the Forgotten by the papers, their ranks seemed to increase every year.

"One of them probably just went door to door 'til someone answered," O'Rourke went on. "Whoever it was threatens our victim but Scutter makes a run for it and boom, he gets shot in the back

Alex looked around the neat and orderly parlor, then back to the body.

"Why would he run if the person at the door had a gun?" he asked.

Danny stepped back into the kitchen, then re-emerged holding a .45 Colt revolver.

"We found this on the kitchen counter," he said.

"Scutter obviously thought he could get to it in time to defend himself," O'Rourke said.

"Did he have anything on him?" Alex asked Danny.

His friend indicated a table beside the door where a ring of keys, a small leather bag, a book of matches, and a billfold had been laid out in a neat row.

"The wallet's empty," O'Rourke said, but Alex reached for the leather bag instead. He picked it up, then set it down again, before turning back to the young detective.

"I'm afraid your theory doesn't hold water, detective," he said, flashing O'Rourke the most insincere smile he could muster.

"Oh, yeah?" he grumbled. "How do you figure?"

Alex picked up the leather bag again and tossed it to him, as O'Rourke caught it, it made a clinking sound.

"No desperate Forgotten man would miss taking his change purse," Alex said. "Also, there's a cabinet full of spirits right there that hasn't been touched." He indicated the liquor cabinet. "Nobody living on the streets would leave that un-plundered, not with the temperature dropping down below freezing every night."

Danny nodded sagely. "Someone desperate would have taken something to help him keep warm."

O'Rourke looked unconvinced.

"Maybe he'd never shot anyone before," he said. "When the gun went off he was scared someone might have heard it and ran a soon as he got the cash."

Alex nodded as if he agreed, then slowly changed to shaking his head.

"I supposed that could be," he admitted. "Until you take into account that Mr. Scutter here was shot by someone he knew."

Both Danny and O'Rourke looked surprised at that.

"I heard you were a runewright," O'Rourke sneered. "Not a clairvoyant."

Alex laughed.

"Nothing supernatural about simple deduction," he said. "Look at the body."

O'Rourke looked down, then shrugged.

"So?"

"So, if he were going for his gun, he'd have been running, don't you think?"

O'Rourke shrugged again, then nodded.

"And if he'd been shot in the back while running, he'd have fallen forward," Alex indicated a spot just inside the kitchen. "And landed on his face. Scutter must have been walking when he was shot, and he fell backwards."

"So the guy shot him before he could run," O'Rourke said with another shrug. "So what?"

"So why did Scutter turn his back on a man with a gun?" Alex said.

"Because he knew him," Danny said with a nod. "A man who worked at a bank and kept a gun handy would never turn his back on a stranger."

Detective O'Rourke looked flustered and his face had gone a bit red, but he rallied.

"Well, if this wasn't about money, what was it about?" he demanded.

"Where's the dog?" Alex asked.

"Huh?" O'Rourke and Danny said in unison.

Alex pointed to one of the pictures on the wall. In it, Scutter knelt behind a reddish-brown German shepherd.

"That one looks recent," Alex said, comparing the face of the man in the photo with the real one on the floor. "So where's the dog?"

"Any of you boys see a dog?" Danny yelled to the cops who were going through the back rooms of the house.

"There's a doghouse out back, but I don't see a dog," came the reply from a cop in the kitchen.

Alex followed Danny and O'Rourke through the kitchen and out into the small backyard. Like the front, it was neat and orderly with a small tool locker up against the rear of the house and a doghouse back by the corner. The grass was lush from the fall moisture except for a circular spot of dirt that seemed to center on the front of the doghouse.

As the trio approached, Alex could see an iron spike that had been driven into the ground near the center of the dirt circle. Attached to it, a heavy chain ran inside the little house.

"Hold it," Alex said once they were about ten feet away. A rusty stain marred the dirt on one side of the circle. "I think that's blood."

"That would explain why the dog isn't barking," Danny said, approaching with caution.

Alex circled around the stain, looking along the line between it and the opening of the doghouse.

"The dog's in there," he said. "Be careful, it might not be dead."

Danny pulled his service revolver and moved carefully toward the opening.

"There's more blood here," he said, pointing to a smeared

line just before the entrance. It looks like our shooter took care of the dog and it crawled inside." He ducked down, then quickly pulled his head back. When no sound came from inside, he took a longer look. "Dead," he pronounced. "Looks like it was shot in the chest, just below the right leg."

"How do you shoot the underside of a dog?" O'Rourke asked.

"You wait till it rears up at the end of its chain," Danny said, standing up so Alex could take a look.

Inside the doghouse, a German Shepard lay on its side. Alex could clearly see the hole in its body. Dark blood clotted and matted the fur around the wound, running down to a sticky pool on the wooden floor. There was blood on the dog's muzzle and Alex reached up to pry its mouth open.

"What are you doing?" O'Rourke asked, stooping down to peer over Alex's shoulder.

"Well," Alex said, extracting some tissue from between the dog's teeth. "Unlike people, dogs don't brush their teeth."

"And?"

Alex backed out of the door, holding the chunk he'd pulled from the dog out into the sunlight for a better look.

"And I was hoping our dead pooch took a bite of whoever shot him, but it doesn't look that way. This is a chunk of fur."

"Probably licked the place where the bullet hit him," Danny said with sigh. "So no real mystery here."

"Well, you're right about that," Alex said, holding the chunk of fur over for Danny to look at. "There's no mystery. This tells us why Scutter, and more importantly his dog, was killed."

O'Rourke laughed out loud at that.

"You're dreaming, scribbler," he scoffed.

Danny looked just as confused, but clearly didn't want to agree with his trainee so he settled for shooting Alex a questioning glance.

"This hair is from a cat," Alex said. "Specifically a tortoiseshell."

"I thought tortoises were reptiles," O'Rourke said, and Alex tried not to roll his eyes.

"How do you know that?" Danny pressed.

"I've tracked down a lot of lost pets in my time," Alex said. "Tortoiseshells are prized by cat fanciers for their color, or rather colors. They resemble the colors on the backs of giant turtles." He indicated the fur. "I see at least three colors of hair here, an orangey-brown, mud-brown, and a yellowish-gold."

"And those are the colors of a tortoiseshell cat?" O'Rourke asked.

Alex nodded.

"Look here," Danny said, crouching down in the center of the dirt circle. He pointed to the stub of a wooden stake that had broken off flush with the ground. "I bet Scutter's dog broke loose and chased down one of the neighbor's cats."

"And caught him," Alex added. "Later, Scutter secured the dog with that metal spike."

"The neighbor comes home," Danny said, picking up the narrative. "He finds his cat dead, then comes over to confront Scutter about it."

"And he shoots his neighbor over a cat?" O'Rourke said, incredulously.

"You don't own a pet, do you, detective? " Alex said with a chuckle. "If you did, you'd know that people get weird and stupid when it comes to their pets. A rich guy once paid me a C-note to track down a tiny little dog that looked like an overgrown rat."

"All right," Danny said, standing up from his examination of the broken stake. "O'Rourke, take some of the boys and re-canvass the block. Find out who owns...or owned...a tortoise-shell cat."

9

O'Rourke looked like he wanted to say something, but just nodded and turned on his heel.

"Thanks," Danny said once he was out of earshot.

"You need to rein that kid in," Alex said. "You're the senior detective here."

"He's not too keen on me," Danny said with a shrug. "Since he wouldn't listen to me, I figured I'd let you put him in his place."

"So this isn't an officially sanctioned police case?"

"No," Danny admitted. "But I'll owe you one."

Alex grinned tightly. Without sanction from the Central Office, he wouldn't be able to bill the department for his time. It didn't matter really; he and Danny always had each other's backs.

"I'll hold you to that," he promised as they headed back to the house.

2

THE ROW

Forty minutes later Alex got out of a cab in Midtown, right on the border of the middle and outer rings. The rings were narrow enough here that he could see the Central Office of Police off in the distance toward the park, and he turned his collar up against the wind as he headed north along the east side of Second Avenue.

An industrial building occupied most of the block, so there were no storefronts along the street. Instead a series of pushcarts were lined up along the side of the building, where street vendors sold their wares. Known as Runewright Row, it housed most of the city's more talented runewrights and many people who sold the various supplies runewrights needed.

Alex often came down here to buy simple inks, pens, and the flash paper he used in his rune work. Lately, however, he'd been coming by almost every day to see Marnie.

Marnie Talbot had never been a very good runewright, but for the last thirty years or so she'd eked out a living on Runewright Row selling whatever runes she could manage. She did have a natural gift for conversation that not only drew people in, but had them coming back again. Marnie was a natural-born saleswoman. If she'd had more talent as a runewright, she probably could have opened a dedicated shop instead of standing by a cart on the roadside year after year.

"And how is my best girl today?" Alex asked as he approached the wheeled cart where Marni sold her wares.

Looking up, she scoffed at him and rolled her eyes. She had a round face with dark skin and eyes, and a mass of kinky black hair she kept tied back, behind her head. Alex guessed she was in her fifties, but her hair showed no signs of gray and her eyes and wits were sharp.

"I've known lots of fancy men like you, Alexander Lockerby," she said with mock indignation. "You only want one thing from me."

Reaching down, she pulled out a shiny blue thermos bottle from under her cart and plunked it down next to a display of her runes for sale.

"You know me too well," Alex said, putting his kit bag down next to the thermos. Reaching into his bag, Alex pulled out an identical thermos, but painted red.

"Is that all you've got for me?" Marnie asked, eyeing Alex with suspicion.

Alex had expected her reaction, and he reached back into his bag, pulling out a small, yellow envelope. Inside were a dozen runes that were too complex for Marnie to write, but had taken Alex all of fifteen minutes to complete. He almost felt guilty at how easy it was for him to do things that most runewrights on the Row couldn't manage at all, but that was the nature of magic. Sorsha Kincaid could do things with a snap of her fingers that Alex couldn't manage with a year's preparation, so it was all relative.

"These should bring a good price," he said, handing the envelope over. "I threw in a couple of restoration runes, and a cleaning rune."

"Bless you," Marnie said, taking the red thermos.

Alex had happened upon Marnie when he'd come to the Row for a couple new packs of flash paper. Of all the rune vendors, Marnie had the one thing no one else could provide for him...good coffee.

Her mother had been a cook on a Mississippi riverboat and she'd learned how to brew coffee that was just shy of legendary. Much to Alex's delight, Marnie's mother taught her daughter all her secrets, and now Marnie brewed coffee right at her cart with the aid of a boiler stone. Ever since Alex had discovered her talents, he'd been coming back every day with an envelope of runes and an empty thermos. He harbored a secret fear that one day some fancy hotel would steal her away for its kitchen, but so far, most people in New York just thought of coffee as something you drank in the morning.

To Alex, coffee was art, and Marnie was DaVinci.

"How are things?" he asked as he reverently placed the full thermos into his bag. He asked the question more out of habit than any desire to engage in a serious conversation, but his attention snapped into focus when Marnie's face fell.

"It's getting pretty thin out here," she said, in a hushed whisper, as if she feared being overheard by the fat balding man in the apron manning the next cart over. "Folks don't need runes much in times like these. Then there's those books keeping people away."

"Books?"

Marnie's face screwed up into a look of disbelief.

"You know," she said as if that explained everything. "Those rune books they've been selling in the five and dimes. I hear they have five minor mending runes in them for a dollar."

That didn't sound right. Mending runes were the staple of a runewright's business. They could fix a cracked cup, restore the handle to a broken pan, or mend a rip in a coat or a pair of trousers. Good mending runes went for at least a dollar apiece and even minor-mending runes cost a quarter. If Marnie was right, whoever was making these books was giving one rune away for free.

"Look around," Marnie whispered, casting a wary eye up the street. "There's a bunch of us that have already gone under."

Alex followed her gaze up the Row. He didn't know everyone here, and some people only came once or twice a week, but the carts did seem further apart than usual and there seemed to be fewer shoppers than he remembered.

He looked back to Marnie to ask more about these mysterious rune books, when a young woman approached the cart. She was a little shorter than average, maybe five foot three or so, with the bronze skin common to the Mediterranean region. Her hair was long and glossy black, and it contrasted well with her blue eyes. She wore tastefully understated makeup, with dark lipstick and only a hint of rouge that gave her a look of innocence that bordered on purity.

"Excuse me," she said in a bright, clear voice. "Someone said you sell coffee here, is that right?"

Alex didn't know who this young woman was, but he decided he liked her.

Marnie took out an old, worn thermos, unscrewed the lid, and poured the contents into a paper cup. Normally she'd put the paper cup into a pewter mug to make it easy to hold without burning yourself, but with the chill weather a hot cup was welcome.

"Is there anything particular you were looking for, dearie?" Marnie asked as she passed the cup over.

"Actually, I need a cleaning rune," she said, her cheeks going a bit pinker than her rouge. "I'm looking for work as a secretary and I got a stain on my best blouse."

Alex marveled that this young woman was having

trouble finding work. Of course the depression left many people out of work, but she was quite pretty and spoke with confidence. She was no Leslie, of course, but then no one was.

Marnie was already starting to haggle with the woman for the cleaning rune that Alex had given her, so he picked up his bag. Before he could head back to the street, the woman touched his sleeve.

"Excuse me," she said. "Would you happen to know anyone looking to hire a secretary? I'm well qualified and have references."

"Uh," Alex said, displaying that rapier wit he was so well known for. "I'm sorry, Miss..."

"Knox," she said with a wide smile full of straight, white teeth. "Sherry Knox."

"Well, Miss Knox, I don't know anyone who's looking right now, I'm sorry."

A look of genuine confusion crossed Sherry's face, as if she hadn't expected that Alex's answer was even a possibility. It was gone just as quickly, replaced by her pleasant smile as she fished in her handbag for a paper card.

"Well if you hear of anything, Mr..."

"Lockerby. Alex Lockerby."

"If you hear of anything, Mr. Lockerby, would you be kind enough to let me know?"

Alex accepted the card, turning it up to read. The image of a crystal ball was printed on the front next to the name Madame Hortense, seer of seers. Underneath the name Sherry Knox and a phone number had been written in ink.

"I tell fortunes down at the Museum of Oddities," she said in answer to his questioning look.

"Sounds like you've already got a job," he said, slipping the card into the pocket of his trench coat. "How come you're out looking for another?"

"Fortune telling is nice," Sherry said with a grin and a wink. "But there's no future in it."

Alex chuckled at the joke.

"All right, Miss Knox," he said. "If I hear of anything, I'll pass it on."

She thanked him and then turned back to Marnie to pay for her coffee and the cleaning rune. Alex watched her for a moment. She was slim and well-proportioned and he already knew she had a sense of humor.

With a sigh, Alex turned and walked toward the corner where he could hail a cab. It had been over a year since Jessica's death and he still felt it. He still compared every woman he met to her. Sherry Knox seemed like a perfectly nice girl, and she was easy to look at...but she wasn't Jessica.

As Alex climbed into a cab and sent it off in the direction of his office, he wondered if anyone ever would measure up.

Twenty minutes later, Alex stepped off the third floor landing and turned toward his office door. He pulled out his pocket watch and pressed the crown, flipping the lid open. Unlike most watches, Alex's pocket watch had four hands inside, in addition to the tiny glowing runes that would grant him access to the brownstone where he lived. Three of the hands were the normal ones any watch would have; hour, minute, and second. The fourth hand was made of glowing red magic. Unlike the normal hands, this one ran counterclockwise, from twelve all the way around to one.

As Alex checked the time, the red hand was pointing to about the seven-minute mark. When Alex had been granted a new lease on life by his mysterious British benefactor, the man had said he'd given Alex a whole year. Alex's mentor, Iggy, had taken that as a challenge and over the course of a couple of months, he cooked up the construct that created the red hand. Whenever Alex opened the watch, the rune would sense his life energy and position the hand accordingly. With the hand pointing between the one and the two, it meant that Alex had a little over one month of life left.

He snapped the watch closed with a shudder. It was both liberating and terrifying knowing more or less how much time remained in your life. He and Iggy had been working feverishly to try to replicate the Brit's life transference rune, but so far, they hadn't cracked it. Every time Alex checked his watch, he was reminded that they were quickly running out of time.

"Well here you are," Leslie growled at him when Alex stepped through the door.

Leslie Tompkins had been Alex's secretary for almost ten years, and she was the heart of Alex's business. A former beauty queen from Iowa, Leslie had the looks of a woman half her age; statuesque with hazel eyes and auburn hair. She also had a great head for business and was responsible for managing the day to day operation of Lockerby Investigations.

"Did you at least solve that case for Danny?" she snapped at him before he could respond.

"I did," he said, knowing she wasn't about to like what would come next.

"But?" she said, sensing bad news on the horizon.

"It's not a paying job this time."

Leslie's face soured and her right eyebrow went up as she scrutinized him.

"That's some friend you've got," she said at last.

"You know Danny's good for work," he said, waving her objections aside. "What's this all about?"

She glared at him, then sat down behind her desk and pretended to make notes on her pad.

"None of your business," she growled.

Alex had known Leslie a long time and he knew that 'none of your business' meant that she was having trouble with Randall again. Randall Walker was the assessor for Suffolk County and he and Leslie had fallen madly in love a couple of years back. Unfortunately, Randall had a couple of kids at home and they objected to his marrying Leslie. While that was good for Alex, it was hell on Leslie, and Alex hated that. He did, however, keep his nose out of it at Leslie's request.

"Well," he said, changing the subject. "You'll be much happier when you see what I brought you." He pulled the thermos out his bag and held it up like a trophy.

As Alex had predicted, Leslie's angry expression melted away to be replaced by a wide smile.

"Ooo," she cooed. "You're forgiven."

Alex put the thermos on her desk and added two new packs of cigarettes.

"You do know how to pamper me," Leslie said as she retrieved a pair of mugs from the middle drawer of one of the office filing cabinets. She opened one of the cigarette packs while Alex poured the coffee.

"Any calls this morning?" he asked as he passed her a mug and she passed him a lit cigarette.

"Yes," she said, some of her old irritation threatening to return. "A couple of important ones, too. I managed to put them off, but I promised to call back as soon as you came in."

Alex sighed and picked up his kit bag.

"Well, you'd better get started," he said, heading for his office. "I'll be writing up the report on the Walker case so just send the first one in when they get here."

"Yes, boss," Leslie called.

Alex sat at his desk staring at the bill he was supposed to be preparing for Caroline Walker. She was a flighty woman with more dollars than sense who believed her short, chubby, balding husband was having an affair. Alex had followed the man for the better part of a week and learned that, once Caroline went to bed, her husband snuck out of the house and went to a quiet bar near their home to read. Alex had even stuck up a casual conversation with the man during one of these outings where he confessed to reading at the bar just to get some peace away from his wife.

He sighed and shook his head as he tried to refocus on the work. It was quite a mess. He almost felt like he'd be doing the unfortunate man a favor if he reported an affair to Caroline.

Before he could ruminate on the implications of that thought, his intercom buzzed.

"Yes," he replied, grateful for the interruption.

"Bishop Cosgrove of the Manhattan Diocese is here to see you," Leslie's voice answered.

Alex hesitated for a moment. He knew that name. Bishop Cosgrove had been Father Harry's superior in the church. Alex had no idea what the Bishop wanted, but he felt sure he wouldn't be interested. Still, the morning had been a bust so far, so he put aside his animus and pressed the key on the front of the intercom box.

"Send him in."

A moment later a short, thin man in a black suit came in. He was entirely bald with brown eyes and white eyebrows in his wrinkled forehead. The suit he wore was of good quality, but not particularly fine or extravagant and he wore the black shirt and white collar that signified his calling. A pair of spectacles were perched on his nose and had the effect of making his eyes seem overlarge and owl-like.

"Mr. Lockerby?" he asked in a soft, tenor voice.

Alex stood and motioned the bishop into one of the two chairs that sat facing his desk.

"How can I help you, Bishop?" he asked, returning to his own seat.

"You are the Alex Lockerby who was taken in by Father Harrison Clementine?" Cosgrove asked, leaning forward in the chair as if he were eager for the answer.

"That's me," Alex said with a nod.

Cosgrove sat back, seeming visibly relieved.

"Saints be praised," he said. "I've come to you about a very serious matter," he went on. "I only hope you can help."

"Well, before we get into your problem, Bishop Cosgrove," Alex said, steepling his hands in front of his mouth as he spoke, "perhaps you could tell me exactly why I should help the man who tried to stop Father Harry from taking me in when my father died? The man who spent the last decade or so trying to throw Father Harry out and shut down the Brotherhood of Hope Mission and then did it before his body was even cold? What, exactly makes you think I'd be interested in helping you?"

3

THE FORGOTTEN

B ishop Cosgrove sat for a moment, taking in everything Alex had said. If he was offended or ruffled, he showed no sign. Alex was about to speak again when he finally sighed, and smiled sadly.

"I understand why you would believe that," he said in a quiet voice. "But like most things in life, there is more to that tale."

He paused for a moment, but Alex just raised an eyebrow, so he went on.

"It's true I tried to prevent Father Clementine from taking you in when your father died," he said. "That had nothing to do with you, and nothing to do with Harrison. It's just that a mission for the poor isn't the best place to raise a teenage boy. I was worried that your presence would distract Father Clementine from his purpose."

Alex scoffed at that.

"You should have known better," he said.

The bishop nodded sagely.

"I won't deny it," he said. "I should have known that no force on earth could turn Father Clementine aside once he'd put his feet on a righteous path. I am happy to admit that I was wrong."

Alex hadn't been expecting that. Father Harry hadn't spoken much about the bishop, but what he had said suggested that he didn't think very highly of the man. Still, Cosgrove wanted Alex's help, so he might just be saying whatever he thought would get him what he wanted.

"As for the mission," Cosgrove went on. "I heard that you visited the new facility last year."

"I saw you're calling it the Brotherhood of Hope," Alex said, trying to keep a lid on his temper.

"That was in honor of Father Clementine," Cosgrove explained. "It's the facility we wanted to build years ago for him, but he was too stubborn to give up the old building."

"Why spend the money to build a new building when the old one was working fine?" Alex asked. Try as he might, he couldn't keep the edge of sarcasm out of his voice.

The bishop actually scoffed at that.

"That old building was a wreck, as well you know," he said. "The maintenance costs just to keep it running were four times what the new building costs to run per year. I never wanted to shut down the mission, Alex. I only wanted to move it to a better facility."

Alex had been taught how to tell when people were lying. Liars tended to fidget or to not look you in the eye. During his explanation, the bishop had maintained eye contact and he sat perfectly still. If the old man was lying, he was very good at it.

"I don't need you to believe me," he said after a short pause. "I'm not here for my own sake, but rather for the people served by the mission. The people Father Clementine loved and served for most of his life."

That was a low blow, using Father Harry's work to strong-arm Alex. The galling thing was that it was working.

"What's your problem, Bishop Cosgrove?" he asked.

"I receive weekly reports from Brother Williams, one of the people who run the Mission."

Alex nodded, he'd met Brother Williams and he seemed like a decent enough fellow.

"Over the last few weeks, the number of poor souls served by the Mission has been going down."

"Isn't that a good thing?" Alex asked.

"Well, yes," Cosgrove said with an earnest nod. "We pray for the day when our services are no longer needed, but I'm sure you're aware that the economy continues to decline, and winter is coming on fast. Historically our services are more in demand now than during the warmer months."

Alex shrugged.

"You're right about it getting colder. Maybe your missing patrons decided to head south and stay warm."

"It's possible," Cosgrove admitted. "But we're missing over a hundred people, Mr. Lockerby. Men and women society has forgotten. People no one cares about but us."

"And you think something has happened to them?"

Cosgrove leaned forward in his chair.

"I don't know," he admitted. "But I haven't slept well since I learned of this."

"And you want me to find out where these forgotten people have gone?"

"Yes, Mr. Lockerby, I came to ask you to do exactly that." He paused and looked at Alex with hard eyes. "I'm not asking for myself, you understand. It doesn't matter what you may think of me. These people are called the Forgotten in the papers and it's truer than even they know." He paused and looked away toward the office window and the city beyond. "If you don't find out what happened to those missing men and women, no one else will. No one else will even look."

Alex ground his teeth. He really wanted to hate Cosgrove,

but he just couldn't bring himself to do it. Clearly he and Father Harry saw things differently, but there didn't seem to be any malice in their disagreement. Worse, the bishop was right. If something bad had happened to the Forgotten, no one would bother to find out what.

"Have you told this to the police?" he asked.

Cosgrove sighed and nodded.

"They respected my concerns, but they made it clear they have too many other cases to deal with."

Alex wasn't surprised. In a city the size of New York, the police were always busy.

"If you're worried about your fee, Mr. Lockerby, I'll be paying you," Cosgrove said. "The laborer is worthy of his hire after all."

"Luke," Alex said with a nod. "Chapter ten, verse seven."

"I see Father Clementine taught you well," Cosgrove said.

"He also taught me that a man's duty is to look after his fellow men, especially those who can't look after themselves."

"Does that mean you'll take my case?" Bishop Cosgrove asked with a faint smile.

Alex nodded.

"I'll go by the mission and talk with Brother Williams," he said. "Are there any camps near the mission?"

"Far too many," Cosgrove affirmed. "Brother Williams will be able to tell you where the closest is."

"All right, Your Eminence," Alex said, rising. "I'll ask around and see what I can find out. It will probably take me a couple of days, then I'll be in touch."

Bishop Cosgrove thanked him and Alex escorted him out.

"What was that about?" Leslie asked once the bishop was gone. She seemed to be in a better mood now that she'd had some of Marnie's coffee and a smoke.

Alex explained his errand while he lit a cigarette himself.

"You think something bad is going on?" Leslie asked.

"If you mean that someone is out there murdering the Forgotten, I doubt it," he said. "Murderers leave bodies in their wake and there's nothing in the papers about the morgue getting extra business. My money's on someone organizing a group to try to make it to Florida for the winter. I'll ask around at the mission and see what I can turn up." He headed back toward his office. "I'll also grab a few finding runes; maybe some of the mission people left something behind I can use to track them."

———

Alex tore a vault rune from his red pasteboard rune book and touched the fragile flash paper to his tongue. The moistened paper stuck to the wall when he pressed it into the middle of the painted rectangle that served as a surrogate door for the vault's magic. Touching his burning cigarette to the paper ignited it and it vanished in a burst of flame that consumed the paper utterly in less than a second. What remained was a silver triangle inscribed inside a circle. Tiny runic letters were inscribed along the inside of the circle and a smaller circle encompassed each of the triangle's three points. Each of these circles held a magic rune of its own and the runes and the characters pulsed with light for a moment before fading.

As the silver rune faded, a heavy steel door melted out of the plaster and clapboard wall, solidifying into place as if had belonged there all along. A brass plate with a large keyhole in the exact center appeared in the middle of the door and Alex withdrew the large skeleton key he kept in his trouser pocket.

Unlocking the door, he pulled it open, revealing his vault. Alex's vault was an extra-dimensional space created by his magic. Most runewrights couldn't create vaults, only the much smaller rune safes, and those that could make vaults usually made one big space where they kept their valuable supplies and did their work. Most runewrights, however, didn't have Iggy for a mentor. Iggy's vault contained an entire house, complete with a functioning kitchen, bathroom, library, parlor, bedroom, and even a surgery. Ever since Alex had first seen it, he'd aspired to create a grand vault of his own. Water and food had to be brought in and stored in a cistern and ice box respectively, but waste water could simply be flushed away into the extra-dimensional void that surrounded the vault, which made clean up easy. Alex had wondered what would happen if people kept removing water from the planet, but he doubted he and Iggy, and any other runewrights who might have discovered this, would make much of a dent.

As Alex stepped inside, the magelights in the ceiling bloomed into light. This close to Empire Tower they had plenty of power to keep them lit. What they revealed wasn't the grand vault Alex aspired to have, but rather a space that looked like it it had been the scene of an explosion in a paper mill. Almost every wall was covered with papers, stuck at odd angles, many on top of others, and all apparently without rhyme or reason. The floor was littered with crumpled and discarded papers, especially around the comfortable reading chair in his small library.

If the arrangement of the papers on the walls seemed random, the subject of each page was not. Each paper held sketches and drawings of runic symbols and runic constructs. Many were similar to each other, but none were the same and all of them represented everything Alex remembered from his encounter with the mysterious Brit a little over a year ago. That encounter had left him with another fifteen or so months of life and enough questions to fill a book.

As he entered his vault, Alex cast his eyes around at the runes adorning the walls. He understood much of what the

Brit had done, but how, exactly, he'd put all the disparate runes together into a cohesive whole still eluded Alex.

He suppressed a curse as his feet sent balls of discarded paper flying. Just over a year ago, before he met the mysterious man, he'd made peace with his reduced mortality, but now that he knew there was a way to defy that particular fate, a way that remained tantalizingly out of reach, it just made him angry.

Moving to his writing desk, Alex swept the papers containing his latest failed musings onto the floor and sat down. Finding runes were the bread and butter of his work. Most people who sought out a private detective needed something found or recovered, so Alex went through the four or five he usually kept in his red rune book fairly regularly. The good news was that he'd become so used to writing new ones that he could refill his book completely in just over an hour.

His writing desk sat next to a side table where he kept the pens, inks, and papers that he used most. Finding runes were complex, and Alex's was even more so. It started with iron-gall ink that had been infused with rust powder for the base shape, then runes done in red, ruby-infused ink for the symbols. Runic letters covered the inside of the main design and described how the magic would link the missing person or object to Alex's brass compass through an object of importance to the seeker or the missing.

It was tedious and exacting work, and Alex had to discard a failed attempt when he tried to hurry.

Take your time. Iggy's words came to his mind as he crumpled up the failed rune and tossed it on the floor with its brethren. *Hurrying makes for shoddy work and shoddy work never made a skillful runewright.*

When at last, Alex finished, he took out his red pasteboard book and turned it over. The book was held together by two short bolts that ran through the edge by the spine and ended in a pair of flat nuts. Using his fingers, Alex removed the nuts and the back cover of the book came off, revealing the inside pages, each of which had two holes in it to accommodate the bolts. He removed the pages as a whole and then took hold of the opposite edge of the pages, turning them over in his hand and shaking gently. This caused the torn bits of pages he'd removed to fall out on his desk. He thought about just sweeping these onto the floor as well, but the state of his vault had been bothering him of late, so he set down the rune pages and swept the page fragments into the little waste bin beside the writing table. He took another few minutes to gather up the sea of discarded paper and stuff them into a larger can by his vault door. Since he did all his work on flash paper a single errant spark could burn down his whole vault if he let it go too much longer.

That done, Alex peeled off the first fifteen or so pages from the pile and loaded them into the front of his book. These were the simple, everyday runes that he might need, everything from barrier runes to keep off rain to mending runes in case he tore his suit coat. Behind these went the new finding runes and finally the other more complex runes he might need. In the very back went five or so blank pages in case he needed to write a rune in the field, and lastly his stack of vault runes. With his book reassembled, Alex put on the back cover, reattached and tightened the nuts, then dropped the book into the left-hand inner pocket of his suit coat.

He paused for a moment, then picked up the scotch bottle that sat on the side table with his inks and poured himself a double. He took a sip as he looked around at the wreck of his vault. It was maddening. He and Iggy and been through the Archimedean Monograph for a year now and they still had only the roughest idea how a life transference construct worked. Draining life energy was easy, it was what got Alex into his current situation in the first place, but taking the life energy from one thing and putting it into something else? That was magic on a level Alex simply didn't understand.

"Well you'd better figure it out soon," he said, remembering the red hand on his pocketwatch. If it was accurate, he only had about six weeks of energy left. He pounded back the rest of the scotch and slammed the glass down on the angled surface of his writing table, letting it slide slowly down to bump against the pencil lip at the bottom.

Thirty minutes later, Alex got out of a cab across the street from the new *Brotherhood of Hope*. He'd been here once before, last year when he tracked Karen Burnham's grandfather to the mission. He'd met Brother Williams then as well, and he seemed a decent sort.

When the nun at the front desk finally managed to track him down, Williams looked exactly the same, a short, pudgy man with a pleasant face and an infectious smile.

"Mr. Lockerby," he said when he recognized Alex. "What brings you back to the Brotherhood of Hope?"

Alex shook the short man's hand and told him about his visit from the bishop. As he spoke, William's cheerful face slid into a worried expression.

"I don't know what to tell you," he said once Alex finished. "It's just as the bishop said. With winter coming on, we should be full up here for supper. Last year we were turning people away, but yesterday there were at least fifty empty chairs."

"Well, if you're turning people away, maybe they just decided to go somewhere else," Alex suggested.

"We haven't had to turn people away so far this year,"

Williams said with a shake of his head. "We expanded the kitchens in the spring."

"What are your patrons saying?"

"They're scared," Brother Williams said. "I've asked about those who have gone missing, but all anyone seems to know is that they're gone."

"All right," Alex said, closing his notebook. "Would you mind if I asked around here for myself? See if anyone can add anything?"

"You're always welcome," Williams said. "You might try two blocks north," he added. "There's a decent sized Hooverville there in a vacant lot."

Hoovervilles were makeshift camps of the Forgotten, named after the former President. With the police keeping the Forgotten out of Central Park, the camps were springing up wherever there was space.

Alex thanked Williams for his help, then made his way into the main hall. It was bigger than the old mission had been, almost double the space, with rows and rows of tables where the city's downtrodden could sit and eat out of the rain and cold. The benches that normally lined the tables had been set up at the far end of the hall where there was a small stage with a simple podium. Alex knew from experience that there would have been a noon Mass. Anyone was welcomed to come in out of the cold and sit; the only price was to attend the Mass.

Several dozen people were sitting at various tables and on the benches. All of them were ragged, dressed in multiple layers of whatever clothes they had. Some spoke quietly with their neighbors, while others slept in their seats, reveling in the warmth of the mission. Alex made his way over to a small group that seemed engaged in earnest conversation and began asking questions. An hour later he gave it up. Everyone in the hall knew that some of their number were gone, but everybody he talked to had a different theory.

The only consistent detail Alex could discern was that none of the mission's patrons personally knew any of the missing people. What he needed was an eyewitness, or at least someone who knew one of the missing people well.

Discouraged, Alex found Brother Williams and thanked him before heading out to locate the makeshift camp.

4
———

THE CAPTAIN

Brother Williams had said the Hooverville was two blocks north of the mission, so Alex just decided to walk. The mission was squarely in the middle of an industrial district, being surrounded by a steelworks, two warehouses, and a fish cannery. A run-down looking five and dime, that obviously catered to the industrial workers, sat kitty-corner across the street. It was in the wrong direction from the Hooverville, but Alex made for it first to stock up on cigarettes. People in Forgotten camps tended to be wary of strangers, but a stranger with a few extra smokes was always welcome.

A sour looking man with a mutton-chop beard and a greasy apron stood leaning on the counter when Alex entered. He had a copy of the Times open on the counter and he looked up with a raised eyebrow when Alex came in. In this part of town, Alex's relatively new trench coat and hat marked him as out of place.

"What can I getcha?" Mutton chops said, straightening up and trying to brush the grease stains from his apron front.

"Four packs of Lucky Strikes," Alex said. As the man

turned to pull the cigarettes out of a display case, Alex noticed a line of brown bags on a shelf behind the counter. "What are those?" he asked.

"I sell bag lunches to the shift guys," the man said. "Sandwiches with a little bag of peanuts."

"Give me two."

If the man found Alex's request unusual, he didn't comment.

"I got ham and liverwurst," he said, taking down two bags from the shelf.

"One of each," Alex said, pulling out his wallet.

Mutton-chops rang up the sale and Alex opened one of the new packs of cigarettes. He kept his in a silver cigarette case and he wasn't about to flash that around a Hooverville. As he pocketed the remaining packs, he saw the paper lying across the counter where the clerk had left it. *Love Triangle Turns Deadly*, the headline read. Underneath it, a bold subheading declared that a woman was caught red-handed after she killed her lover in an effort to hide their affair. The story wasn't particularly interesting, but Alex hadn't yet seen the paper today and Iggy would expect to discuss it over dinner. There was probably time to read the headlines on his walk, but he wanted to stay focused on the problem at hand. He bought a paper anyway and tucked it into the pocket of his trench coat for later.

"You hear anything about people turning up missing around here?" he asked as he stowed the bag lunches in his kit.

The man started to sneer, but stopped as if considering his answer.

"I don't know about anybody disappearing," he said. "But I ain't seen Lefty in a week."

"Who's Lefty?"

"Lefty's this red-headed Irish bum," Mutton-chops said

with a sour expression. "He's always comin' around looking for work. Like I'd hire an Irish with only one hand. I wouldn't get ten minutes of work out of him a day."

"He's missing his right hand?" Alex asked.

"How did you know that?" Mutton-chops said in a startled voice, as if Alex had just performed some kind of magic trick.

"Guy's name is Lefty," Alex said with a chuckle, then he picked up his kit and headed back outside.

Alex smelled the camp well before he could see it. These kinds of places all smelled the same, a sour mix of unwashed bodies, uncollected refuse, and despair.

The camp was located on an open piece of ground between two industrial buildings. From the smell of it, one of them was a glue factory and Alex resisted the urge to hold his handkerchief over his nose as he approached. The camp itself resembled jetsam floating on still water, a collection of crates, boxes, tarps, cardboard, and what looked like salvaged bedsheets. All these materials were strung together into makeshift shelters that looked none too waterproof or warm.

Scattered throughout the camp were metal drums, several with active fires in them. Alex knew that during the day, the residents of these camps would scour the city looking for any wood they could find. Come nightfall all of the barrels would be lit to provide the occupants of the camp with some meager warmth before they took to their makeshift shelters to sleep.

"Hello there," Alex called to a group huddled around one of the barrels. Residents of these kinds of camps were usually wary of strangers, especially well-dressed ones. While Alex's clothes weren't particularly fine, they did mark him as one of the fortunate few that still had a job in these dark times.

"What do you want, mister?" a burly man with shaggy black hair asked. Everyone at the fire had turned to look at Alex, their eyes full of caution and suspicion in equal measure. Alex pulled the open cigarette pack from his pocket and shook it until he could grab one.

"I was looking for a warm place to have a smoke," Alex said, putting the cigarette in his mouth. He held out the pack as he reached the fire barrel. "Care to join me?"

The others in the group, two ragged men and a scrawny woman with a weathered face, all looked to the man who had spoken. He was tall with broad shoulders and a square jaw in a face that had gone thin from not enough food. His eyes were brown and hard, and they held Alex's gaze for a moment, before he shrugged and took a cigarette.

"If you're bringing the smokes, you're welcome enough," he said.

Alex shook more cigarettes out of the pack and offered one to everyone around the fire barrel.

"So why are you really here?" the leader asked, once he'd taken a long drag off the cigarette.

"You know the *Brotherhood of Hope?*"

"Sure," the woman answered. "They got decent food there and the nuns ain't too preachy."

"The brothers who run it say that people are going missing around here," Alex said. "You folks hear of anything like that?"

The air around the fire suddenly went chilly as the people exchanged uneasy glances. It was clear they knew something but didn't want to talk about it. Whether they were involved, or just worried that saying what they feared out loud would make it too real, Alex couldn't tell.

"Where are my manners?" Alex wondered as the pause

stretched out uncomfortably. "I'm Alex Lockerby. I'm a private detective."

"We don't want any trouble," a short man with sunken cheeks said. He looked like he wanted to leave, but the warmth of the fire made him think better of it.

"Listen here," the square-jawed leader said. "Whoever you're looking for, they're not here, and even if they were, we wouldn't rat them out to a private dick."

"Nothing like that," Alex said. "I don't have papers on anybody." A lot of private detectives worked for the police and the courts, tracing down wanted men or bail jumpers. Alex offered the group another cigarette and they hesitantly took them. "I was raised by the father who ran the old mission," he explained. "The bishop who runs this one tells me that suddenly people who come regularly aren't showing up."

"Maybe they got jobs," the woman said, a note of challenge in her voice.

The economy being what it was, that wasn't likely, but Alex resisted the urge to scoff. These people weren't living in camps, huddled around meager fires, because they were lazy or stupid. The stock market crash had ruined a lot of people's lives. As an orphan himself, Alex could easily have ended up in a place like this, so he was cautious not to make light of these people.

"If that's the case, I'll go tell Bishop Cosgrove the good news," Alex said. "He'll be thrilled. But, that's not what's going on," he said, looking around at the dirty faces clustered around the fire. "Is it?"

"Folk have been going out and just not coming back," the square-jawed man said. "Some folks say they just got tired of the cold and decided to move on, but I reckon that's bunk."

Alex offered him another cigarette, which he immediately took.

"Why do you think it's bunk?"

"Because they don't come back for their stuff," the short man said, looking around as if he expected some dire creature to swoop down on him for daring to speak.

Alex nodded. That was suspicious. There were bums even before the depression, men and a few women who simply wanted no part of modern life and wandered from place to place as they willed. Most of these professional wanderers would hop a train south to Florida or Texas for the winter, but none of them would go without taking their few possessions with them.

"Where do you think they went?" Alex asked, puffing on his cigarette.

The short man shrugged.

"Don't nobody care," Square Jaw muttered, casting Alex a dark look.

"Let's say I care," Alex said.

"There was this fellow who came around."

All eyes turned to the tall, emaciated man who'd stayed quiet up to now. He had sallow skin and dark, beady eyes in a sunken face that made his nose look beak like. A worn bowler hat was pulled down over his ears and he wore a threadbare suit coat that was both too broad and too short.

"What fellow?"

"Like you," he continued. "Fancy clothes, handing out sandwiches. He said there was work to be had up north somewhere."

Square Jaw scoffed at that.

"Just another glad-hander," he said. "The Navy uses 'em to drum up recruits sometimes."

"Sometimes they work for cargo ships," the woman said. "Looking to Shanghai people like us."

"People here don't pay 'em no mind," Square Jaw said. "At least the smart ones don't."

37

"Do you think that's what happened?" the short man asked. "Someone Shanghaied the missing people?"

Alex thought about it. That would explain why people might leave but not come back for their gear.

"How many people are missing?" he asked.

Square Jaw shrugged.

"No way to tell," he said.

"At least ten people are gone from here," the tall man said. "And they didn't just get jobs or decide to leave town. There used to be a woman here, Hortie Mills—"

"Pete here was sweet on Hortie," Square Jaw said, jerking his thumb at the tall man. "Wasn't you, Pete?"

Pete looked ruffled, but continued.

"Hortie went out gathering one day and never came back," he said, his voice earnest. "She wouldn't do that."

"Why not?"

"On account of Willie," the woman said, an indignant fire suddenly in her voice.

"Willie is her son," Pete continued. "He's seven."

Alex felt his stomach drop. Memories of his own youth rushed back to him, especially the moment when he'd been informed that his father was dead and he hadn't a relation in the world.

"Where is Willie now?" he asked.

"He's with me and mine," the woman said, her tone challenging Alex to say anything about it. "I've got a daughter, Sadie. She's five."

"Is there anyone who might remember this recruiter?" Alex asked. "The one who was passing out sandwiches?"

"You might try Lefty," the short man said. "He's always looking for work and he ain't particular about what it is."

Alex remembered the red-headed Irishman the five and dime clerk had mentioned. If he was as tenacious as the clerk

38

said, it was a cinch he would have talked with any recruiter that came through.

"Where can I find Lefty?" he asked.

"Back there," Square Jaw said, pointing at one of the better constructed shelters. "Normally he'd be out looking for work, but he got roughed up by some toughs yesterday."

"What happened?"

Pete shrugged.

"Some people don't like Irish."

Alex reached in his pocket and pulled out two of his sealed cigarette packs. He tossed them to Square Jaw and Pete.

"Share the wealth," he said, indicating the others. He then dug into his kit bag and passed the two bag lunches to the woman.

"For Willie and Sadie," he said. She accepted them suspiciously, but there was gratitude in her eyes.

Alex left the group and headed back to the shelter Square Jaw had indicated. He'd wanted to keep one of the lunches in case he had to loosen Lefty's tongue, but the thought of a couple of kids in this place was too much. The depression hadn't hit Manhattan as hard as the rest of the city. Most of New York's wealthy had moved to the island to be as close to the Core as they could, and it had the effect of making Manhattan one of the wealthiest places in the state. It also made most of the rest of the city markedly poorer by contrast.

Lefty's shelter was better constructed than those around it, and Alex could see the shiny ends of nails used to secure the odd bits of lumber that made up its frame. Broken bits of wooden boxes had been used to make walls and the roof looked to be made of several scrounged sandwich boards. The gaps had been sealed up with mud mixed with plaster and on the whole, it looked fairly sound and waterproof.

"What do you want, stranger?" a voice from inside called before Alex could knock.

"I'm looking for Lefty," Alex said. "The guy at the five and dime by the mission said he might be looking for work."

There was a pause that stretched out for most of a minute, then the heavy curtain that hung in the door was pulled back, revealing a man. He was younger than Alex, maybe in his late twenties, with a pale face and hair the color of carrots. A large, purple bruise was visible on his cheek and he had a black eye.

"I'm Lefty," he said, his voice guarded. "And I'm always looking for honest work. Just who are you?"

"What happened to your face?"

Lefty shrugged.

"I was looking for work and someone took offense," he said with a shrug.

"Were you stealing food while you looked for work?" Alex asked. It was common for shopkeepers and grocers to go after thieves, especially in these times.

"I was not," he growled, stepping out of the hovel and standing up straight. He was dressed like the other occupants of the Hooverville, but his clothes looked clean and brushed and he'd slicked down his hair. No hand protruded from the right sleeve of his coat, telling Alex he had the right man.

Lefty took a step closer, just inches from Alex's chest. Alex could see over the top of his head, but the smaller man didn't back down; that meant he still had some self-respect, so he probably wasn't stealing.

"Good," Alex said, offering him a cigarette from his open pack.

Lefty looked at the pack with undisguised hunger in his eyes, but then he looked back up at Alex.

"So, what's this work you've got?" he said.

"It's easy work," Alex said with a shrug. "I just need some information, and I'm willing to pay for it."

He explained about the mission and Bishop Cosgrove and the man who'd come with sandwiches, then offered Lefty the cigarette pack again. This time Lefty took one. Alex offered him a light as Lefty indicated a couple of dilapidated crates they could use as stools.

"I remember this fellow you're talking about," he said once they were seated. "He was all smiles and big talk, about having more jobs than he could fill. I signed up right away, but once he got a look at me, he turned me down flat."

"Not a fan of the Irish?" Alex asked. New York had been flooded with Irish immigrants since the days of the potato famine, and many New Yorkers resented them, especially recently with jobs being scarce.

Lefty shook his head.

"No," he said, holding up the stump of his right hand. "It was this. Bastard took one look and said they couldn't use me."

"Do you remember where he said these jobs were?"

He shook his head.

"Somewhere close," he said. "The guy wasn't specific."

"Did anyone from here go with him?" Alex asked.

"I don't know," Lefty shrugged. "I'm not here most days."

Alex sighed and shook his head; this wasn't going anywhere. He thanked Lefty and offered him the last, unopened pack of cigarettes.

"You said this was about people going missing," Lefty said, taking the offered pack. "How come you didn't ask me about that?"

"You said you weren't here most days," Alex said. "Why? Do you know someone who went missing?"

"Yeah," he growled. "The Captain's been gone for two

41

weeks now, not that any of them care." He nodded in the direction of Square Jaw and the others.

"Who's the Captain?"

"Old sailor," Lefty said. "He and I hit it off right away when he saw I knew how to tie a proper knot. And 'cause he's left-handed, like me." Lefty held up his remaining hand, and Alex briefly wondered if Lefty was left-handed by birth or necessity.

"How long have you known the Captain?" Alex asked. If they'd only met in this camp, it couldn't have been too long.

"About two months," Lefty said. "People here said he must've gone south. You know, hopped a train to Florida, but I know better. I was the only one who ever talked to him. The Captain was a sailor in the Great War, served on a supply ship called the *Amphion*."

"Why does that mean he didn't go south?" Alex asked.

"Because the *Amphion* was sunk by the Germans," Lefty said. "The Captain said that after floating in the Atlantic for a day waiting to be rescued, he never got cold again. Weather didn't bother him. He didn't go south because of the cold and he doesn't have any family left. If people are going missing, then the Captain is one of them."

Alex thought about that. Just because the Captain claimed to have survived cold water for a day didn't mean he was immune to the weather. Lefty had only known the man for a few months, so it was still possible the Captain had family and went to be with them, or he could have just moved on. Still, it was a place to start.

"This Captain fellow have a name?"

"Dobson," Lefty said.

"He got a first name?"

"I'm sure he does," Lefty said, "but none that he ever told me. He's a big fellow with a grey beard and he always wears one of those wool navy coats."

Alex nodded, writing the details in his flip notebook. An old sailor with a beard and a pea coat who goes by the moniker 'Captain' would fit the descriptions of hundreds of men in the city, maybe thousands, but he wrote it down anyway. When you didn't have anywhere else to start, even a long shot was worth taking.

"Thanks, Lefty," Alex said, closing his notebook and rising. he reached into his pocket, pulled out his wallet, and extracted a fiver.

"What's this for?" Lefty asked, somewhat suspiciously as he took the offered bill.

"I said I had a job, remember?" Alex said. "Jobs pay."

Lefty stood quickly and licked his lips.

"Well, if you ever need a good hand, so to speak," he said with an earnest chuckle, "I'm your man."

Alex looked at him for a moment. Being a private detective was pretty much a one man show and he regretted that he didn't have any work to offer.

"If I run across anyone who's looking," he said. "I'll be sure to mention your name."

Lefty looked a bit deflated, but nodded with a smile.

"Thank you, kindly," was all he said.

5

MARITAL AFFAIRS

There wasn't any chance of getting a cab in this neighborhood, so Alex headed back toward the mission. A few blocks further on would take him near enough to the mid-ring to find a crawler station. As he passed the grubby five and dime, he stopped in to call his office.

"Lockerby Investigations," Leslie growled at him when the call went through.

"Hello sunshine," he said. "What's the news?"

"Sorry boss," she said, most of the irritation melting from her voice. "How did it go at the mission?"

"Not sure," Alex said. "People are definitely going missing; the only question is, did they just move on, or is there something else at work here?" He thought of Hortie and Willie as he said it. Clearly she wouldn't have moved on without her son, but that didn't mean she couldn't have simply had an accident and been injured or killed. "I'm going to have to check the hospitals and the city morgue to learn more."

"Well, before you do that, you need to come by the office," Leslie said, some of her usual cheer filling her voice.

"There's a client here who's been waiting for you for over an hour."

Alex stifled a groan. His office was literally on the other side of Manhattan and he'd have to go past the Morgue just to get there.

"Take his number and tell him I'll call him first thing tomorrow," he said.

"I did," Leslie said, "but he insists on seeing you today."

Alex pulled out his pocket watch and flipped open the cover. The black hands pointed at three fifty-three. Between the *Brotherhood of Hope* and the Hooverville, he'd used up most of the afternoon. By the time he got back to his office and met with this new client, it would be after five and the morgue would be locked up for everyone except police. He could try to have Danny get him in, but he was probably still busy with his murder case.

"All right," Alex sighed, snapping the pocket watch closed. "I'm still over by the mission, so I'll have to take a crawler to the inner-ring. I'll catch a cab from there, so figure on about thirty minutes."

Leslie said she would inform the client and hung up. With thirty minutes of travel to kill, Alex bought a paper, then pulled up his collar and headed for the crawler station.

As it turned out, Alex had been generous in his estimation of the travel time from the *Brotherhood of Hope* and his office. By the time he trudged up the stairs and entered his office it was eight minutes to five. The offices of Lockerby Investigations consisted of two rooms: the outer office, or waiting area, and Alex's private inner office. The waiting area was a long rectangle with a window against the far wall, right behind Leslie's desk. A half-dozen file cabinets occupied the left wall, along with an end table that held their coffee pot. Along the right wall were two couches, in decent condition, and the door to the private office just to the side of Leslie's desk.

A solid looking man in his thirties sat on the couch with his legs crossed. He had a chiseled face with sharp cheek-bones and a Roman nose under light blue eyes. His hair was slicked back, and Alex could only tell that it was naturally black because of the man's pencil mustache. The suit he wore was relatively new, immaculately clean, and his shoes were well polished.

Outwardly, the man seemed at ease, but Alex immediately noted the overflowing ashtray on the little table that separated the two couches. He knew that Leslie always emptied those ash trays once a client left. Based on the amount of ash and butts in the tray, the man must have gone through the better part of two packs while he waited.

"Alex," Leslie said in a voice that carried both stress and relief.

The man on the couch rose immediately without putting down his cigarette.

"This is Paul Masterson," Leslie said, stepping around her desk. "Mr. Masterson, Alex Lockerby."

Alex held out his hand as Masterson suddenly realized he still had his cigarette.

"What can I do for you, Mr. Masterson?" Alex said as Masterson turned to drop his cigarette into the overflowing ash tray.

"Thank goodness you're here, Mr. Lockerby," he said in a voice that seemed self-assured in spite of his obvious agitation. "I need you to help get my wife out of jail."

Alex resisted the urge to raise an eyebrow at that.

"I'm not an attorney, Mr. Masterson," he began, but Paul waved him silent.

"No, no," he said. "You don't understand; my wife has

been accused of murder. I need you to prove that she didn't do it."

Leslie made a small coughing noise in her throat and Alex glanced at her. She was holding up a copy of the Times, turned to the headline just below the fold. It read, *Love Triangle Turns Deadly*.

Alex turned back to Paul and smiled.

"Of course you do," he said with no trace of the weariness he suddenly felt. "Let's go into my office."

Alex poured himself a scotch and one for the agitated Paul Masterson.

"Now, why don't you tell me why the police think your wife murdered someone," he said, passing Paul the glass.

"She was caught right there, Mr. Lockerby," Paul said, downing the scotch in one go. "Standing over the body with the gun in her hand."

Alex raised an eyebrow at that. He knew from experience that most criminals and their families professed their innocence, even in the face of overwhelming evidence, but he was interested to hear what justification Paul would give.

"So she did kill someone," Alex said. "Do you know why?"

"That's just it, Mr. Lockerby—"

"Call me Alex."

"That's my problem. June...that's my wife, she didn't even know that guy. She never met him before in her entire life."

"You spoke to her?"

Paul nodded as Alex poured him another drink.

"They let me see her over at the jail. She says she doesn't even remember shooting him."

Well, that's convenient.

"I know what you're thinking," Paul went on, his voice

earnest. "That's what anyone would say to beat a murder rap, but I'm telling you it's true."

"Okay, Paul," Alex said, sitting back behind his desk and opening his notebook. "What makes you think your wife didn't shoot the victim?"

"First off, we don't even own a gun," Paul said.

"There are plenty of places in the city to buy a gun," Alex said. "Most pawn shops have one or two lying around."

"Then there's the victim," Paul went on, undaunted. "He's a bookkeeper and he lives up in the Bronx. We live on the south side, Alex, almost an hour away."

"I read about this case in the paper," Alex said. "They're saying he was your wife's lover."

Paul's eyes got hard and he paused for a minute to get control of himself.

"My wife was happy," he said at last. "She didn't have a lover, much less one who lived an hour away."

"What do you do for a living, Mr. Masterson?"

"I'm the head of the sales department for the Dixie Cup Company here in New York," he said.

That actually made sense. Paul was clearly distressed, but he was keeping his emotions in check and making his case with facts, ideal mannerisms for a salesman.

"How long have you and your wife..."

"June," Paul supplied.

"How long have you been married to June?"

"Almost fifteen years," he said. "We were high school sweethearts."

Alex made a show of writing this down to give himself time to think. Fifteen years was well beyond the preverbal seven-year itch, but it was plenty of time for a housewife to grow bored.

"I tell you she was happy," Paul said when Alex brought

this up. "We only moved here a year ago. My job pays more than we ever had before, and she was enjoying her life."

"All right," Alex said at last. He had more questions, but he'd have to find those answers for himself. Clearly Paul believed his wife and nothing Alex could say would shake that belief. "So June was happy, she liked her life here, and she wasn't having an affair. Why do you think she shot the bookkeeper?"

Paul shook his head, a desperate, hopeless look flashing briefly on his face.

"Mr. Lockerby," he said. "I have no idea. She says she didn't, but the police say she did. I know she's not lying to me, but she doesn't remember leaving our house and she doesn't remember how she got to the Bronx."

"But that's where the police found her," Alex said. "Standing over a still-warm body with a literal smoking gun."

Paul nodded, then hung his head.

"I don't know what to tell you, Mr. Lockerby," he said. "All I know is that June was happy here, happy with me. She didn't have a lover, she didn't have a gun, and she didn't have any reason to shoot a stranger from the Bronx."

"Okay, Paul," Alex said, flipping his notebook closed. "I'll take your case. First thing tomorrow I'll go to the Central Office of Police and talk to the detective in charge of June's case, see what they know. After that, I'll go talk to June and see if she remembers anything else."

"Tomorrow?" Paul said, looking stricken. "Can't you go see her now, tonight? I told her I'd find someone to help. I can't bear the thought of her in that place."

"Visiting hours are over," Alex said. "Since I'm not her attorney, they aren't going to let me see her till tomorrow." Paul drew in a breath to argue but Alex held up a hand to silence him. "Nothing I can do will get her released," Alex continued. "They'll have a bail hearing sometime tomorrow.

The best thing you can do is go find a lawyer to represent her."

"All right," Paul said, his stoic exterior firmly back in place.

"I require a day's fee in advance," Alex said. "Pay my secretary and leave her a number where I can reach you. I'll call you tomorrow after I've seen June."

Paul thanked Alex and let himself out. Alex pulled his own copy of the Times from his kit bag and re-read the headline story. The man June Masterson was supposed to have killed was one Hugo Ayers of the Bronx, a bookkeeper. The reporter who wrote the story didn't have many details about Hugo or June, but he seemed quite certain the killing was based on an affair. He probably got that detail from one of the beat cops on the scene, which meant the police had some evidence that such an affair existed.

That's not good news.

If there was evidence that June and Hugo knew each other, if they'd been seen out together, or if there were cabbies who delivered her to the Bronx on a regular basis, then the motive of an affair was probably true. Alex wouldn't enjoy telling Paul Masterson that.

With a sigh, he set the papers aside and checked his watch. It was almost five-thirty, so the morgue would be closed. He could still try going by a few hospitals to see if Hortie or the Captain had been admitted, but that would be a long process. If they'd been in an accident and were unconscious, the hospital might not even have their names.

A knock at the door brought him out of his musings.

"I'm going to head home," Leslie said, leaning on the frame of the open door.

"Everything okay?" Alex asked, remembering her earlier bad mood.

"Randall was supposed to be in town tonight," she said.

Randall Walker was her on-again, off-again beau and the Assessor for Suffolk County. Leslie liked him and he seemed like a good guy, but their relationship wasn't going anywhere, and Leslie knew it. Still, she was in her mid-forties and while her beauty queen good looks hadn't begun fading yet, that was a battle that time would eventually win.

"I'm sorry," Alex said and meant it.

"What do you think about our client?" she said, changing the subject.

Alex shrugged, then stood up.

"I think it looks bad for his wife," he said, tucking his flip notebook into his shirt pocket. "I'll go see her in the morning."

Leslie chuckled darkly.

"He seems to think she wasn't having an affair," she said.

"You think she was?"

She sighed and shook her head.

"People always disappoint you, kid. It's a law of nature."

Alex gave her a sly grin.

"Even me?"

"No," she said, her sour expression evaporating into the usual smile she wore. "You're always there for me."

"Likewise," Alex said, slipping into his trench coat and grabbing his hat. "I guess we're just stuck with each other."

She shook her head at that but laughed anyway.

"Depressing, isn't it?"

"Not at all, M'lady," Alex said in his best British accent. He switched off his office light and offered Leslie his arm. "Who else would I share a cab with at six o'clock on a Monday?"

Leslie rolled her eyes, but took his arm.

"Charmed, I'm sure," she said, and they walked out together.

———————

Ten minutes later, Alex wished Leslie good night and trudged up the stone steps of the brownstone he shared with his friend and mentor Dr. Ignatius Bell. The front door was painted white and had an oval, stained-glass window in it. By all appearances, it wasn't the most secure of barriers; the door itself wasn't even locked, but that was a deception. Iggy had put several layers of runes on the door, all keyed to a very specific runic construct. Without it, a squad of men with a battering ram would be kept at bay as long as the construct lasted.

As he approached the door, Alex took out his pocket watch and pressed the crown, releasing the spring-loaded cover. When he'd looked at his watch earlier, he'd seen the red hand and the normal black ones, but nothing else. Now, in proximity to the door, a complex ring of tiny, pulsating runes hovered above the glass of the watch and the runes holding the door in place released.

"Is that you, lad?" Iggy called once Alex exited the glassed-in vestibule just inside the front door. Given the second set of protection runes on the inner, vestibule door, the question was largely rhetorical, since only Iggy and Alex had the runes that would open both doors.

"Yes," Alex said, hanging up his hat on the row of pegs beyond the vestibule and then hanging his coat on the tall rack just inside the library door. He expected to find Iggy in the library. On these cold evenings, Iggy could usually be found in one of the two wing-backed chairs that faced the fireplace with a well-worn pulp novel in hand.

"I'm in the lab," Iggy called, obviously anticipating Alex's next question.

Alex turned left and passed along a short hallway to the kitchen. When Iggy first moved into the brownstone, he'd painted a red line on the wall in the shape of a door. This meant that he didn't have to draw one with chalk every time he wanted to open his vault and Alex had copied the idea for his office. The space the painted door outline normally occupied was gone and the heavy door to Iggy's vault stood open. There was a time when Iggy forbade Alex from entering his vault, but those days were long over, so Alex rapped politely on the wall near the door and entered.

The first time Alex had entered his mentor's vault, he'd been amazed by how comfortable and orderly it was. The first room was a large, open area that contained a surgery and storage for Iggy's medical supplies. Beyond that, up a flight of stairs was an elevated bedroom and to the left, through a short hall was a kitchen and a small dining room. Iggy had spent the time to mold the floor to look like tile and the walls to look like brick, something Alex hadn't bothered with.

Iggy's vault was largely the same as it had been, but now the surgery table and the magelights that illuminated it had been moved into a new alcove on the right side. In its place, lab tables and equipment had been added in a double row. It reminded Alex of Jessica's lab. Piles of papers and notebooks covered much of the other tables. Like the papers in Alex's vault, these had drawings of runic constructs on them as mentor and student tried to decipher the construct that had given Alex more life.

"Come in, Alex," Iggy said, standing behind a table with two enormous bell jars on it. Each was illuminated by a large overhead magelight, and Alex could see a cluster of winged insects in one of them.

"How's it going?" Alex asked. He tried to keep a positive note in his voice, but for a year now the answer had always been the same.

"I think I'm on to something," Iggy said.

Alex's head snapped up at the words. This wasn't the usual

platitude where Iggy would say he was making progress and urge Alex not to give up, this sounded like the old man was actually excited.

Quickening his step, Alex moved to the table. Now that he was closer, he could see that one jar was filled with brown winged insects. The second jar appeared empty at first, but Alex caught sight of a single insect clinging to the side of the glass.

"What's all this?" he asked.

"Rhithrogena Germanica," Iggy said, peering over the jar from the opposite side of the table. "Or, more commonly, the brown mayfly. I've been getting a steady supply from a friend at Colombia."

"Why?" Alex asked.

"This particular insect is remarkable for one important reason," Iggy said, grinning at Alex and sending his bottle-brush mustache bending upward. "Once they reach their adult stage, they only live for about twenty-four hours."

"I'm not sure we can get much in the way of life energy from them," Alex said, squinting through the glass at the mass of insects.

Iggy held up one finger, then went to the stand where he'd hung up his suit coat. Withdrawing his green rune book, he returned to the table and tore out one of the pages. This he stuck to the jar with only one insect in it.

"Now watch," he said as he lit a match and ignited the paper. Alex recognized the rune once the paper burned away and left the construct hanging in the air. It was the same one he'd painstakingly inscribed inside the back cover of his pocket watch, the one that created the red clock hand.

As the rune faded away a red ring appeared above the bell jar. Without a clock face for reference, it was impossible to tell what it meant.

"Unlike your watch, the color matters here," Iggy said.

"I've tested hundreds of mayflies and calibrated this rune as precisely as I can. The red color means that this fly is down to less than twenty percent of its life energy."

Alex looked through the glass, but the bug just looked like a bug.

"Now watch this," Iggy said, tearing five more pages from his book. He pasted three of them around the jar with the mass of insects inside, and one on the top; the last paper he stuck to the other jar with the single insect.

With a wink and a nod, he struck a match and lit the flash paper on the second jar. As it burned, all the other rune papers ignited as well, bursting into a glowing web of complex constructs all connected together.

As Alex watched, the insects in the first jar shivered and began to fall to the bottom in a heap. He felt the hair on his arms stand up as the magic worked; it felt familiar. A moment later, the red ring above the single mayfly turned yellow, then orange, green, and finally blue.

"Does that mean what I think it means?" Alex asked, not daring to hope he could believe his eyes.

Iggy's grin got even wider and he wiggled his eyebrows in a very self-satisfied fashion.

"I've been keeping this mayfly alive for five days now," he said. "I think we've got a workable construct."

Alex couldn't keep the grin off his face as he looked down at the mayfly clinging to the side of the jar. As he watched, the blue halo that hovered over the jar went suddenly white in a burst of light that dazzled him. It didn't last long, flaring in a blinding pulse before the entire ring burst in a shower of sparks. When Alex could see again, he found the lone mayfly lying at the bottom of the bell jar. The spot where it had been clinging to the jar was covered in goo that had burst from inside the unfortunate insect.

"Or not," Alex said.

6

MORIARTY

Iggy swore, something he almost never did, and threw his rune book on the floor. Alex just stared at the ruptured body of the mayfly. Whatever had gone wrong had caused the insect to explode from the inside.

"Did it absorb too much life energy?" Alex asked.

Iggy sighed and shrugged.

"No way to tell," he said. "That seems likely, but it could be that the stress of absorbing life energy built up until the creature couldn't take it. Then again, it might be something else entirely."

Alex sighed and nodded. He'd been genuinely excited about Iggy's discovery; they'd been working on the life transfer construct every night since the unknown Brit had used it on Alex, trying to suss out how it worked. The basics were simple, it was just a life rune used in reverse, but that was the trick. Some runes could be easily used in reverse, but life runes had no basis for that. It shouldn't have been difficult, but the more Alex and Iggy delved into it, the harder it turned out to be.

"Okay," Alex said, throttling his disappointment. "What

do we do now?"

"I need a drink," Iggy growled, stooping to pick up his rune book. He stormed out of the vault, heading toward the library.

Alex took a last look at the two jars with their dead mayflies, then followed. He shared Iggy's frustration, but with only six short weeks left to him, he felt the need to hurry.

He found Iggy in the library sitting in his usual chair trimming the end from a cigar.

"It's cold in here," he said as Alex entered. "Light the fire, would you?"

Alex did as he was instructed, then sat down in the second chair, separated from Iggy by a small reading table that held a Tiffany lamp and two ash trays.

"Here," Iggy said, passing Alex a cigar and his cutter. "This problem calls for a good think, and nothing oils the brain like a fine cigar and some brandy."

As Alex trimmed his cigar, Iggy rose and opened the liquor cabinet that stood beside the window. He filled two large snifters about a third of the way, then set a fancy wooden stand on the reading table between the chairs. Each snifter fitted into the stand at an angle, suspending the brandy over a small tea candle. Once lit, these would warm the liquor prior to drinking.

"All right," Iggy said finally, once he'd lit the warmer, and then his cigar. "Let's go over it again. Walk me through everything you remember about Moriarty."

Alex didn't want to suppress a groan, but he did anyway. With every failure, Iggy wanted to go back over Alex's time with the mysterious Brit, who Iggy had dubbed 'Moriarty' after his famous villain. Alex was pretty sure that this Moriarty wasn't a villain, but at least the name gave them something to call him.

Alex puffed on his cigar, then recounted again the incident in the slaughterhouse, filling in as much detail as he could remember. He tried to recall every symbol on the blue rune Moriarty had used to kick off his construct, every line and connection of the floating circle of symbols that had surrounded him. Unfortunately the particulars of the construct seemed to swim and change in his memory, much as they had appeared to do at the time.

"It's all right, lad," Iggy said, once Alex had lapsed into a frustrated silence while trying to recall minute details of the individual pieces of the life transfer construct. He blew out the tea candles and passed Alex one of the snifters. "Take a break and have some of this."

Alex took the glass, careful to hold it by the stem. They sat in silence, puffing their cigars and sipping warm brandy for a long time. Alex tried to recall more details, but the more he thought about it, the more the entire memory seemed to slip away.

"What I don't get is why Moriarty's construct was so inefficient," Iggy said at last.

Alex looked at Iggy with a raised eyebrow, but said nothing.

"Think about it," Iggy went on. "He used fifty hogs and only managed to give you fifteen or sixteen months of life energy. Hogs live about ten years each, that's five hundred years of life energy he had to work with, and he only managed to pass you less than one percent of it."

Alex thought back to the mayflies in the bell jars. He hadn't counted the ones in the first jar, but there couldn't have been more than twenty.

"Did you use the same number of bugs each time you tried that?" he asked his mentor.

Iggy nodded.

"So you only needed twenty or so mayflies to fully refill

the life of one," Alex said. "To give it a whole additional day of life."

Iggy nodded again.

"It's not as good as it sounds," Iggy cautioned. "Mayflies all have the same lifespan, whereas pigs are significantly shorter lived than humans, so the ratios aren't the same. Still, I bet if we did the math, we'll find out that our construct is still more efficient than Moriarty's."

"But that doesn't make sense," Alex protested. "He's had years to work on this, maybe more than one lifetime. Why would our first attempt be better?"

"Why indeed?" Iggy said.

Alex thought about it as they sipped their brandy in silence.

"Maybe he was in a hurry," Alex said at last.

"I thought of that, but it doesn't seem likely," Iggy said. "Moriarty pulled you out of the drink around midnight, and you said that when he showed you that the city had been purged of Dr. Burnham's fog, it was some time in the early afternoon. That means he had at least twelve hours to prepare. That's more than enough time."

Alex shrugged. Iggy was right, there were a few runes that required days to write, but all of them depended on lesser constructs that needed time to take effect before the next step in the writing process could be completed. If the life transfer rune depended on that, Moriarty wouldn't have been able to finish, and if he had the rune already prepared, then the whole question was moot.

"I suppose Moriarty must have deliberately weakened the rune," Iggy said. "Made it less efficient. He told you the first time was hard on the body."

"Yes," Alex admitted. "But that mayfly didn't explode until the fourth time."

Iggy stroked his chin and nodded.

"What if that's it?" Alex asked. "Right before the mayfly exploded, the life detector went white. What if you just transferred too much life energy into it and its body simply couldn't take it?"

"If that's what happened, why didn't it explode the first time?"

Alex didn't have an answer to that. If the problem was too much energy, the bug would have burst on the first try.

"What if it's like a pressure tank?" Alex said.

"How so?"

"Well, when the gas company stores coal gas in a tank, they keep it under pressure," Alex explained.

"Hence the name, pressure tank," Iggy said.

"Yes, but if you put too much gas in a tank..." Alex suggested.

"It can weaken the tank," Iggy said, catching on. "So if we put too much life into that mayfly, it might have been okay for a few times, but over time it weakened the creature until —" He spread his hands apart in a gesture meant to represent an explosion.

"If that's the case, it would make sense that Moriarty's construct was less efficient. He didn't know how much my body could take."

"So he dumbed down the rune to be as basic as possible," Iggy finished. He grinned and drained the brandy from his snifter. "I think we have a working theory," he declared. "I'll get some more mayflies from my friend tomorrow and start testing it." He sighed and sat back in his chair, tension visibly leaving his frame.

Alex hadn't noticed, but his own muscles suddenly ached as if he'd been clenching them.

"What do you want to talk about now?" he asked Iggy. Then with a grin, he added, "How about we figure out how Moriarty shut himself inside a vault?"

Iggy's serene expression soured.

"You know that's not possible," he chided. "You were probably delirious from the life transfer and imagined it. I've been through the Monograph a dozen times in the last year and there is absolutely no possible way to open a vault from the inside. If Moriarty had done that, he'd be very dead right now."

Alex didn't bother to stifle his grin. Of all the parts of his story, how Moriarty had obviously been inside the brownstone, or how he'd somehow put an invisible rune on Alex while he slept, it was the vault that bothered Iggy the most. He simply couldn't accept that. Alex couldn't really blame him. Runewright lore was replete with stories of practitioners who'd closed their vault doors from the inside, never to be seen again. It was the one rule of learning the vault rune, never close the door from the inside. Still, Alex knew what he had seen. Whatever rune lore Moriarty possessed, it enabled him to close himself inside his vault and live to tell the tale.

That thought fired Alex's imagination.

"Mind if I take a look at the Monograph for a few hours?" he said as nonchalantly as he could.

"No," Iggy growled. "There's nothing in there about opening a closed vault from the inside. Let it go."

Alex was about to protest when Iggy went on.

"Tell me about your day. Did you get any interesting clients?"

Alex sighed. Talking about his day was far less interesting than reading the monograph, but he'd raised Iggy's hackles with the vault question, so he knew the old man wouldn't budge.

"You saw that case in the paper about the woman who shot her lover?" Alex asked.

"Of course," Iggy said, tapping the ashes off his cigar.

"Her husband came in to see me. Says his wife didn't

know the victim and has no memory of the event. He wants me to prove her innocent."

"If the papers are to be believed, that could be difficult," Iggy said. "As I recall, she was found standing over the body with the murder weapon still in her hand."

"I'll go see her tomorrow and hear the story directly. Any idea what might cause memory loss?"

"Oh, a lot of things," Iggy said sagely. "A blow to the head, overuse of certain painkillers, then there's deliberate drugging."

"How would drugging someone get them to commit murder?"

"If you mean commit a specific murder, that's highly unlikely," Iggy said. "Some experiments during the Great War showed that people under the influence of certain drugs or alchemical substances became very suggestible, but nowhere near what you'd need to order them to kill a specific stranger."

"What if she did know the victim?" Alex wondered. "Would that make a difference?"

"I suppose it's technically possible," Iggy said after considering the questions for a long minute. "But I'd say it was very unlikely. If someone other than the housewife wanted the victim dead, there are much easier ways to go about it."

"What about sorcery? Could a sorcerer do it?"

Iggy shrugged.

"I have no idea," he admitted. "Why don't you ask Sorsha? I'm sure she'd know."

Alex shuddered at the thought.

"Is she still vexed with you?" Iggy asked with a smirk.

The old man knew very well that Sorsha was still angry at Alex. She'd practically burst into tears when Alex showed up alive after disappearing over the side of the *Tripoli* in the North Atlantic. Her attitude had changed, however, when he told her the harrowing story of how he'd used a buoyancy rune to stay afloat and then swam to shore over the course of eight hours. Sorsha was nobody's fool, and she knew that story was a lie. Even though buoyancy runes did exist, it was something Alex would never have occasion to keep in his rune book.

The problem, of course, was that if he told her the truth, that some powerful runewright had been watching him and plucked him out of the ocean because he had big plans for Alex, that would raise far too many questions. She'd be certain to assume that Moriarty had the Archimedean Monograph and if she believed that, she'd never leave Alex alone. Worse, she might jump to the conclusion that Alex and Iggy had the Monograph and if that happened, they'd have to go on the lam. There was no possibility that Sorsha would keep that information to herself, not with her bosses in the US government looking for the Monograph. Alex didn't like lying to the sorceress, but he simply couldn't take the risk of telling her the truth.

Alex puffed on his cigar, turning his mind back to the case of June Masterson. If she was the victim of some plot to make her the patsy in a murder, it was an excessively complex plot. He'd learned over the years that the more complex the explanation to a murder, the more likely it was to be wrong. While it was true that some killers went to great lengths to hide their crimes, their reasons for committing the murder were almost always simple.

"Greed, jealousy, and passion," he said, blowing out a lopsided smoke ring.

"The triumvirate of murder," Iggy agreed. "Figure out which one of those motivated this killing and you'll know who's behind it. Any other cases?" he added.

Alex told him about the missing Forgotten and his conversation with Lefty.

"I dare say you're already planning to check the morgue and the hospitals," Iggy said in a bored voice.

Alex nodded.

"What if you don't find anything?" Iggy pressed.

"Then I'll visit more Hoovervilles," Alex said. "If it's only a handful of people that have gone missing, they might have been Shanghaied onto a cargo ship."

"What if it's more?"

"If a lot of people are missing, and they aren't in the morgue or the hospital, then someone is keeping them prisoner somewhere, maybe an off-the-books workhouse?"

"That might explain why your mysterious recruiter didn't want a one-handed man."

Alex nodded. It was possible, but not very likely. The idea that someone in the city was grabbing up the Forgotten for some slave labor job was repellant, but the problem was that the Forgotten weren't well fed or highly skilled. Whoever tried something like that would have to train them, house them, and keep them warm and fed. Alex imagined it would be cheaper just to hire legitimate workers.

He sat, thinking through the problem, until Iggy opened the ornate chest that sat against the wall beside his chair and pulled out one of his pulp novels.

"What if you could open more than one door?" Alex asked suddenly. "Into a vault, I mean," he said in response to Iggy's questioning glance. "If you had two doors, and one was always open, then you could close the second one without being afraid of being trapped inside."

"Tosh," Iggy muttered, turning his attention back to his book. "You know very well that the rune that creates the key, also creates the vault."

Alex did know that; it was the rune carved on the flat part of his vault key. Unlike other runes, the vault rune didn't degrade with time because, technically, it was only used once, the first time the vault was opened. After that it required a separate vault rune to call the door into existence.

No two vault runes were identical, even ones written by the same person since tiny variations in pressure and form made each one unique.

"In order to do that, a runewright would have to be able to make an exact copy of his vault rune," Iggy went on. "Or rather he'd have to have an exact copy of most of it. The part of the construct that created the vault would have to be identical, but then he'd have to write a new part to create a second key."

"So you're saying it is possible," Alex said, giving Iggy a sly grin.

"I know you think you're funny," Iggy grumbled. "But runes are serious business."

Alex started to press the joke, but something stopped him. For some reason he thought about Moriarty's fishhook rune. It came, unbidden to his mind. He could see it, glowing and spinning in the depths, right before its master had tugged on the line and pulled Alex across the miles that separated him from the city. It made no sense for that to leap to mind when Alex was talking of vault runes, yet there it was.

His thoughts were interrupted when his stomach rumbled, and he remembered that he'd missed lunch.

"Is there any dinner?" Alex asked, pushing the thoughts of vaults and fishhook runes from his mind.

"No," Iggy declared in a voice that dared Alex to say anything about it. "I was quite busy all afternoon."

"All right then," Alex said, crushing out his cigar and standing up. "Let's go down and see Mary. I'm buying."

Iggy regarded him with a critical eye, as if weighing the worth of such a suggestion, then he snapped his book closed and set it on the reading table.

"Excellent idea," he declared.

65

7

HARDBALL

The Manhattan Central Office of Police was a ten-story building south of Central Park near the core. It was the main location for the detectives that served the island, at least from the Bronx south, and housed the holding cells, evidence storage, secretarial, and administration departments. Smaller precinct buildings housed the local beat cops and served as temporary holding facilities when needed.

As the hub for police work in Manhattan, the Central Office never closed. Its lobby consisted of a long series of high counters where police sergeants fielded public requests for assistance day or night. Despite all that, the office did maintain hours for people wishing to visit incarcerated loved ones, or pick up records, or property, and even for irritating private detectives who wanted to ask questions. As such, Alex went by Runewright Row on his way into town the following morning to get his thermos of coffee before arriving outside the marble and glass entrance of the Central Office.

Most of the small precinct stations were just a floor or two in a regular building, with nothing more than a sign cut in the shape of a police shield to announce their presence. The Central Office, however, was the home of the Chief over the entire island. As such, it had a gleaming marble facade and glass doors with frosted police emblems in the center of each.

Normally the office opened at nine, and Alex timed his arrival perfectly. As he entered, a pudgy beat cop was unlocking the door that led back to the building's bank of elevators. Despite the fact that the holding cells were in the basement, Alex pushed the button for the fifth floor, where the detectives were housed. He'd decided he'd better talk to the detective who had caught June Masterson's case before he saw her. If he knew what the police had on her, he would know what questions to ask to fill in any gaps.

When he arrived, he swung by Danny's desk to get an update on the tortoiseshell shooting, but Danny was either out on a case or not in yet. A quick round of questions later and he was directed to the desk of Detective Clive Lowe of Division Two.

Lowe turned out to be an average sort of fellow in almost every way. He was average height and weight, with average looks, an average suit, and mud-brown hair with light brown eyes.

"What is it?" he demanded when Alex approached his desk.

"Hear you caught the Masterson case?" Alex said.

"You a reporter?" Lowe asked.

Alex shook his head and handed over one of his business cards. Lowe rolled his eyes when he read it and then handed it back.

"What's a private dick doing in this mess?"

Alex shrugged and put on his friendly smile.

"The husband hired me," he said. "Wants to make sure everything is what it appears to be." Alex didn't bother explaining that Paul Masterson thought his wife was inno-cent. Detective Lowe wouldn't want to hear that, and then he might not cooperate.

"That was quick," Lowe said but then he shrugged and stood up. "Look, I've got to go see my Lieutenant about another case, so what do you want to know?"

"Who'd she shoot?"

Lowe picked up a flip notebook like the one Alex used and opened it.

"Hugo Ayers," he said. "Mr. Ayers was forty-one, he was a bookkeeper, and he lived alone in a Bronx apartment building."

"You sure it was June who shot him?" Alex asked, scrib-bling in his own notebook.

Lowe gave Alex a scrutinizing glance, then looked back at his notes.

"Two witnesses saw Mrs. Masterson enter the apartment building lobby about one twenty-five yesterday afternoon," he said. "She walked up to the second floor, knocked on Mr. Ayers' door, and when he opened it, she shot him three times in the chest. A neighbor who works the night shift heard the shots, came running out into the hall, and found Mrs. Masterson standing over Mr. Ayers with the gun in her hand."

He flipped his notebook closed and stood up.

"Now if you don't mind," he said, rising. "I have to go see my Lieutenant."

"Why did the papers think there was an affair?" Alex asked. "June is at least ten years younger than Ayers."

"We found a letter at her place," Lowe said taking his suit coat off the back of his chair and putting it on. "She confessed to the affair, said Ayers threatened to tell her husband, and that she intended to shut him up for good."

That didn't make sense. If she intended to silence Ayers to cover up the affair, why write a letter exposing it? Maybe so her husband would understand if she got caught or if Ayers managed to kill her? He'd have to ask June about it, assuming she remembered doing it.

"Where is June?" he asked as Lowe turned to leave.

"I think they already came for her," Lowe said.

"You mean her attorney?" Alex asked.

That finally got a rise out of Lowe. He turned and looked at Alex like he was crazy.

"No," he said. "The coroner. She hung herself in her cell last night."

The holding area under the Central Office consisted of several large cells for holding drunks or minor offenders and three rows of individual cells for more important prisoners. June Masterson had been held in the furthest row from the elevator, which was used for female prisoners when the occasion called for it.

A bored cop in a stained blue uniform led Alex along the hall to the third row, then down about halfway.

"This is the cell," he said, jerking his thumb at it.

The cell was a rectangle, slightly longer than it was wide and had a single metal cot along the back wall. The front wall was entirely made of bars with a heavy, barred door in the center. Otherwise, it was empty, though there was evidence that the floor had been mopped recently.

"Who found the body?" Alex asked.

"Officer Tredwell," the cop said. "She's in charge of female prisoners."

"Is she here?"

"No," the cop said in his bored voice. "She was pretty shook up, so the Sergeant sent her home."

"Did you see the body?"

The officer brightened at that.

"Oh, yeah," he said with a macabre grin. "She was hanging from that pipe, right there."

A thick iron water pipe ran across the ceiling, and Alex could see where some of the paint had rubbed off the sides. Alex looked at the bed, but the single sheet over the mattress looked undisturbed.

"What did she use to hang herself?"

"Her blouse laced up in the back," the cop said. "She took the string out of that, tied it around the pipe, then jumped off the bed."

Alex gave the man a sour look. He was entirely too happy to be relating the details of June Masterson's death.

"Open it up."

The cop fished out his keys and unlocked the barred door. There wasn't much Alex could see from inside, but he wanted to be thorough. The pipe along the ceiling was pretty high up, but easily reachable if you stood on the bed. A fragment of string was still tied around the pipe where June had hung herself, dangling down an inch or so.

"Who cut her down?" Alex asked.

The cop shrugged.

"I wasn't here for that." He sounded disappointed.

Alex looked back at the fragment of string dangling from the pipe. He would have expected the police or the coroner to have cut June's body down, but the loose end of the string looked frayed. He climbed up on the cot for a better look.

"Hey," the cop objected. "What do you think you're doing?"

"You said you saw the woman hanging," Alex said, more to stall the man than out of any desire to know.

"I already told you I did," he said. "Now get off there."

Alex tugged the tied string along the pipe until he could see it clearly. It wasn't as thick as he would have expected, but it seemed sturdy. He rubbed it between his fingers and he could feel the frayed fibers.

"This wasn't cut," he said. "I think it broke."

"That sometimes happens when you try to get a body down," the cop said. "Now come out of there."

Alex climbed down off the cot and exited the cell.

"The detective in charge of the case said the coroner came for the body," Alex said.

"What did you expect?" The cop sneered as he shut the door.

"Thanks," Alex said, more out of general politeness than in any acknowledgement of the bored cop's assistance. He turned and walked back toward the elevator as the cop locked up the cell. His feet seemed to get heavier and heavier as he approached.

June's body would be over at the city morgue a half dozen blocks away. That wouldn't be a problem, Alex had been there many times. What he was dreading was the phone call he was going to have to make when he reached the Central Office's enormous lobby.

The New York City Morgue was only five minutes from the Central Office of Police by car, but it took Alex the better part of an hour to reach it. On his way out of the Central Office, Alex had called Paul Masterson to give him the news of his wife's suicide and arrange to meet him at the city morgue. When he finished, Alex decided to walk the six blocks to the morgue to clear his head.

In his years as a private investigator, Alex had only had to make that kind of call five times before. Making the phone call that changed people's lives forever never got easy.

By the time he reached the New York City Police Auxiliary building, his walk had helped to clear his head. The Auxiliary building stood five stories high and housed the records office, secretarial pool, and the financial clerks for the police department. The basement was entirely dedicated to the morgue.

The lobby of the building looked like any lobby in any professional building in the city, except for the uniformed officer sitting behind the desk in the lobby. Alex had visited the morgue enough that the officer behind the desk recognized him when he pushed through the outer door and went back to reading his paper as Alex made his way to the elevators.

When the doors slid open, Alex found himself looking at an attractive young woman in a white blouse and a green skirt. She had an hourglass figure with a slim waist, big brown eyes, and her short fingernails were painted a bright red. She was in the act of touching up her matching lipstick in a hand mirror when the doors opened, and she seemed startled to see anyone.

Alex smiled and got in, punching the button for the morgue, but the elevator went up instead of down.

"Hi," he said as the young woman put away her lipstick and compact. "I'm Alex."

She gave him an appraising look, then smiled.

"Betty Sorenson," she introduced herself.

"You're in the secretarial pool," Alex said. It was a statement rather than a question.

Betty looked confused for a second, then she flashed a million-dollar smile.

"I'm sure we haven't met," she said. "I think I'd remember you."

"It's your fingernails," Alex said. "They're cut short so you don't break them on the typewriter keys."

She held up her hand, looking at her nails, then laughed.

"Is that what they're teaching you over at Central?"

She obviously assumed Alex was a detective and he felt no desire to disabuse her of that notion. Even here, PIs weren't liked.

He was about to answer, but the elevator stopped and Betty got off.

"Nice to meet you, Alex," she said as the door closed behind her.

I must be losing my touch, Alex thought as the car started back down. He was only in his mid-thirties and still young, except for his unnaturally white hair.

When the doors opened again, Alex found himself in the morgue. The floors were made of a dark green tile that ran up the walls to about waist height and the light fixtures in the main hallway were too far apart, giving the place a gloomy, bereft look. Alex knew from experience that if he turned right, he'd end up in the large refrigerated room where the dead were kept for as long as the police needed them. To the left were two operating theaters flanked by glass observation rooms. In the center, just opposite the elevators, was the coroner's office, the property room, and a supply closet.

Since June Masterson's body had just come in that morning, Alex expected it would be in one of the operating theaters, so he turned left and made his way down the hall. The first theater was empty, so Alex proceeded to the second. There was a body on the table inside, but when Alex approached, he found it to be a man of advanced years with a knife wound in his chest.

"Who the devil are you?" a strange voice assaulted him.

Alex turned to find a thin, athletic-looking man in shirt-sleeves who had just entered by the back hallway. He carried a clipboard in one hand and had a white doctor's coat slung over his arm. His face was imperious and he had chiseled features and a pointed jaw that gave the look weight. A heavy gold wedding band, set with a heart-shaped ruby in an antique design, adorned his left hand and the chain to his pocket watch had a gold fob. By all appearances, he was well-to-do and in his mid-thirties.

"Hi," Alex said, putting on a friendly face. "I'm Alex Lockerby. Is Dr. Anderson around?"

The man ran a critical eye up and down Alex before returning to his face.

"Dr. Anderson retired," he said in a curt, crisp voice. Alex noticed a trace of Midwest in his accent, but city, not rural. He probably hailed from Chicago or Detroit. "He moved to Arizona to take care of his ailing sister. I'm Dr. Daniel Wagner," he went on. "This is my morgue now and I don't appreciate you detectives just popping in to bother me. If you have a question about a case, call the records department, that's what they're for."

Alex didn't know that Anderson had a sister or that she was sick. Iggy probably knew, but it wasn't likely Iggy knew Anderson had gone to Arizona as that seemed to be very sudden. As for Wagner, Alex could already tell he was going to be trouble. Still there was no reason to lead with the stick when you had a perfectly good carrot to try.

"Well, it's nice to meet you, Dr. Wagner," Alex said, offering the man his hand. The doctor looked from the hand to Alex but didn't shake. "I think we got off on the wrong foot," Alex said, withdrawing his hand. "I'm not with the police department—"

Wagner waved Alex silent with an exasperated expression.

"Reporters aren't allowed in here," he said in a condescending voice. "Leave at once or I'll call the desk sergeant and have you forcibly removed."

Alex laughed at that. He knew he shouldn't have, but he couldn't help himself.

"What is it you find so amusing?" Wagner demanded.

"I think it's funny that you think the cops would waste a sergeant on this job," Alex said. "The guy up at the desk is Charlie Cooper and he's been on the force for almost forty years. They gave him this job as a sort of unofficial retirement."

Wagner's eyebrows did their best effort to grow together as he scowled.

"Despite that," he said in a tight voice. "I'm sure I can find someone to come over here and arrest you."

Alex put up his hands in a gesture of supplication.

"Easy, Doc, I'm not a reporter," he said, reaching into his shirt pocket for one of his business cards. "A woman was brought in this morning from the Central Office. She was accused of murder but then killed herself. Her husband hired me to dig into the murder."

Wagner took the card, but his look of disgust didn't lessen when he read it.

"I don't know what could have possessed Dr. Anderson to make him associate with a low-rent pretend detective," he said, throwing the card in Alex's face, "but I'm absolutely certain I'm not going to. Get out right now or I'll have you arrested."

Alex raised an eyebrow at that. The Morgue was a public building and while the cops could ask him to leave, they couldn't arrest him just for being there.

"On what charge?" he asked.

"I'm sure I can invent something by the time they get here," Wagner said, an edge of steel creeping into his voice. His arrogant expression managed to get even more so, and the ghost of a self-satisfied grin crossed his lips.

To his credit, Alex actually spent a few seconds thinking about the potential ramifications of any action he might take. Much of his job depended on his having access to the morgue and, more importantly, to the coroner himself.

Clearly Wagner wasn't going to play ball. Not willingly at any rate.

Okay, it's the stick then.

Alex let an amused smile spread across his face and then he laughed. It had the desired effect on Wagner, whose arrogant look faltered.

"You think I'm joking?" he fumed.

Alex shook his head.

"No," he said. "I just find it funny that you think you can blow in here and play hardball with the big boys. That weak beer you just served might have been a big deal wherever you came from, but this is New York, the biggest city in the world. If you want to threaten someone here, you're going to have to do better than that."

Wagner bristled and seized the receiver of the phone on the little desk by the operating theater's back door.

"Before you do something you'll regret," Alex said, speaking quickly, "let me tell you what's going to happen if you make that call."

Wagner hesitated and his arrogant look came back.

"All right," he said. "Amuse me."

Alex took out a cigarette and lit it.

"First off, I noticed your ring," Alex said nodding at Wagner's left hand. "It's an heirloom from your wife's family."

"How could you know that?" Wagner demanded, his arrogance turning to confusion.

"It's a claddagh ring," Alex explained. "That's Irish. Your last name, Wagner, that's German, so it's a cinch the ring comes from your wife's family."

"I could have gotten it from my mother," Wagner countered.

"But you didn't," Alex said with a chuckle. "You're a married man, so the heart should be pointing toward the hand, not away. If you'd gotten that ring from your mother, she would have taught you how to wear it properly."

"I'm failing to see how the way I wear my ring puts me in any danger if I have you arrested, Lockerby."

"Don't get ahead of the story," Alex said. He indicated Wagner's clothes. "You dress awful tony for a coroner, that plus the ring tells me that it's your wife's family who's rich."

Wagner raised an incredulous eyebrow and gave Alex a bored look.

"Again, I fail to see how that matters in the slightest."

"To the cops it doesn't matter at all," Alex confirmed. "But when I got on the elevator to come down here, I met an absolutely enchanting young woman by the name of Betty Sorenson. Her short fingernails and the fact that the elevator dropped her off at the third floor tell me that she's a secretary in this very building."

"There are several dozen secretaries on the third floor," Wagner said, sounding tired.

"Yes, but Betty was coming up from the morgue," Alex said. "I bet I can count on one hand the number of reasons a secretary would be down here, and the first three would be 'because she's having an affair with the coroner.'"

A look of surprise with a hint of fear darted across Wagner's eyes, but it vanished almost as it arrived.

"You have no proof of that."

Alex chuckled as he puffed on his cigarette.

"I don't really need any," he said. "Once I tell your wife about my elevator ride with the attractive and buxom Miss Sorenson, I'm sure she'll get the picture."

Wagner opened his mouth to argue, but Alex talked over him.

"You see, Betty was touching up her lipstick when I got on the elevator. As I'm sure your wife knows, there's usually only two reasons a woman does that; either she just ate something, or she did something to smudge it. You were very careful to remove any evidence of Betty's lipstick from your face and neck, Wagner, but when you got dressed, you forgot that you were wearing your lab coat when Miss Sorenson came down."

Wagner's eyes darted to the coat in his hand. Along the edge of the collar was a dark red stain.

"That's Betty's color, isn't it?" Alex said in the casual voice one might use to point out an available cab. "I'm sure your wife will find that very interesting."

Dr. Wagner put on a brave face and shrugged.

"I've been meaning to divorce her anyway," he said.

Alex laughed in his face.

"Don't try to kid a kidder, Doc. I know what a coroner makes. You didn't buy those snazzy clothes and your gold watch chain on a coroner's salary. That's your wife's money and if she goes, so does your gravy train. You're not going to divorce her. Not ever."

Wagner glared daggers at Alex for a long moment, then he put the phone receiver back in its cradle.

Alex just smiled and took another drag off his cigarette.

"Welcome to New York, Doc," he said.

8

JUNE

"You sure about this?" Alex asked Paul Masterson. His client had arrived at the morgue just after Alex had convinced Dr. Wagner to be helpful and so he'd wheeled June's body into one of the operating theaters and covered it with a sheet.

Alex could tell that Paul was shaken but he held himself together with a stiff upper lip attitude that Iggy would have approved of.

"I need to say goodbye," Paul said. He was standing in front of the door, but made no move to open it.

Alex took hold of the knob and turned it. That seemed to stir Paul, and he walked into the room. His posture was rigid and his hands didn't tremble as he pulled the sheet down from June's face. Alex knew the stricken look on the man's face; he'd worn it himself, just last year when he'd had to say a similar goodbye to Jessica.

"I've got the man she shot set up in the other theater," Wagner hissed as he approached. While his voice wasn't loud, it carried, and Alex cast him a dark look before pulling the door to the operating theater closed. Wagner cast him a dark look in return. He'd made it clear that he didn't appreciate this kind of intrusion in his morgue, but since Alex had him over a barrel, there wasn't much he could do about it.

"If there's nothing else," he said, "I've got paperwork."

"Just a minute," Alex said as he started to turn away. "I want to see your reports on these two." He indicated June and the other theater where the body of Hugo Ayers lay.

"Reports?" Wagner scoffed. "This is a closed case," he said, not bothering to hide his disdain. "She killed him and then herself. There isn't any need for an autopsy or even a preliminary examination."

Alex ground his teeth. Anderson wouldn't have done such shoddy work; he at least did a visual inspection of every body that came through his door.

"I'll want to examine both of them once the husband is gone, then," Alex said.

"Do whatever you want," Wagner growled.

"One more thing, Doc," Alex said as the man turned to leave. "There's been a report that some of the people from the Hoovervilles and the Forgotten camps have gone missing. You seeing any of them turn up here?"

"Some of them always turn up here," Wagner said. "I have four at the moment. Two stab wounds, one that was hit by a cab, and one who died of exposure."

That all sounded fairly ordinary, and it wasn't enough to account for the numbers that were missing. Alex thanked him, more out of habit than any actual recognition of Wagner's contribution, and the man stormed off.

The threat to expose his affair would keep Warner complacent for a while, but he was probably already destroying any evidence of his connection to Betty Sorenson. Alex's threat probably wouldn't work again. He'd have to figure out some other way to get access to the morgue. It was too important to his work.

80

Deciding to worry about that later, Alex opened the door and entered the operating theater. Paul was just standing by the body, looking down at June's face. Even in death, she was pretty, with dark hair and fair skin.

"I don't understand any of this, Mr. Lockerby," Paul said. His voice was soft and distant, as if the words were having to find their way out of him. "I saw her just yesterday. She was upset, of course, but I told her I'd hire someone to figure all this out. She believed in me." He turned to Alex. "She always believed in me."

"I'm sorry, Paul," Alex said. "I can still look into this if you want, but I'd understand if you wanted to call it off. I won't charge you for the time I put in."

"No!" Paul said. It was almost a shout and his voice echoed off the ceramic tile that covered most of the room. "No," he said again once the echoes had died away. "I know my wife," he insisted. "She wouldn't have killed herself. She was Catholic, it's a mortal sin."

Alex put his hand on Paul's shoulder.

"People sometimes do desperate things when they lose hope," he said.

"No," Paul insisted again, though his voice was soft this time. "June would never have killed herself."

"If you're thinking someone at the Central Office of Police was involved," Alex said, shaking his head, "that isn't very likely."

"But it's not impossible," Paul said.

Alex sighed.

"No," he admitted. "It's not impossible."

"I want you to find out what happened to my wife," Paul said, the muscles in his jaw tightening. "I want to know why she went to the Bronx and shot someone she didn't know. I want to know why she wrote a letter confessing to an affair I know she wasn't having. And I want to know how she came to be...to be hanging in that cell."

Alex looked him in the eye for a long moment. He saw a man who was adrift, like a ship without a rudder, just looking for a port, any port. Alex had seen that look before. Nothing he could say would dissuade Paul from pursuing the answers he so desperately sought.

"All right," Alex said, clapping him on the shoulder. "I'll give you one more day."

Paul opened his mouth to protest but Alex cut him off.

"I'll take a look at this letter June supposedly wrote," he said. "Then I'll go have a look at Mr. Ayers' apartment in the Bronx. I'll see what I can find out."

"What if there's nothing there?" Paul asked.

Alex give him a reassuring smile.

"We'll cross that bridge if we come to it."

Paul thanked him and then left to make arrangements for June's body with the police clerk on the second floor. Alex waited until he had gone before pulling the sheet off June's body.

She was naked under the sheet, her clothing having been removed by one of the orderlies who worked under Wagner. A wooden crate sat under the gurney and Alex pulled it out into the light. It contained everything June Masterson had been wearing when she was found hanging in her cell.

Carrying the box to the desk against the wall, Alex laid out its contents; a green blouse with a lace up back, a gray, knee-length skirt, a pair of black flats, a brassiere, a pair of bloomers, and the heavy cord she had used to hang herself. Alex ran the cord through his fingers and found where it had been cut, undoubtedly to get the body down. It wasn't torn like the string in the cell had been, and this cord was heavier.

Clearly someone else had tried to hang themselves before June, but they didn't have a strong enough string. When it broke, they probably thought better of it and no one had noticed the string still tied around the iron pipe.

Satisfied that he understood the discrepancy, Alex examined the other articles of clothing. All of them were perfectly ordinary and contained no clues at all as to why a mid-ring housewife would have killed a Bronx bookkeeper.

Apart from the obvious explanation.

After putting the clothing back in the box, Alex went over the body in detail. There was a deep gouge around her neck where the cord had strangled her, but that was no surprise. Alex got out his multi-lamp and oculus and went over June's neck and hands with silverlight. If someone had covered her mouth and forced her head into the makeshift noose, he would expect to see smears around her mouth and prints on her face, but the light revealed nothing.

Frustrated, he turned his attention to her extremities. Several of June's fingernails were broken but there were scratches on her neck where she'd clawed at the cord. That wasn't suspicious, though, most people who hung themselves panicked at some point and tried to break free. The only other odd thing was that June's left foot was twisted at a funny angle and the skin around her ankle was covered in a large bruise.

Alex didn't have the medical training to know if her ankle was broken, and he doubted he could get Warner to help. Still, you had to be careful when cutting down a hanging person. The police had probably dropped June's body when they were cutting her down.

Finished but unsatisfied, Alex covered June back up and moved to the second operating theater. The Bronx bookkeeper, Hugo Ayers, was laying on a gurney like a slab of so much meat. Wagner hadn't even bothered to cover him.

"Nice," Alex muttered. He was starting to think that

instead of finding a way to work with Wagner, that he needed
to just get him fired.

Half an hour later, Alex had to admit defeat. Hugo's
clothing was perfectly ordinary and his cause of death was
obvious from the three .38 caliber holes in his chest. Detective Lowe had said that June shot Hugo when he opened the
door to his apartment. The grouping of the bullets backed up
that statement. The only strange thing was that Hugo was a
short, dumpy, balding man with a large mustache. Not exactly
the dashing figure Alex would have expected a bored housewife to take up with.

Maybe he's got money.

Alex went down to the cooler and retrieved a sheet to
cover Hugo, then packed up his kit. He would have to hope
that there was something in June's letter or Hugo's apartment
that would shed some light on these deaths, because the
bodies weren't telling him anything.

Alex stopped in at a drugstore down the block from the
morgue to use the phone. He could have called from the box
in the lobby of the morgue, but the drugstore had two things
the morgue lacked: a lunch counter and decent coffee. Before
he'd discovered Marnie and her magic brew, Alex had made a
point of ferreting out all the places in the city where he could
get a good cup of joe.

"Hey, Mr. Lockerby," a skinny man with curly blond hair
and a white apron greeted him from behind the counter.
"Haven't seen you in a while. You want lunch?"

"The usual, Charlie," Alex said, digging out his wallet.
"And can you give me change for a buck, I need to use the
phone."

Charlie took the bill and opened the register. While he

counted out the change, Alex leaned on the counter. A large display that used to hold shaving razors was now filled with several rows of thin cardboard books, some blue and others red. The cover showed what looked like a cartoon cat with an enormous grin and the words *Happy Jack* were printed above it.

"Didn't figure you'd need one of those," Charlie said, returning with a handfuls of change.

Alex cupped his hand to accept the money, then nodded at the display.

"What is that?"

"Rune books," Charlie said, picking up one of the red covered books. "They got six mending runes in this one for a buck."

The price of one dollar was clearly marked on the cover but Alex couldn't believe that. Dropping his change in his pocket, he took the book from Charlie. As he suspected, the runes inside were minor mending runes, much less powerful than a standard mending rune. Still, six for a dollar was a good price. Most runewrights on the row sold this kind of rune for a quarter apiece.

"How many of these do you have?" Alex asked, tucking the red book back on the shelf with its brethren.

"I got twenty of these mending books and ten of the general purpose ones." Charlie indicated the blue covered books.

Alex picked up one of those and paged through it. There were two mending runes along with some barrier runes, binding runes, and a couple Alex recognized but didn't use. The runes themselves were competently made, nothing special though. The one thing all the runes in the Happy Jack books had in common was that all of them could be written without special inks, just a pencil would do.

"How's this Jack guy making a living at these prices?" Alex asked.

Charlie just shrugged at that.

"I don't know about that, Mr. Lockerby. All I know is they sell out pretty quick."

Alex shrugged and returned the booklet to the display. As Charlie started in on the poached eggs and toast, Alex moved to the back of the store where the phone booth stood.

His first call was to Detective Lowe at the Central Office. He needed to get into Hugo Ayers' apartment and since it was Lowe's case he would have to give permission. All that assumed the police still had a man on the door of the apartment. Standard procedure was to secure a murder scene for at least the first twenty-four hours.

When Lowe's desk phone buzzed on for over a minute, the police operator came back on the line.

"Your party doesn't answer," she said in a bored, nasal voice. "Is there somewhere else I can transfer your call?"

Alex knew that Lowe might be out, so he already had a contingency plan.

"Detective Danny Pak, please."

"Just a moment," the operator said, and the line clicked over to the regular buzzing sound that indicated a ringing phone on the other end.

"Detective Pak," Danny answered a moment later.

"How'd it go with the tortoiseshell shooting?" Alex asked.

"We found the guy. It was just like you figured, Scutter's dog got loose and messed up the neighbor's cat. The guy claims he shot Scutter when he offered to pay for the dead cat."

"Scutter offered to pay and the neighbor shot him anyway?" Alex asked, a bit stunned by that.

"He said that it was obscene to try to put a price on the life of his cat."

Alex whistled. He knew some pet owners were a bit nutty when it came to the objects of their affections, but this took it to a whole new level.

"Hey, remember when you said you'd owe me a favor over that case?" Alex said, segueing into the reason for his call.

Danny chuckled.

"Let me guess, you're calling to collect."

"You heard about the girl who supposedly shot her lover, then hanged herself down in the cooler?"

"Yeah," Danny's voice suddenly got serious. "That's all over the station. There are a bunch of tabloid reporters camped out in the lobby. I even saw a guy from the Times. Needless to say, the Captain wants it dealt with quickly and quietly."

"They're already on that," Alex said, then he explained about Dr. Wagner and his belief that the case was already closed. "Do you think they will have pulled the uniform off of Ayers' door?"

"Probably," Danny said. "If they want this to go away, they would have turned the apartment back over to the building owner so he can rent it out again."

That was actually good news. The owner would have to clean up the place, arrange to get Ayers' belongings out, and replace the carpet where Ayres had died. Even if Ayers had died instantly, there would be blood loss.

Alex explained about Paul Masterson and his wanting Alex to look into his wife's actions leading up to her death.

"Can you call over to the super and tell him to let me in?" Alex asked.

"Sure," Danny said. "Do you know where Ayers lived?"

Alex pulled out his notebook and read Danny the address. He'd gotten it from the identity card he'd found in Ayers' pocket when he went through the dead man's pants.

"I'll call over there and give them the usual story," Danny said, then he hung up.

Danny and Alex had done this dodge many times. Most building superintendents wanted to cooperate with the cops, against the inevitable times when they'd need a friendly police officer. Danny would call and say that the police were sending over a consultant to look over the scene and would they please let him in, then he'd give the super Alex's name. It worked better than a skeleton key.

Alex checked the lunch counter, but the clerk in the white apron was still cooking his food, so Alex dropped another nickel into the phone.

This time it was Iggy who picked up. Alex told him about his experience at the morgue with the new doctor and that Anderson had retired to Arizona to be with his sister.

"I knew this was coming," Iggy said, with a sigh. "Sarah has been sick for some time. She must have taken a turn for the worse for Dr. Anderson to leave so suddenly, though."

"What are we going to do about this new guy?" Alex asked. "I don't think I can hold his affair over his head for much longer. He's probably already burning any connection between himself and Betty Sorenson."

"No doubt about that," Iggy said. "But it's been my experience that men who pick up a new mistress within a few weeks of starting a new job tend not to be moderate in their habits."

Alex grinned and nodded even though Iggy couldn't see him.

"You mean this probably isn't the only skeleton in the good doctor's closet."

"Just so."

Alex changed the subject, telling Iggy about his plans to check out Hugo's apartment.

"If that's a bust, then I'm out of leads," he said. "Unless someone created a magical doppelgänger of June."

"Maybe you should call Sorsha," Iggy said with a chuckle.

"I wonder what Andrew Barton is up to these days?" Alex replied. Barton was better known as the Lightning Lord, one of New York's six resident sorcerers and the provider of much of Manhattan's electrical power. Alex had worked for him before and Barton seemed to like him.

"Coward," Iggy said, then he bid Alex good luck and hung up.

This time when Alex checked the counter, his plate of poached eggs and toast was waiting for him. His stomach rumbled at the sight, but instead of leaving he pulled another nickel from his pocket and dropped it into the phone.

"Lockerby Investigations," Leslie's voice greeted him.

"Hey doll, it's me," he said. He explained about what happened with June and how Paul wanted Alex to keep investigating. "I'm headed up to the Bronx to check out the dead bookkeeper's apartment. It'll probably take a few hours."

"Things are quiet here," she reported.

"Got time to go to the records office?" Alex asked.

"I can fit that in. What do you want me to look up?"

"Pull the license for a Doctor Daniel Wagner; he's in charge of the morgue now."

"Do you want to know anything specific?" Leslie asked. Alex could hear the scratching of her pencil as she wrote down what he'd told her.

"Find out as much as you can about him," Alex said. "Where he went to medical school and where he practiced before he came here."

"All right," Leslie said. "Anything else?"

"Yeah. Once you get back, start calling the places where Wagner worked. Find out if he was involved in anything shady or scandalous."

"Dig up the dirt," Leslie said. "Gotcha, boss."

Alex hung up the phone and headed back to the counter where his rapidly cooling eggs waited for him beside the display of rune books. He still didn't know anything definite about June Masterson or Dr. Wagner, but at least he had the ball rolling.

9

THE BOOKKEEPER'S PAD

The apartment of Hugo Ayers was on the second floor of a neat, five story building on the south end of the Bronx. It was only a few blocks from Willis Pawn, the shop where Alex had traced a missing silver hair-brush during the case where he'd met Leslie. The last time Alex had been here, he'd had to walk home because the Bronx was outer-ring and by the time he walked back into Manhattan, the crawlers had stopped running.

This time Alex arrived by cab, right in front of Ayers' building. The juxtaposition of the two experiences reminded him just how far he'd come from his tiny basement office in Harlem.

Ayers' superintendent was a short, fussy-looking man, with a well-trimmed mustache and spectacles, who made it abundantly clear that he didn't appreciate the police wasting his time.

"I'll be in my office on the first floor if you need anything further," he said when he let Alex into Ayers' apartment. "Be sure to lock up when you leave."

"Did you know Mr. Ayers?" Alex asked before the man could retreat.

The superintendent hesitated, but then shrugged.

"Just to speak to," he said. "We weren't close."

"Was he a man of regular habits?" Alex asked.

Anger flashed across the superintendent's face and his mustache bristled.

"If you mean did he spend his nights galavanting all over town, then no," he said. "Mr. Ayers was a quiet, respectable man." He hesitated then looked away. "Or at least I thought he was."

"So you never saw him bring a girl back here?"

"Of course not. I'm not running a bordello."

"Do you know where Mr. Ayers worked?"

"He was a bookkeeper," the super said, not meeting Alex's gaze. "He had lots of clients."

"Did he have any debts, maybe money trouble?"

The super looked uncomfortable but Alex just waited for him to speak, letting the silence stretch out uncomfortably.

"He had a few late rent payments in the spring," the man said. "He said that he'd lost a couple of important clients."

Alex completely understood the feast and famine cycle created when you worked for yourself.

"What about lately?" he asked.

The super shrugged.

"His rent is on time."

Alex thanked him and the little man withdrew. He stood in the hallway for a moment, looking through the open door of Hugo Ayers' apartment. Beyond the door was a sitting room with well-made furniture and an oriental-style carpet covering the floor. A large red stain covered the edge of the carpet closest to the door.

According to what Detective Lowe had told him, June Masterson had stood in the hall when she shot Hugo. That would match the stain on the rug, but it didn't make much sense. If Hugo knew June, why didn't he step back when he saw it was her? Did she just shoot the moment he opened the door?

He didn't have any way to answer those questions since, according to Lowe, no one had seen the shooting.

Pushing those thoughts from his mind, Alex stepped inside, pulling the door closed behind him. The sitting room was neat and orderly, though sparsely decorated, and the furniture was of decent quality. A small freestanding liquor cabinet held a half-dozen open bottles of various spirits, but nothing too fancy.

An opening led into a small kitchen with a folding dining table that was set up for one person. There were no dishes in the sink and the counter had been wiped down; clearly Hugo Ayers was a man of meticulous habits.

Not the sort to get involved with a married woman.

Behind the kitchen was a small study with several book-shelves, a reading chair, and a desk. Alex continued past it without stopping to survey the rest of the apartment, which consisted of a small bathroom and bedroom. Like the kitchen, the other rooms were neat, clean, and orderly.

Hugo's possessions were all of good quality, but not extravagant. That plus his late rent payments suggested that if he had money, he'd only come into it recently. If he didn't have money, then he would have to have brought any potential lovers back to his own apartment, rather than shelling out for a hotel.

Alex checked the bedroom closet, the dresser, and Hugo's hamper but didn't come up with a stitch of clothing a woman would wear. The top dresser drawer had a small box with a set of gold cufflinks and a pair of antique silver wedding rings in it, but they were heavily tarnished with no signs of recent wear.

Probably family heirlooms.

Frustrated, Alex turned to his multi-lamp. Sweeping the bedroom with silverlight yielded the usual signs of habitation, but nothing that would suggest that Hugo brought a lover into his bedroom. Alex swept the rest of the house for good measure, but came up just as empty.

With a sigh, he put back his equipment and turned his attention to the study. Next to the writing desk was a shelf, with a row of ledgers. As a bookkeeper, Hugo Ayers would have worked on his various employers' books, but those records would have stayed at the client's offices. That meant that the ledgers on the shelf must be the ones for Hugo's business.

Alex searched through them until he found the one for 1936. He wasn't terribly familiar with accounting notations, but from what he could make out, several of Hugo's clients had stopped paying him back in April and May. Then in June a new client appeared, labeled 'Ashford.' According to Hugo's books, Ashford payed considerably more than Hugo's other clients.

Alex didn't know what kind of business Ashford might be and it was getting late enough that he probably didn't have time to go down to the records office and search through business licenses. As it was, it would be after five by the time he got back to his office.

Heading to the kitchen, Alex picked up the cradle of the telephone on the little dining table. If Leslie didn't have anything for him, he might just head home.

"Are you still in the Bronx?" Leslie asked once the call connected. "I need you to come back to the office as quick as you can. There's a couple of clients waiting for you. They say their daughter has been kidnapped."

As he predicted, it was just after five when Alex got back to his office. The moment he stepped through the door, a tall, thin man in a fancy suit stood up from where he'd been sitting on the waiting couch. Beside him a plump woman with pleasant features and dark circles under her eyes was gripping her hands together so tightly that her knuckles were white.

"Mr. Lockerby," the man said, helping the woman to her feet. "Thank heaven you're here. We need you to use your finding rune to locate our daughter."

The man was taller even than Alex with a mop of blond hair and a goatee with a handlebar mustache. His shirt was silk and his pinstripe suit was expertly tailored. The woman had raven black hair that was done up tastefully, framing a round face. She wore an elegant if understated dress of a dark blue fabric and her high-button shoes were the latest fashion.

Clearly they had money, which was an obvious reason why someone might have taken their daughter.

"I'll be happy to help you, Mr..."

"Fredrick Westlake," the man introduced himself. "And this is my wife Isabel."

Alex motioned in the direction of the door marked *Private*.

"If you'll come into my office," he said, "I'll see about finding your daughter."

He conducted them to the upholstered chairs in front of his desk, then sat down opposite and took out his notebook.

"Tell me what happened," he said.

The Westlakes exchanged worried glances.

"You have to hurry, Mr. Lockerby," Fredrick said in an urgent voice. "I asked around and everyone said you're the man to find our Vivian. Use your magic."

Alex put down his notebook and planted a look of calm assurance on his face.

"I will, Mr. Westlake," he said in his most soothing voice.

95

"But the magic works through me. The more I know about your daughter and the circumstances, the better it will work. If I try to use it now, just knowing her name, it might not work at all."

Isabel Westlake made a sound that reminded Alex of a wounded cat and Fredrick put his arm around her.

"I assure you," Alex said before either of them could speak. "This is the fastest way to find your daughter."

"All right, Mr. Lockerby," Fredrick said in a resolved voice. "What do you want to know?"

"How old is your daughter?" He guessed that the West-lakes were in their forties so that could put Vivian anywhere from ten to twenty-five.

"Just eighteen," Isabel said, speaking for the first time. She had a pleasant voice to match her face.

"Is this the first time she's disappeared?" Alex asked.

The Westlakes exchanged another telling look.

"No," Fredrick admitted. "We recently discovered that Vivian has been sneaking out of the house at night to go to nightclubs. But that's not what happened here."

"We'll get to that in a minute," Alex said, making notes. "How did you find out where she'd been going?"

"We have money, Mr. Lockerby," Fredrick said. "I've done very well for myself, but we weren't always so blessed."

"We don't flaunt our money, Mr. Lockerby," Isabel said. "And we never spoiled Vivian the way other rich folk do."

"What does that have to do with your daughter sneaking out?"

"She didn't have money of her own," Fredrick said. "So she stole things from around the house to..."

"To pay for the nightclubs," Alex finished.

"I noticed something missing from one of the curio cabinets and went to ask her about it," Isabel said in a quavering voice.

"That's when we learned she wasn't in her bed," Fredrick added. "Naturally, we waited up and confronted her when she got home."

"And how did she take that?" Alex asked, pretty sure he could guess the answer.

"Not well," Fredrick admitted. "I threatened to disinherit her if she didn't fall in line."

"She said she'd behave from now on," Isabel said. "But we put away everything in the house that was valuable just the same."

Fredrick nodded sadly, looking at his wife.

"Locked it in the basement," he said. "We thought that was the end of it. I mean she couldn't get into nightclubs without money."

"But today when I went to check on her, she was gone," Isabel said.

"Did she take a bag with her?" Alex asked. "Clothes, makeup, that sort of thing?"

"No," Isabel said. "That's why we think someone took her."

"You think someone was taking advantage of her," Alex guessed. "And when the gravy train stopped, they decided to get money out of you."

They didn't answer, but Fredrick nodded.

"Have you received a ransom demand?"

"Not yet," Fredrick said. "But she's only been gone since just before noon."

"Does Vivian have any well-heeled friends?" Alex asked. "Someone who might be willing to help her, take her in?"

"She has several society friends," Isabel said. "But their parents wouldn't be a part of such a thing."

Alex wasn't sure about that. Still, a wealthy socialite who had an appetite for nightclubs was more likely to run into seedy characters there than with her society friends.

"Is that enough?" Isabel asked. "For you to use your rune, I mean?"

"Almost," Alex said. "I'm going to need something that belonged to your daughter. Something she cared deeply about."

Fredrick looked alarmed at that and Isabel pressed a handkerchief to her eyes, attempting to stifle a sob. Alex was genuinely confused.

"What's wrong?" He said.

"The reason she didn't take any of her things is because she sold them for cash," Fredrick admitted. "Anything she had of any value."

"All of her treasured things are gone," Isabel sobbed.

Alex had to think about that. Without something personal with a connection to Vivian, the finding rune wouldn't have anything to latch on to. He considered using the Westlakes themselves, but he doubted Vivian was very happy with them at the moment, which might cause resistance to the rune.

"You said she sold valuable objects from around the house," Alex said. "Was any of it something personal to you? Preferably something she took recently."

Isabel looked up and nodded.

"She sold a silver picture frame that belonged to my grandmother," she said.

"That's how we discovered the thefts," Fredrick added. "Isabel noticed immediately when it went missing."

Alex took out his rune book and tore out a finding rune, setting it on his desk. He then took out the rolled map and cigar box he kept in the filing cabinet on the back wall.

"I want you to think about that frame, Mrs. Westlake," he said, rolling the map out onto the top of his desk. He weighed it down with the four jade figurines from the box, then took out his brass compass. "Can you see the frame in your mind?"

"Yes," she said, closing her eyes.

He took out his rune book again and tore out one of the blank pages from the back. Folding it, he put it in the palm of his hand and lit the paper with the touch tip on his desk. The Westlakes jumped at the fireball, which was a perfectly normal reaction.

"Notice it didn't burn my hand," Alex said, showing his unmarked palm to Isabel. "It just feels hot for a moment."

She didn't look terribly convinced, but he showed her how he intended to put the rune paper in her open hand while she touched his compass which sat atop the map of Manhattan. Reluctantly, she put out her hand. Alex could tell she was terrified, but her love for her missing daughter was more powerful than her fear.

"All right," Alex said, lighting the metal match in the touch tip. "Think about that picture frame. Think about your grandmother and all she meant to you."

He touched the burning match to the flash paper, and it vanished in an instant. The orange finding rune remained behind as the fire burned away, spinning slowly over Isabel's palm. After a minute it shuddered and stopped, then burst into a shower of sparks that disappeared before they reached Isabel's hand.

Alex moved her hand and checked the compass beneath. Its needle was not pointing north. Being careful not to lift it and break its contact with the map, Alex slid the compass along the east side of Central Park. The needle kept pointing south, toward the core. Eventually, he found a spot where the needle turned around and he moved the compass in circles until he found a place where the needed pointed inward the whole time.

"Is Vivian there?" Isabel asked in a faint voice.

"No," Alex admitted.

"Then what's all this for?" Fredrick exploded. "You're supposed to find our Viv."

Alex put up his hands in a gesture of patience.

"And that's what I'm doing, Mr. Westlake," he said. "You don't have anything I can use to link to your daughter's location, but this," he pointed to the spot the compass indicated. "This is where I'm going to find a pawn shop with your wife's missing mirror for sale."

"But how does that help you find Vivian?" Isabel asked, her voice getting desperate. "The frame wasn't special to her."

"Probably not," Alex said. "But I'll bet that frame isn't the only thing your daughter sold to the pawnbroker. If I can find something that was hers, it will have a stronger connection."

"The brooch," Fredrick said with a nod. Alex gave him a questioning look and he went on. "We got her a fancy gold brooch when she finished school. It had pearls around the edge. If she needed money, it would be easy to sell."

"Did she like it?"

"She was ecstatic when we gave it to her," Isabel said.

"All right," Alex said. "I'll see if I can find the brooch."

"What if you can't?" Fredrick interrupted.

"If I can't, I'll look for personal things she might have sold," Alex said. "Once I have one of those, I'll cast the rune again and that will lead me to Vivian."

For the first time since Alex met them, Isabel seemed to relax, as if a heavy weight had been lifted off her shoulders.

"What do we do?" Fredrick asked.

"I want you to go home—" Alex began.

"We can't just go home and wait," he said. "We'd go mad."

"If this is a kidnapping, whoever took your daughter might call to ask for a ransom," Alex pointed out. He didn't believe Vivian had been kidnapped, not after the story the Westlakes told him. Vivian was a petulant child who'd lost her favorite toy and was now having a temper tantrum. Still, he would move much faster without her parents tagging along, so he indulged their kidnapping theory.

"Go home and wait by the phone," he continued. "As soon as I know something, I'll call."

"What if we hear from the kidnapper?" Fredrick said.

Alex took out one of his business cards and jotted Leslie's number on the back.

"This is my secretary's home number," he said, passing the card to Fredrick. "If anything happens, call her."

Fredrick accepted the card gratefully and Alex walked them out.

10

CHINCHILLA

The battered brass compass Alex used with his finding rune led him to a swanky part of the inner-ring, close to the core. A line of high-end shops ran along the street, their neat, orderly window displays advertising everything from clothing to jewelry. At the end of the row, one shop had an entrance that faced the corner. It too was neat and clean with a well-constructed window display, and the marquee above the door read *Empire Merchandise*. It was nicer than the pawn shops Alex was used to, but to be fair, it catered to a higher class of clientele than Alex was used to.

The proprietor of *Empire Merchandise* was a rotund man with thick arms, a bald head, and an affable manner who sat behind a well-ordered glass counter smoking a cigar. When Alex came in, he laid aside the paper he'd been reading and stood with a smile.

"Welcome," he said, running a practiced eye over Alex. "How may I direct you?"

Alex consulted the compass and found it pointing to a shelf off to one side that was stacked with all manner of silver items. Most of them had begun to tarnish a bit so Alex spotted the gleaming antique picture frame easily.

"How much for that?" he asked, dropping the compass into his coat pocket.

"Ah, you have a good eye," the proprietor said, taking the frame down and setting it gently on the counter. "I just got this piece in. It's solid silver and in the Louis the XIV style."

Alex picked it up and felt a tingle in his hands. With the frame and the compass this close together the magic that connected them was palpable.

"How much?" Alex asked, setting it back on the counter.

"For that?" The man asked, as if the question was a surprise. "I couldn't let that go for less than twenty-five dollars."

That meant he'd take twenty for it. *Empire Merchandise* might be a high-end pawnbroker that catered to the many rich folks who were hit hard by the stock market crash, but haggling was a staple of every hock shop in every city the world over.

"Tell you what," Alex said, reaching into his pocket and extracting a twenty and a five from his wallet.

"I'll give you the twenty-five," he put the cash on the counter. "And you tell me all about the little girl who sold it to you."

The clerk's affable smile evaporated.

"You a cop?" he asked, ignoring the money.

Alex shook his head and handed over one of his business cards.

"Nothing like that," he said as the proprietor read the card. "The girl's been stealing stuff from her family home and living it up on the town."

The clerk's face soured, but he rallied and handed Alex his card back.

"No court will hold me up for buying stuff that belonged to the girl's family," he said.

Alex expected this reaction. If the Westlakes wanted to make trouble for the man, they could file a police report saying the items were stolen and then he'd be on the hook for receiving stolen goods.

"The girl's gone missing," Alex said, adding a five to the pile of cash on the counter. The man's face blanched.

"I don't know anything about her, other than her name, Vivian Westlake," he said. He was about to go on when Alex cut him off.

"Relax," he said. "Vivian's family hired me to find her. As it said on my card, I'm a runewright, so I need something of hers in order for my finding rune to work. I figure something she sold you early on."

The man looked flustered and took out a handkerchief to mop his perspiring brow.

"I don't know," he said, uncertainty in his voice.

"Her parents mentioned a brooch," Alex said. "Gold and fancy, with pearls all around it."

"Yes," the proprietor said, nodding. Then his face fell. "I'm afraid I sold that already. A young man came in and bought it for his girl."

"Do you have a name?"

He shook his head.

"I'd never seen him before or since."

"What about other stuff?" Alex asked. "She must have sold you lots to keep up with her lifestyle."

"Just a moment," the man said. "Let me get my book."

He disappeared into the back room and returned a moment later with a thick, leatherbound book.

"You put dates in there?" Alex asked as the proprietor began paging through it.

"Yes," he said. "I'll find out when she sold me the brooch, then see what else she brought in around then."

It took a few minutes, but the tubby proprietor finally located the entry.

"Here it is," he said. "According to this she also sold a silver comb and brush set and a chinchilla coat."

The brushes would be something Vivian would have used every day, but unlike Leslie's silver brush, they wouldn't be special to her. With her parent's money, they were probably just ordinary things to her. The coat was a different story, however. Chinchilla fur was popular and valuable. Alex would bet it cost Vivian a lot to part with it.

"You still have the coat?" he asked.

"Yes," the proprietor said. "But I'm not letting that go for less than three hundred dollars, I don't care if the girl is missing."

Alex didn't have that kind of cash on him, but he didn't need to buy the jacket, just borrow it. He explained the procedure for using a finding rune and reluctantly, the man conducted Alex into his back room where he laid the coat on a large table. It was long, like Alex's trench coat with grey and black sections sewn together in a pattern that reminded Alex of a tile roof. He wasn't much for expensive things but the coat had a sumptuous feel as he ran his hand over it.

"Amazing," the pawn shop owner said with a grin. "Think of how your girl would look at you if you gave her one of these."

Alex thought about it and he had to admit, any girl he knew would be over the moon to have something like this.

Except Sorsha, but she probably already has three.

"Too rich for my blood," he said, pulling his map and cigar box from his kit. He turned the jacket over, exposing the lining. There was no way the man would let Alex ignite the rune paper within ten feet of the coat, so Alex didn't bother to tell him how the rune worked. He lit a cigarette, set up the map, compass, coat, and rune paper, then ignited it.

The rune blazed to life as the flash paper vanished. The pawn shop proprietor was so enthralled that he didn't even protest the brief fireball that had erupted right in the middle of his storage room.

Carefully, Alex removed the coat and handed it back to the stunned pawnbroker. Unlike when the spell had locked on to the picture frame, this time the needle seemed to waver back and forth as if it didn't have a firm hold on Vivian. Alex moved it around the map, eventually narrowing it down to a four-block radius on the opposite side of the core.

"What does that mean?" the pawnbroker asked, peeping over Alex's shoulder.

"The rune is having trouble finding the girl," Alex explained. "I've seen this before; it likely means she's underground."

The man looked at Alex sharply.

"That doesn't sound good," he observed.

Alex shrugged as he rolled up the map and returned his jade figurines to the cigar box.

"She spent the money she got from you going to night-clubs," he said. "There's a dozen of them in that part of town and most of them are built below street level."

The pawnbroker checked his watch.

"It's only six-thirty," he said in a scandalized voice.

"And most of the clubs don't open till seven," Alex said. "I figure she's found herself a sugar daddy and she's holed up in one of them."

"So how will you find her?"

Alex took the brass compass and held it up.

"Once I get closer, this will point me right to her," he said. "Do me a favor. Figure out what she sold you and put it aside; I'm sure her parents will want to buy it back."

The man scoffed at that.

"You obviously don't know rich people," he said. "If you tell them I've got their things, they'll come down here with an attorney and police and threaten to close me down if I don't just give it all back."

Alex was a bit surprised to hear that. He'd done exactly that many times, but he was used to small time thefts where the victims couldn't pay to get back their stolen property. If he had the right measure of the Westlakes, they could buy this whole store and not miss it.

"I'll tell them they need to buy the stuff back," Alex said. "It's not your fault their daughter stole it."

"I doubt that will be much help," the pawnbroker said in a resigned voice.

"Listen, if they give you a hard time, tell them you'll have to file a police report declaring all the things their daughter sold you as stolen," Alex said. "They aren't going to want her name on an official police report and hushing that up will be way more expensive than just paying you."

The man's round face brightened at that.

"That's pretty good," he said with a conspiratorial wink, then he offered Alex his hand. "Thanks."

Alex shook it, then picked up his kit and headed out to look for a phone booth.

"Are you going to be home for dinner?" Iggy asked once Alex got him on the phone.

"That's why I'm calling," Alex said. "I picked up a new case and I'll need to see it through." He explained about the Westlakes and their missing daughter.

"You think she's in danger?" Iggy asked once Alex finished.

"No, I think she's mad at her parents and she's run away from home."

"Perhaps," Iggy said, drawing out the word.

Alex always felt the hairs on the back his neck stand up when Iggy talked like that.

"You think I missed something?"

"No," he said. "You're probably right. Unless the young lady wasn't only supplementing her lifestyle by stealing from her parents."

Alex hadn't considered that. Vivian Westlake was stealing from her parents, but what if that money wasn't enough to pay for her high living? Usually a woman didn't have to buy her own drinks, but the nightclubs near the core were expensive places. What if she owed money to someone who didn't want to hear that her father might disinherit her?

If this was an actual kidnapping and not just a fit of youthful pique, Alex could be walking into a hornet's nest.

"I'll be careful," he told Iggy.

"Good lad," Iggy replied. "Now I'm anxious to hear about June. Did you learn anything new?"

Alex sighed. In the wake of the Westlake's panic over their daughter, he'd almost managed to forget about June's suicide.

"I went by the apartment of Hugo Ayers, the man she was supposed to have murdered," he said, resisting the urge to curse. "I don't care if June wrote a confession saying they were having an affair, if Hugo ever had a woman in that apartment, I'll eat my hat."

Iggy didn't respond right away, and Alex could tell he was thinking over what he knew about the case. He lit a cigarette as the silence dragged out between them.

"I don't know, lad," he said finally. "If June wasn't having an affair with this man then someone forced her to kill him."

"And to write that confession?" Alex added.

"I suppose that's possible," Iggy said, and Alex could hear the doubt in his voice. "But that's a lot of work just to kill a man. Is there any reason someone would want to kill Mr. Ayers?"

"He was a bookkeeper," Alex offered, prepared for the question. "That means he knew his clients' secrets, at least the ones that have to do with money."

"Any of his clients likely to have financial secrets worth killing for?"

Alex was less prepared for that question, even though he knew Iggy would ask it.

"Not that I can see," he said. "Ayers did lose some clients earlier in the year, and I haven't had a chance to look into that."

"That seems like a long time to wait to kill him," Iggy observed. "It's not impossible though. Anything more recent?"

"He has one new client, some company called Ashford. I don't know what that is yet, but I'll figure it out tomorrow."

"Ashford? As in William Ashford?"

Alex shrugged at that.

"Don't know," he admitted. "Is that something I should know?"

Iggy tisked at him.

"I'm disappointed in you, boy," he said. "You're supposed to be reading the entire newspaper, not just the police blotter and the agony columns."

Alex started to protest, but Iggy cut him off.

"Because," he said, "if you had read the whole paper, you'd know that there's an election in two weeks."

"I know that," Alex protested. "Mayor Barnes is up for re-election. According to the papers he's supposed to be a shoo-in."

"All true," Iggy admitted. "But do you know who his challenger is?"

Alex suppressed a groan.

"William Ashford?"

"Correct," Iggy said. "And there's nobody better at having secrets that need hiding than a politician."

"Right," Alex said, feeling foolish. Now that Iggy reminded him, he remembered Ashford's name. He was the son of a former Senator with political aspirations and enough money to indulge them. "I'll find his campaign office tomorrow and find out what Hugo Ayers did for him."

"Good lad. Now, have you eaten anything?"

"I'm calling you from a diner near the area where Vivian Westlake is. I'll grab a sandwich while I wait for the clubs to open." He checked his pocket watch and saw it was only eight minutes to seven.

"Well get going then, and be careful," Iggy said.

Alex promised he would, then hung up and went to flag down the waitress.

Eight minutes and one mediocre pastrami sandwich later, Alex stepped out onto the sidewalk in front of the diner. There were two nightclubs just up the block and he'd planned to start with those. All he needed to do was walk by the front and see if the compass needle turned as he passed. If they weren't the ones he was looking for, he'd grab a cab and follow the needle to wherever Vivian was holed up.

Consulting the compass, Alex crossed the street. He was almost across when someone shouted a warning. A car came tearing through the intersection right at him and Alex barely had time to fling himself out of the way before it careened past.

As Alex landed hard on the sidewalk a tremendous crash erupted behind him, filling the air with the sounds of breaking glass and tortured metal. It took Alex a second to shake off the effects of his landing and by the time he stood up he could hear running feet converging on him.

"Are you all right, young fella?" a voice with an Irish accent asked.

Alex turned to find himself confronted by an older uniformed policeman. He had a strong jaw and a fluffy gray mustache under green eyes.

"I think so," he said. His shoulder and arm were sore, but nothing felt broken. Turning, Alex looked down the road where the car had been heading. It hadn't gone far, plowing into a parked delivery truck and skidding sideways into the street.

Alex turned and limped toward the wreckage, his leg protesting. Already bystanders were gathering, trying to see what happened. When Alex reached the car, he found the driver slumped over the steering wheel.

"Stand back everyone," the cop said, catching up. "Is he all right?" That last was directed at Alex.

Reaching in through the broken window, Alex took hold of the man's coat and pulled him back from the steering wheel. He appeared to be a middle-aged man, with slicked back dark hair and bad skin. He was also quite dead, his lifeless eyes still open and staring at Alex.

"Poor fella'," the cop said. "I don't know what he thought he was doin', though. The way he took off, it was like he was tryin' to hit ya."

"What do you mean by that?"

The cop pointed back down the street in the direction the car had come from.

"I was walking my beat when I saw him over there," the officer said. "He was still there when I came back, just sittin' in his car with the motor runnin'. I was about to tell him to move along when he just took off."

Alex was certain he'd never seen the dead man before. It was probable that the dead man saw the cop coming and simply didn't want to talk to him. He glanced at the diner and then at the dead man. Between his unsatisfactory sandwich and the call to Iggy, Alex had been in the diner for about fifteen minutes.

"How long does it take you to walk your beat?" he asked the officer.

"About a quarter of an hour," he said. "Why?"

Alex glanced around, but no one seemed to be paying undue attention to him.

"No reason," Alex answered, then he clapped the cop on the shoulder. "Thanks for the warning."

He left the cop to sort out the traffic accident and headed up the sidewalk toward the nightclubs. As he went, he told himself that the accident was just that. The dark-haired man had taken off too fast and lost control of his car. Nothing to worry about.

"Yeah," he said out loud in an effort to convince himself. "Nothing to worry about."

11

THE NORTHERN LIGHTS

I t took Alex almost an hour to find Vivian. When the finding rune first located an area just north of the core, he figured she'd taken refuge in one of the nightclubs she frequented. Unfortunately, the two closest to the five and dime where he'd called Iggy were a bust. As he passed them the compass needle barely moved, so he hailed a cab and followed the little needle father inside his target area.

"Stop here," he told the cabbie as the needle swung around suddenly. He hadn't been paying much attention to the street and once he'd paid his driver, he found himself standing in front of a swanky looking nightclub. Art Deco sconces ran along the front, concealing purple neon lights that cast a ghostly glow on green painted walls. The single door leading to the street was also ringed in concealed purple neon, illuminating a heavy, iron bound door painted white. Above the door hung a large panel of frosted glass with multiple neon lights behind it in colors of green, blue, and purple. Solid metal letters had been mounted to the front of the glass and where they blocked the glow of the neon, Alex could read the name, *Northern Lights*.

Muffled band music bled out through the door and the well-dressed man standing in front tapped his toe in time. In the early days, club doormen would have challenged Alex at a fancy place like this, but his fortunes had come up of late.

"Welcome to the Northern Lights," he said as Alex approached, stepping back to take hold of the door and pull it open.

Alex tipped his hat to the doorman as the brassy music washed over him. As he expected, the club itself was below street level and he had to descend a short staircase down to the floor. A girl in a white uniform coat with silver accents took his hat, coat, and kit bag, then Alex made his way to the bar.

It was still early but at least half of the tables were full of couples and groups that had come to eat and dance. Alex scanned the room but didn't see anyone he thought might be Vivian.

"What can I get you?" the barman asked. He was young and handsome with a silver vest over a white shirt.

"Scotch on the rocks," Alex ordered. As the man went to get the drink, Alex pulled the compass out of his pocket and checked it. The needle was pointing toward the back of the club where the band was playing on a short set of risers. To their right was a heavy curtain covering an opening where, presumably, the back rooms were located.

"Is the manager available?" Alex asked as the barman brought him his drink.

"The owner is in his office," he said, pointing to a staircase on the opposite wall from the band. "Up those stairs."

Alex thanked the man, then finished his drink.

At the top of the stairs was a short hallway that ended in a heavy door marked *Private*. To the left was a door with the word *Office* written in white paint on a frosted glass panel. On the right, a similar door was labeled *Engagements*.

Alex guessed that behind the central door were apartments. That worried him. He'd assumed she was underground, but the living spaces were upstairs. That might mean that Vivian was not here of her own volition.

The thought made him hesitate as he approached the office door. He'd left his 1911 and his knuckleduster in his vault. Some clubs had ties to the mob and Alex didn't want to have a gun on him if a club owner had him searched.

In any case, it was too late to change his mind now, so he stepped up to the door and rapped on the frame.

"Come," a voice called from inside.

Alex opened the door and found himself in an elegant office. Like the club below, it had deco accents, including the purple light sconces from outside, though done in frosted glass to cast more light. A dark mahogany desk stood in the middle of the room with filing cabinets on one side and a comfortable-looking couch on the other. Two chairs sat in front of the desk with enough space between them to leave a sort of aisle. It reminded Alex of his own office, just bigger and a lot more opulent.

A broad shouldered man in an expensive suit sat behind the desk. He had a flat face with a square nose, a square jaw, and hard blue eyes. His hair was black, except at the temples where a trace of gray had crept in, though he looked to only be in his thirties. An accounting book sat open on the desk in front of him, illuminated by a brass lamp.

Another man sat easily on the couch with his legs crossed. He was reading a paper, but his dark eyes swept over Alex when he entered. Even sitting down, this man was big and Alex had no doubt this was the proprietor's bodyguard.

In front of the desk stood a short, thin man with deeply tanned skin and a full head of slicked-back hair. He wore a tuxedo and he stood with an earnest posture, leaning slightly forward.

"Just a minute," the man behind the desk said to Alex, then he turned to the standing man. "So you don't know who ordered the wine?"

"No, sir," the man said.

"And now it's just gone?"

"I think it may have been mistakenly served to another party."

The man behind the desk stood up in anger and leaned across the desk.

"You lost track of a 1919 Cabernet?" he shouted. "That's a two hundred dollar bottle and you're saying it just got served to some random guest."

The thin man started to stammer but the speaker waved him silent.

"You're fired, Fairherst," he said. "Get your things and get out."

Fairherst looked like he wanted to argue, but bowed his head and nodded.

"Yes, sir," he said, then turned and withdrew.

The man behind the desk sat back down, watching Fairherst until he left the office, then his gaze shifted to Alex.

"What is it?" he asked, his voice still forceful but polite.

"I was told the owner was up here," Alex said. "Is that you?"

"George Sheridan," he said. "That's me. Now what can I do for you?"

Alex crossed the floor to the desk, pulling out one of his business cards as he went.

"My name's Alex Lockerby," he said. "I need a few moments with Vivian Westlake."

George's eyes hardened considerably at that and his eyebrows threatened to merge in the middle of his forehead. Before he said anything, however, he glanced at the card.

"What's a private dick want with Viv?" he asked.

Alex relaxed a bit at that. George had called her Viv,
instead of Vivian or Miss Westlake. Obviously it was a pet
name, which meant they were probably on friendly terms,
and that meant she probably wasn't a prisoner in the club's
basement.

"Her parents hired me to find out what happened to her,"
Alex explained. "She hasn't been home in over a day and
that's not normal for her."

"Did they tell you how they threw her out?" George
asked.

Alex put on his friendly smile.

"I don't ask about my client's motives, Mr. Sheridan," he
said. "I just do what they pay me to do. In this case, they
wanted me to find Vivian and make sure she was all right."

"And they want her home?"

"They do."

"Miss Westlake is of age, Mr. Lockerby," George said with
a raised eyebrow. "What she does and where she goes are
none of her parents' concern anymore."

That answer surprised Alex. Sheridan's initial reaction
seemed to indicate that he had sheltered Vivian as a favor of
some kind, one he'd be glad to be done with. Now, however,
he seemed to be taking her side. If Vivian told him that her
parents threw her out, he must know she had no more access
to money, and Alex doubted she was such good company that
George would want her hanging around.

"That's true," Alex said. "And I'm not here to deliver an
ultimatum. I just need to see Miss Westlake and let her know
that her parents want her to come home."

"Well I've got a message for the Westlakes," George said,
an edge of anger creeping into his voice. "Vivian doesn't want
anything to do with them. Now shove off."

"You should reconsider that," Alex said, keeping his voice
friendly. "The Westlakes are going to want assurances that

their daughter is safe. If I go back to them and say that she's here but you didn't let me see her...well, rich people can make a lot of trouble if they want to."

George Sheridan stood up at that, his face flushed with anger.

"Are you threatening me, scribbler?" he demanded.

"Of course not," Alex said easily. "I'm just trying to save everyone involved a lot of trouble."

"Beck," George snapped.

The man on the couch put down his paper and stood. He was at least an inch taller than Alex's six-foot one and he outweighed Alex by thirty pounds of solid muscle.

"Throw this bum out," George continued. "And don't be gentle about it."

Alex put up his hands in a placating gesture, but the man-mountain Beck advanced on him. He had a determined expression on his face and his hands balled into fists.

Since there didn't seem to be any reasoning with George or his man Beck, Alex touched his thumb to the ring on the third finger of his left hand. Exerting a tiny amount of will, he activated one of the flash runes on it and blinding light flared up in the room. Alex had shut his eyes tight as the flash went off, but he was still seeing purple dots when he opened them.

To his chagrin, he found that Beck hadn't stopped his advance. He had clearly been blinded but he lunged forward, attempting to bowl Alex over, aiming for the spot where he'd been standing. Alex hadn't actually moved, so Beck caught him on the side of the head with a wild, flailing blow

Alex saw more stars and staggered back out of the blind bodyguard's reach. He kicked over one of the chairs and Beck went for the sound, stumbling as his legs hit the overturned furniture.

Taking advantage of the distraction and his adversary's blindness, Alex shook his head to clear it, then quietly let himself out of the office. He descended the stairs quickly but without giving the appearance of hurrying. The blindness induced by the flash rune would last another thirty seconds or so.

He retrieved his things from the coat check girl and managed to make it out onto the street before any meaningful pursuit could be organized by Beck. Just down from him the thin man Sheridan had fired, Fairherst, was getting into a cab. Alex ran up behind and pushed in after him.

"Mind if I pay for your ride?" Alex asked when Fairherst began to object. "Get going," he told the cabbie. As they pulled away from the Northern Lights, he watched out of the taxi's rear window as Beck burst out the club door onto the sidewalk, looking wildly in all directions. Alex resisted the urge to wave at him.

"Where are you going, Mr. Fairherst?" Alex asked.

"The Astor hotel," he said, then added. "The restaurant manager there has been trying to hire me for a while."

"Astor Hotel," Alex told the cabbie. This close to the core, it didn't take long and Alex bade Fairherst good luck as he stepped out.

"Where to now?" the cabbie asked.

Alex gave the cabbie the address of the Westlake home, then gingerly prodded the left side of his head with his fingers. Beck had only struck him a glancing blow, but he could already tell he'd have a black eye in the morning. He was very glad the man hadn't gotten in a better shot.

Twenty minutes later the cab dropped Alex off in front of a large, inner-ring home with a neat lawn and rose bushes out front. They were dormant on account of the cold weather, but Alex would bet they were amazing in the summer.

A short man with a bow tie and striped waistcoat answered the door, then invited Alex to wait in the foyer. The house was laid out in a U shape around the marble-tiled foyer, with doors leading off to other rooms on the right and left side. A grand staircase occupied the far side of the space, running up to the second floor where more doors were visible through the balusters of the railing.

"Mr. Lockerby," Isabel Westlake exclaimed, rushing out of a side room that appeared to be an elegant parlor. "Is Vivian with you?"

"Not at the moment," Alex said. "But I know where she is."

"Then you must go and get her," she said, pain clearly evident in her voice.

"That's a bit more complicated than it sounds," Alex said.

"Why?" Fredrick asked, following his wife out into the hall.

Alex explained about his encounter with George Sheridan and his refusal to let Alex see Vivian.

"I don't care what he says," Fredrick said, anger flowing over his face. "I'm paying you to get my daughter back."

"With respect, Mr. Westlake, I'm not the police," Alex said. "If I go in there and try to force your daughter to come with me, the cops will arrest me for trespassing and kidnapping."

"But she's clearly being held against her will," Fredrick insisted. "Otherwise this Sheridan fellow would have let you see her."

"You could be right," Alex said. He pulled out his flip notebook and tore out a page he'd prepared in the cab. "If you tell that to the police, they'll send someone over there to talk to your daughter. Sheridan won't be able to stop them, and they'll figure out what's going on."

"Who's Detective Pak?" Fredrick asked, squinting at the paper.

"He's a friend of mine over at the Central Office," Alex said. "Tell him what I told you and he'll find out what's really going on with Vivian."

"That's an unusual name," Fredrick said.

"Danny is of Japanese descent," Alex said. "That's not a problem, is it?"

Fredrick hesitated before answering and Alex fought to keep from getting angry. He'd seen enough of the seedy side of human nature to believe that who a person's parents were made very little difference when it came to who they chose to become.

"No," Fredrick said at last, looking up from the paper. "I have a company that deals in oriental furniture, so I have lots of contacts in the Far East. It's just that Pak isn't a Japanese name, it's Korean."

"Well, I wouldn't know about that," Alex responded. Truth be told, Alex knew Pak wasn't Danny's real name, it was Takahashi. Danny and his sister Amy had changed it because their father was a bigwig in the Japanese Mafia. Alex had never given any thought to their new last name, but he did wonder why they would have picked one from another culture. Maybe he'd ask Danny about it if he got the time.

"Anyway, Danny's a good egg," Alex said. "Tell him I sent you and he'll take good care of you."

"Thank you, Mr. Lockerby," Isabelle said, taking his hand and squeezing it. "We didn't mean to be so forceful and we appreciate everything you've done."

"Will I be able to reach Detective Pak at this hour?" Fredrick asked.

Alex nodded.

"He told me he was working the late shift all this week." He tore another page out of his notebook and passed it over.

"This is the address of the pawn shop where Vivian sold your things. The owner bought them in good faith, so you'll have to buy them back, but I figured you should know where to get them if you want them."

Isabell thanked him as Paul went to telephone Danny, then Alex headed out into the dark city in search of a cab.

When Alex finally managed to get home, it was after nine. Iggy usually retired at nine, but Alex found him hard at work in his vault. His bell jars were filled again, a handful of mayflies in the first and a lone one in the second.

"Just in time," he said with a twinkle in his eye. "What happened to you?"

Confused, Alex just looked at him until Iggy pointed to his eye. Alex touched the side of his face and it stung.

"I had a disagreement with a human mountain," he said.

Iggy walked to a cabinet and pulled out a screw top container.

"Rub that on it before you go to bed and that shiner will be gone by morning."

Alex thanked him and tucked the tin in his pocket.

"I think I've got it this time," Iggy said, turning back to the bell jars.

"You don't have enough bugs in this one," Alex observed. "There were more last time."

Iggy winked at him and his mustache bristled.

"I still think my rune is more efficient than Moriarty's," he said. "So instead of trying to weaken the construct, I'm just using fewer Mayflies."

That made sense. The transfer of life energy should be the same either way.

"Now, let's give it a try."

Iggy handed Alex three rune papers and had him stick them all around the sides of the first bell jar. Iggy then stuck a fourth paper to the top of the second jar and lit it with his gold cigarette lighter.

All four runes flared to life as one and blue symbols of power appeared around the first jar and over the second. Alex felt a tingling in the air as the power of the runes activated and a moment later the mayflies in the first jar all dropped dead. A red halo appeared above the second jar but, as they watched, it shifted to orange.

Alex and Iggy stared through the glass of the second jar at the single Mayfly, but it didn't appear to be doing anything.

"Did it work?" Alex asked.

Iggy sighed and straightened up.

"We won't know till tomorrow morning," he said. "If the color of the detector rune is any indication, this Mayfly has another twelve or so hours left to it."

With nothing to do but wait, Iggy led Alex out to the library for a smoke.

"You didn't tell me about the missing Forgotten when you called earlier," he said once they were seated and Alex had made up the fire.

"Nothing to tell," Alex said. "The morgue was a dead end."

"Have you tried the hospitals?"

"Haven't had time," Alex said. "I suppose I could look in on a few tomorrow, but if the missing people haven't turned up there I don't know what else to do."

"What about your friend at the tabloids?" Iggy asked.

Alex did have a good relationship with Billy Tasker, a writer for the *Midnight Sun*, one of the city's more notorious and sensational tabloids. He was the one who had dubbed Alex the *Runewright Detective*.

"What's he got to do with this?"

Iggy shrugged and puffed on his cigar.

"Maybe nothing," he admitted. "But if there really is an epidemic of missing people from the camps, that seems like the kind of things a tabloid would know about."

Alex hadn't thought of that. It made sense; the Forgotten weren't written about in the serious newspapers. Most people wanted to forget they existed, hence the name. But tabloids thrived on that kind of story. If there were any rumors about missing Forgotten, Billy would know about it.

"I'll call him in the morning," Alex said, taking a cigarette from his silver case.

"Now," Iggy said, blowing a smoke ring toward the fireplace. "Tell me how things went with the missing girl."

"What makes you think I found her?"

"Because you're home, dear boy," he said with a self-satisfied smile.

12
———

RELIGION AND POLITICS

T he morning dawned crisp and cold with frost entirely covering Alex's bedroom window. He'd spent several hours the night before going through the Archimedean Monograph looking for anything he might have missed the last dozen times he'd been through it. Unfortunately the book stubbornly refused to change to suit his desires. There were amazing ideas in there, some he was itching to try, but nothing that would help Iggy refine the life transfer construct.

Alex wasn't one of those people who bounced out of bed at sunrise, ready to meet the day. Usually he needed a liberal amount of coffee to get his synapses going. This morning, however, he found himself up and dressed by eight. As it turned out, all of his reading in the Monograph had yielded one idea. It had nothing to do with Iggy's construct, but Iggy hadn't let Alex help much with that anyway, so he felt justified in working on a project of his own. When he saw the frost on his window, he knew it was time to test it.

Iggy had stayed up even later than Alex, reading the latest

pulp novel in his collection in an effort to clear his head. As a result, the kitchen was cold and dark when Alex made his way downstairs. Normally the lack of a pot of brewing coffee on the stove would be a serious hindrance, but *The Lunch Box* was only two blocks away and they had started opening early since the summer. He'd walk over and get his coffee there, along with some poached eggs and toast.

Stepping outside, Alex pulled the lapels of his trench coat closed against the cold. His breath steamed and the air stung his face. It was perfect.

Normally he kept his rune book in the inside left pocket of his suit coat, but this morning Alex had taken the precaution of tucking it into the outside pocket of his trench coat. Removing it, he flipped through the pages until he found what he was looking for. It resembled a standard barrier rune, one of the first runes Alex had ever learned. Many runewrights knew it and they sold them on street corners when it rained. When activated, a barrier rune would protect the user from rain for about an hour.

This rune looked similar to the basic barrier rune, two interlocking triangles, with minor power symbols inside each of the six points, all written with a pencil. This rune varied only slightly, but the difference was important. Alex had added a circle that filled the inside of the shape, where the triangles intersected. Inside that, he'd written a rune that translated loosely to the word 'temperance'. To Alex, it looked like a fish swimming in such a tight circle that its body turned inward in a spiral. The circle and the rune were done in ruby infused ink and shone red against the dull gray of the pencil lines.

Just as he would do with a barrier rune, Alex licked the flash paper and stuck it to the brim of his hat. He lit it with his morning cigarette and the paper vanished in a puff of fire. The magic washed over him and he shivered as he felt it touch his skin. Like the standard barrier rune, the new version created a bubble of invisible magical energy around him. Almost immediately the cold dissipated and Alex stopped shivering. His clothes and coat were still cool, but the chill in the air was gone.

Alex skipped down the steps of the brownstone and turned south along the sidewalk. He hadn't been sure this new construct would work but now that it had, he couldn't help grinning. About a week ago, he'd come across an idea in the Monograph for a temperance rune, something that would prevent paper from getting too hot. It was supposed to keep books from burning in the event of a fire, and there was a long paragraph on the bottom of the page about the loss of Alexandria. The problem, noted by yet another author, was that the rune simply didn't last long enough to be practical.

Alex had thought that if the rune could prevent paper from heating to the point where it would combust, it might be able to keep water from freezing. He'd tried that in the icebox with a mug of tea and an hour later it came out still hot. As far as he could tell the temperance rune kept whatever object or body it was cast on at the same temperature it started at for the duration of the effect. After that it was a snap to add it to a barrier rune and grant himself temporary immunity to more weather than just rain.

As he walked, Alex marveled at how well the construct worked. He could still feel the wind, but it no longer stung his face, and he didn't have to put his hands in his pockets. This was the sort of idea that could make him a fortune. If only there were a way to mass produce them. That was the inherent weakness of runewright magic, of course. Each rune was a handcrafted work of magic that, once used, was extremely temporary. A runewright could only make as many per day as his body and his talent would allow.

He thought about the Happy Jack rune books he'd seen in

the five and dime. Whoever owned that company must have hundreds of runewrights working round the clock to produce so many constructs. Alex wondered if he could do something like that.

As soon as the thought came, he dismissed it. The barrier rune was simple and most runewrights knew it. But the temperance rune was something he'd only seen in the Monograph. If he started producing powerful constructs with new, formerly unknown runes, someone would connect the dots about who had found the legendary book of rune magic. That was heat Alex simply didn't need, his temperance construct notwithstanding.

A little over an hour later, Alex jumped out of a cab and hurried into the building that housed his office. His climate rune, as he decided to call it, had expired during the cab ride and the short trip from the car to the building lobby nearly froze him.

"You're in early," Leslie said when he stepped into the outer office.

"Lots to do," he said, taking off his trench coat and hanging it on the coat rack beside the door. "I need you to set up a meeting for me," he continued. "As soon as possible."

Leslie picked up her notepad and pencil then looked at him expectantly.

"I need to meet with someone who works for William Ashford's political campaign," he said. "I want to talk to them about Hugo Ayers."

She raised an eyebrow at the request but said nothing.

"I've got to make some calls of my own," he said, heading for his office. "Let me know as soon as you have something."

Alex's first call was to the office of *The Midnight Sun*, a tabloid with a reputation for printing gossip, the more salacious the better. They also had an interesting tendency to break stories that seemed to be the worst kinds of slander that later turned out to be proved true. Alex knew this was because one of their lead writers was actually a legitimate reporter, Billy Tasker.

"Billy, it's Alex," he said when Tasker picked up the other end of the line. "I need to pick your brain."

"I was hoping you'd have something juicy for me," Billy replied. "Things are slow over here."

"That bad?"

"You have no idea. Right now the only thing on today's front page is a story about how some political candidate put a hex on Mayor Banes."

Alex felt the hair on his arms stand up.

"That candidate wouldn't be William Ashford, would it?" he asked.

"Yeah. He's been rising in the polls and no one knows why. Sure he's got bills and sandwich boards all over the city, and he's done some radio, but no one had heard of the guy a month ago."

"So your editor decided on Hexes?" Alex asked with a chuckle.

"Don't laugh," Billy said. "It sells papers."

"Do you think there's something going on with Ashford?" Alex said.

"Why?" Billy asked, his voice shifting from affable to suspicious. "Are you looking at him for something?"

"His bookkeeper was murdered."

"And...?"

"And I'm looking into it," Alex said.

"But you'll call your old pal Billy if it turns out Ashford is involved somehow, right?"

"Of course," Alex said; he even meant it. Mostly. He had no intention of letting Billy or anyone else drag June's name through the mud, but Billy was a good source and Alex needed to keep him happy.

"So what did you call me about?" Billy said.

Alex told him about the missing Forgotten and how both the mission and the Hoovervilles were noticing.

"I haven't heard anything like that," Billy said after a long pause. "I've got contacts at the hospitals and they haven't reported any mysterious accidents or deaths. Now that I know about it, though, I'll keep my ear to the ground."

"Call me if you hear anything." Alex said.

Billy promised that he would, and Alex hung up. His next call was to Bishop Cosgrove at the Manhattan Diocese. The Bishop was not happy to hear that Alex had no new information for him.

"Sorry," Alex said. "I've checked everywhere I know and found nothing. The only conclusion left is that the missing people moved on."

"I know you know your business, Alex," Bishop Cosgrove said. "But this just feels wrong to me. I won't tell you the Almighty is speaking to me or anything so dramatic, but I'm worried. I've been overseeing missions in this city since before the crash. I can tell you for a fact, I've never seen anything like this in all my years."

Alex stifled a sigh and pinched the bridge of his nose. There really wasn't anything more to do, but he could hear Father Harry in the back of his mind telling him that the missing Forgotten needed someone to speak for them.

"All right," he said. "I'll keep looking, but I can't promise I'll find anything."

"That's all I can ask of you," Cosgrove said. "Thank you, Alex. May God watch over you and inspire you."

Alex thanked him and hung up. He could still go by the hospitals and check their morgues, but Billy had said there was nothing there and Alex believed him. Dr. Wagner might have lied to him about not seeing Forgotten coming through the city morgue. He wasn't likely to let Alex in the morgue again, but Alex could simply go around him and ask Danny. If Forgotten bodies were being sent to the morgue, a beat cop or detective would have had to fill out a report.

He reached for the phone before he remembered that Danny was on nights this week. At this hour, he would be home in bed.

"Maybe Dr. Wagner hasn't covered his tracks yet," Alex said, resolving to try the city morgue. Before he could put out his cigarette and get up to leave, however, Leslie tapped on the door.

As Alex looked up, she pushed the door open and leaned on the frame. She was always well dressed, but her outfit today was designed to be eye catching. Her blouse plunged low, her skirt was up over her knees with a long slit that reached up to her mid-thigh. She also wore stockings with high heels. As a former beauty queen, Leslie always looked good, but today she was obviously making an effort.

"You look nice," he said.

She favored him with her million-dollar smile.

"Randall's in town," she said.

Alex didn't comment on that. Her on-again-off-again beau had stood her up last week and Alex knew better than to get in the middle of that.

"I talked to a man named Malcom Jones," Leslie said, sparing Alex the need to comment on her love life. "He's William Ashford's campaign manager. He'll be at their office all day and said you can come by any time to meet him." She tore a page off the top of her note pad and held it up.

Alex stood and buttoned his coat.

"I'm done here anyway," he said.

"Any luck with the missing people from the Hoovervilles?" she asked, passing him the paper with the address of Ashford's campaign office.

"No," he admitted. "But I'll keep looking. Is there anything on the docket I need to know about?"

"A couple of record searches," she said. "I'll start on those after lunch."

Leslie was as good as Alex when it came to digging around in the city's various records offices and newspaper archives, maybe better. He knew the work was in capable hands.

"Let me know if anything comes up that I need to know about," he said, picking up his kit bag and putting on his hat. "I'm going to try to see Danny after I meet with the guy at Ashford's campaign, but I'll call before I do."

Leslie gave him an encouraging smile and Alex donned his trench coat and headed out.

The headquarters of William Ashford's campaign for Mayor wasn't what Alex had expected. One could argue that New York was the most powerful and influential city in the world, so being its mayor was a big deal. The building where the cab dropped him off was older and not in the best repair. There were bits of crumbling brick around the eaves and some of the windowsills were warped and peeling. It was located almost at the outer edge of the mid-ring, north of the park in an area that was mostly homes and small businesses.

Alex would have thought himself in the wrong place except for the large *Ashford for Mayor* sign in the lobby window. There wasn't an elevator, so Alex walked up the three flights of stairs to reach the heavy door with another advertisement for Ashford on it.

Beyond the door was a large open space where several people worked at desks. Most were typing various things while a few others were on the phone. Everyone looked busy, but with the election just a week away, Alex expected more activity.

"Are you from the Tribune?" a man in a well-made suit asked, noticing Alex. He looked to be in his early thirties with slicked back brown hair and a baby face. His accent marked him as British and educated. As Alex shook his hand, he noticed a small, round tattoo on the inside of the man's wrist that appeared to be a coin.

"Misspent youth," the man said, noticing Alex's noticing. "I joined the Royal Navy right at the end of the Great War."

Alex raised an eyebrow at that; he didn't look old enough to have served in a war that ended almost twenty years ago.

"I was only sixteen and very enthusiastic," he said. "I'm Malcom Jones, I'm the campaign manager."

"Alex Lockerby," Alex introduced himself. He was about to explain why he was here, but the smile drained away from Jones' face.

"You're the private detective," he said. "I spoke with your secretary. She said you wanted to ask about poor Hugo." He shook his head. "Terrible business."

Alex pulled his hand free of Jones' grip since the man seemed to have forgotten he still held it.

"Can you tell me what Mr. Ayers did here?" he asked.

Jones glanced around at the room, but no one seemed to be paying them any attention.

"Let's go into my office," he said, indicating a plain door in the right-hand wall. He led the way and Alex followed into a small room with a desk and some comfortable chairs. A few folders were neatly stacked on one side of the desk and a bookshelf behind it held books and decorative things, including a bust of George Washington.

"Have a seat," Jones said, moving around to the far side of the desk.

"Is there some reason we're meeting in here?" Alex asked once they were both situated.

Jones looked like he was weighing his answer carefully then he sighed.

"I suppose it's not really a secret," he said. "You see, I was brought on as campaign manager four months ago."

Alex remembered Billy Tasker suggesting that Ashford's campaign took off recently.

"Whenever I take over a political campaign, I always have an audit done of their books," Jones continued. "I asked the city auditor for the name of a good, independent man and they recommended Hugo."

"You said you do an audit whenever you take over a political campaign," Alex said. "Do you do this sort of thing often?"

Jones nodded with a cockeyed grin.

"I'm a professional campaign strategist," he said with obvious pride. "I've run campaigns in Virginia, Maryland, Maine, and here in New York. I'm proud to say that most of my candidates have won, though, of course, you can't win them all."

Alex jotted this down in his notebook. He'd never heard of a professional political adviser, but it was probably like any other job.

"So why do you do an audit when you get hired to run a campaign?"

Jones laughed at that.

"You'd be amazed the shenanigans that operations like this get up to," he said. "Whenever you have lots of people responsible for posting bills or running newspaper ads, you find corruption. It's a side effect of spending so much money in such a short amount of time."

"And did Hugo find any of that corruption?"

Jones' face clouded over and he sighed.

"Yes," he admitted. "We had to let several people go for misappropriating funds. One fellow had an expense account so he could take wealthy potential donors to lunch."

"Let me guess," Alex said. "He was using it to court dancing girls."

"I see you're no stranger to politics, Mr. Lockerby," he said with a laugh.

Nothing could be further from the truth, of course. Alex hated everything about politics and ignored it as often as he could. He did, however, have a pretty good understanding of human nature.

"I went through Mr. Ayers' apartment," Alex said, changing the subject. "It looks like he worked here since you came on four months ago. Was he still auditing the books?"

"No," Jones admitted. "He finished the audit in about a week He did such good work that I hired him on for the duration of the campaign."

"You said you fired the people who'd been stealing money. Any of them make threats, maybe mention Hugo?"

"Not that I'm aware of," Jones said, his face clouding over. "What, exactly, are you getting at, Mr. Lockerby? I thought Hugo was killed because of an illicit love affair."

Alex fixed the man with a grin.

"You knew Hugo," he said. "Did he seem like the kind of man to have an affair with a married woman at least ten years his junior?"

Jones got a look of confusion and revulsion.

"I wouldn't have thought so," he admitted. "But that woman who shot him was caught red handed, wasn't she? And the paper said she left some kind of confession, explaining why she did it."

"Yes," Alex said. "That is what the papers said, but if there's one thing I've learned in the detective business, it's not to believe everything I read."

"You think Hugo's death has something to do with his work here?"

Alex shrugged.

"You said it yourself, there's a lot of money moving around a political campaign. Maybe someone didn't like getting fired. Maybe they blamed Hugo."

"And enticed a young woman with a husband and a life to shoot him in cold blood?" Jones said with a raised eyebrow of disbelief.

Alex had to admit, when he put it like that, it did sound a little crazy.

"I'm just doing my due diligence," he said. "The papers are probably right, but I get paid to make sure."

"Well, I don't know what I can tell you about this sad business, Mr. Lockerby," he said. "All I, or anyone here, really knows about Hugo was that he was a good bookkeeper."

"If it's okay with you, I'd like to see Mr. Ayers' desk," Alex said. "Maybe there's something there that can shed some light on what happened."

He expected Jones to turn him down, but the man just shrugged.

"I can't let you see the campaign books, of course," he said. "But those are in the office safe anyway. I suppose there's no harm in it."

He stood and led Alex to a desk in a little room off the main office. It was neat and orderly, just like Hugo's apartment, with a single desk in the center of the room. A brass lamp stood atop it and there was a locking filing cabinet on one wall.

"What's in there?" Alex asked, gesturing at the cabinet.

"Those are the personnel files for everyone on the staff and our freelancers," he said. He took hold of the top drawer and tugged on it to confirm that it was locked, then turned to go.

"Let me know when you're done," he said, then he left Alex alone in the little office.

13

THE WHEEL OF FORTUNE

It was just past noon when Alex stepped out of the lobby of the Ashford Campaign's building and into the frigid Manhattan air. He'd spent almost three hours going over Hugo Ayers' office and hadn't found a thing. There was a thick book with copious notes about the campaign's financial transactions, detailing who was being paid and for what. Alex had expected to find something suspicious in all of that, but the transactions were very straightforward and pedestrian. He wondered why Hugo bothered keeping such detailed notes of the dozens of small, ordinary transactions the campaign had on a daily basis. When he asked, Malcom informed him that such record keeping was required by the State Board of Elections.

Alex should have known.

By the time he'd finished going through Hugo's notes, the only thing he had discovered was a headache.

The bookkeeper's desk, like his apartment, was neat and Spartan with no evidence that he had a paramour of any kind. The drawers contained nothing more than the tools of the bookkeeper's trade: pencils, erasers, a slide rule, notebooks, and the ruled paper favored by financial record keepers. There was even a green eyeshade to reduce strain from the harsh overhead light. What wasn't there was anything that might hint that Hugo Ayers was anything other than he appeared; a quiet, competent, unattached bookkeeper.

The only thing that had seemed out of place was a hand-bill announcing the opening of the new skycrawler line that ran from South Harlem over to the Bronx. Since the ribbon cutting was due to take place at the seventh avenue station, and that was only two blocks from the campaign building, Alex assumed Hugo planned to attend, so that was a dead end as well.

Standing on the sidewalk, Alex looked up and down the street, but there wasn't a cab in sight. Since he hadn't thought to call for one before he left Ashford's headquarters, Alex turned east along the road and started walking. He considered using one of his climate runes, but the weather had warmed up tolerably and the bitter chill in the air had gone.

Exactly two blocks later, Alex reached Seventh Avenue. On the opposite side of the street, a scaffolding had been erected around the new skycrawler station. Since the grand opening was in less than a week, workmen were scrambling to finish construction on the raised platform that was the station itself. Alex couldn't board the elevated crawler here since the functioning part of the line was further south, so he ducked into a corner drugstore to call a cab from there.

After he called for a cab, Alex dropped another nickel into the phone's slot and dialed his office. He'd promised to call Leslie and it was already after noon.

"I'm sorry sir," the operator said after almost two minutes. "Your party doesn't answer."

That was strange. Leslie was going to run some record searches, but the city offices would all be closed for the lunch hour.

"Is there another number you'd like to try?" the operator pressed when Alex didn't respond.

"Yes," he said, digging out his rune book. He flipped to the little pocket in the back and pulled out the business card of Paul Masterson. This time the line connected on the second ring.

"Did you find something?" Paul asked once Alex identified himself. "Anything?"

There was a pleading desperation in Paul's voice and it grated on Alex's conscience. He was absolutely certain June hadn't been having an affair with Hugo Ayers, but if that was true, why would she have killed Hugo?

Why would she have killed herself?

"I'm pretty sure that your wife didn't know Mr. Ayers," Alex said, choosing his words carefully.

"I already know that," Paul said, irritation born of stress giving an edge to his voice.

"Yes," Alex said in a calm, placating voice. "Now I know it too. That means that this is either an elaborate frame up, or somebody blackmailed your wife into killing Ayers and then herself."

"She was from Wisconsin, for God's sake," Paul said, his voice coming out in a sob. "She didn't have any dark secrets, nothing anyone could have used to force her to do such horrible things."

Alex didn't know June, but he knew better than to believe that. There was always a way to get to someone if you worked hard enough. Of course that begged another question: who wanted Hugo Ayers dead that badly? Getting the kind of leverage you needed to force someone to kill would take a lot of work. It would have been much easier to just find a mob hitter who was willing to freelance. That suggested that whoever had forced Jean's hand already had leverage on her, and that meant it was likely someone from her past.

"Listen Paul, I'm sure you're right" Alex lied. "If you want me to stop all this, just say the word."

A long silence stretched out over the wire, then Paul said, "No."

"Well, in that case, I want you to call your building's superintendent and have them let me into your apartment."

"Why?" There was an edge of anger in the question.

"If someone forced June to do this, they would have had to contact her at your home," Alex explained. "And," he rushed on before Paul could protest, "if this is a frame up, they would have had to take your wife from there. In either case, whoever did this might have left evidence behind. If I can find it, I have a good chance to figure out what really happened. If someone else is involved, I might be able to prove it."

"All right," Paul said with a heavy sigh. "Do whatever you need to do, I've got no secrets. I'll telephone the super."

Alex thanked him, then took down the address of the building and hung up. He knew that June and Paul's apartment was a long shot, but since Ayers was a dead end, he didn't have much choice. If the apartment was a bust, Alex would have to tell Paul the investigation was a dead end and the police version of the story would be the official one. June would be known as a murderess who killed herself to avoid a public trial.

Alex wondered how Paul would go on if it came to that.

The drug store didn't have a lunch counter, so Alex went back outside to wait for his cab. The address that Paul had given him was on the far side of the core in the south side mid-ring, which meant he'd be going right past East 42nd.

"Where to?" the cabbie asked as Alex climbed into the car.

"Runewright Row," he replied.

———

By the time Alex's cab pulled up next to the wide sidewalk that made up Runewright Row, the weather had turned cloudy and cold again. Alex considered using another of his new runes, but igniting it in front of fellow runewrights would lead to questions he didn't want to answer. Buttoning his trench coat against the wind, he paid the cabbie and then headed north along the row.

When he'd been here earlier in the week, the number of pushcarts and sellers had been fewer than he was used to, but now they were positively thin. Several carts stood by themselves, with large gaps between them and their neighbors. The gaps were too frequent and too large to be explained by the bad weather.

"Alex," Marnie said as he approached her cart. Her wizened face broke into a smile and her breath steamed in the frigid air. "I didn't think I'd see you today."

Alex tried to come by at least four times a week, but if he hadn't made it by noon, it usually meant he wasn't coming.

"I was passing by," he said with a grin and a shrug. He looked up at the gray sky and shivered. "It's exactly the sort of weather for a hot cup of coffee. Please tell me you have some ready."

Marnie's face fell.

"I sold out at lunch," she admitted. "I'm brewing some more but it won't be ready for a bit. I've got your thermos," she said. "But I'm sure it's cold by now."

Alex put down his kit bag and extracted the empty thermos.

"I'll take it anyway," he said. Cold coffee wasn't ideal, but he had a boiler stone for heating up coffee back at his office. Once he got back there, Marnie's coffee could easily be made drinkable again.

He passed over the empty thermos and accepted the full one in return. Normally, Alex would have brought runes to trade, but he hadn't anticipated coming by today, so he didn't have anything prepared. Marnie would have to make do with cash.

"That's too much and you know it," Marnie said as he passed her a five dollar bill.

"It's all I've got," Alex lied.

A look of gratitude ghosted across her haggard features and the fiver vanished into the front pocket of her apron.

"In that case you have to stay until the fresh coffee is ready," she said. "I insist."

She checked the pot on the far end of her cart. It sat on a block of wood to keep it from scorching her pushcart. Inside the pot, Marnie had added a fragment of a boiler stone. Once the contents began to boil, she'd remove the stone with a pair of tongs and the coffee would be ready to drink, though a bit hot at first.

The coffee pot was just beginning to steam, so Alex didn't mind waiting. Being ten minutes later to Paul and June's apartment wasn't likely to make any difference.

"Did I hear there's no coffee?" a woman's voice interrupted. She sounded familiar to Alex, but he couldn't place her.

Turning, he found the job seeker from the other day approaching. She was clad in a light coat that was some color between purple and red, and she looked cold. Her raven hair was tied together behind her head and the rest hung down over her shoulder, providing a dark barrier between the coat and her olive skin.

"Miss Knox," Alex said, finally remembering her name. She was the fortune teller who was looking for secretarial work. "What brings you out in this weather?"

She favored him with a crooked smile.

"Same as you, I expect," she said. "I need a hot cup of coffee."

"It'll be a few minutes, dear," Marnie said.

"How goes the job hunt?" Alex asked as Marnie busied herself with the brewing pot.

Sherry shrugged and looked a bit sheepish.

"Lots of people want me to tell their fortune," she said. "Not so many want a secretary."

Alex was surprised to hear that. Sherry didn't have Leslie's incredible good looks but she was attractive in a girl-next-door sort of way. She shouldn't have had too much trouble landing a job.

Maybe she can't type.

"Where is everybody?" Sherry said, pointing to the largely empty row.

"Gone off to work for that factory," Marnie grumbled, warming her chapped hands around the coffee pot.

"Happy Jack?" Alex asked, getting a dark look and a nod in return.

Clearly Marnie thought that any runewright who would leave the row for paying work was some kind of sell out. Alex looked up and down the street, taking in the gaps in the usual line of carts. If he had to guess, a full third of the occupants of the row were gone, maybe a bit more.

"You sure they're all working on those rune books?" he asked.

"Some slick fellow came down here the other day," Marnie said with a curt nod. "Said there was good pay to be had for any runewright who could do a minor mending rune."

"Is that hard?" Sherry asked.

Marnie shook her head.

"Most folks can do it, but you'd think they'd have more pride."

Alex didn't think that. Most factories had boilers to run steam powered machinery, that meant that in this weather, they were warm. He ran an appraising eye over Marnie's clothing. Her coat was thin and the gloves on her hands had holes in most of the fingers. It might cost him his source of good coffee, but Marnie could use easy work in a warm place.

He was about to suggest that she take the work when Sherry spoke up.

"It's cold," she said, suppressing a shiver. "What say I tell your fortune while we wait?" She directed herself to Alex.

Caught off guard, he muttered something that sounded positive and Sherry smiled. She pulled a pack of large cards from the pocket of her coat and moved to Marnie's cart.

"Do people really ask you to do this in job interviews?" he asked as Sherry began shuffling the cards.

She smiled and nodded.

"Oh, yes," she said, enthusiastically. "It's all the rage these days."

Alex had a hard time believing that. Fortune telling wasn't real magic, it was an entertaining show, a spectacle for the gullible or the bored. Sherry seemed to sense Alex's hesitation and she smirked.

"Come on, Mr. Lockerby," she urged. "It'll be fun."

"I'd like to see it," Marnie said, moving to stand behind Sherry.

"All right," Alex said, doing his best not to sigh as he said it. He really didn't have time for this, but since he'd already said he was waiting for coffee he couldn't just leave.

"Let's see who is surrounding you," Sherry said. She cut the deck and then pulled one of the large cards from the top. Turning it over she placed it on the worn surface of Marnie's cart. The face of the card depicted a man in a flowing robe standing under a spreading tree. He had a crown on his head and a medallion hung round his neck with a five-pointed star on it.

"The King of Pentacles," Sherry declared with a raised eyebrow. "An auspicious beginning."

"What does it mean?" Marnie asked, already being drawn into the spectacle.

Alex resisted the urge to say 'nothing.'

"It could mean many different things," Sherry said. "Traditionally, the suit of Pentacles represents the earth, but Pentacles are also symbols for magic. The King usually represents prosperity or security."

"How do you know which of those things it means?" Marnie pressed.

Sherry gave her an enigmatic smile and placed her hand back on the deck.

"You have to let the story play out," she said. "Once we have more pieces, it gets easier to decipher the meaning of each card."

She turned over the next card, revealing the image of a tree with a sturdy branch sticking out from it. Below the branch a man was suspended from a rope that appeared to be wrapped around one of his feet.

"The Hanged Man," Sherry said. "A portent of sacrifice or danger, it could also mean someone in need of help."

Sherry reached for the next card.

"How many cards do you draw?" Alex asked, interested in the performance if not the fortune.

"Every reading is a story, Mr. Lockerby," Sherry said.

"Call me Alex."

"Well, Alex, it's just like reading a book," she explained. "I keep drawing cards until the story ends."

She turned over the next card. This one had a handsome

woman seated on a wooden chair. A crown of brass sat on her head and she held a glass orb with the five-pointed star inside it. This card came off the deck upside down from the others, but Sherry didn't turn it over, instead laying it in line as it had been drawn.

"The Queen of Pentacles," she said. "But she's inverted."

"What's that mean?" Marnie asked, her voice barely a whisper.

"The Queen represents practicality and determination, but because she's upside down, it reverses the meaning."

"So, frivolity and sloth?" Alex asked with a chuckle.

"More like selfishness or jealousy," Sherry said. She turned the next card, revealing a man and woman clutched in a passionate embrace. "The Lovers," she said.

Well, things are starting to look up, Alex thought. Unless that represented Paul and June Masterson.

It doesn't represent anyone, he reminded himself. *She's not seeing the future.*

"The High Priestess," Sherry declared, laying down a card with a woman clad in an elaborate robe. "I think these are all the people in your present orbit Alex."

"A King, a hanging man, an upside-down queen, some lovers and a priestess," Alex recited. "Quite the motley crew."

Sherry grinned at that, putting her hand back on the deck.

"Let's see what role you will play?" She turned over the next card, laying down the image of an armored man with an oversized sword, seated on a horse. When she saw the image, Sherry grinned. "I should have known, the Knight of Swords."

"So what's it all mean?" Marnie asked again.

"We're not quite done," Sherry said. She pointed to the cards she'd laid out. The first five cards, representing people, were laid out next to each other in a row. The knight card, representing Alex, had been placed below that row in the center, directly beneath the inverted queen.

"I think they are grouped together like this," Sherry went on. She placed the King and the Hanged Man so they were touching and did the same for the Lovers and the High Priestess. The inverted Queen she left alone above the knight.

The position of the Queen's wand and the knight's sword made it look as if they were locked in battle.

"What now?" Alex asked, interested in the story Sherry was weaving. She was really quite good at this and he wondered why she wanted to give it up. Surely someone with her skills as an entertainer could make good money.

"Now we discover what obstacles stand between you and the others." Sherry turned over a card depicting what looked like a lighthouse. Like the Queen, this card was inverted, and Sherry placed it between the pair of the King and Hanged Man, and the knight.

"The Tower," Sherry said. "It represents disaster, but inverted it can mean disaster avoided."

"So I'm supposed to avert some disaster between these two?"

Sherry cocked her head, as if considering Alex's words, then she nodded.

"Yes," she said. "It could mean exactly that, but in my experience the cards are never quite that direct. The hanged man represents a person in jeopardy and the inverted tower is between you and them."

"What about the King?"

"He represents stability," she said. "Abundance. Perhaps it means some sort of patron, a benefactor for someone in jeopardy."

"And I'm supposed to what?" Alex asked. "Bring them together to avoid disaster?"

Sherry looked up at him across the cards. It the gray light of the cloudy afternoon, her dark eyes seemed to reflect the purple backs of the deck in her hand.

"I think you have the right of it," she said with a serious nod. She turned over the next card, placing it between the inverted Queen and the knight. "The Inverted Moon," she said, though Alex couldn't tell that it was upside down. "Illusion, misrepresentation, and fear," she said.

Without stopping to explain, she turned over one more card. This one had a pinwheel on it like the kind carnival barkers spun to award prizes at a county fair. Sherry placed the card between the lovers, the high priestess, and the knight. As she did it, her mouth crooked up in a self-satisfied smile.

"Okay," Alex said after a moment of silence. "What story does it all tell?"

Sherry looked up and fixed Alex with a serious gaze.

"You already know this one," she said, pointing to the first group. She moved her finger over to the other side of the pattern and pointed at the lovers and the hanged man. "The Wheel of Fortune represents change," she said. "You will be confronted with a great change, one that will affect the lives of all these people."

"And I have to sort it all out for them?" he guessed.

Sherry pointed to the knight card, at the enormous sword he carried.

"Beware, Alex," she said. "In this story, you are the Knight of Swords. The sword can cut in both directions."

"So, if I'm not careful, I could screw up these people's lives even more?"

"Yes," Sherry said with no trace of amusement or self-consciousness.

"What about the Queen and the Moon?" Alex asked.

This time the look Sherry gave him was troubled.

"The Queen might be a person," she said. "Trapped or bound in an illusion or a lie."

"So I have to free her?" Alex guessed.

"Be careful," Sherry said. "The sword—"

"Cuts both ways," Alex finished. "I know. Well, that was very interesting—"

"I'm not finished," Sherry said in a firm voice. Her eyes were locked on his with an intensity that bordered on passion and they'd regained their purple reflection. "The Queen is of the earth element," she said. "That could mean anything from stability to magic."

Alex didn't see how that helped but he waited for her to finish.

"It could also mean that the Queen isn't a person," she said. "She might represent the earth itself."

"So the earth is caught up in a lie and needs me to free it," Alex said, barely managing to hide the sardonic smile threatening to spread across his lips.

"Not the planet," Sherry said. "The people."

Alex's mind flashed back to a darkened room in the attic of a slaughterhouse. What was it Moriarty had said? He wanted Alex to be his lever, a lever to move the world. A shiver ran up Alex's back and his mind snapped into sharp focus.

"So, according to the cards, I have to save everyone on earth?" he said. He intended to sound sarcastic, but his voice came out raspy. "The cards seem to think very highly of me."

Sherry didn't answer, but moved her finger to point at the oversized sword in the knight's hands.

"The sword cuts both ways, Alex," she repeated, her voice low and solemn. She looked up at him with an enigmatic expression that was neither smile nor frown. "It might be your destiny to save the world...or you might be the one who destroys it."

14

VIVIAN

A lex finally arrived at the modest apartment of Paul and June Masterson just after one o'clock. The building superintendent, a fat woman with a motherly disposition, let him in and lingered, asking questions about what had happened to June. It was clear she was both shocked and tantalized by the story and wanted more details than the papers had provided

Alex thanked her curtly and hustled her out. He wasn't usually that brusque, but the meeting with Sherry Knox had bothered him. All the way over in his cab, he'd reviewed what she'd said in his mind. He had no illusions: no magic was capable of seeing the future, but Sherry's reading had come uncomfortably close to Moriarty's words. It had to be a coincidence, but Alex hated coincidences.

There's no such thing as coincidence in murder. Iggy's words rang through Alex's mind. As far as he knew, Sherry wasn't involved in a murder, so he took a deep breath and forced the memory to the back of his mind. If it still bothered him later, he'd relate the experience to Iggy and see what his mentor thought.

"He'll think I'm an idiot who's reading meaning in tea leaves," Alex said out loud, then he set down his kit bag and got to work.

First, he walked through the Mastersons' apartment, just letting his mind observe it. The counters were clean and there weren't any dishes in the sink. A basket sat beside the kitchen table with a cloth draped over it; the word 'Mending' had been stitched across it with burgundy thread. The basket was empty except for a sock with a hole in the toe and its mate.

In the bedroom, everything was in order. A laundry hamper was half full and no clothes were left out. Even the bed was made.

Alex wondered if Paul had been back since June's death.

With nothing obvious out of place, Alex began opening drawers and examining the shelves in the closets. Based on what he knew of Paul, he doubted June was some kind of criminal mastermind. If she was hiding correspondence or gifts from a lover, they'd be in the usual places. When that didn't yield anything, Alex started looking for false bottom drawers or hidden panels behind walls or in the backs of cupboards.

An hour later he had to admit defeat. June Masterson wasn't hiding anything. She had no jewelry stashed where her husband wouldn't be likely to see it, no love letters carefully hidden away, and no inconvenient blackmail notes concealed under her mattress.

The police had taken the note June had written confessing her affair with Hugo, but the trash can was still mostly full, so Alex went through it. He found an old shopping list and a note from a neighbor about some misdirected mail, but nothing else handwritten. There were two red covers for empty Happy Jack rune books, which explained the empty mending basket, but nothing of significance.

Alex sat at the kitchen table for a quarter of an hour puzzling through what he knew. The lack of any crumpled drafts of June's confession bothered him. If June had really been leaving a letter behind for her husband, she would have rewritten it at least once. The idea that she just wrote out what she wanted to say on the first try simply wasn't creditable.

It gave weight to the idea that she'd been forced to write that note. A note someone else had probably written in advance. But who? And why? And how?

Alex didn't have answers for any of those questions. He didn't even have theories. It had to be that Hugo was the target and June was just the killer's weapon, but as far as Alex could tell, there was no reason to kill Hugo. He didn't work with the kind of information that would compromise his clients, and he didn't have any clients with mob connections.

The mayoral race seemed like it provided the most possibility for a motive. If the campaign was up to something and Hugo found out, that might put him at risk. But the campaign had to report their every move to the state, who undoubtedly would send in auditors. If they were doing something off the books, Hugo wouldn't have known about it. Also, the only way for that theory to work was if someone in Ashford's inner circle had a connection with June, one that came with serious blackmail material.

That just wasn't likely.

Too many coincidences.

Alex knew there was nothing left to find in the Masterson's apartment, but he picked up his kit bag and pulled out his multi-lamp and oculus just the same. He spent half an hour going over the place again and found nothing.

Admitting defeat, he packed up his kit and checked the time. It was getting on toward three. Leslie would be at the archives doing her research, so he couldn't call her. Instead he headed down to the street and caught a cab, telling the driver to drop him off in front of the Central Office of Police.

Danny Pak looked tired when Alex arrived at his desk half an hour later. He had dark circles under his eyes, and he sat with his shoulders slumped forward. Clearly the night shift wasn't agreeing with him.

"You look like hell," Alex said when Danny finally caught sight of him.

"Last night went late," he said, a tired grin dragging its way onto his face.

Alex sat down on the corner of Danny's desk and took out a cigarette, then offered one to Danny.

"What happened?" Alex asked, lighting his cigarette with his brass lighter as Danny used a paper match on his. "You catch something interesting after dealing with the Westlakes?"

Danny raised an eyebrow and some of his color seemed to come back.

"You mean your clients didn't tell you?" he asked. "The club owner had their daughter locked up in his back room. We had to bust the door down to get her out."

That didn't sound right. When Alex had met George Sheridan, the club owner freely admitted that Vivian West-lake was there. Why would he do that if he was actually holding her hostage? And why, when he knew Alex would go straight to the family, did Sheridan still have her in his club when Danny and the cops arrived?

"We took her back to her parents," Danny continued. "She was pretty glad to see them."

"What did Sheridan say when you got there?" Alex asked.

"He wasn't in," Danny said. "But after he tried to throw

you out earlier, the Lieutenant had us get a warrant. When we searched the place, we found Miss Westlake locked in a storage room behind the bandstand."

None of this jibed with Alex's meeting. Sheridan definitely thought of himself as a tough guy, but he didn't seem stupid.

"What did Vivian tell you?" he asked.

Danny shrugged.

"Just that she'd thought Sheridan was a good guy. I guess he told her that her parents hired you and she got cold feet, wanted to go home. That's when Sheridan locked her up."

Alex nodded. It still didn't make much sense, but maybe the reason Sheridan had gone out was to find a place to stash Vivian.

"Well at least she's home safe," Alex said. The whole thing was still bothering him, but with Vivian home, his work was done. "Did you manage to nab Sheridan?"

Danny smiled and nodded.

"He came waltzing in just as we were leaving, demanding to know why we were there. He's cooling his heels downstairs in holding as we speak."

"What's his story?"

"He clammed up quick," Danny said. "Demanded to see his lawyer. But Callahan knows him. The little weasel used to run with the Rosono Crime Family, but he was a minor player."

"Does he still have mob ties?" Alex asked. He'd been leery of the Rosonos since he helped Danny bring down their inside man at the police department, former DA Acheson Smith. As far as he knew, Lucky Tony Casetti, who ran the family, hadn't expressed any interest in either him or Danny, but his ears perked up whenever the Rosono name came up.

Danny shrugged.

"Who knows? I'll let the state's attorney figure it out."

"Well, good job. Keep this up and you'll make Lieutenant before you're thirty."

"Keep making me look good," Danny said with a chuckle.

"Yeah," Alex said, glancing around to see if anyone might be paying attention to them. "About that. I need to get a look at a police file. The one on the Ayers murder."

Danny's brows knit together for a moment, then he remembered.

"You said Detective Lowe had that case? You know I'm not supposed to go snooping in other detective's cases."

Alex shrugged, then checked again to see if they could be overheard.

"With June dead, the case is closed, right?"

"Yeah," Danny said in a noncommittal tone.

"So the file is probably already on its way over to the archive. I just need you to pull it for a few days."

"You think there's more to this?" Danny said. Alex started to answer, but Danny held up his hand. "Do you have any evidence that something's wrong with this case?"

"No," Alex admitted after a long pause. "But everything about this stinks. I've been over both their apartments, and Hugo Ayers' office, and there's nothing. No evidence that they even knew each other, much less were secret lovers."

"She wrote a confession," Danny said. "According to the papers it was in her own handwriting."

"That's why I need to see the file," Alex explained. "Something about this is off, and I don't know what it is yet."

Danny gave him a hard look.

"I could get in real trouble if Lowe or his lieutenant find out about this."

"You know I wouldn't ask if it wasn't important." When that didn't sway his friend Alex added, "I'll get you a dinner invite to the brownstone. Lord knows you don't eat well with

Amy gone." Iggy was an excellent cook and he was fairly stingy with dinner invitations.

Danny held his gaze for another moment, then sighed and nodded.

"I know one of the girls in the file room," he said. "I'll have her pull the file, but it'll take a few hours. Come back tomorrow."

Alex thanked his friend, then headed for the elevators. Once in the lobby, he stopped to call Leslie, but again he got no answer. Whatever research she was doing must have been more difficult than she thought.

With Leslie still out, there wouldn't be any new work waiting for Alex at his office. But with Vivian safe at home, he could collect the rest of his fee from the Westlakes.

The home of Fredrick and Isabel Westlake looked much more impressive in daylight. It was a modest Victorian number complete with a wraparound porch and a tower. Located in the inner ring just up against the Core, it had an air of opulence about it without the over the top pretension to wealth so common to Core homes. A wrought iron gate with an intricate art nouveau pattern encircled the small yard and, even though it was full winter, Alex could tell that the Westlakes employed a groundskeeper.

He wasn't expected, so he just walked up the cobbled path that led from the sidewalk and rang the bell. A plump man in an expensive suit answered the door after a few moments. He was in his forties by the look of him, with thick brown hair cut in an older style and calculating eyes. The latter he ran over Alex, apprising the visitor to his house.

"Yes?" he said in a voice that marked him as a New

Englander. "Come in," he said once Alex explained the reason for his visit.

He led Alex through a small foyer to an elegant sitting room full of comfortable couches and chairs all arranged in a semi-circle. A large fireplace occupied the far wall of the room with a mantle of polished redwood that supported all manner of framed photographs and knick-knacks. A sideboard ran along the opposite wall, laid out with empty dishware that would be filled with hors d'oeuvres when the Westlakes entertained.

"Wait here, please," the butler said. Alex assumed he was a butler, but he'd never really understood the various ranks and positions of the staff employed by rich people. The butler turned and left, presumably to announce Alex's presence, so Alex busied himself by walking around the room and looking at the photos and the bric-a-brac.

Above the fireplace was a decent sized painting of Fredrick and Isabel, obviously done many years ago. Below the painting, in the center of the mantle was a photograph of a young woman that Alex assumed was Vivian. She looked a bit like Isabel, but hadn't inherited her mother's simple beauty. Vivian appeared to be in her teens in the picture, with frizzy hair and an unfortunate amount of acne.

Moving on, Alex found pictures of the Westlakes in locations all over the world. He stopped to look closer at one that showed Fredrick and Isabel in a vineyard. This one included Vivian, but she looked to be about six.

"My biggest failure," Fredrick's voice came from behind Alex.

He turned to find the man standing in the doorway with a smile on his face.

"Pardon?" Alex asked.

Fredrick nodded at the picture.

"That's the Mist Valley Winery," he said. "It's in California. I bought it as an investment back in seventeen." He chuckled to himself. "They had an excellent wine and great prospects, but then..."

Alex nodded. Two years later Prohibition had been signed into law.

"They are making a bit of a comeback," Fredrick went on. "But it takes time to produce a good wine. I don't expect it to start paying off for at least another ten years."

Alex put the picture back on the mantel.

"How's Vivian?" he asked.

Fredrick closed his eyes and sighed.

"It's good to have her home," he said. "It seems her experience has shaken her, though."

"I'm sorry to hear that."

"Don't be," Fredrick said. "It's like we got our old Vivian back. Thank you, Mr. Lockerby."

"I'm glad I could help," Alex admitted.

"I trust you're here about your bill," Fredrick said, reaching into the pocket of his suit coat. He pulled out a thick leather wallet and began pulling twenty dollar bills out of it. "What do I owe you?"

"Twenty-five each for the two runes I used and another twenty-five for the day."

Fredrick paid him and Alex tucked the bills into his trouser pocket.

"If you ever need anything from me," Fredrick said as he ushered Alex back to the front door, "don't hesitate to ask."

Alex laughed at that.

"Just tell your friends that if they need a detective, I'm the guy to see," he said.

"Mr. Lockerby?" a soft voice asked.

He turned to find Vivian descending the broad, curving staircase. At least he assumed it was Vivian. Unlike the unfortunate girl in the photograph on the mantel, this woman was stunning. Gone was the frizzy hair and acne, replaced by long, jet black hair that shimmered and flowed as she moved. Her face was utterly flawless. Alex would have chalked that up to the expert use of makeup, but the large, purple bruise across the right side of her face showed that she wasn't wearing any.

"I apologize for my appearance," she said in a lilting voice. "But when Edwards said you were here, I simply had to meet you."

Alex really didn't care why she bothered; he was enchanted. She stepped off the stairs and glided across the foyer to stand before him.

"I wanted to say thank you," she said. "For helping me."

"It was no trouble at all," Alex said, meaning it. He wanted to let it go at that, but he just couldn't help himself. "When I met with Mr. Sheridan, he said you were staying at the *Northern Lights* voluntarily. What happened?"

She blushed slightly but didn't look away.

"It's true," she said. "I did go to George when I...when I left here. He said I could use one of the spare rooms at the Club; he has a half-dozen for when important people stay."

That was a polite way of saying when they were blind drunk. High profile patrons who didn't want to have pictures of them falling down drunk would often be offered rooms by high end nightclubs.

"Apparently he was planning to woo Vivian," Fredrick said. "Convince her to marry him so he could get his hands on her money when her mother and I are gone."

Alex nodded, stroking his chin. This made more sense.

"So, when I showed up, he realized he was out of time," he said. "But why bother locking you up?"

"He was having a marriage certificate made," Vivian said, looking away for the first time. "He has friends at city hall who could make it look official."

"I'm glad you managed to spook him, Mr. Lockerby," Frederick said.

"After you came by, George asked me to marry him," Vivian explained. "Just like that. Well, of course I refused. That's when..."

"When he gave you that shiner and locked you up," Alex finished, feeling his hands tighten into fists. He should have done worse to Sheridan and his goon than just blinding them.

"It's a blessing in disguise," Fredrick said.

"Yes," Vivian said, raising her chin so her purple cheek became more visible. "If he hadn't shown his true colors, I might still be there, instead of here where I belong."

"With people who really care about you," Fredrick said, putting his arm around her.

"Well, I'm glad I could be of help," Alex said.

Vivian thanked him again, as did Frederick, then Alex returned to the street and headed for his office.

15

THE LAWYER

I t was almost four when Alex stepped through the door into his office waiting room. Leslie had finally returned, and she greeted him with an electric smile. She usually smiled, but this was her happy smile, the one she only brought out on special occasions.

"I take it your search went well?" he said.

A shadow passed across Leslie's face. She was very good at doing the kinds of research a detective agency needed, but she didn't particularly like it. The city archives were always dusty and if she had to go to the library, the old men who frequented the place always ogled her.

"I found everything we need," she said, dismissively. "It's on your desk whenever you're ready to call the clients. How was your day?"

He shrugged as he took off his trench coat and hung it up.

"I still can't make heads or tails of the Masterson case," he said. "I'm pretty sure June shot Hugo Ayers but I can't for the life of me figure out why." He crossed to Leslie's desk and offered her a cigarette.

"Was she having an affair with the bookkeeper?" she asked.

Alex lit the touch tip on the desk and offered her a light.

"No," he said as she puffed her cigarette to life, staining the other end with her dark red lipstick. "I'd be willing to bet a month's earnings she never even met Hugo Ayers before she shot him."

Leslie leaned back in her chair and blew out a puff of smoke.

"Did someone force her to do it?" she asked.

"I don't see how," Alex said, lighting his own cigarette and returning the match to the body of the lighter.

"So it's a frame-up."

"That makes the most sense, but why June? It would be much easier to frame some two-bit thug, make it look like a robbery."

"Put it out of your mind," Leslie said after a long pause. "Focus on something else. You're too caught up in this."

Alex nodded. It was good advice. Sometimes the only way to solve a problem was to let it stew in the back of his mind. Eventually his brain would come up with some new angle.

"What else did you do today?" Leslie asked when he didn't respond.

"I closed the Westlake case," he said, digging the seventy-five dollars out of his pocket and putting it on the desk. As he told Leslie about his meeting last night with George Sheridan and Danny's subsequent rescue of Vivian, Leslie pulled the cashbox out of her lower right desk drawer. She counted out the bills, added them to the considerable stack in the box, then noted down the amount on a notepad. Once she finished, she shut the box and returned it to her desk.

"So how was your day?" Alex asked once she finished.

"I told you," she said. "I put all the research on your desk."

"That's not what I meant," Alex said, giving her a hard look. "I called just after noon and you were out. All the city offices close for lunch, so I know you weren't doing research."

She blushed and Alex nearly fell over. Leslie was a master at concealing her emotions, it was a survival skill from her days as a beauty queen.

"Randall took me to lunch," she said, blushing even more.

"That must have been some lunch."

She sighed.

"It was," her dreamy look evaporated and she regained the control Alex was used to. "I didn't want to spring it on you this way, but...Randall asked me to marry him."

A strange mix of emotions warred inside Alex. His agency's success was in no small part due to Leslie and her business acumen. What would he do without her? He wasn't enough of an optimist to believe that he'd ever be able to replace her. At the same time, he felt relief. Randall had intended to propose to Leslie over a year ago, but one of his children had objected. Leslie had taken that hard.

"What about his daughter?" Alex asked.

"'He's been working on her and she gave him her blessing," Leslie said, unable to keep the electric smile from spreading across her face.

"You're not wearing a ring," Alex pointed out.

Leslie reached into her center drawer and pulled out a satin bag. From inside, she removed a simple gold band with an emerald on it and slipped it on her hand.

"You would have noticed," she said.

"I'm happy for you," he said, and meant every word. He wasn't happy for the effect her leaving would have on his business, but he kept that bit to himself. "When's the big day?"

"December twentieth," she said. "We want to honeymoon over the Christmas holidays."

Alex tried to keep the distress he was feeling from showing on his face, but he must have let some slip.

"We've still got a month to find a replacement," she said, putting her hand on his. "And after we're back from the honeymoon, I'll come into the city a few days a week and help train her. I promise."

"Sorry," Alex said.

"I knew you'd take it hard, kid," she said, lifting her hand to his cheek. "We've been a team for over a decade."

"And we work well together," he said. The realization that she was leaving suddenly hit him and he felt lost. This time he managed to keep it from his face.

"I'll put an ad in the Times tomorrow," Leslie said. " There are plenty of job seekers these days. We should be able to find someone quickly."

Alex put his cigarette in the ash tray on Leslie's desk and dug out his rune book.

Flipping to the back cover, he pulled a business card out of the stitched pocket. The printed name said Madame Hortense, but underneath that was written, Sherry Knox.

The very first time Alex had met her, she'd been looking for secretarial work. She'd seemed surprised that Alex didn't know of any, even though she didn't even know his name at the time.

His mind raced back over his two interactions with her. All he really knew was that she was a fortune teller at the Museum of Oddities, entertaining people with fanciful tales made up from her cards. Based on the reading she'd done for him, she was good at her job.

As Alex recalled the reading she'd done earlier, he remembered one of the interactions she'd predicted. He would be faced with change because of a pair of lovers. He knew card reading was just a form of storytelling, but he felt a chill just the same. According to Sherry, that change also involved another woman, represented by the High Priestess card.

"Hey kid," Leslie's voice broke into his thoughts. "You all right?"

"Yeah," he lied, recovering himself quickly. He handed her the card. "I want you to dig up everything you can on this woman."

"Madame Hortense?" Leslie read with an incredulous look.

"I met her a couple of days ago and she was looking for work as a secretary."

Leslie raised an eyebrow, then tucked the card into her purse.

"That's fortunate," she said.

"Yes," Alex said. "It's quite the coincidence."

He wondered just how much Sherry would have to know about his life to have arranged that meeting. It didn't seem possible, but he hadn't exactly been hiding his activities. How had she known about Leslie, though?

His thoughts were interrupted by the sound of his office door opening. He turned just as a slim older man in an expensive suit entered. He had a shrewd face and walked with a slight limp.

"Can I help you?" Leslie asked, walking around her desk to take the man's hat.

"Are you Alexander Lockerby?" he asked Alex, ignoring Leslie.

"Call me Alex. Is something I can help you with Mr. —?"

"Hardwick," the man said. "Arthur Hardwick, of Finch, Hardwick, and Michaels."

Alex recognized the name. Mr. Hardwick was the senior partner in one of Manhattan's finest law firms.

"I take it you have a client who needs my services," Alex said, motioning toward his office door. "Won't you come in?"

"What makes you think I'm not here with a summons for you?" Hardwick said.

Alex chuckled at that.

"When lawyers want to serve papers, they send a secretary," he said. "If they want information, they send a junior partner. Senior partners only come when they're representing a client in trouble."

Hardwick's face split into a devious grin.

"You'll do," he said. "I represent Mr. George Sheridan, whom I believe you met last night. He would like to retain your services. Shall we step into your office to discuss it?"

Alex bristled but kept his temper in check.

"Of course," was all he said.

"I have to tell you, Mr. Hardwick," Alex said as he sat down at his desk, "last night your client tried to have one of his goons rough me up at his club. I'm not inclined to help him."

If this admission startled Hardwick, the man hid it well.

"I understand that," he said. "But I believe you might be the only man in New York that can help George."

Alex sat back in his chair and steepled his fingers together.

"I was hired by Vivian Westlake's family to find her," Alex said.

"Since she's been found and returned to her family, I'm guessing your obligation to them has been discharged," Hardwick said. "That should leave you free to take my client's case."

"Oh, I'm certainly free," Alex said. "But the police found Miss Westlake locked up in your client's club with a bruise on her face. I'm not seeing a lot of use for a detective in this otherwise open and shut case."

"That's exactly the point," Hardwick countered. "The police have it all wrong."

Alex raised an eyebrow at that. He wondered what story George Sheridan was trying to sell. It would have to be a good one to overcome the mountain of evidence against him.

"Vivian Westlake went to *The Northern Lights* club of her own free will," Hardwick said. "When she got there, she told George that she'd left her family and that she was ready to marry him."

"Marry?" Alex said, not bothering to hide his skepticism.

"You need to understand, Mr. Lockerby, this was not the first time Vivian Westlake patronized my client's club. They have a long association going back almost a year."

"And you have evidence of this?"

Hardwick nodded.

"They were regulars at several upscale restaurants," he said. "I already have two signed statements confirming that and there will be more before long."

"Okay," Alex said. It did make sense that Vivian didn't choose George at random, they must have known each other.

"Had they ever discussed marriage?"

"George had proposed to Vivian on several occasions," Hardwick said. "She always rejected him, but not this time."

"She says that marriage was all his idea. That he locked her up so he could have a bogus marriage certificate made up."

"George wouldn't have had to lock up Vivian," Hardwick said in a firm voice. "Because they were already married."

That took Alex by surprise.

"Can you prove that?"

Hardwick hesitated then shook his head.

"Unfortunately no," he said. "The certificate proving the marriage is missing."

"That's convenient."

"Let's assume for a moment that George is telling the truth," Hardwick said.

"That would mean that Vivian hit herself in the face to fake that bruise," Alex said.

"Yes, it would mean just that," Hardwick said. "Vivian and George get married, but she gets cold feet. She wants out, and your arrival gives her just the opportunity she needs. She waits until George leaves the club, then destroys the marriage certificate, fakes an injury, and locks herself in the storeroom. When the police arrive, she tells them the story they want to hear, and George ends up in jail."

"Why would Vivian go through with a marriage just to frame her new husband before the ink is even dry on the license?"

Hardwick shrugged and shook his head.

"I have no idea what was in her mind, but I know that if she claimed George was trying to force her to marry him that she's lying. They were married by a justice of the peace in the county courthouse yesterday morning."

"If that's true, there will be a duplicate certificate on file with the city," Alex said.

"Which is where you come in," Hardwick pressed. "Eventually the certificate will end up in the records office, but since it was only created yesterday—"

"It's still working its way through the bureaucracy," Alex finished.

"You wouldn't believe the number of offices a marriage license has to go through before it gets filed. I need you to use your much-touted finding rune to track it down. With that, I can prove that Vivian's story is false and the police will release my client."

"All that will prove is that George didn't need to get a fake license," Alex said. "It's still a long way from proving that he didn't hit Vivian and lock her up."

"If she's his wife, he's allowed to hit her," Hardwick pointed out. "And everyone in the club knows that the store-room door can't be unlocked from the inside. Once I have that certificate, I can create enough reasonable doubt that no jury will convict George."

It wasn't a bad story, but it still had plenty of holes, not the least of which was Vivian's bruise; Alex doubted she could have done that to herself. Still, Hardwick didn't have to prove that George didn't kidnap Vivian, all he needed to do was raise doubts with the jury, and if Vivian had lied, there would be plenty of doubt to go around.

Alex looked at Hardwick who just sat, watching him expectantly. It would be an easy enough job. Tomorrow morning when the offices opened, he'd find the justice who'd performed the marriage and use him and something of George Sheridan's as a focus to locate the certificate. He'd have it wrapped up by lunch.

Still, Alex didn't really like George and this whole affair was a mess he was well rid of.

"If George is telling the truth," Hardwick said, sensing Alex's decision wasn't going his way, "then that certificate will turn up sooner or later. All you'd be doing is making it sooner. If George is lying, then you won't find anything, and you still get paid."

Alex regarded the lawyer for a moment. He understood why the man was so highly paid — he made convincing arguments. And he was right. Another consideration was that, if Alex performed well on this case, the law firm of Finch, Hardwick, and Michaels might want to use him again. Big law firms always had clients in need of investigative work, which would bode well for Alex.

"All right," he said. "First thing tomorrow I'll go over to the county clerk's office and track down the license. I'll need something from your client though, to make the finding rune work. Preferably something that meant something to him and to Vivian."

"You'd have to ask him about that," Hardwick said.

Alex pulled out his pocketwatch and flipped open the cover. The red ring that gauged his remaining life sat at one, indicating he had maybe four weeks of life left.

Give or take.

He ignored that, focusing on the watch's normal hands which indicated that it was four thirty-five.

"You said he's in lockup over at the Central Office?"

Hardwick nodded so Alex continued.

"I'll have to see George in the morning then. I won't make it over there by five."

The lawyer chuckled at that.

"Lawyers can see their clients anytime they want," he said. "And they can bring whomever they want."

Alex snapped his watch closed. He generally didn't have a good opinion of lawyers, but they definitely had their uses.

"I'll get my hat," he said.

16

GEORGE

The same cop who had shown Alex around the cell where June Masterson hung herself was on duty at the front desk of the cooler. Since the only people who were supposed to be down there after five were police, he sat with his feet up on the reception desk reading a pulp novel. A steaming coffee cup and half a sandwich were within easy reach and he wore a smile of serene contentment, rather than the bored look he'd had before.

His expression changed when Alex stepped out of the stairwell, souring like he suddenly smelled something bad.

"We're closed," he drawled, his bored voice returning. "Visitors are only allowed between ten and five."

"I figured you were missing me," Alex said. "So I came by to see how you were doing."

The cop's face changed from boredom to anger and he stood, setting his book aside.

"He's with me, officer," Arthur Hardwick said, stepping out from behind Alex.

The cop hesitated for a moment before he recognized the lawyer.

"Mr. Hardwick," he said in a voice that clearly indicated that he didn't like lawyers any more than he liked private detectives. "What brings you by tonight?"

"I'm here to see George Sheridan," Hardwick said in a no-nonsense voice. "Mr. Lockerby is assisting me."

The cop looked like he would love nothing more than to say no and send Alex and Hardwick on their way. Unfortunately for him, the law was quite clear about attorneys having access to their clients.

"Sign in here," he said, picking up a clipboard and handing it to Hardwick.

Arthur wrote his name and the name of his client on the provided line, then signed next to it. Alex had to do the same, then the cop motioned for them to follow.

"This way."

He led them down the hall, past the drunk tank and the communal cells for people only being held overnight, to the block of individual cells. A half dozen men were cooling their heels there and the cop led them all the way down to the end where George Sheridan sat sullenly on a metal bunk. His slicked-back hair was a bit disheveled and he'd taken off his coat and his tie, but he seemed none the worse for his arrest.

"It's about time, Arthur," he growled as the cop unlocked the door.

"You pay me because I'm good at my job, George," Hardwick said as he stepped inside. "Not because I'm fast. You remember Mr. Lockerby, of course."

Alex stepped into the cell behind Hardwick and the cop closed the door and locked it. Even though the entire front of the cell was just bars, he immediately felt like it had gotten smaller.

"Give a shout when you're ready to leave," the cop said, then turned and walked back toward the front.

"Nice to see you again," Sheridan said in a voice that

clearly indicated he wasn't at all happy to see Alex. "At least I can see you this time."

Alex didn't bother hiding his grin at the memory of setting off the flash rune in Sheridan's office.

"Take it easy, George," Hardwick intervened before Alex could speak. "You do want Mr. Lockerby's help, correct?"

Sheridan glared at his lawyer for a second, then his expression softened.

"I apologize," he said, both to Hardwick and Alex. "This whole thing has got me a bit out of sorts."

"Now, I've talked to Mr. Lockerby," Hardwick said, "and he's willing to help find that marriage certificate, but he needs something from you."

Hardwick looked to Alex.

"I need something that will connect you to the certificate," he said. "I'm assuming you signed it?"

Sheridan nodded.

"Did you use your own pen by chance?"

"No," he answered. "The clerk at the county building had one on the desk."

Alex thought for a minute. The connection between Sheridan, Vivian Westlake, and the marriage certificate would be tenuous at best. While the certificate was of tremendous importance, Sheridan had probably only touched it long enough to sign his name. He'd need something stronger in order for his finding rune to form a link.

Assuming this marriage certificate actually exists.

"Is that it?" Sheridan said when Alex didn't respond.

Alex explained how the finding rune worked and why having a strong connection was so important.

"Tell me about your marriage" Alex finished. "How did you come to ask Vivian to marry you?"

"It was her idea," Sheridan said. He stood up and started to pace the short length of the cell. Hardwick immediately sat down on the vacated bunk. "She showed up a couple days ago in the morning, said she'd had a fight with her folks and needed a place to stay."

"How did you know her?"

Sheridan chuckled at that.

"Everybody knows Viv," he said.

Alex wasn't surprised at that. Vivian was gorgeous, which would make her memorable.

"She's always the life of the party," Sheridan went on. "Been coming around my place for about a year now. A couple of months ago we started going out, dinner, the pictures, that sort of thing."

"So you weren't surprised when she asked you for a place to stay?" Alex asked.

"Nah," Sheridan said. "We've got a half dozen rooms in the back for when important guests have had a bit too much to make it home. I just put her up in one of those."

"So how did the subject of marriage come up?" Hardwick asked. Alex hadn't noticed, but the lawyer had taken a pad of paper from his briefcase and was making notes.

"After she got situated, I went to see her," Sheridan said. "I told her she should go back home and hash things out with her parents. I mean, she can't just stay with friends for the next ten years, right?"

Alex wanted to keep disliking Sheridan, but the man seemed to genuinely care about Vivian.

"Anyway," Sheridan went on. "She tells me that she needs to make a change, take charge of her own life. That's when she says that we should get married."

"And you didn't think that was just her desperate attempt to make sure she had a roof over her head?" Hardwick asked.

"Of course I did," George scoffed.

"Then why did you go through with it?" Alex asked.

Sheridan regarded him for a moment before speaking.

"How much do you know about the nightclub business?" he asked.

"Nothing," Alex admitted.

"Well she's a fickle mistress," he said. "Clubs live and die on publicity. Some photographer for the Times sees the right Broadway starlet in your club and suddenly you're the place to be. Somebody picks a fight and it gets out of hand — no one comes around anymore, and you're done."

Alex hadn't really thought about it, but that made sense. He'd never been one for the nightclub scene, but the society pages were full of stories about what important person went to which club.

"Then if you manage to stay in business long enough, you become an institution," Sheridan said. "Like the Rainbow Room or the Cotton Club, but even then, you're not safe. When Cab Calloway left to be in the pictures, the Cotton Club folded like a gypsy tent."

Now Alex understood.

"So you married Vivian because of her parents' money," he said.

"Damn right I did," Sheridan said with no trace of embarrassment. "If things went south at the Northern Lights, we'd have that to fall back on. Of course it didn't hurt that Viv's a real looker. The way I saw it I was coming out way ahead in the deal."

"Then what happened?"

Sheridan shrugged and leaned against the wall of bars.

"We went over to the county offices and got hitched."

"Don't you need a blood test to get married?" Hardwick asked.

"Not if you slip the clerk a C note, you don't," Sheridan said.

"Who performed the ceremony?" Alex asked.

"A Justice of the Peace," Hardwick answered. "I talked to

him, but he doesn't remember George or Vivian. Apparently he performed twenty-two marriages that day."

"Look," Sheridan said, irritation creeping into his voice. "We don't need the Justice of the Peace or the clerk or anybody else. There's a signed certificate out there with both our names on it that proves I'm being set up by that little tramp."

"And I can track it down," Alex said in a placating voice. "But it'll go a lot faster if I can use a finding rune. Did you give Vivian anything to mark the occasion? Did she give you a ring?"

"Sure, we picked one up on the way there," he reached into his pocket and pulled out a simple gold band, holding it out to Alex.

"I don't think that will help," he said. "Neither of you owned it long enough."

Sheridan looked suddenly startled and walked to where he'd laid his suit coat on the bed. After digging around in the various pockets, he grinned and produced a small, silver ring with a diamond mounted in it.

"I gave this to Viv," he said. "It was my grandmother's. She left it on my desk after I went out. I guess she didn't want to be caught wearing it when she told her story to the cops."

"But she wore it up till then?" Alex said.

"Yes," Sheridan said with a nod. "I remember seeing it on her hand when I went to tell her about your little visit."

A wide smile spread across Alex's face as he looked at the ring.

"That will do nicely." He took the offered ring and dropped it into his coat pocket.

"All right," he said. "As soon as the county clerk opens in the morning, I'll use the ring to cast a finding rune and locate your paperwork."

"Why not cast it right now?" Hardwick said.

"The link created by a finding rune will fade over time," Alex said. "It's best when it's fresh."

Hardwick and Sheridan exchanged a look, then the latter turned to Alex.

"Thank you for your help, Mr. Lockerby," he said. "I know you probably don't want to work with me, and I appreciate it."

Alex was impressed; it actually sounded like Sheridan meant it.

"If the certificate is in the county building, I should have it by ten," he said. "If it's been moved, it will take longer, but I should have something for you by noon at the latest."

"All right," Hardwick said, putting his pad back in his briefcase. "I believe that's it, then. Call the guard," he said to Sheridan. "We'll see you in the morning."

<hr />

Alex stepped out of a cab in front of the brownstone. It had been a long day and he was exhausted. He knew that when he opened his watch to unlock the runes holding the front door closed, the red hand inside would be there, measuring what was left of his life. It was a feeling he thought he'd come to grips with a year ago when he'd been certain of his impending mortality.

Apparently he hadn't put it behind him. The stone steps that led up to the stoop seemed very long all of a sudden. Deciding to do what most people do when faced with unpleasant realities, Alex put off climbing the steps and took out his cigarette case. Selecting one at random, he held it between his teeth as he swapped his case for his brass lighter.

As he flicked the lighter to life a car backfired in the road and he started, nearly dropping the lighter.

"You're getting jumpy," he admonished himself.

He wasn't expecting the second backfire, but he managed not to jump when it came. This time something cracked against the heavy stones that flanked the stairs.

Someone was shooting at him.

Alex bolted up the stairs before the thought had taken full possession of his mind, reacting on instinct. His hand dug into his vest pocket and pulled out his pocketwatch, thumbing the release that would open its lid.

A third and fourth shot rang out, forcing Alex to turn and duck, hiding his head with his free arm. The five shield runes on his suit coat would protect him if the bullets hit him in the torso, but he could still get shot where the coat didn't cover.

He felt the runes holding the door release just as the fourth shot slammed into the glass of the door. The glass was protected by some of Iggy's more serious runes, so the bullet just bounced off it, but the red hot metal slug rebounded and hit Alex in the neck.

Stifling a curse, he brushed at his throat and tried to open the door at the same time. A fifth shot rang out, but the bullet hit the wall well over Alex's head. Ignoring his stinging neck, Alex jerked the door open and threw himself inside. As he hit the carpet in the vestibule, he kicked the door shut with his foot.

Lying there on the floor, Alex waited for more rounds to hit the brownstone's facade, but nothing came. Whoever was out there must have decided they missed their chance.

That wasn't all they missed.

Putting his elbow on the floor, Alex tried to push himself up to a sitting position but winced as pain erupted in his arm. The shield runes would stop bullets from penetrating, but they still hurt when they hit. Since he couldn't remember being hit, he figured he'd done this to himself when he dove onto the hardwood floor of the vestibule.

Moving carefully to avoid putting pressure on his left arm, Alex got to his feet and peered through the stained glass window in the door. There was no sign of the shooter and the street opposite appeared empty.

"What are you doing?" Iggy's voice came from behind him.

"Someone just took a shot or five at me," he said, turning to find his mentor standing at the inner vestibule door. "But they're gone now."

"Are you hurt?"

Alex leaned down to pick up his hat and winced at the pain in his arm.

"I landed funny on my arm," Alex admitted. "But mostly it's my pride that got hurt. I didn't even see the guy."

"You working any mob cases?" Iggy asked, stepping back so Alex could move out of the vestibule and into the house proper. "Maybe something with a jealous husband?"

Alex shook his head as he hung up his hat and gingerly removed his trench coat.

"No," he began but stopped. "But, yesterday, when I went to look for Vivian Westlake, a car almost hit me."

"Let me see that arm," Iggy said once Alex managed to get out of his coat. "Do you think it was the shooter?"

"No," Alex said, holding out his arm for Iggy. "The driver hit a parked delivery truck. He was killed."

"Sounds like he lost control," Iggy said, probing Alex's arm.

"Maybe, but a beat cop saw the whole thing. He said it looked like the guy was trying to hit me."

"Does this hurt?" Iggy asked, pressing on Alex's elbow.

Grunting as the pain in his arm spiked, Alex nodded.

"Just a sprain, I think," Iggy said, letting go. "You'll be

right as rain in the morning, but don't lift anything heavy before then."

"What? You don't have a potion for that?"

"Of course I do," Iggy said, as if the very idea were insulting. "But they cost about ten dollars to buy and I think that's a bit much for a simple sprain."

Alex couldn't argue with that logic. Ten dollars was a high price to pay for something that would go away in a few hours on its own.

"Call me crazy," Alex said as they crossed the library, heading for the kitchen. "But I don't think whoever took a shot at me was a mob enforcer. They shot five times and only came close to hitting me once."

"That doesn't mean anything," Iggy said, opening the door to his vault. "They might have been using a gun they weren't familiar with."

"A hitter for one of the families wouldn't make that kind of mistake," Alex pointed out.

"I thought you said you didn't have any mob cases."

Alex told Iggy about George Sheridan and how he'd approached Alex to prove he'd been legitimately married to Vivian.

"Danny said Sheridan had ties to the Rosonos," he finished.

"Even if that's true, the car tried to hit you before you went looking for Vivian," Iggy said. "If it was trying to hit you, then the Rosonos couldn't have sent it. You hadn't even met Sheridan yet."

It was a good point. Most of Alex's current cases were records searches that didn't involve money or some large, disputed inheritance. The only other things he was working on were the missing Forgotten and looking into Paul Masterson's wife. Neither of those cases seemed to be going anywhere, so they weren't likely to have motivated a killer.

A killer with access to multiple assassins, he reminded himself, since the driver of the car was quite dead. Frankly the only person Alex could think of that might want him dead was Dr. Wagner, the new police coroner. But unless his wife's family was in the mob, and that wasn't very likely since he worked for the police, he wouldn't have access to multiple potential killers either.

Iggy led Alex into his vault to the tables where he'd set up his Mayfly experiment. The Mayfly from the previous night was still crawling around in its bell jar, so Alex took that as a good sign.

Assuming that's the same one.

"So," Iggy said as he began setting up his new transfer rune. "Do you believe Sheridan? About Vivian making up the kidnapping story."

"It makes more sense than that Sheridan just left her locked in his storeroom for the cops to find," Alex said. "He had to know her parents would go to the cops for sure after he threw me out."

"I think you're right," Iggy said.

"But that still doesn't make much sense. Why would Vivian do that?"

Iggy considered that for a moment.

"I suspect the idea of defying her parents was intoxicating for her," he said. "But then, once she'd gone through with the marriage..."

"Reality set in," Alex finished, catching Iggy's train of thought. "She's embarrassed, maybe scared, so she cooks up a story to make Sheridan out to be a bad guy."

"If she knew about his mob connections, it would have been easy for her to come up with such a plan."

Iggy began sticking rune papers to the various bell jars.

"Well, that explains it," Alex said, feeling better now that he had a rational reason for Vivian's behavior.

"All right," Iggy said, pointing to the lone Mayfly in its own jar. "I used my new transfer rune on this one twelve hours ago. Let's see where we are." He pointed to a rune paper on top of the jar and Alex lit it with his cigarette.

The paper erupted and a moment later a red ring appeared, hovering above the jar. There was only a sliver of the circle left, it reminded Alex of the red hand in his watch.

"Now these," Iggy said pointing to the remaining papers.

Alex lit them in the order Iggy indicated and, once the last one vanished, the group of Mayflies in the second jar shuddered and died. As they fell, the red ring above the single bug's jar expanded. It ran around in a circle, turning blue as it passed the three o'clock position, and finally stopping around nine o'clock.

"Did it work?" Alex asked.

Iggy nodded, his eyes sparkling.

"I'll need to test it for a few more days just to be sure it's safe, but this looks very good. The new rune isn't transferring a full life's worth of energy, only about a third."

"So when do we try it on me?"

"Not until we're sure," Iggy said. He held up his hand to silence Alex, who was prepared to point out that he didn't exactly have a lot of time to spare. "I know," Iggy said, "but you need to trust me on this. Your watch says you have time left, so let's make sure this works."

Alex wasn't thrilled by the idea, but as usual, Iggy had a point. Then there was the former Mayfly in the solo jar. The poor thing absorbed so much life energy that it had burst from within. That wasn't something Alex was eager to try.

"All right, Iggy," Alex said, the exhaustion of the day finally washing over him. "We'll do it your way. For now, however, I'm going to bed. I've got a full day of hunting down missing things tomorrow, starting with the county clerk's office, so I need some sleep."

"Alex," Iggy said as he turned to leave. "Someone shot at you tonight and whoever's behind it might have tried to kill you before."

"I'll keep my eyes open," he said.

"Take your automatic," Iggy called after him. "You might have to shoot back next time."

17

THE PAWN

A lex's alarm clock rattled to life at eight and by the time he was awake enough to silence it, the spring had entirely wound down. He hadn't slept well and what dreams he could remember involved being shot at by the ghost of June Masterson who, for some inexplicable reason, wanted to find George Sheridan's marriage certificate.

The offices of the county clerk were located in the courthouse, which would open promptly at nine, so despite his desire for another few hours of sleep, Alex dragged himself out of bed and dressed. He wouldn't have time for breakfast, but the disturbing night had left him without an appetite anyway. It did inspire him to open his vault before he left his room and visit his gun locker, though.

Opening the cabinet revealed Alex's selection of weaponry. His .45 caliber 1911 and a .38 revolver hung on pegs on the left side with a stack of full magazines and boxes of shells for each gun, respectively. One of the magazines for his 1911 had an X on the bottom, rendered in white paint. That was the one with the highly illegal spellbreaker bullets.

The right side of the cabinet had a tall, vertical space that held his Browning A-5 semi-automatic shotgun with several boxes of shells. Next to that was a new addition that Alex had taken as payment for an off-the-books case he'd done for Admiral Tennon who ran the Navy Yard. Alex had tracked down a ring of thieves who had been stealing medical supplies and potions from the yard's supply depot. In return, the Admiral let him pick a reward from the armory. Alex had picked a military style Thompson sub-machine gun.

The Thompson stood next to the A-5 with a stack of four box type magazines that held thirty rounds each. He wanted to upgrade to the much larger drum magazines favored by gangsters, but if he was being honest with himself, he couldn't imagine a situation where he'd need the Thompson's fire-power in the first place. If that ever happened, he was already in way over his head.

On the inside of the door that covered the gun cabinet hung Alex's shoulder holster, a long, Bowie style boot knife, and a knuckle duster made of steel and covered with runes. The knuckle duster already gave Alex a serious advantage in a fistfight, but the runes he put on it would make any blow feel like being hit by a truck. It would also leave the area numb for a few minutes. Recently, Alex had added three flash runes to the top where his thumb could reach them, in case he needed to make a hasty exit.

Ignoring the more powerful weapons, Alex took down the shoulder holster and slipped it on. He put one of the regular magazines into the 1911, then inserted it into the holster under his left arm. Two more full magazines went into the elastic straps under his right arm. Last, Alex dropped the knuckle duster in his right-hand coat pocket.

Before he left his vault, however, he checked to make sure the shield runes on his suit coat were intact. All five were still there, meaning none of the bullets from last night had actually hit him. It would be nice to put more of the defensive runes on his coat, but shield runes didn't work well in groups. When you had more than five in close proximity, they would cancel each other out over time.

Next, Alex examined his flash ring. Due the the size of the ring, he could only keep four flash runes on it at any one time. He'd used one in George Sheridan's office two nights ago, so this ring only had three. It would take about an hour to put a new flash rune on the ring and Alex didn't have the time. Three would have to do.

Feeling about as prepared as he could be, Alex closed his vault and headed downstairs to call a cab. If he got one quickly, he could still reach the courthouse when it opened.

The New York County Courthouse was an enormous marble structure done in the Greek style, complete with columns and a frieze along the front. Due to unfortunate timing, it was located in the south side mid ring fairly close to where the outer ring began, having been built before Barton took over Empire Tower. Alex had heard a rumor that the city was holding up approving Andrew Barton's new power relay tower until he extended the inner ring down to the courthouse. Alex wasn't sure that was how Barton's power network functioned, but when did the government ever care if something they wanted was possible?

A small group of people were standing on the marble steps, shivering in the frigid air when Alex arrived, and he joined them as they waited for the doors to be opened. He'd taken the precaution of using a climate rune before he left the brownstone, so the New York morning didn't bother him.

Most of the people waiting in the cold looked like attorneys, though Alex expected they were the most junior of their respective firms. There was no way Arthur Hardwick would be here at this hour, freezing his briefs off while he waited for the court.

A few minutes later, the doors were opened by a balding policeman and the people filed in. The office of the Justice of the Peace was on the third floor, but Alex didn't bother talking to him. Hardwick had said the man who had performed George and Vivian's wedding didn't remember it.

Assuming there was a wedding in the first place, he reminded himself.

A placard on the wall informed him that the county clerk's office was located on the main floor in the rear of the building, so Alex headed there. No matter what the Justice of the Peace remembered or didn't, if there was a record of the wedding, the clerks were the place to start.

"I'm here about a marriage certificate," he told the bespectacled man behind the counter when he entered. He had a harried look and was busily scribbling in a large record book. Behind him several other people were working at typewriters.

"I told you people we'd call when we found it," the man snapped. "You can stop bothering us and tell your boss that we work a lot faster when we're not bothered every few hours."

"I'm sorry?" Alex said. He knew that Hardwick had been over yesterday looking for the missing certificate, but Alex was reasonably sure no one else from Hardwick's office had been by in the interim.

The clerk seemed startled as if he expected Alex to protest.

"Oh," he said. "I thought you had come to harass me about those damn missing marriage licenses, like the others."

"People have been bothering you?" Alex said. Since this clerk was in a talkative mood, Alex might as well see if he could learn something.

"It's nothing," the man said with a sigh. "Records don't go missing very often but it seems like when they do, that's when someone comes looking for them. Usually they're just mis-filed, but it can take a few days to track them down. A lot of paperwork goes through this building on a daily basis."

Each of the people at the typewriters had a stack of papers waiting for them that were several inches high.

"I can imagine," Alex said. "It looks like you could use some help."

The clerk laughed at that.

"The city doesn't do anything until five years after it's needed," he said. "But I can dream."

"I'm Alex Lockerby," Alex said, handing the clerk one of his cards. "And today is your lucky day."

The clerk squinted at the card in confusion. "The runewright detective?"

Alex was about to explain his presence when the clerk's sullen demeanor vanished and he grinned. "Hey, I read about you," he said. "You're that guy who helped catch the Ghost Killer a few years back."

"Yes," Alex admitted, trying and failing to sound modest. "And now I'm here to help you. Mr. Hardwick paid for me to use my finding rune to locate your missing files. Apparently he needs one of them pretty bad."

The clerk considered that for a long moment and Alex could see his emotions warring across his face. Clearly he'd had enough of Hardwick and the whole missing marriage license but, like most people, he'd never seen anyone do significant magic up close.

"Can you really find the missing licenses?" he asked at last.

Alex explained that he could find the one Hardwick wanted using George Sheridan's grandmother's ring, and that as long as the other missing documents went to the same place, they should be easy to recover.

"Even if they're not," he went on, "no one is pestering you about those, so you can find them in your own time. This will solve your immediate problem."

The clerk looked skeptical, but eventually nodded.

"How does it work?" he wondered.

Alex produced his kit and rolled out a heavy piece of vellum. This had an intricate stabilization rune drawn on it, just like the one on the floor of his office, hidden under the rug. Stabilization runes worked in concert with his finding rune, refining the link between Alex and the sought object. He used to use them a lot, but creating them in the field required a big patch of open floor space, chalk to draw with, and a green candle that Alex would use to drip wax at certain key points in the construct. The mat was more difficult to make and used much more expensive materials, but it could be easily transported and set up. It would go bad eventually, as the magic faded with use, but Alex could always make another.

Alex added his brass compass onto the stabilization rune and then placed Sheridan's ring on top. Since he was relatively sure the missing license was still in the courthouse, he didn't bother using his map of the city; it would just point to where he already was.

Folding up the flash paper with the finding rune on it, Alex placed it on the ring and compass, then lit it with his brass lighter. This time when the orange finding rune flashed into existence, the stabilization rune below it glowed briefly as well. This also happened when Alex used finding runes in his office, but the rug hid the glow.

A moment later the finding rune stopped rotating and disappeared in a shower of orange embers. The needle of Alex's battered brass compass turned from north and pointed off to the west.

Alex dropped Sheridan's ring in his pocket then rolled up

the vellum stabilization rune and returned it to his bag. "I think we've got it," Alex said to the clerk. "Are you up for a treasure hunt?"

By this point everyone in the office had gathered around to see and the clerk flashed Alex an eager smile.

Following the compass, Alex wandered around and through the various offices and hallways until he came to a locked door with the word *Records* painted on it. Once the clerk unlocked the door, Alex led them through rows of packed shelves down to one marked, *Death Certificates*, and then to the shelf at the end.

"In there," Alex said, pointing to a thick folder sitting about eye level.

Since Alex was taller than most, the clerk had to reach up to pull the folder down. It only took him a few minutes to find the missing paperwork.

"Figures," he said, returning the folder to its place on the shelf. "Some idiot mixed these up with the death certificates. Probably means some of the death records are in the marriage section."

Alex looked over the clerk's shoulder at the file on top. It was, indeed a marriage license declaring that, as far as the city of New York was concerned, George Sheridan and Vivian Westlake were husband and wife. Alex did note that Vivian's signature was rough and jerky, while George's was smooth and flowing.

Maybe she was under duress when she signed?

"Now that you found it," Alex said to the clerk, "can I take that one on top over to the Central Office of Police? Mr. Hardwick needs it to get his client out of jail."

The clerk's smile evaporated.

"Of course not," he said as if Alex had asked him if he could fly. "Official paperwork has to stay here until it's moved over to the hall of records."

Alex felt a headache coming on.

"If Hardwick needs this," he said, holding up the paper, "then you'll need to have an official copy made."

Alex was very proud that he managed not to roll his eyes at that.

"Where do I do that?" he asked.

"Right this way," the clerk said, then he led Alex back to his office. "Copies are five dollars and take three days," he said.

Alex pulled out his billfold and put a ten on the counter.

"What say I wanted it today before noon?" he asked.

The clerk looked around, but no one appeared to be watching, then he took the bill and stuffed it into his pocket.

"Come back at noon," he said. "I'll have it ready."

Alex promised that he would, then headed back to the lobby, stopping at the bank of phone booths to call his office. Leslie's voice hadn't lost any of its chipper energy.

"Did you have any luck?" she asked.

"Yeah, Turns out Sheridan and Vivian are legally married. They're making a copy of the official certificate for me. It should be ready by noon."

"Danny called for you," Leslie said once Alex finished. "He said he got that file you wanted and it's on his desk. He also said he was going to bed and that I should tell you not to bother him for at least eight hours."

Alex chuckled at that.

"All right," he said. "I'm going to head over to the Central Office and get a look at that file."

"You can tell Sheridan the good news while you're there," Leslie said, then she hung up.

At the Central Office, Alex crossed the large lobby and

headed for the elevators. He had a momentary thought of stopping down at the cooler and telling Sheridan that he'd be a free man by one o'clock, but Sheridan was an ass, so Alex decided to let him stew a while longer. Instead, he headed up to the fifth floor.

The file on the Ayers shooting was on Danny's desk, so Alex sat down and began to go through it. Most of the pages were as he remembered them, but Detective Lowe had added notes on June's suicide and the evidence found in her apartment and on her person.

Her handwritten note confessing to an affair with Hugo Ayers was there, and Alex read through it. It was plain and straightforward, saying that she had been having an affair with Hugo, that he had rejected her for someone new, and that she couldn't accept that. Her intention to kill Hugo was plain and there was a note from Lowe stapled to the letter that said the handwriting matched June's.

Alex read through the letter several more times. Something bothered him about it, but he couldn't put his finger on it. He took out his own notebook and transcribed the words of the letter so he could study the text later.

Setting the letter aside, he picked up the last item in the folder, an envelope containing three pieces of paper. The first was a complete list of all the items found in June's handbag when she was arrested: a compact mirror, a tube of lipstick, a clean handkerchief, a rain bonnet, a wallet with twenty-two dollars inside, a box of cartridges for the .38 she'd used to shoot Hugo, and two receipts. It all seemed perfectly ordinary except for the bullets, but since June was on a mission to murder a man, Alex supposed they weren't really out of place either.

He put the list back in the envelope and pulled out the two remaining pieces of paper, the two receipts that were found in June's handbag. The first was a clothing claim ticket for a laundry around the corner from the Masterson's apartment. Alex remembered seeing it when the cab dropped him off there. He jotted down the number on the ticket, then picked up the second receipt. This was a sales receipt from a place called Garvey Pawn and recorded June's purchase of the .38 special she'd used to kill Hugo, and a box of shells.

No doubt the same ones found in her handbag, Alex thought, turning the receipt over. He found the back blank, so he put it back in the envelope and closed the case file in frustration.

He'd wondered where June got the gun, and now he knew. With a name like Garvey Pawn, the shop had to be near Garvey Park and that was right in between June's apartment and Hugo's. It was a bit strange that she waited to buy the gun, but she probably didn't want to be recognized buying it by someone who lived near her.

Thoroughly unsatisfied, Alex wrote Danny a thank you note and dropped it on top of the file, then headed back to the elevators. He still had an hour to kill until his copy of the marriage certificate would be ready and his head was buzzing like an angry beehive due to his fitful night's sleep. He was tempted to go the diner across the street for something to eat and coffee, but he needed the coffee more than the sandwich and he knew where he wanted to go for coffee.

18

LEFT BEHIND

arnie was bundled up in several layers when Alex arrived on Runewright Row. Alex had taken the precaution of using a climate rune this time, so he felt fine in his trench coat, but she was shivering and standing very close to her coffee pot, using its heat to warm her hands. He felt guilty in his invisible bubble of warmth, but even if he shared one of his runes with Marnie, it would only last an hour. It was a bandage, not a solution.

"You need some gloves," he said, somewhat sheepishly.

"Alex," she said, her face splitting into a smile. "Three days you've come to see me and the week's barely half done. I think that's a record."

"My cases are keeping me up late," he said. "I need the coffee, and I just can't resist your smiling face."

She laughed at that.

"Liar," she said. "But I can get you coffee."

Alex removed the empty thermos from his kit bag and passed it over. He hadn't packed it this morning since he didn't anticipate being near the Row, but he always washed it with the dinner dishes at the brownstone, then stored it in his vault. That made it easy for him to duck into the janitor's closet at the Central Office and retrieve it before heading for Marnie's cart.

Marnie accepted the thermos and filled it from the tall coffee pot. She usually had a thermos ready for him, but if he hadn't shown by ten, she'd just pour it back into the pot.

"There you go," she said, handing it back.

Alex accepted the thermos and returned it to his kit. He'd set his bag on top of her cart and when he took it down, he noticed that most of her runes for sale were the same as they'd been when he came on Monday.

"How's business?" he asked as casually as he could.

Marnie's perpetual smile cracked, and her eyes shifted side to side.

"It's not good," she admitted. "I used to go through a dozen mending runes a day, and more on the weekends. People wanted minor restoration runes, binding runes, and barrier runes when it was raining. I'd even sell the odd lesser finding rune for people who'd lost things. This week I've only sold twenty runes. If those Happy Jack vandals keep going, they'll put us all out of business."

Alex glanced up and down the Row. There were fewer vendors today than there had been yesterday, nowhere near the numbers from a month ago.

"How many have gone to work for Happy Jack?""

Marnie shrugged and a rare sneer crossed her face.

"Traitors," she muttered. "Every one of them sold the rest of us out."

Watching Marnie shiver in the November air, Alex wasn't sure he agreed with that.

"They're writing runes in a warm factory for a decent wage," he said. He didn't actually know what Happy Jack paid, but it had to be at least what a person could make on the Row or the missing runewrights wouldn't have taken the work.

"They're forcing the rest of us out of business," Marnie said. "If those rune book makers didn't have any runewrights to put out their books, there'd be plenty for the rest of us."

Alex sighed and put his hand on Marnie's shoulder.

"But they do have runewrights," he said. "And they're going to keep putting out their books. There's nothing anyone can do about that."

She looked at him, shocked at first, but her look gradually lost its passion, changing to a deep sadness.

"What will the rest of us do?" she asked.

"Go join the others," Alex said. "You're just as skilled as anyone else on the Row and it's honorable work."

She shook her head, and cast her eyes side to side as if she feared being overheard.

"I don't trust them, Alex," she said, genuine fear in her voice. "Something's not right."

"I'm sure it's fine," Alex said, resisting the urge to roll his eyes. Change could be a frightening thing for someone as set in her ways as Marnie. She'd been selling her runes here for almost two decades after all.

"No," she insisted. "It's not. John and Benny went to that place and they haven't been back. Not even to say hello."

Alex didn't know John, but he remembered Benny, a short, bespectacled man who made a warming rune that would keep food from cooling off for over an hour. It was a big hit with housewives whose husbands didn't have a fixed schedule. Alex had gotten the original idea for his climate rune from Benny's work.

"They're probably just busy," Alex assured her.

"We were friends for ten years, Alex," she said. "And they haven't come back once. None of the people who went have."

Alex didn't find that strange at all, but he didn't say so.

"I'll tell you what," he said. "I'll go by Happy Jack and talk to Benny. While I'm there I'll take a look at the place and make sure it's on the up and up."

Marnie took his hand with her cold one and squeezed it.

"Thank you," she said, relief plain in her voice.

"But," Alex went on, "if everything's okay, I want you to go get a job there."

She let go of his hand and scowled at him.

"Who's going to make your coffee if I do that?" she demanded, defiance in her voice.

"I'll give up coffee if I have to," Alex said.

"Liar," Marnie said.

"I mean it," Alex said.

She looked like she would argue, but her look softened.

"You go to that factory," she said. "You'll see what I mean."

"And if I don't?"

"Then I'll go," she said. Her look was still defiant, but her voice betrayed that.

Alex didn't particularly want to stop by the Happy Jack rune company, wherever that was, but if it got Marnie off the street and out of the weather, he'd do it.

"All right," he said.

Alex was running almost an hour late when he finally made it back to the Central Office. He'd planned to be there by noon but ended up in a heated argument with the clerk at the courthouse. They had the official copy of the Sheridan-Westlake marriage certificate ready for him, but they wanted another ten dollars for making it. It was nothing less than highway robbery and Alex protested. Vigorously.

In the end he paid the clerk and took his overpriced piece

of paper. As a wiser man than he once noted, you can't fight city hall.

He rode the elevator down from the Central Office lobby to the basement where the cooler was located. He expected that George Sheridan would be very happy to see him. When he got there, however, nothing could be further from the truth.

"There you are," Sheridan's voice greeted him when he stepped off the elevator. "I should have known you'd show up now."

Sheridan was standing at the little cage window that led into the prisoner property room. He wasn't handcuffed or escorted by a guard, which Alex found unusual.

"You're being released?" he asked.

Sheridan chuckled and rolled his eyes.

"I should have guessed you weren't any good as a detective," he said. "Why do you think I'm standing here? Of course I'm being released."

Alex was pretty sure no one else had gotten a copy of the marriage certificate before him.

"What happened?" he asked.

A cop in the property cage returned with a small box and began passing Sheridan's personal effects to him through the little window in the cage.

"My lawyer threatened to sue Vivian's parents if she kept lying," Sheridan said. "She must have known it was only a matter of time before we came up with the certificate, so she confessed."

Alex hadn't anticipated that, but he hadn't expected to actually find a marriage license for George and Vivian in the first place. It was shaping up to be a day full of surprises.

"So I guess you don't need this?" Alex said, holding up the envelope the courthouse clerk had given him.

"What's that?" Sheridan said, busily stuffing his wallet and keys into his trouser pockets.

"What you sent me to find," Alex said. "Your marriage certificate."

Sheridan laughed and shook his head.

"You really are bad at this," he said. "Vivian confessed to the marriage, so I don't need that."

"I don't care," Alex said. "You asked me to get it and I got it."

"Well I'm not paying for late work," Sheridan said, dropping a pocketwatch into his jacket.

"You hired me," Alex said. "And this paper you wanted cost me twenty bucks."

Sheridan found that immensely funny.

"Keep it," he said, signing a receipt the cop in the cage handed him.

Alex normally would have threatened Sheridan at this point, but since he was standing in the police lockup with at least three cops as witnesses, he bit his tongue.

"Aw, what's the matter, Lockerby," Sheridan said as he headed for the elevators. "You gonna cry?"

Alex dropped his hand into his jacket pocket, letting his fingers slip into the holes in his knuckle duster. He had a momentary thought of taking the elevator up with Sheridan and leaving him an unconscious heap when he left the lobby, but too many cops would see him get in the elevator.

He let go of the knuckleduster but froze as Sheridan's words echoed in his mind.

You gonna cry?

As the elevator door closed on Sheridan, Alex turned and ran for the stairs, all thought of the nightclub owner and his overpriced marriage certificate were gone.

By the time Alex reached the fifth floor, he really wished he'd taken the elevator. Panting from the exertion, he pushed open the stairwell door and made his way to the area reserved for division five.

"Danny, I need you to come with me to the morgue," he said when he reached his friend's desk. Danny Pak was seated behind a stack of paperwork with a pen in one hand and a blotter in the other. He looked up as Alex spoke; his eyes were bloodshot with dark circles under them.

"What?" he said, taking a moment to process what Alex said. "Why?"

"Because June Masterson didn't kill Hugo Ayers of her own will."

"What?" Danny demanded, more forcefully this time.

"Someone forced her to do it," Alex went on. "I think they used magic, but they might have drugged her or used hypnosis, I don't know. That's why I need to examine her body again."

Danny just sat, looking at him for a long moment.

"Someone forced her to kill her lover with magic?" he said. "Do you have any idea how crazy that sounds?"

Alex picked up the file that was still sitting on the corner of Alex's desk and pulled out the envelope with the list of items taken from June's handbag.

"Look here," Alex said, putting the list down on top of Danny's paperwork and pointing to one particular item.

"One clean handkerchief," Danny read. "So?"

"Think about it," Alex said. "If you were on your way to murder someone you had been sleeping with, would you be calm?"

"Probably not," Danny admitted. "What's that got to do with a handkerchief?"

"It's clean," Alex said. "Don't you think she would have

201

shed a tear or two on her way to violently murder a man she had feelings for?"

"Maybe this is her backup handkerchief," Danny said, pointing to the list.

"There's one way to be sure," Alex said with a sly grin.

"Let me guess," Danny said. "Go over to the morgue and look at June's body?"

"Even if they cleaned her up, I should be able to see if her makeup ran using silverlight," Alex said.

"Maybe she wasn't wearing any," Danny suggested.

Alex shook his head at that.

"A nice, mid-ring housewife? Of course she was wearing makeup."

"So why do you need me?" Danny said with a resigned sigh.

"Have you met the new coroner?"

"No."

"Well I have, and he doesn't like me."

Danny just looked at Alex, shaking his head.

"You know," he said in an admonishing voice, "you might try being nice to people."

"Who's got time for that?" Alex said with a laugh.

"All right," Danny said, putting his pen back in his pocket. "I'll get my coat, but you're really going to owe me for this."

"You know I'm good for it," Alex said.

As Alex predicted, Dr. Wagner wasn't thrilled to see him back in the morgue, but before he could have Alex thrown out, Danny flashed his gold detective shield at him. After that he sullenly wheeled June's body into one of his operating theaters and withdrew.

Alex got out his oculus and his multi-lamp, clipping the

silverlight burner into the latter. Once he had it lit, he passed the beam from the lamp carefully over June's face.

"Any signs of her makeup running?" Danny asked.

Alex shook his head and passed over his oculus for Danny to put on.

"What are all these?" Danny asked, pointing to marks on June's face that only he could see. "They look like freckles."

"Blood spatter," Alex said. "You can see it on her hands too. She must have been close to Hugo when she shot him."

"I don't see any signs that her makeup ran," Danny said. "But that just proves that she didn't cry, or if she did, she touched up her makeup before she shot the guy."

"Even if she did, there would still be signs," Alex said.

"Maybe she hated the guy," Danny proffered. "So she wouldn't have cried."

"Not according to her note," Alex said. "In the note she left behind she said that he rejected her and she couldn't live without him."

"Okay," Danny admitted, taking off the oculus and handing it back. "How do you force someone to kill another person? Is there a rune for that?"

Alex shrugged.

"I wouldn't have thought so," he said. "But then I wouldn't have thought alchemists could produce an artificial plague or that a killer could send an anchor rune through the mail."

He put the silverlight burner aside to cool and took out the ghostlight one.

"So how do we prove that someone used a type of magic that no one's ever heard of to make a mid-ring housewife kill a random bookkeeper?" Danny asked.

"First we have to prove that it was magic in the first place," Alex said, igniting the ghostlight burner with his lighter.

"Couldn't it just be simple blackmail?"

"No," Alex said, strapping on the oculus. "If someone had blackmailed June into killing a stranger, she definitely would have cried."

He pointed the greenish light at June's body and slowly played it up and down over her. Then he had Danny help him lift June's body on its side and he ran the light over her back.

"Hurry up," Danny said after a minute. Clearly, he wasn't comfortable touching the nude body of a dead woman.

Alex nodded and Danny rolled June back in place.

"Did you find anything?"

"There aren't any runes on her body," Alex said, slipping off his oculus and handing it to Danny. "But have a look."

"She's glowing," he said once he'd put it on.

"What you're seeing is magic residue," Alex said. "Since there aren't any runes drawn on the body, it probably isn't rune magic, but that still leaves sorcery and alchemy."

"Can you be sure?" Danny asked. "I mean couldn't she have just taken a cold remedy potion or something?"

Alex shook his head.

"Something that minor would have faded by now," he said. "Someone definitely used powerful magic on June before she died. I'm betting it means that June killed Hugo Ayers under the effect of that magic."

Danny gave Alex a hard look.

"How the devil are you going to prove that?"

Alex thought about that for a long moment before answering.

"I have to find out who wanted Hugo Ayers dead," he said. "Once I know the who, I should be able to figure out the how."

"I thought you'd already dug into Ayers' life. Who do you think is involved?"

"Hugo had about a dozen clients, but none of them jump

out as suspicious," Alex said. "Then there's William Ashford's campaign for mayor."

"Where Ayers handled the money," Danny said. "You do know that money is the single most common motive for murder."

Alex nodded. Danny was right, of course, but Hugo hadn't been with the campaign very long. It was just as likely to be one of his long-term clients.

"First, I need to find out if there are actually any spells or potions that can be used to make a person kill," he said.

Danny laughed.

"Do you think anyone will admit to knowing something like that?"

"Yes," Alex said with a sigh. "I know a couple of people who won't bother to lie to me."

Danny laughed harder at the look on Alex's face.

"I take it the Ice Queen is still mad at you?"

"When was she ever not mad at me," Alex said.

"Do you want me to go with you?" Danny said. "You know, for protection or in case someone has to identify your body."

"Thanks, but no," Alex said, giving Danny an unamused look. He checked his ghostlight burner, but it was still too hot to put back in his kit bag.

"In that case, I've got to get back to doing real work," Danny said, heading for the elevator. "If you're still alive by dinner, remember you owe me an invite."

"I'll see what I can do," he said.

As Danny disappeared in the elevator, Alex finished putting away his other gear. Since it would be a few minutes before his burner was cool enough to stow, Alex left the operating theater and headed for the office to tell Dr. Wagner that he was done.

A short hallway connected the operating theater with the

coroner's offices and several empty gurneys lined the far wall. One of them had boxes of supplies and other things piled on it. As he passed, Alex noticed a heavy blue coat sitting on top of a box of other clothes.

The thought of Marnie huddling around her coffee pot in the November cold went through his mind and his fists clenched. While he might not be able to help her with his all-too-temporary climate rune, he could simply buy her a better coat. Call it a down payment on future coffee or something so she wouldn't feel bad taking it.

He was almost past the box of clothes when he realized what he had actually seen. Turning, he picked up the coat and held it up. It was a thick, coarse weave fabric that stank like sweat, smoke, and whisky. Each of the heavy buttons had an anchor stamped on it.

It was a sailor's pea coat.

Alex opened the coat and looked at the inside pocket. Above it was label where a single word had been stitched.

Dobson.

"Dr. Wagner?" Alex called down the hall. "Where's the body that belongs to this coat?"

"Where's your Chinese cop friend?" Wagner said, slinking out of his office a few doors down the hall.

"Danny's Japanese," Alex growled. "And he had to get back to work. Lucky for you," he added.

"What a charming department this city runs," Wagner said, unimpressed by Alex's implied threat. "Now, since your reason for being here is gone, I suggest you leave as well. The Central Office may tolerate unqualified amateurs running around their building, poking their noses in where they don't belong, but I don't."

Alex crossed his arms over his chest and gave the doctor a wolfish smile.

"I'll leave when I'm good and ready," Alex said, being sure to draw himself up to his full six-foot-one stature. "Unless you want me to drive by your house after I leave and have a chat with your wife."

Wagner's face flushed and his hands clenched into fists. Alex half-expected the man to take a poke at him. After a tense few second's the doctor's hands relaxed, and his face slid into a sneer of disdain.

"After tomorrow it won't matter," he said. "Then I don't ever want to see you here again, with or without your little cop friend."

He turned to leave but Alex held the dirty pea coat out into his path.

"Where is the man who came in with this?" he demanded.

Wagner looked at the coat and shrugged.

"In the cold room, of course," he said as if that should have been perfectly obvious.

"I want to see him," Alex said.

Wagner glared at him for a long moment.

"Fine," he muttered, then led Alex down the hall to a large heavy door. When the doctor pulled it open, Alex felt a wall of cold air come pouring out. Inside were about two dozen wheeled gurneys, most with covered bodies on them. Wagner waved at the far corner of the room where five bodies were lined up.

"Based on the smell of that coat," he said. "I'm guessing your dead man was a vagrant. That's where we leave the bodies bound for the city's common grave."

"Which one?"

Wagner rolled his eyes.

"How should I know?" he said. "You're supposed to be a detective."

With that he turned and left. Alex waited until he heard the doctor's office door close before pulling out a climate rune and sticking it to his hat. He also took out a cigarette and lit them both at the same time. The bubble of comfort surrounded him as the first puff of the cigarette filled his lungs, and both were wonderful. He was tempted to just stand there in the refrigerated room until he'd smoked through the cigarette, but he finally felt like he was making progress on his cases and he didn't want to lose momentum.

One by one, Alex checked the covered bodies. Three were women, and two were men. All of them had a gaunt, desperate look, even in death. Of the men, one had the olive complexion that came with a Latin origin, so Alex moved to the last one.

This man could easily be Lefty's missing friend Dobson, also known as the Captain. He had a thick, scraggly white beard and a hard, haggard face. His body was emaciated, as if it had been a while since he'd eaten properly, but his skin was loose. This implied that his malnutrition was something recent. Alex knew that if this was indeed the Captain, he would have eaten well at the mission, well enough not to be mere skin and bones.

Smoothing out the skin on the man's forearm, Alex found a tattoo of the Navy's anchor emblem. That was certainly a good sign, but what clenched it was the name tattooed above the anchor.

Amphion.

It was the name of the Captain's ship, the one that been sunk by the Germans in the big war. The number forty-two was tattooed after the name, presumably the number of his fellow sailors who survived the disaster. Lefty had said there weren't many.

"All right, Captain," Alex said, opening his kit. "What do you have to tell me?"

Now that he knew this was the Captain, Alex did a more thorough examination. It was obvious that wherever the Captain had been, he hadn't been eating well. There were bruises on his body, but not where Alex would expect them if the man had been in a fight. The most pronounced bruising was on the back of the man's thighs, as if he'd been sitting on a hard bench for extended periods.

The left side of the Captain's face had lines of bruises in a grid pattern. It looked like he'd run face first into a wire fence. Curious, Alex checked the clipboard hanging off the end of the gurney. According to the police report, the Captain had been found dead on a sewer grate in the south side outer-ring. The official cause of death was listed as exposure.

Lefty had told him that the Captain was immune to the cold weather. More likely he was just smart. Because the underground temperature was a constant fifty-two degrees, sewers were always a source of warm air as the cold city air sank down through their grates, driving warm air upward.

"I guess the cold finally caught up with you, eh Captain?" Alex said, setting the clipboard aside.

The only other strange mark on the body was a dark stain on the man's right hand. Initially Alex thought it was ink, but the Captain was left-handed. The mark seemed to stain the skin, soaking through the outer layers.

"Frostbite," Alex concluded. Not surprising given the way the Captain had died.

With a sigh, Alex set the dead man's hand down. So far, nothing about the corpse indicated foul play. He was about to cover the body when he decided to look further. Taking out his silverlight burner, he went over the body in detail. Under the light, the bruises stood out more sharply, but they didn't reveal anything new. A urine stain covered the Captain's upper legs, probably the result of his bladder releasing when he died.

None of what the lamp revealed was especially useful until he got to the stain on the right hand. Whatever it was, it wasn't frostbite. Under the silverlight, it glowed brightly. Alex took off the oculus and examined the mark again. It still looked like ink, so Alex examined the fingers of the Captain's right hand. He found an indentation in the middle finger and the pad of the thumb, right where Alex would expect them. He had similar callouses on his own hands from all the writing he did.

"I guess you were lying about being left-handed," he said, setting the hand back down.

Something about the fluorescing stain on the Captain's hand bothered Alex. He put his oculus back on and laid his notebook on an empty gurney. Opening it to a page full of notes, Alex shone the lamp at it. His fingerprints on the paper lit up brightly, but the writing he'd done did not. Alex turned to a page where Leslie had written a client's address. While Alex always carried a pencil, Leslie used a pen when she wrote notes at her desk. The ink from Leslie's pen did not react under the silverlight either, though Alex could clearly make out her small fingerprints alongside his.

He turned back to the captain and the stain on the dead man's hand glowed brightly even before the light was directly on it. Whatever was all over the captain's hand, it wasn't ink.

"Are you still here, scribbler?" Wagner's voice came down the hall.

Knowing that his time was almost up, Alex dove into his kit and pulled out a wrapped leather case. Unsnapping the clasp that kept it rolled up, Alex gave the bundle a flick with his wrist that sent the strip of leather across the empty gurney. As it unrolled, it revealed a set of tools. In the middle were a series of sharp, pointed surgical knives and a small glass vial with a threaded brass lid.

Working quickly, Alex took out one of the knives and the vial. He turned the Captain's hand over and deftly sliced off a small bit of the skin of the man's palm. When Iggy had shown him how to do this, Alex had been queasy, but now he performed the task with dispassion.

Lifting the little square of skin on the tip of the knife, Alex transferred it to the vial and screwed the top on. He was just putting the knife back in his roll-up tool kit when Wagner pulled the heavy door to the refrigerated room open.

"Oh," he said with a scowl. "I figured you'd have frozen solid by now."

"Sorry to disappoint you, Doc," Alex said, rolling his tool kit back up and stowing it in his kit bag.

"Well since you're still breathing, I guess you don't belong here," Wagner said.

Alex thought about pushing him, but that was just a waste of time. He had everything he'd come for and now he had investigations to pursue.

"See you 'round, Wagner," he said, picking up his kit and pushing past the man.

"I rather doubt it," Wagner called after him.

Alex had a momentary thought of introducing the smug doctor to his knuckle duster, but that would definitely get him banned from the morgue in perpetuity. Something about Wagner's smugness bothered Alex, though, tickling his memory.

"He said it wouldn't matter if I talked to his wife after tomorrow," Alex said, recalling the doctor's words as he opened the elevator door. "That son-of-bitch."

Alex punched the button for the third floor instead of the lobby.

When the doors opened, a sign pointed him to the left to reach the secretarial pool.

"Miss Sorenson?" he said, when he reached the little desk where Betty sat. He could see what Wagner saw in her; she was quite lovely.

"The private detective," she said, a smile blooming on her face. "What brings you back?"

"Is there somewhere we could talk for a minute?" Alex asked.

"I haven't had my smoke break," she said with a raised eyebrow.

Chuckling, Alex took his silver cigarette case out of his coat pocket and offered one to Betty. It wasn't that long ago he, himself, had to depend on the kindness of others for smokes.

Betty selected a cigarette from Alex's case, then stood up.

"This way," she said, and led him out of the office and down the hall to a small break room.

"So," she said as Alex offered her a light. "What's this all about?"

"I'm going to go out on a limb and say that your boss isn't here today," Alex said, lighting a cigarette of his own.

Betty looked impressed at that.

"How did you know?"

"Because Dr. Wagner down in the morgue isn't as open minded about private detectives as you are," Alex said. "That day we met, he tried to have me thrown out. I saw your lipstick on the collar of his doctor's coat and threatened to expose your affair unless he gave me access."

"I am not—" Betty began, but Alex cut her off.

"I don't care what you do with your life, Miss Sorenson. That's not why I'm here."

"Then why are you here?" she demanded, her pleasant smile and demeanor gone. "Are you going to blackmail me too?"

Alex didn't laugh, but he wanted to.

"Blackmail is such an ugly word," he said. "I prefer extortion."

"I don't like either one," Betty sneered.

"Apparently the good doctor doesn't much like them either," Alex said. "I was just down in the morgue and he told me that I wouldn't be able to blackmail him after tomorrow. That's how I know your supervisor is out of the office today."

Her nervous anger wavered, and her brows knit together.

"I don't understand," she said.

"He's planning to lodge a complaint against you when your boss gets back," Alex said. "He's going to make sure that if his wife ever hears the name Betty Sorenson and comes looking, you won't be here."

"He's going to get me fired?" Betty gasped. "But I need this job!"

"Then I suggest you get some blackmail material of your own," Alex advised her. "Surely he's written you. Maybe a love note, or an invitation to a secret rendezvous?"

Her look of panic slowly faded, replace by a devious smile.

"Yes," she said. "I do have a few things like that." Almost as soon as she said it, her face fell again. "I can't show that to my boss," she said, turning a bright pink. "He'd fire me."

"It's not for your boss," Alex said. "It's for Mrs. Wagner."

The devious smile returned, but Alex figured he'd better spell the whole scheme out. Betty didn't seem to be very bright.

"Before your boss gets back, call Wagner," he said. "Make it clear that you and he are over and that, if he ever bothers you again, you'll take your evidence to his wife."

Satisfied that he'd done all he could, Alex gave Peggy another couple of cigarettes, wished her luck, and headed for the street. For the first time in days, he had several solid leads. He wanted to head for the brownstone and enlist Iggy's help in figuring out what the black substance on the Captain's hand was, but that was just a curiosity. As far as he could tell, the Captain died of natural causes.

June, on the other hand, was another matter. Someone had used her as a weapon, then thrown her away like so much garbage. He needed to find out who and how. For the how,

Alex was going to have to talk to someone about a more powerful magic than runes. It was a bad idea, but it was the only one he had.

"Chrysler Building," he told the cabbie who stopped to pick him up.

The Chrysler building was actually fairly close to the city morgue, so Alex reached it before he had time to come up with a better idea. Even the elevator to the sixty-fifth floor seemed to go quickly and before he knew it, he found himself standing outside the steel and glass doors of Kincaid Refrigeration Enterprises, Inc. Like most things associated with Sorsha, the doors were elegant, refined, and seriously overdone.

The double doors came together in the center with an image of her flying castle rendered on them in a mixture of engraving and added layers to give it depth. The castle was rendered in brass with rays of energy radiating out from it done in metal that had been blued. It reminded Alex of the elevator doors in Empire Tower and he wondered if Sorsha were trying to keep up with the opulent style of Andrew Barton. Sorsha was rich by any measure, but Barton's fortunes made her look like a pauper.

Above the image of the castle and the cold rays were two frosted windows. They had been made to look like a frosted window on a cold morning with a ring around the edges of the glass. The doors were impressive, Alex had to admit that, just like their owner.

He took a deep breath, and pushed the right hand door open. Beyond it was a large reception area where an attractive young woman was speaking on the phone behind a marble topped desk. She had hair that shone like burnished copper and brown eyes that tended toward a honey color. Alex could tell from her voice that she'd grown up in the south, Georgia or South Carolina from the tone of her accent. As she spoke, Alex found himself enchanted by the honeyed flow of her accent.

"Welcome," she said to Alex once she hung up the phone. "Do ya have an appointment?"

Alex presented her with one of his business cards and put on his best, Sunday-go-to-meeting smile.

"I don't," he said. "Just tell Miss Kincaid that I'm here."

The girl looked at the card and one of her coppery eyebrows shot up.

"The Alex Lockerby?" she said in a skeptical voice.

"Uh," Alex managed. "As far as I know I'm the only one."

Her interest in him up to this point had been that of a well-trained, and no doubt highly paid receptionist, but the grin that began to spread across her face was anything but professional. She looked like a kid on Christmas.

"Well, it's nice to finally put a face to the name," she said. "Just wait here for a li'l minute and I'll see if Miss Kincaid is in."

For most receptionists, that would be a lie designed to give their employer the chance to brush off an annoying caller, but with Sorsha there was a very real chance that she had left the office without her receptionist's knowledge. Alex knew from experience that there was a garage complete with a floater limousine built right into the exterior wall of the building.

Of course Sorsha was a sorceress, so she could always teleport herself in and out of her office whenever she wanted, as well.

Alex shuddered at the thought of that. He'd had the displeasure to travel by teleportation on several previous occasions and he had no desire to ever repeat the experience.

Miss Burnside?" Sorsha's

He diverted the memory of instantaneous travel by watching the receptionist's receding form. Like her employer, she wore slacks with a button-up shirt. Alex didn't much care for the progressive style where women wore men's clothes, but he had to admit that the form of a receding woman in pants was a very pleasant sight.

"Are you quite finished ogling Miss Burnside?" Sorsha's frigid voice came from uncomfortably close behind him.

20

OTHER POSSIBILITIES

Alex managed not to jump, and turned as slowly as he could. Behind him stood the Ice Queen herself, her platinum blonde hair shining in the bright lights of the office like a halo. She wore a white button-up shirt with a narrow tie and slacks. The only consideration for her sex was the custom jacket, tailored to emphasize her small waist and the modest flare of her hips, and the burgundy color of the slacks and the tie which matched her lipstick. Her arms were crossed, and her brows were knit together in a look of profound disapproval.

Even angry and wearing pants, she was beautiful. Now that Alex thought about it, he reckoned she was more beautiful when she was angry.

"Why are you here?" she demanded. Alex took a breath to answer, but she interrupted. "I'd like the truth this time. Assuming you're capable of that."

Yep, Alex thought. *She's still mad.*

Alex was tempted to tell her an obvious lie just to get a rise out of her, but something in the Sorceress' look warned him away from that impulse. He'd always been able to tell when he was pushing Sorsha too far. As he looked her in her hard, dangerous eyes, he realized that was a line he'd crossed just by coming to her office.

"Is it possible for a sorcerer to force someone to commit a murder against their will?" he asked, deciding to go for honesty.

Sorsha raised an eyebrow at that, but her imperious gaze held fast.

"With the right blackmail material, I imagine it's possible to force a person to commit all kinds of deplorable acts," she said. "But, since that's hardly unique to sorcerers, I'm going to assume you mean magically."

Alex nodded.

"Yes," he said. "Is it possible to use magic to compel a person to act against their will?"

"Am I to assume your question is not academic?"

"No," he confirmed.

Her look shifted, softening to something between dangerous amusement and genuine curiosity.

"And you suspect me?" There was a distinct note of challenge in that simple statement.

"No," Alex admitted. "If I had evidence that led me to conclude that you murdered someone, you'd know it because I'd completely disappear, and you'd never see me again."

The dangerous look melted into a dazzling smile that reminded Alex of Leslie's, though much more predatory.

"There now," she said, reaching up to pat him on the cheek. "You can be sweet when you try."

Alex wasn't sure how his open admission that he'd flee the city out of sheer terror rather than try to bring her to justice was sweet. Then again, Sorsha was a woman in a decidedly male world, both in business and in magic. The idea that she was dangerous probably was a compliment.

"Let's go to my office and you can tell me why you want to know about magic and murder," she said.

Without waiting for an answer, she swept away, heading down a broad hallway. As he hurried to follow, Alex caught a glimpse of Miss Burnside, Sorsha's secretary, standing to one side. She'd clearly been watching the proceedings and had a look of undisguised mirth on her face.

What has Sorsha been saying to her employees about me?

Alex had been to Sorsha's offices once before, but it had been after hours, so he hadn't met any of the Ice Queen's staff. He could only guess what they'd heard from their boss and her two FBI lackeys.

Assuming she still works with the FBI, Alex thought. He hadn't had a lot of contact with Sorsha since the events of a year ago.

Before he had time to ponder any further, Sorsha reached a large glass door and pulled it open. She just stood there, holding it, waiting for Alex to enter. Since arguing with her would be useless, Alex took off his hat and entered the office first.

He'd never been in Sorsha's office proper but nothing in it surprised him. She had a large desk made of white oak with an inset slab of marble for a top that dominated the back side of the space. The walls were painted a bluish white color and an enormous window dominated the back wall. There was a small loveseat off to one side with a coffee table in front of it and a liquor cabinet to the side. In front of the desk were two small, uncomfortable looking chairs.

"Have a seat," she said, moving past him and around her desk. Before she sat down, she did the trick where she reached into thin air and pulled some small object into her hand. In this case it was an elegant cigarette case made of copper and inlaid with ivory. "Cigarette?" she offered.

Alex was well past depending on the kindness of strangers for his cigarettes but he took one with a smile. He reached into his pocket for his lighter. Sorsha put her cigarette in her mouth and puffed on it. As she did, her ice-blue eyes flashed, and the tip of the cigarette glowed with fire.

"Show off," Alex said with a grin, squeezing the side of his lighter which flipped the cap up and struck the flint. She gave him a haughty smile that had just a tinge of insincerity and then sat down.

"Now," she said, blowing smoke. "Tell me why you think a sorcerer might be able to control another person with magic."

Before Alex could answer, the door behind him opened. He turned to see the secretary, Miss Burnside, looking apologetic.

"I'm sorry, ma'am," she said to Sorsha. "But Director Stevens is on the phone."

Sorsha's brows knit together again, this time in a look of irritation.

"Very well," she said, standing up. "I'll take it in the conference room. Excuse me a minute," she told Alex. She headed for the door but stopped on her way out to have a whispered word with Miss Burnside.

Alex wondered what that was about once the frosted glass door was closed. He'd met Director Adam Stevens once before a few years ago. He was the head of the FBI's New York office.

I guess Sorsha is still working with them.

A moment later the door opened, and Alex didn't have to guess about Sorsha's ties with the Bureau. Standing in the door was one half of Sorsha's assigned FBI team, Agent Aissa Mendes. She was younger than Alex, probably in her late twenties, with olive skin, dark eyes, and a mass of unruly, curly hair that she had somehow managed to tie back behind her head. She wore the standard, durable business suit that other FBI agents wore, though she substituted a skirt for the usual trousers. The last time Alex had seen Agent Mendes she'd been a trainee and he could see the butt of the pistol sticking out from under her left arm. That had been caused by the fact that Mendes was quite busty and the shoulder holster simply hadn't been designed to account for breasts. As she stood in the doorway now, however, she had clearly worked out that problem. The only sign that she was armed was a slight bulge to the side of her left breast.

"Agent Mendes," Alex said, standing quickly and hoping the movement covered the fact that he'd just been staring at the young woman's chest.

"Mr. Lockerby," she said with a slight nod. If she'd noticed him staring, she didn't acknowledge it. "It's been a while."

"Did Sorsha send you in here to keep an eye on me?"

Mendes chuckled but shook her head.

"Actually, she wanted Agent Redhorn, but he went to lunch. I guess she was afraid I'd fall victim to your charms."

As she said it, Mendes' face shone with mirth and Alex laughed too.

"I'll tell her you held out against my libertine ways," he said, then remembering his manners, he fished out his silver cigarette case.

"Thanks," Mendes said, crossing to where Alex stood and selecting a cigarette. She reached up and took his cigarette, using it to light her own before handing it back. "So," she said, after taking a puff. "You and the boss, is there some history there?"

Alex raised an eyebrow at that.

"No," he said.

Mendes gave him a skeptical look.

"You sure about that? she asked. "Because you two carry on like an old married couple."

Alex hadn't really thought about it. There was a time, back when he'd first met the Ice Queen, when they might have meant something to each other, but those days seemed very far away.

"I'm sure," he said.

Mendes raised a speculative eyebrow at that and looked like she was about to say something when the door opened and Sorsha came back in. She seemed a bit surprised to see Mendes, but if it irritated her, nothing showed.

"That's my cue," Mendes said to Alex. "It was nice to see you again, Mr. Lockerby."

With that, Agent Mendes withdrew and Sorsha went around her desk as before.

"I'm sorry," she said, sitting down. "I'm handling security for the Mayoral debate on Saturday and things keep changing."

"Isn't the election next week?" Alex asked, struggling to remember what he'd read about it in the papers. "That's kind of late to be having a debate."

"It's going to be on the radio," Sorsha said. "Normally that's easy, but a bunch of important people are going to be there. Even Andrew is coming, so the arrangements are maddening."

Alex was surprised to hear that New York's most famous sorcerer, Andrew Barton, was going to be attending. Barton was rarely seen outside his offices in Empire Tower.

"What's the Lightning Lord doing at a political debate?" he asked.

Sorsha shrugged.

"He's fighting with the city about his new power tower," she said, dismissively. "I guess he's backing the challenger. That would certainly explain why he's rising so quickly in the polls. Andrew can buy a lot of advertising."

Alex found that particular detail to be very interesting and it reminded him of his reason for being in Sorsha's office.

"So tell me," he said. "If a sorcerer wanted to murder someone, could they use magic to force a patsy to do it for them?"

Sorsha shook her head and her platinum hair bounced back and forth.

"I don't know of any way to do something like that," she said. "But I don't think it would matter."

"Why not?"

She gave him a hard look, her ice-blue eyes boring into him.

"Because, if a sorcerer wanted someone dead, there are plenty of easier ways to do it."

"What if they wanted the death to not raise suspicion?" Alex countered. "Like if there was a ready-made killer to be apprehended."

"No," Sorsha insisted. "Sorcery can't do what you're describing."

Alex fixed her with a challenging look.

"You've stopped me from controlling my own body on two occasions," he said in an even voice. "If you can do that, what's to stop you from moving someone around like a marionette on a string?"

Sorsha rolled her eyes at that.

"You mean this?" she said, snapping her fingers.

The instant she made the sound, Alex found himself unable to move. The sensation would have given him the shivers if he had been able to shiver.

"I assure you," Sorsha went on, looking him right in the eyes with her sparkling blue ones. "This isn't about controlling your body so much as it is about making the air around you too dense for you to move. Think of it like a fly trapped in amber."

Alex wanted to tell her what she could do with her explanation, but he couldn't move his jaw to speak. As uncomfortable as he was, Sorsha didn't look like her usual calm self either. Beads of sweat had broken out along her forehead and her hands were trembling slightly.

"Even if I could march you around like a toy soldier, it still wouldn't be worth it," Sorsha said. "This requires a tremendous amount of effort and I have to be able to see you for it to work. Besides," she said, a wicked grin splitting her face. "If I wanted to kill you, all I'd have to do is apply a bit more pressure."

As she said it, Alex suddenly found that he could no longer breathe.

"Keep up the pressure for a few minutes and you'd suffocate. Anyone finding your body would think you choked on food or died of an aneurysm. The coroner would find that you died of natural causes, not murder."

Sorsha gasped and her body shook for a second, then Alex could move again. More importantly, he could breathe again.

"Don't..." he panted. "Don't do that."

Sorsha grinned at him, panting almost as hard as he was, but said nothing.

"You seem to have given that a great deal of thought," he said, once his breathing returned to normal. He gave her a penetrating look and she matched it.

"Yes," she said at last. "I have. There are many people who are jealous and fearful of sorcerers. I have to be careful every day, everywhere I go. And yes, I have thought a lot about how to defend myself."

"By making sure you make defending yourself look like natural causes?"

She finally looked away, rolling her shoulders in a slight shrug.

"Fewer questions that way," she admitted. "Less chance of someone's families trying to sue you for defending yourself."

Alex wanted to be offended by her practical approach to killing but he just couldn't. He'd killed men in life or death situations before and it helped to have thought through what your actions would be ahead of time. It was practical, efficient, and a bit cold blooded — just like Sorsha herself.

"Okay," Alex said. "I guess I'm not looking for a sorcerer."

He stood up quickly, but Sorsha motioned for him to sit back down.

"What makes you think magic compelled someone to commit murder?" she asked, mopping her forehead with a handkerchief from her desk.

Alex hesitated, then sat back down. He wanted to be away from the powerful and capricious sorceress, but he'd come to her for a reason, so he might as well see it through. Pulling out his notebook he went over the facts of June's case with her, along with his conclusions.

"So a woman kills a man that she claims in a letter is her lover," Sorsha summarized. "But you don't buy it. You think someone used magic on her, forced her to kill a stranger and then herself?"

"I know how it sounds," Alex said, a bit defensively. "But if there's a connection between June and Hugo, I can't find it, and how else do you explain the magic residue on June's body?"

"Easy," Sorsha said. "Maybe she drank a potion prior to her death. The police may have used a potion to try to revive her when they found her."

Alex had to admit, that was a possibility.

"So you think I'm chasing shadows?"

Sorsha sat back in her chair and raised her hand to her chin.

"I want to say yes," she admitted. "But I've learned to trust your instincts. Let me see your notes."

Alex handed over his notebook, then sat in silence as Sorsha flipped through the pages that related to June Masterson.

"So the police think she hung herself with the lace tie from her blouse?" Sorsha asked after a few minutes.

"Yes."

She nodded and went back to reading. After a minute she looked up at him with a strange expression, then handed his notebook back.

"You're right," she said in a quiet voice. "I don't know why June Masterson shot the bookkeeper, but she most definitely did not hang herself of her own free will."

Alex was caught by surprise. He'd expected Sorsha to tell him he was crazy, then throw him out.

"What do you mean?" he managed as he accepted his notebook back.

"You noted that there were two cords tied around the pipe June used to hang herself," Sorsha said. "Describe the one that June used."

Alex closed his eyes and pulled the image of the cord into his mind. He tried to describe it as best he could, but it really was just a bit of string used to tie up the bodice of June's blouse.

"That's why I know June didn't kill herself," Sorsha said when he finished. "A peasant blouse doesn't need a heavy cord to keep it closed. What you're describing is much too heavy for that style of blouse."

"Maybe she lost the original and had to replace it with what she had on hand," Alex suggested.

Sorsha shook her head.

"You said in your notes that when you examined June's body, she had a broken ankle, right?"

"Yes," Alex admitted. "It appeared broken."

"And that there were two cords tied around the pipe in June's cell, a broken thin one and the one June was hanging from?"

Again, Alex nodded.

"That's because the broken cord was the one from June's blouse," Sorsha said. "When she tried to use it to hang herself, it snapped and she fell."

"Which explains the broken ankle," Alex said, starting to see where Sorsha was going with this. "But if you're right, where did she get the second cord?"

Sorsha smiled at that.

"She must have had help from someone," she said. "Someone in the police lockup must have brought her the cord she used to hang herself when the first one broke. They probably helped her get back on the bed with her broken ankle too."

Alex didn't like the implications of that. At the time June hung herself, visiting hours were over and the cooler was locked up tight. The only people in the basement of the Central Office at that time were the other prisoners and the cops on duty.

"You find out who it was that helped June kill herself," Sorsha went on, "and that will lead you to whoever is behind it."

If Alex ever wondered why the FBI hired Sorsha as a consultant, he knew now. She'd just expertly sussed out a clue that he'd missed entirely.

"I hope you find them," she said when Alex didn't respond. "And I hope they just used blackmail to force June to do their bidding."

"Why?" Alex asked.

"Because," Sorsha said, giving him an earnest look. "If

someone's found a way to magically make people their slaves, that's utterly terrifying."

Alex hadn't really thought about it that way. Sorsha was right.

"Be careful," she admonished him.

Alex nodded, tucking his notebook into his shirt pocket.

"I will," he promised.

21

JOB OFFERS

Alex thought about his conversation with Sorsha on the elevator ride back to the marble and brass lobby of the Chrysler Building. Most people considered sorcerers to be almost mythical beings, custodians of incredible power, demi-gods in their own right. The idea that being a sorcerer was akin to having a target on one's back was something Alex hadn't even considered.

Sorsha had come into her power when she was in her early twenties. It was hard to imagine her having to come to grips with that and the knowledge that there were suddenly people who wanted you dead.

The bell in the elevator chimed and Alex opened the door. Pushing thoughts of the Ice Queen from his mind, he made his way across the lobby to the phone booths by the door. Sorsha didn't know it, but she had given Alex a lead, one he intended to follow up on right away, but he needed to call Leslie first and check in.

"What's the good word, boss?" Leslie said once he reached her.

"Not much right now," he admitted. "I'm going down to

the core to run down a lead, but it's pretty thin. Any calls come in that I need to deal with?"

"Just Paul Masterson," she said. "He called yesterday and again this morning. What do you want me to tell him?"

"I'm convinced June didn't kill herself, but I can't prove it yet," Alex said. "Let him know I'm still on the case until he tells me to stop."

There was a short pause then Leslie spoke.

"You need to talk to him yourself," she said. "Soon. He's not holding up very well."

"Can't say as I blame him," Alex said. "I'll call him tomorrow. Hopefully I'll know more by then."

"I'll tell him."

"One more thing," Alex said, remembering his conversation with Marnie. "See if you can find the address for the Happy Jack company. They make those rune books that have been popping up everywhere."

Leslie said that she would, then the line went quiet.

"Is there something else?" Alex asked when she didn't hang up.

"I looked into that girl you told me about, Madame Hortense, also known as Sherry Knox."

Something in her voice rang the warning bell in Alex's mind.

"And?" he prompted.

"And as far as I can tell," Leslie said, "she didn't exist three years ago. She's lived in the same boarding house for the last year and a half and I traced her to two others before that, but the reference she gave before the first one was a fake."

"What about her work?"

"I called her boss down at the Museum of Oddities and pretended to be her bank," Leslie said. "Before she worked there, she was a secretary at the Museum of Natural History. When she got that job, she didn't have any references at all

231

and no history. Her personal file over there is mostly blank."
She paused for a minute, then went on. "Basically she doesn't
exist before 1934."

"So Sherry Knox is as much an alias as Madame Hortense," he said.

"That's my guess."

"Okay," Alex said, intrigued more than annoyed. "Keep
that under your hat if she calls."

"I can always tell her to get lost for you," Leslie offered.

Alex thought about that but the idea that Sherry was
living incognito like Iggy made him curious.

"No," he said at last. "I want to do a bit more digging
first."

"You're the boss," Leslie said in a voice that clearly indicated her disapproval.

Alex thanked her and hung up. Normally he would have
caught a cab, but there was a skycrawler station right in front
of the building. Since all sky crawlers eventually went to
Empire Station, the hub of Andrew Barton's network for the
centipede-like busses, Alex climbed up to the platform.

It was time to see another sorcerer.

The trip to Empire Station only took a few minutes, but it
felt even shorter. Alex's mind ran at full speed, not with the
cases he was supposed to be working on but rather with the
strange affair of Sherry Knox. He'd managed to forget about
the reading she'd done for him, but Leslie's mention of her
brought it thundering back into his mind.

There were three branches of magic: sorcerers, alchemy,
and runes. None of them had any power to see the future,
and as far as Alex knew, no one had such power. But
somehow Sherry had hit very near the mark with her 'save

the world' comment. Was she just buttering him up, hoping he'd help her find a job? That had to be it, but it still seemed like a strange thing to predict to a random stranger.

Unless meeting her wasn't random, he thought.

Had she engineered their meeting? Shadowing Alex to determine the best place to encounter him? He went to Runewright Row at least three times a week for coffee, it would be an excellent place to lie in wait for him.

That would mean that her looking for a job as a secretary was a setup. She'd known that Alex was in need of a secretary and made herself available.

Alex shook his head as the thought entered his mind. That couldn't be right, because he'd met Sherry two days before Leslie told him she was getting married. Could Sherry have been watching Leslie as well?

Not by herself.

That thought made Alex sit up straight in his seat. Without appearing to, he looked around the crawler at the other passengers. No one seemed to be paying any special attention to him.

I'm jumping at shadows, he thought, settling back into his seat.

The kind of tailing he was thinking of would require a group of people to pull off. Sorsha and her FBI lackeys could manage it with the bureau's resources, but it would be well beyond most people.

So if Sherry didn't have people following Leslie around, it wouldn't be possible for her to know that Alex would be looking for a secretary.

Unless she really can see the future.

Alex banished the thought as quickly as it came. Humans moved forward through time, but could only look backward. Either Sherry was part of some large organization that was keeping tabs on him or she really was what she seemed to be, a young woman who liked good coffee and was looking for a job.

Iggy had once told him about a principle in science where the simplest solution to a problem was usually the right one. It applied in detective work too and it dictated that Sherry wasn't an agent of some sinister power, just a person looking for a job. It was a coincidence that she happened to be looking for the exact kind of work Alex needed done.

"And we know how much I love coincidences," he muttered to himself as the crawler slowed to a stop at Empire Station.

He got up and shuffled off with his fellow passengers, glancing around again, just to be sure he wasn't being followed. When the answer to that question was 'no' he felt a bit foolish and pushed the thoughts of Sherry out of his mind. He'd come to Empire Tower to meet with New York's preeminent sorcerer, the Lightning Lord himself, Andrew Barton, and he needed to be focused. Sorsha had mentioned that Barton would be attending the upcoming mayoral debate and that he was currently feuding with the city. That meant that Barton was supporting William Ashford, and if that was the case, then Barton might know Hugo Ayers. After his talk with Sorsha, Alex didn't believe Barton could have magicked June Masterson into killing Hugo, but he might know something about why Hugo was killed.

Or Sorsha might be wrong and Barton is actually a magical murderer who can make me jump off the top of Empire Tower for figuring that out, he reminded himself.

In either case, Alex needed his mind clear and sharp. Always good advice when meeting with sorcerers.

―――――

"I'm sorry, Alex," Gary Bickman said in his proper British

accent, once Alex had made his way up to the offices of Barton Electric. "Mr. Barton isn't in right now. Even if he was, he's already late for a meeting."

Bickman nodded off to one side of the cavernous lobby where a half-dozen men in fancy suits waited. Several of them had the kind of leather folios favored by lawyers and one was carrying a sturdy tube usually used to hold blueprints. All of the men looked annoyed and irritable.

Alex did not envy the Lightning Lord his meeting, though from the look of the waiting men, none of them had the gumption to stand up to a sorcerer.

"I only need five minutes," Alex said. "When do you expect him?"

Bickman opened his silk tuxedo jacket and withdrew a gold pocketwatch from his vest pocket. Alex had gotten Bickman the job as Barton's valet and gatekeeper and it seemed to be working out well for the little man.

"He was supposed to be back from a meeting with the county commission over an hour ago," he said. "He's been having a problem getting approval for his new electric tower in the Bronx. I honestly couldn't tell you when he'll be back."

Alex checked his own battered brass watch, studiously ignoring the tiny sliver of the red life meter. It was almost four o'clock.

"I can wait a bit," he said.

Bickman glanced nervously at the waiting men in their expensive suits.

"I'll let him know you're here when he comes in," Bickman said, leaning close so as not to be overheard. "But I can't promise anything."

Alex grinned and clapped the smaller man on the shoulder.

"Don't worry about that," he said. "If he can't see me, he can't see me."

Bickman seemed to relax at that. Clearly being Andrew Barton's gatekeeper came with a fair amount of stress. At least from the look of it, Bickman was being well compensated for the trouble.

Alex thanked him and set off to the other side of the enormous lobby from the lawyers. They were seated on the right side, where comfortable couches and chairs had been arranged around low tables. A row of sumptuous wooden phone booths, decked out with etched glass doors and polished brass fittings, lined the wall beyond them. On the left side of the lobby was something Alex hadn't seen in any business office he'd ever visited, a fully stocked bar complete with a barman. It had a polished mahogany counter with a brass rail and tall, comfortable bar stools.

"Can I get you something?" the barman asked as Alex mounted a stool at the far end.

Alex put his kit bag on the bar and withdrew the thermos Marnie had given him. It had been hours since he'd seen her, but her coffee wouldn't have gone cold in that time.

"Can you get me a coffee cup?" he asked, setting the thermos on the bar.

The barman smiled and produced an empty ceramic cup, then went back to polishing glasses. Grateful for the silence and the solitude, Alex unscrewed the lid of the thermos and filled the ceramic cup. Not bothering to recap the thermos, Alex picked up the cup and drank. Coffee always made him feel better, but Marnie's coffee had a magic of its own. The feeling of renewal and vigor that washed over him made him realize just how tired he'd been. He'd spent the bulk of the week chasing down leads about June Masterson and getting involved in the drama that was Vivian Westlake's life and he had precious little to show for it. He hadn't even been paid for the work he did for George Sheridan.

With a sigh Alex raised the cup back to his lips and

drained it. He'd just started pouring a second cup when a voice from behind him made him jump.

"Lockerby!"

It was Andrew Barton's voice. Alex turned to find the Lightning Lord himself striding across the marble floor from the direction of the elevator. He wore a fashionable blue suit but not an overtly expensive one. His hair looked a bit grayer than Alex remembered and there were lines around his eyes that hadn't been there before. He had the look of a man who carried a great many responsibilities.

Across the lobby, the lawyers had all stood up in expectation and now several of them were casting Alex dark looks. For his part, Barton seemed to be glad not to have to deal with them yet.

"I was just thinking about you and here you are," Barton continued. "I wanted to talk to you about—" He stopped suddenly and sniffed then pointed at Alex's thermos. "What's that?"

Alex's brows knit together in confusion.

"Coffee?" he suggested, wondering where Barton had been that he didn't know what coffee smelled like.

Rather than answering, Barton picked up the thermos and held it under his nose, inhaling deeply.

"That's not coffee," he said, a genuine smile of pleasure splitting his face. "May I?"

Alex shrugged and offered Barton his cup, but the Lightning Lord just tipped the thermos, pouring the liquid out onto his other hand. Before it reached his hand, the liquid stopped and began to swirl as if contained by something. As Alex watched, a ceramic cup, much like the one he held, materialized around the coffee, held in Barton's left hand.

What is it with sorcerers? Bunch of show offs.

Alex wondered if he ever used his magic, meager though it was, in front of others like Barton and Sorsha did.

"You're a liar, Lockerby," Barton accused him after taking a tentative sip of the dark liquid. "This isn't coffee, it's nectar. Did you make this?"

Chuckling, Alex shook his head.

"Don't tell me it's that gorgeous secretary of yours," Barton continued. "I've been wanting a reason to steal her away from you."

"No," Alex said. "And she's recently engaged."

"Pity," Barton said, sipping from the cup again. "Where did you get this?"

"A runewright friend of mine makes it."

"There's a coffee rune?" Barton said, seeming genuinely interested.

Alex was about to shake his head, but he honestly had never thought about it. Iggy had been supplying Dr. Kellen with glassware he etched with runes to help her with her potion brewing. What if Marnie was doing the same thing?

"Not that I know of," he said. "But we runewrights don't exactly share our secrets."

"Ask your friend if he wants a job," Barton said, refilling his cup from the thermos. "The coffee down in the terminal is swill. Even my own chef can't seem to make a decent cup."

Alex was ashamed to admit it, but his gut reaction was to put Barton off. Marnie was his secret source for good coffee, after all, and he didn't want to share. After a moment, he realized he was being childish. Alex wanted Marnie out of the elements, and brewing coffee for commuters in Barton's terminal or even just for Barton himself would be a plumb job. Alex wouldn't be able to trade her runes for coffee anymore, but it wasn't like he couldn't afford to just buy it.

"I'll let her know," he said.

"Her?" Barton said, perking up. "Better and better."

Alex hid the smile that spread across his face at the thought of Barton coming on to Marnie.

"Can we talk for a minute?" he asked. "I wanted to ask you something about a case I'm working on."

"Walk with me," Barton said, heading for the elevator up to his office, and still firmly in possession of Alex's thermos.

Alex quickly laid out the story of June Masterson and Hugo Ayers ending with June's body radiating residual magic.

"No," Barton said as the elevator doors opened on his palatial office. "A sorcerer couldn't do what you're describing."

"Are you sure?" Alex asked, remembering how until just a moment ago he wouldn't have conceived that there was such a thing as a coffee rune.

"The human body is far too complex for a sorcerer to just take it over and drive it around like a stolen car," Barton said, pouring the last of Alex's coffee into his cup. "A sorcerer has to understand the systems we're working with to do magic, that's why most of us do fairly simple things, like make power or refrigeration disks. What you might be looking for is some kind of alchemy, though. Maybe a potion that made whoever drank it easily suggestible?"

Alex hadn't considered alchemy, but it wasn't a bad theory.

"Does the name Hugo Ayers ring a bell?" Alex asked.

Barton thought for a moment then shook his head.

"Should it?"

"He was the bookkeeper for William Ashford's political campaign."

Barton raised an eyebrow at that.

"And you think because I'm supporting Ashford, that I might have wanted him dead?"

"No," Alex lied. "But I thought you might know if there was any reason someone would. I can't find anything in Hugo's life that's suspicious, but someone had him killed."

Barton laughed.

"If you're asking if Ashford is doing something illegal, let me set your mind at ease. That lump isn't smart enough to be tricky."

That didn't make any sense to Alex and it must have showed on his face.

"Why do you think I'm helping to finance his campaign?" Barton went on. "The mayor and the city council want me to put up my first satellite tower on the south side to support a few government buildings. I want to put it up in the Bronx, so they're holding up my permits. Ashford is the kind of man I can control once he's in office."

The dichotomy of practicality and chicanery in that statement boggled Alex's mind.

"I'm just glad Ashford came along," Barton went on. "Until a few months ago there wasn't anyone who could challenge Mayor Banes."

Alex hadn't thought about it, but Barton was right, Ashford wasn't even a contender until a month or two ago. Something about that tickled his memory, but he couldn't remember what.

"Anyway, enough of that," Barton said, handing Alex back his empty thermos. "I've got an offer for you. I want you to come work for me."

Alex raised an eyebrow at that. Barton had offered him a job in the past, but this time it seemed to come out of nowhere.

"I told you last time," he said. "I don't think you'd like me working for you."

"Not as a detective or anything like that," Barton said. He looked like he was going to go on, but he hesitated, choosing his words. "How much do you know about sorcery?"

"I know you cast spells that are nigh unto permanent," Alex said. "You live a long time, and most of you seem to like to show off."

Barton laughed at that last bit, but he did nod in agreement.

"Like everything else in life," he said, "there's a limit to what a sorcerer can do. At most we can maintain somewhere around three hundred spells at any given time."

Alex wasn't sure that made sense. Sorsha had to have thousands of her cold disks operating all over the country, to say nothing of the magic that connected Barton's etherium generators to the tens of thousands of magelights and apartment buildings all over Manhattan.

"We get around that by enchanting the raw materials first, then cutting them up into pieces," Barton said when Alex voiced his concern. "The problem I'm having is that each of my generators requires a spell to keep it working."

Alex thought about that for a moment, doing some quick math in his head.

"You're going to run out of spells before you've powered the whole city," he guessed. "To say nothing of powering the state."

Barton nodded grimly.

"I've come at this every way I can think of," he said. "But there's just nothing I can do about it. Soon, I'm going to have to stop making my etherium generators or find a way to channel more power through them. That's when I thought of you."

"I'm not sure I can tell you anything about sorcery that you don't already know," Alex admitted.

"Not sorcery," Barton said, an enigmatic smile on his face. "Runes." Before Alex could ask what on Earth Barton was talking about, he went on. "I think it might be possible to combine sorcery and rune magic. Make my spells more efficient or help them to cover a wider area."

Alex thought the Lightning Lord was grasping at straws.

"I know it sounds crazy," he said, reading Alex perfectly.

241

"But just because something's never been done, doesn't mean it can't be done. Just look at the world we live in. Do you realize that less than a generation ago the only way to get around was on horseback?"

"Okay," Alex said. "Let's say it's possible. I still don't think I can help you."

Barton shook his head and grabbed Alex by the arm.

"It doesn't matter what you think, Alex," he said. "I want you to come work for me and help me figure it out. I'll pay you well."

It was tempting, Alex had to admit. He'd seen the apartments Barton kept in the Tower for his important employees and they were palaces compared to where he'd grown up.

"No," he said at last. "I appreciate it, but I like what I'm doing just fine."

Barton looked like he was on the verge of exploding in anger, but after a moment he just sighed.

"All right," he said. "But I want you to give it some thought on your own. If you can help me with this problem in any way, I'll make it worth your while."

Alex thought about that. Frankly, now that Barton had put the idea in his head, he wouldn't be able to not think about it. The idea of combining two disparate forms of magic was a tantalizing puzzle.

"I'll let you know if I think of anything," he said.

22

GHOSTS

Alex walked slowly through the little churchyard just south of the core. It wasn't particularly large, but there were many gravestones crowded together inside. Some were big, while others were just flat marble rectangles jutting up out of the winter brown grass. He stopped for a few minutes to pay his respects to Father Harry, then moved on to the edge of the yard where a gray stone wall separated it from the street beyond.

"Hi, Jess," he said, kneeling down by a simple marker. The name on the stone said *Andrea Elizabeth Kellen*, but Alex just couldn't bring himself to call her by her right name. He'd known her best as Jessica.

"I'm sorry it's been a while since I've been by. I'd tell you it's because I'm out solving lots of cases and helping people with their problems, but that'd be a lie." He sighed. He told her about the cases he was working and how none of them seemed to be going anywhere. "I guess I did find Vivian Westlake for all the good that did," he said with a laugh. "I used to think I was smart, but you know better than that, don't you?"

He spent a few more minutes talking to the stone, then he stood up and put his hat back on.

"I need to go talk to Linda," he said. "I figured I'd better come see you first. I'm sure she'll ask if I've been by."

Alex stood there for a long moment, as if he expected Jessica to answer, but she didn't. She'd gone on to whatever mysteries lay beyond this life and there was nothing he could do about it. He wondered what Jessica would tell him to do if she could.

"She'd tell you to get on with living your life," he said to the empty churchyard.

Determined, he tugged his hat down firmly on his head and looked down at the simple stone again.

"See you 'round, Jess," he said, then he turned and headed back along the winding path toward the iron gate that guarded the entrance to the churchyard. As he went, he caught sight of a man in a grey overcoat standing near the spot where Sorsha Kincaid's butler, Hitchens, had been buried. With the sorceress' penchant for wearing men's clothes Alex thought it might be her at first, but Alex could tell that the man was larger than the diminutive sorceress.

Alex passed by the man who stood, looking down at a stone in much the same way he had, and stepped out into the street to hail a cab. When he managed it, he gave the cabbie an address he knew very well, but hadn't visited in almost a year.

"Sure thing, mac," was all the cabbie said.

———

The alchemy shop of Dr. Andrea Kellin looked much the same as it had a year ago when Alex and Jessica had been ambushed in the back yard. That thought brought a host of memories back to Alex as he stepped out of the cab and handed the driver a five spot. The only real difference was that the name on the sign now read Linda Kellen instead of Andrea.

Linda was Andrea's daughter. She had contracted polio as a young woman and had nearly died of the dread disease. Andrea had given everything, including her health and eventually her life to cure Linda, and she'd been successful. Two months after Andrea's death, her cure had her daughter out of the iron lung where she'd spent six years. A few months after that, Linda had been well enough to return home and resume her mother's work. She didn't have her mother's medical degree, but she made up for that with an absolute talent for alchemy.

Within six months, Linda had managed to rebuild her mother's clientele and have the business flourishing again. Alex was happy for her, he really was. Linda was a good kid, but she reminded him so much of her mother that coming here was always hard.

Andrea had always closed her shop promptly at five, mostly to give herself time to work on the cure for Linda. With that motivation gone, Linda stayed open till six-thirty, so the neon sign out front was still lit and the shop was open when Alex mounted the stairs to the porch.

The bell over the door jingled as Alex opened it. The room beyond was exactly as he remembered it with rows of shelves packed with various potions, salves, and elixirs. Powdered ingredients that were meant to be mixed with other things stood in sealed jars inside a glass display case, along with open bins of raw ingredients for home remedies. Along the back wall, behind the display cases that made up the counter, were dozens of pictures from Andrea's life, including her medical degree. A beaded curtain hung in the doorway that led from the shop area back to the rest of the house.

"Just a minute," an achingly familiar voice called. A moment later a young woman with red hair came pushing through the curtain. She wore a simple green blouse with a tan skirt and moved slowly with a crutch under each arm. While she had recovered almost completely from the polio, her body had suffered a great deal of atrophy during her long stay in the iron lung.

Alex had to remind himself that this wasn't Jessica. Linda was twenty-seven and had all of her mother's good looks. They could have been twins.

"Alex," Linda said, her face lighting up. "What brings you here?"

"I actually need your help on a case," Alex said, dropping his hat onto the glass counter. He told her about June and what he suspected. "Is there any kind of potion that could have lowered June's will? I mean enough so that someone could have convinced her to kill?"

"Men have been using liquids to lower women's resistance for centuries," June said with a chuckle. "But I don't know of anything that would make a person that suggestible while leaving them lucid enough to commit a murder across town."

Alex sighed and nodded. He'd been expecting that answer; it would fit in with how his week was going. Still, he had held out hope Linda might have something for him.

"How goes your rehabilitation?" he asked, changing the subject.

"I'm taking potions that help my muscles get better," she said. "It's slow going, but I should be able to walk without these in another year or two."

She nodded at the crutches.

"Have you been to see mom?" she asked then. Her voice was both stern and soft at the same time.

Just like Jessica.

He nodded.

"I told her about my case," he said. "She didn't have any suggestions either."

Linda laughed at that but there was sadness in her eyes. She'd spent the last decade largely separated from her mother, and now Andrea was gone. Having lost both his real father and his surrogate, Father Harry, Alex could relate.

He made small talk with her for another quarter hour, then excused himself and headed back out to the street. He'd never catch a cab in this part of town, so he walked west toward the park and the skycrawler station by the Museum of Natural History.

The weather had turned cold and Alex pulled another climate rune from his book and stuck it to his hat. He retrieved a cigarette from his silver case, feeling ridiculous with the rune paper hanging off the front of his hat. Flicking his lighter to life, Alex glanced around as he lit the cigarette and then the rune paper. At this hour and in this weather, there weren't many people walking the streets in this quiet neighborhood, just a businessman who seemed to be looking for a particular house, stopping in front of each one he passed to check the number.

With his bubble of warmth in place, Alex made his way to the skycrawler station. He didn't have to turn and look behind him to know that the businessman in the gray suit was following him. Whoever he was, he was good, but he'd made the mistake of standing too close to the path in the cemetery. Alex had got a decent look at his back when on his way out of the churchyard and he noticed how the man stood, slightly off kilter, as if one of his legs was longer than the other. The businessman had on the same gray overcoat and stood slightly off kilter when he paused in front of each house.

Struggling not to hurry, Alex walked slowly in the direction of Central Park West. He was still in a residential neighborhood and many of the houses were dark, meaning whoever was ghosting Alex would have to stay close to avoid losing him. As he walked, Alex could feel an itch growing between his shoulder blades. He was wearing his suit coat with the shield runes in it, but that didn't make the thought of being shot in the back any more pleasant. Still, the man in the grey overcoat had followed him to the churchyard and that was a much better place for an ambush than a street lined with houses.

As he neared the end of the block, Alex strained to hear the trailing footsteps of the man in the grey overcoat. A large hedge lined the road to his left and as Alex reached the cross street, he ducked to the side behind the obscuring greenery and took off running. After a few yards, the hedge parted where a gate led to the house on the corner. Without hesitation, Alex vaulted over the gate and thrust his hand into his coat, pulling his 1911 free.

The sound of running feet grew louder as the man in the grey overcoat gave chase. Alex leaned close to the gate, holding his pistol up next to his face. As the man drew even with the opening in the hedge, Alex lashed out with the butt of the weapon, catching his pursuer in the shoulder.

It would have been better if Alex had hit the man in the face, but he let out an alarmed cry and stumbled from the unexpected blow, going down in a heap on the sidewalk. Alex leaped back over the gate, but his shadow wasn't ready to give up, rolling onto his front and springing up to his feet.

"Don't," Alex said, leveling the 1911 at the man's face.

Obediently, he froze, then raised his hands, showing them to be empty. The street was dark, and the brim of the man's hat cast an impenetrable shadow across his face.

"Who are you?" Alex demanded. "And who are you working for?"

The man chuckled in a decidedly high-pitched voice.

"You already know that," he said.

Alex knew the voice, but it took him a minute to place it. When he did, he leaned in with his pistol and flicked it upward, catching the brim of his shadow's hat and knocking it off. Beneath it was a ball of curly hair that had been tied up to hide under the hat and Alex swore.

"Agent Mendes," he said, straightening up and putting his 1911 back in the holster under his left arm.

"Took you long enough," she said, leaning down to pick up her hat. Despite the fact that Alex had clubbed her in the shoulder, she flashed him an amused grin. "I've been on you since you left the boss's place. How did you make me, anyway?"

Alex had to admit he was impressed. With her hair tied up under her hat and the bulky overcoat hiding her curvy figure, she'd made a very passable man.

"You cock your hip when you stand," he said. "It's a way to accentuate your figure. When I saw you in that overcoat, I assumed you were a man who had one leg shorter than the other. It was distinctive enough to be memorable."

She cocked her head slightly and a pensive look spread over her face.

"I'll have to work on that."

"Dare I ask what you're doing following me all over town?"

"Boss lady thinks you're in danger," she said, turning her head as if she expected someone to be lurking nearby. "She sent me to keep an eye on you and keep you out of trouble."

Alex laughed at that and Mendes' thick eyebrows tried to grow together in an expression of anger.

"She must think very highly of your skills," Alex said. "Even I have trouble managing that."

"I can imagine," she said in an unamused voice. She reached up and tugged at a cord that bound her curly hair up. It came free and her hair bounced down around her head. "So," she said, putting her hat back on. "Where to now?"

"Nowhere," Alex growled. He was quite capable of taking care of himself and he didn't want or need a chaperone. "You can go back to the Ice Queen and tell her I'm fine."

Mendes fixed him with a stern look.

"You know I can't do that," she said. "You can either let me come with you or I'll just follow you like before, but either way I'm not going anywhere."

Alex seriously considered telling her off, but he doubted it would make a dent. Mendes was a junior agent and in a test program for female agents. She'd have to go above and beyond the expectations of her job to stand out and she knew it. There was no way he'd be able to convince her to just go home and put her feet up.

"All right," he sighed. "You can come."

Without waiting to see if she was following, he turned back toward the park and started walking.

"You never said where we were going," she said, falling into step beside him.

Alex thought about that for a moment. He'd planned to go home, but Iggy would be out at the slaughterhouse making arrangements to use the transference rune. If all went well, they could try it tomorrow night, but in the meantime that left Alex without any dinner.

"You ever hear of a diner called *The Lunch Box?*" Alex asked.

"No," Mendes replied, her face brightening. "But I haven't had anything to eat since breakfast."

"In that case, you'll love it."

———

Alex slid into a booth in the diner while Doris the waitress filled a ceramic cup with coffee for him. She didn't ask him if he wanted coffee, she knew him far better than that. The coffee at The Lunch Box wasn't terrible, but it was nowhere near what Marnie could do.

When Alex had been new to the detective game, he'd spent a lot of time in diners, mostly while he was staking out cheating husbands. In those days, he'd always ordered the same thing, poached eggs on buttered toast. It was cheap and relatively filling. Nowadays, Alex found he'd developed a taste for it and even though he could afford more elaborate meals, he always ordered the same thing.

"The usual, Alex?" Doris asked as Agent Mendes took off the bulky overcoat and hung it up on a peg by the door.

"Yeah," he said. "And one for my friend here."

Doris looked at Mendes in her suit coat and trousers and rolled her eyes before hurrying off the the kitchen.

Mendes slid into the booth opposite Alex. She was taller than Sorsha but still shorter than Alex and she sat up straight in her seat to keep close to his eye level. Of course she might have simply not wanted her considerable chest to overhang the table too much.

Mendes gave new meaning to the term 'busty.' Alex wondered if she had to have her FBI standard suit coat altered so she could button it.

"So, what's the usual?" she asked, dragging Alex's attention away from her chest.

Alex had ordered for her on instinct and now he was a bit embarrassed by his choice. Still he explained his dinner choice and where his taste for eggs and toast had come from. She listened patiently and laughed at the story.

"It's all right," she said when he was done. "My mother made me eggs and toast all the time, so it reminds me of home."

"Where is home, exactly?"

Mendes told Alex about growing up in Arizona, the child of a town sheriff and a teacher. Alex then regaled her with tales of some of his more interesting cases until the food came.

"So how did you meet the boss?" Mendes asked before finishing off her toast.

Alex was about to answer when the glass behind him exploded in a shower of glass and a bullet slammed into his shoulder. Grunting in pain, he grabbed his 1911 and slid out of the booth. Another shot rang out and Alex felt the air pressure as it whizzed past his head so close he could feel its heat.

Out on the sidewalk in front of the diner, Alex could see a man leveling a pistol at him. Screams and cries of startled and terrified diner patrons erupted as Alex took aim.

The man outside fired first, sending a bullet painfully into Alex's arm and throwing off his aim. Alex let loose two shots, but both went wide. The man returned fire but missed Alex.

This time, taking more careful aim, Alex put two shots into the man's torso. The surprised man tried to level his gun again, but strength left him and he collapsed to the sidewalk, unmoving.

"Get on the phone and call an ambulance," he called over his shoulder to Mendes. "We need to take that guy alive if we can." He stood from his crouch and started for the door, but Mendes hadn't answered. She was new to the job, and Alex remembered his first time being shot at. A thing like that tended to rattle a person.

Turning back he intended to get her moving, but she wasn't in the booth at all. A tight knot formed in Alex's stomach as he saw her lying prone on the floor. Her eyes were closed and a widening pool of blood was spreading rapidly from a wound in the side of her head.

23

DEATH AT DINNER

lex paced back and forth across the lobby of the New York Hospital like a tiger in a cage. He'd paid a cabbie twenty bucks to get him here in under fifteen minutes and the man had made it, but Alex had no idea if that had helped. Nurses had rushed Agent Mendes into their operating theater as soon as Alex arrived, but the only thing he knew about head wounds was that when they were caused by bullets, they were usually fatal.

He pulled out his cigarette case, but when he opened it, he found it empty. Swearing, he stuffed it back into his left coat pocket and turned toward the little counter where the hospital sold medical supplies.

"Stop," he growled after he'd taken a step. "Get a hold of yourself."

Instead of the medical counter and a fresh pack of cigarettes, Alex turned toward the row of phone booths on the front wall. He entered the nearest one and closed the door behind him then dropped a nickel in the slot.

"There you are," Iggy exclaimed when the line connected.

"I saw police cars out in front of The Lunch Box when I got home, and Doris told me someone shot the woman you were with."

Alex took a deep breath and told his mentor what had happened. The more he spoke, the angrier he got.

"It should have been me," he exclaimed once he'd reached the end. "I knew someone might be after me and I should have sat facing the window. I might have seen the shooter in time."

"Or he might have shot right through Agent Mendes just to get to you," Iggy pointed out. "As it was, your shielded coat stopped at least two shots that might have hit someone else. And it's not like you button your coat when you sit down, so you might have been killed by the first shot."

Alex didn't want to accept that, but it made sense. On top of that, he knew that regret and second guessing accomplished nothing. No amount of magic could change the past.

"How is she doing?" Iggy asked when Alex didn't speak.

"No one's told me anything yet."

"Well, go have a smoke and calm down," Iggy suggested. "And call me when you know something."

Alex promised that he would and hung up. He felt better after talking to Iggy, but he couldn't help thinking that if he hadn't caught Mendes following him, she wouldn't be fighting for her life upstairs.

"I need a cigarette," he said to no one.

He made his way to the medical counter and bought a pack of cigarettes. Sticking one in his mouth, he emptied the rest into his silver case.

"You Lockerby?" A thick necked man in a black fedora asked, walking up to him as Alex lit the cigarette. He wore a cheap suit and had a gold detective badge on his belt.

"Yeah," Alex said with a sigh. He didn't know this detective but he did spend a fair amount of time at the Central Office so this man might know him.

"I'm Detective Zimmerman, I hear someone took a shot at you outside an east side diner."

It wasn't a question, so Alex just nodded.

"Witnesses said you shot the gunman, then left the scene to bring a victim here."

"That's about it," Alex said, too tired to be difficult for the sake of being difficult.

"Yeah, I've got a problem with that."

Alex's fuzzy brain snapped back into focus as the neckless detective consulted his notebook.

"Well that's what happened," Alex said, not sure where the man was going.

He looked up at Alex then back at his notebook.

"You see, that's my problem," he said. "The dead guy we scraped up off the sidewalk was named Dexter Stevens. You ever heard of him?"

Alex shook his head.

"We found an identity card in his pocket," Zimmerman said. "Stevens was a salesman for Maceys Department Store. Not exactly the kind of guy to shoot up a diner full of random people."

"What are you getting at, Detective Zimmerman?"

"Well," he said, finally looking up from his notebook. "It looks to me that you didn't shoot the guy who shot at the diner. You shot an innocent bystander by mistake."

Alex searched his memory. He was certain the man he shot had been pointing a gun at the diner. The fact that he only seemed to be a random stranger wasn't surprising, it was exactly like Hugo Ayers' murder.

Not that Zimmerman will believe that explanation.

"Did you find a gun on Mr. Stevens?" Alex asked.

Zimmerman consulted his notebook again.

"We did find a .357 revolver near his body, yes, but we can't say that it belongs to Stevens."

"Make sure your boys run a paraffin test on the body," Alex said. "You'll see that he's the gunman."

"Are you telling me how to do my job?" Zimmerman said with just the trace of a smile.

Alex was about to respond that someone needed to, but he managed to choke back the words.

"Of course not," he said, pasting a friendly smile on his face. "I'm just answering your questions."

"Well that's not much of an answer. You see, I think you just shot out of the diner without looking and you killed a poor salesman on his way home from work."

"Lockerby!" a man's voice erupted through the hospital lobby.

Alex turned to see Mendes' partner, Agent Redhorn, bearing down on him at a fast walk. Redhorn was average height and slim, but something about the way the man carried himself broadcast that he was not one to be trifled with.

"What the hell happened?" he demanded as he stormed up to Alex and Zimmerman.

The latter plucked his badge from his belt and stuck it in Redhorn's face.

"This is a police matter," he said. "You need to step away."

Something flashed in Redhorn's eyes that made Alex want to take a step back, but the FBI man simply pulled out his own badge and held it up for Zimmerman.

"This man and the shooting you're investigating are now a federal matter," he growled. "Now beat it, flatfoot."

Zimmerman gave Redhorn a look of pure hatred, then flipped his notebook closed and walked away grumbling.

"Now," Redhorn said, turning his murderous gaze on Alex. "What the hell happened to my partner?"

Alex related his experience at the diner concluding with his harrowing ride to the hospital.

"And just what was Agent Mendes doing having dinner with you?" Redhorn demanded, much in the manner of an overprotective father whose daughter got home late from a date.

"What was I supposed to do?" Alex growled back at the FBI man. Between Zimmerman and Redhorn he'd had enough of people thinking he was somehow the bad guy in this scenario. "Did you expect me to leave the poor kid outside to just watch me eat from across the street? She hadn't had anything to eat since breakfast."

"You were supposed to let her do the job I sent her to do," Sorsha Kincaid's voice cut into the conversation.

Alex turned to find the sorceress striding up from the direction of the door. She wore a button-up shirt and vest over a pencil skirt, looking much more feminine than she had earlier. As she approached, Alex wondered how many times a day she changed her look.

"A job that didn't need doing," Alex protested.

"Clearly it did," Sorsha countered.

"No," Alex pushed back. "If she hadn't been there, she wouldn't have been shot."

"No, if she'd been doing her job she wouldn't have been shot," Sorsha said, stepping uncomfortably close to Alex, her ice blue eyes glaring up into his.

"I'm sure you can discuss who's fault this is later," Redhorn said. "But I'd like to know how my partner is doing."

"They won't tell me," Alex said, not breaking eye contact with Sorsha.

"Where was she shot?" she asked.

"In the head," Alex said.

That got a reaction and Sorsha gasped. She turned and

strode purposely toward the reception desk by the doors that led into the hospital proper.

"She'll get answers," Redhorn said, his voice milder. "Thanks for getting Mendes here so quickly." It was a grudging admission, but Redhorn stated it simply.

"Alex?"

Alex turned to find Danny Pak striding across the lobby.

"I need to come here more often," Alex said. "Everybody I know seems to end up here."

"Did you come about Vivian?" Danny said as he drew near. "Who called you?"

Redhorn noticed the gold shield clipped to the breast pocket of Danny's coat and his brows knit together.

"I already told your partner to buzz off," he said in a warning voice. "This is a federal matter."

Danny looked from Redhorn to Alex and then laughed. Not prepared for that, Redhorn just looked shocked.

"Who's the stiff?" Danny asked.

"This is Agent Redhorn of the FBI," Alex said. "He's one of Sorsha's."

Redhorn looked like he might just choke on his own outrage, so Alex went on.

"This is my friend, Danny Pak. He's not here to arrest me."

"Have people been trying to arrest you?" Danny asked, his curiosity piqued.

Alex didn't want to go into it.

"Later," he said. "What's this about Vivian? Do you mean Vivian Westlake?"

Danny nodded.

"She's here. The family butler called the cops saying the Westlakes had collapsed at dinner. By the time we got there, Fredrick and Isabel were dead and Vivian was barely clinging to life. They brought her here."

Alex was stunned.

"Do they know what happened?"

"Looks like poison of some kind," Danny said with a shrug. "Apparently the cook is missing too."

"Why would he poison his employer?" Redhorn asked. "Did Westlake owe him money?"

"Don't know," Danny said with a shrug. "I've got to take Vivian's statement, then I'm headed over there. You want to tag along?" This last was directed at Alex.

Alex looked at Redhorn, but he was watching Sorsha who was having an animated discussion with someone in a doctor's coat.

"Go ahead," he said at last, then he turned back to Alex. "But we will be having a conversation later about you putting my partner in danger."

"Looking forward to it," Alex lied as Redhorn started across the lobby in the direction of Sorsha and the doctor.

"Let's go before he changes his mind," Alex said, tugging at Danny's coat as he headed for the elevators.

Vivian Westlake looked terrible. Her face was pale, her eyes were bloodshot, and her voice was hoarse. The doctor caring for her had objected to anyone seeing her until Danny shoved his detective badge in the man's face and threatened to arrest him.

"I don't know what to tell you," Vivian managed to say. "We were just having dinner then suddenly my stomach hurt. I remember falling out of my chair, but I must have blacked out because I woke up here."

Danny asked her a few questions while Alex just listened. Even sick and pale Vivian was a beautiful woman, so different from the acne riddled teen she had been. Her glossy raven hair spilled out over her pillow like it had been arranged for a fashion magazine shoot. Alex understood what George Sheridan saw in her.

"We were celebrating," Vivian said, pulling Alex's attention back. "My dad had George served with divorce papers."

That was fast, Alex thought. *It must be nice to have a lawyer on retainer.*

Danny thanked Vivian, then Alex wished her a swift recovery and they withdrew to the hall.

"What's her prognosis, doctor?" Danny asked the white-coated man.

"She's very weak. We'll have to keep an eye on her for a few days, but I suspect that if whatever killed her parents hasn't taken her by now, she's probably going to recover. She's a very lucky young woman."

"Do you know what she was poisoned with?" Alex asked.

"No way to tell for certain," the doctor said with a shake of his head.

Danny thanked him and led Alex down the hall toward the elevator.

"I'm heading over to the Westlakes," he said as they waited for the car to arrive. "It sounds like we're looking for the cook, but when rich people get murdered, the powers that be want all the I's dotted and the T's crossed."

"Are you sure they were murdered?" Alex asked. "It might be an accident."

"Why did the cook go on the lam then?"

Alex shrugged.

"He probably saw what happened and figured he'd be blamed."

"Maybe," Danny said but he didn't sound convinced.

The car arrived and Danny pulled the gate open. Alex was tempted to let the whole thing drop. The Westlakes weren't his clients anymore and neither was Vivian's soon-to-be ex-husband. He should just go home and get some rest. Still, he hadn't had much luck with his cases of late and this seemed straightforward enough. Either the cook poisoned them or he didn't. Then there was Fredrick and Isabel. He'd liked them. They seemed like decent people and if he could help find out what happened to them, he aught to try.

"Mind if I tag along?" he asked Danny as they got on to the elevator.

Two patrol cars were waiting outside the Westlake's inner-ring home when Danny and Alex drove up. Since the coroner's van was absent, Alex assumed Dr. Wagner's people had already been by to pick up Fredrick and Isabel. It might have helped for Alex to see the bodies, but under the circumstances he really didn't want to.

When he followed Danny into the house, a uniformed officer conducted them to the dining room. It was large and tastefully appointed with a long table of carved walnut taking up the center of the room, directly under a chandelier that had been made with magelights in mind. A large china cabinet stood against the back wall and a long window dominated one side of the room. Below the window was a low sideboard with a gleaming silver service set out on it. These were only decorative since the meal was on the table.

A Persian carpet, woven of green and gold threads, covered the hardwood floor and Alex could see pools of drying vomit on it. From the look of it, all three of the Westlakes had thrown up their meal when whatever killed them had started to take effect.

The family meal consisted of a glazed ham with new potatoes, green beans, and rolls that looked light as air. An open bottle of wine stood in a silver bucket on its own stand. The bucket had once contained ice, but was now full of water. A coffee pot was also on the table and each place setting had a cup and saucer, though one of them had the cup turned over.

While Danny talked with the officer who had taken charge of the crime scene, Alex circled the table twice, being careful to keep his distance and avoid the vomit.

"Find anything?" Danny asked as Alex completed his second circuit.

"You first," Alex said, still staring intently at the table.

"The butler found them about fifteen minutes after they began eating," Danny said, reading from his notes. "Mr Westlake was dead by then, but his wife and Vivian were still alive. Mrs. Westlake died while they were waiting for the police and an ambulance." He looked up from his notebook and gave Alex a penetrating look. "Now, what do you see?"

"This wasn't an accident," Alex said.

Danny nodded at that and pointed at the carpet.

"They threw up," he said. "Means whatever it was, it was probably concentrated. A deliberate dose."

"That's the way I figure it," Alex said.

"So something in the food?" Danny said. "Maybe the wine or the coffee?"

"We can rule out the coffee," Alex said, pointing at the overturned cup at one of the place settings. "Whoever sat there didn't have any. We can also rule out the rolls and the potatoes. Whoever sat at the far end of the table didn't use their butter knife and there are no potatoes on that plate either."

Danny moved to inspect the settings, then nodded.

"So it has to be the wine," he concluded. "I don't think they could have eaten enough of the ham or the green beans to kill them if the poison was there."

Alex pulled out his chalk and rune book, drawing a

doorway on the front wall. Two minutes later he was back from his vault with his kit bag.

"Let's see for sure," he said, pulling a round phial with a rubber stopper from inside his kit. Popping the stopper out, he sprinkled some of the powder inside on the wine bottle and on the nearest wine glass. That done, he took out his multi-lamp and clipped the ghostlight burner into it.

"What's that?" Danny asked.

"Toxicity powder," Alex explained. "It's an old alchemists' trick to detect when a potion has gone bad. With my lamp," he said, lighting the burner and closing the front, "the powder will glow in the presence of toxic substances."

He put on his oculus and adjusted the lenses. When he shone his lamp at the wine glass, the liquid inside glowed brightly. He turned the lamp on the wine bottle, however, and only the lip glowed.

"It's the wine, all right," he said, handing the oculus to Danny. "I don't know if your investigators can figure out what it is, but you ought to have that bottle tested."

Danny handed back the oculus, then called one of the uniformed officers to bring in the Westlake's butler.

"How can I help, sir?" the plump butler said in a weak voice as he arrived.

"Who picked out the wine for dinner?" Danny asked.

"Mr. Westlake."

"Did you get it for him, or did he get it himself?"

"He brought it up," the butler said. "It was already here when I set up for dinner, so I started it chilling."

"Did you open it?"

The butler shook his head.

"No, sir. Mr. Westlake always opened the bottle, but I did pour."

Danny wrote all this down, then thanked the butler, who turned to leave.

"One more thing," Alex asked before the little man could leave. "Do you keep the house keys as part of your duties?"

"Of course," the man said, looking slightly offended. "Mr. Westlake trusts...trusted me implicitly."

"Thanks," Alex said, and the butler withdrew.

Danny gave Alex a penetrating look, then rolled his eyes.

"Spill it," he said. "I know that look, you've figured something out and you want to impress everyone with how clever you are, but it's late and I'm tired, so out with it."

Alex resisted the urge to laugh. His friend knew him too well.

"The cook isn't your man," he said. Alex pointed to the bottle in the silver bucket. "That's from the Mist Valley Winery," he said. "If you look closely, you can see the year on it — 1919."

Danny looked then shrugged.

"So?"

"So that's an expensive bottle of wine, a California wine from before prohibition," Alex explained. "Fredrick Westlake was an investor, so it makes sense he'd have one or two, but they'd be locked in the wine cellar where the cook couldn't get them, and he certainly couldn't have gone out and bought one."

Danny considered this, then nodded.

"So the cook saw that the Westlakes died during dinner and figured he'd be on the hook for it. Are we looking at the butler then? Is that why you asked about his having the keys?"

"No," Alex said. "It's possible he did it, but I don't think so. He'd have a better story if he'd planned this."

"Then why are the keys important?"

"Follow me." Alex led Danny out into the foyer where the butler waited and had the pudgy man conduct them to the cellar door. When they reached it, Alex tugged on the handle. "Locked," he said.

"Of course it's locked," the butler said, somewhat abashed. "I run a well-ordered household."

"Then how did Mr. Westlake get that bottle of wine you found on the dining room table?" Alex asked.

The butler looked startled and just stammered.

"Someone else provided the wine," Danny said, catching on. "They left it on the table and Jeeves here thought that Westlake had done it, while he thought the butler got it."

"Exactly," Alex said.

"So who put it on the table?" the butler demanded. "Are you suggesting Mrs. Westlake or Miss Vivian did it?"

"No," Danny said. "They didn't have keys either, right?"

"Oh," the butler said, embarrassed. "Of course, you're right."

"So who got the wine?" Danny said, turning to Alex. "It would have to be someone who knew the family's dining routine and had access to the wine cellar."

"You don't mean me," the butler squeaked but Alex waved him silent.

"There's another option," he said. "Someone who knew the Westlake's dinner habits and had access to another bottle of Mist Valley wine."

"There isn't anyone who fits that bill," Danny said.

"Sure there is," Alex replied. "Vivian's not-yet-ex-husband owns a nightclub and he's a connoisseur of domestic, pre-prohibition wines. Also, he's spent a lot of time with Vivian, so it's quite likely he knew the family's dinner procedures."

"But why would a nightclub owner poison the Master?" the butler asked.

Alex shrugged.

"They served him with divorce papers today, maybe he was angry."

"Or maybe he didn't want that divorce to go through,"

Danny suggested. "If the Westlakes die before it's final, he inherits everything."

"That sounds like motive to me," Alex said. "Now, how much would you wager that his fingerprints are on that bottle?"

Danny looked back toward the dining room and grinned. "No bet."

24

THE TRAIL

The next morning Alex stumbled downstairs to the brownstone's kitchen well after the sun had come up. To his surprise Iggy was sitting at the dining room table with the Archimedean Monograph open in front of him. Alex knew something wasn't right with this picture, but he was at least two cups of coffee short of figuring out what.

"Pot's on the stove," Iggy said, anticipating Alex's need. He ran a practiced eye over Alex, then pointed to his chest. "Fix your tie."

Alex ignored the tie comment and opened the cupboard, extracting a mug, then poured coffee into it from the pot on the stove. Two cups later, he walked to the glass door that separated the kitchen from Iggy's greenhouse and checked his tie in the reflection. In the fuzz of his pre-coffee morning, he'd put the tie on backward with the short end in front.

Grumbling, he pulled the tie off and started to re-tie it.

"Why are you in here reading?" he asked. Iggy usually read in his wingback chair in the library. It had better light during the day and the fireplace at night. "Is something wrong with the transference rune?"

Iggy looked up with a sigh.

"No," he said after a long moment. "I'm confident it will work, and our little mayfly friend is still doing well."

"Trying to figure out Moriarty's vault?" Alex hid a grin behind his coffee cup. The subject of Moriarty closing his vault door behind him when he left Alex alone in the attic of the slaughterhouse was a sticking point for Iggy.

"You were clearly delirious," his mentor said, looking back down at the Monograph. "I've read this enough to know that there's no way to open a vault door from the inside, and I'm not willing to attempt it just to prove the point."

It wasn't cowardly, Alex knew. Runewrights who shut their vault doors from the inside were never seen again. The implications were pretty clear: if you closed the door to your vault, it would become your tomb.

"What if Moriarty had more than one door," Alex said as the coffee started firing his synapses.

"Don't be absurd," Iggy said, irritation in his voice.

"Think about it," Alex protested. "If there was another door into his vault, that one could have been left open."

"Except you and I both know a runewright can only have one vault key," Iggy said. "The rune that creates the vault links it to the key when you cast it. You can't do it again without breaking the link to the original key."

Iggy was right, of course, and Alex knew it, but he knew what he'd seen in that slaughterhouse attic.

"It's impossible," Iggy continued, a note of finality in his voice.

"Wasn't it you who told me that if you remove the impossible and nothing remains, then some part of the impossible, must be possible?" Alex countered. He was baiting Iggy and he knew it, but Alex resented Iggy's dismissal of what he'd seen.

Iggy looked up from his book and gave Alex a patronizing look.

"How is Agent Mendes?" he said, changing the subject. Clearly, he'd been wanting to work the conversation around to the subject, but hoped Alex would do it for him.

"I don't know," Alex shrugged. He told Iggy about his encounter with Detective Zimmerman and later with Agent Redhorn and Sorsha. "When Danny showed up, I just wanted to get out of there. I should have stayed."

"There wasn't anything you could do," Iggy said. "It was probably best to get your mind off of it."

Alex had managed to put the shooting out of his mind, but now it was back and bothering him just as much as it had the previous night.

"Did Zimmerman say who the shooter was?" Iggy asked.

"A nobody," Alex responded. "He was a salesman at Macy's. We'd never met. I'm going to dig into that today, but I'll bet you a steak dinner that he didn't have any reason to be shooting up a diner last night."

"Just like June Masterson," Iggy observed. "And before you start blaming yourself for that man's death, remember that he was shooting into a crowded diner."

"I know," Alex said. On a rational level, he understood that he'd made the only real choice available to him, but that didn't stop him from feeling like he'd committed murder somehow.

Someone committed murder, he corrected himself. Someone sent Dexter Stevens to kill him. Whoever did that killed Stevens just as surely as if they'd shot him themselves.

"It has to be Ashford," Alex said, running through his shallow suspect pool in his head. "Or someone on his campaign."

Iggy considered that for a moment, then reached for his cigarette case and shrugged.

"Politics is a dirty business," he said, "but what makes you think Ashford wanted to have his bookkeeper killed? Did he see something he shouldn't have, or maybe the campaign was funneling money to the mob?"

Alex shook his head.

"I don't know," he said. "New York is the biggest, wealthiest, and most powerful city on earth. That's reason enough to want to be mayor."

"Well that sounds like a hunch," Iggy said, lighting a cigarette. "And a pretty thin one at that."

And hunches are the hallmark of shoddy detective work.

Iggy didn't say it, but Alex remembered the hundreds of times he had said it. And as annoying a saying as it was, Iggy was right.

"What should I do then?" he asked with a defeated sigh. "The only person who can tell me what Hugo Ayers might have known is Hugo, and he's past asking."

"It seems to me," Iggy said, shutting the Archimedean Monograph and standing, "that if you want to know who's behind the murder of Hugo Ayers and the attempts on your own life, you need to find out how the assassins are connected."

"I'm not sure June and the shooter from last night are connected," Alex said, not really sure where Iggy was going with this line of thought.

"You're forgetting the unfortunate fellow in the car," Iggy said. "After last night, I'm inclined to agree with you that whoever is behind this is using magic to compel otherwise innocent people to murder."

"I thought you said that was impossible."

Iggy puffed on his cigarette for a moment, then shrugged.

"The likelihood that one person had blackmail material

on three seemingly random people isn't high," he said. "Besides, as you very intelligently pointed out, if you eliminate the impossible and nothing remains…"

"Some part of the impossible, must be possible," Alex finished.

"That means that whoever is doing this must be connected to June and the others in some way," Iggy said. "Find the connection and it will lead you to your murderous magician."

Iggy had a point. June didn't cast a control spell on herself. Alex was reminded of the fishhook rune Moriarty had put on him; he would have had to do that in the brownstone while Alex slept. That kind of delicate spell work required proximity and time. If the mind control rune was the same, then all the assassins' lives would have intersected with whomever was controlling them.

It was a place to start, which was more than Alex had when he got up that morning.

"Now," Iggy said, heading into the library to return the Archimedean Monograph to its place on the bookshelf. "Let's head over to the hospital and see how Agent Mendes is doing."

After asking directions from a helpful nurse, Alex found the room where Agent Mendes was recovering. She lay at the end of a row of beds in a darkened room with a dozen other unconscious people.

"It looks like she's asleep," Alex said, squinting down to the last bed. He almost didn't recognize Agent Mendes. Her mass of tight curly hair had been shorn and her head was almost entirely wrapped in a bandage.

"No," said Iggy, pushing past Alex. He pointed at the

metal stands next to each bed with a glass bottle hanging from it. Each sleeping patient had a rubber tube connected to their arms that ran up to the bottle. "That's dream syrup," Iggy said. "These patients are being kept asleep so they can heal."

"Is that bad?" Alex asked, hurrying to catch up with Iggy.

"Not necessarily," Iggy said. When he reached the bed with Mendes, he picked up the clipboard hanging from it and began reading.

Alex looked over Mendes' sleeping form. The bandage that had been wrapped around her head bulged out over her right ear. Her normally olive skin appeared pale and her lips were cracked and dry. She didn't look good, but at least her breathing appeared regular.

"Ah," he said after a minute. "Luckily, the bullet didn't hit her straight on. It caught her in just behind the temple and ricochetted off her skull."

Alex tried to picture that and winced. It didn't sound very lucky.

"What does that mean?"

"Who are you?" a new voice asked.

Alex turned to find an older, pudgy man in a white doctor's coat bearing down on them. He had thick fingers, like sausages, bloodshot eyes, and his face was round and squishy. As non-threatening as he looked, the man strode with the purpose of someone in charge. Alex guessed he must Mendes' doctor.

"You used a major mending rune, I see," Iggy said, still reading from the chart. "Not how I would have handled it. At least the scar will be covered by her hair."

"Well, thanks for your opinion," the doctor said. "But I'm in charge of this patient and this ward so I'm going to have to ask you to leave."

"You should have used a standard mending rune in

concert with a purification elixir to reduce the chance of infection," Iggy said, still reading from the chart.

The doctor's face got slightly red and he grabbed the clipboard out of Iggy's hands.

"That would have made her recovery take two weeks," the doctor said. "Now are you leaving, or do I have to summon a policeman?"

"True," Iggy said, looking up at the man for the first time. "But with the major restoration rune, her skull fracture is healing too fast. It causes serious pain."

The doctor's face went full red and he stepped up nose-to-nose with Iggy.

"Which is why we're keeping her asleep," he growled. "I hate it when you amateurs come in here and try to tell me my business."

Iggy chuckled at that.

"If you knew your business, doctor," he said, putting dismissive emphasis on the word 'doctor,' "you'd know that with severe head trauma it's better to keep the patient awake, that way you can detect any potential brain injuries while there's still time to heal them. By the time Agent Mendes here wakes up, it will be too late to do anything if she's suffered brain trauma."

"Brain trauma is very unlikely with these kinds of wounds," the doctor blustered. Alex could tell from his tone that he wasn't as confident in his position as he had been.

"Seeing as how this woman is a federal agent working with Sorsha Kincaid," Iggy said, pushing past the doctor and heading back toward the hall, "you'd better hope so."

Alex had seen Iggy take people down before. His mentor had very little patience for ignorance and self-importance. He flashed the doctor an amused grin and then followed Iggy out into the corridor.

"Idiot," Iggy grumbled as they headed for the elevator.

"Will Agent Mendes be all right?"

"I think so," Iggy said, giving him a smile and a nod. "That doctor might be an idiot, but he was right about one thing, brain injury isn't terribly likely with this kind of wound. I'd rather have done it the right way just in case, though."

Alex took a deep breath and let it out. He could almost feel the tension leaving his body. Iggy had been right, Mendes being shot wasn't his fault, but he still felt responsible to some degree.

"All right," he said as the elevator car arrived. "I'm going to the office."

Iggy nodded at him.

"Call me if you figure out the connection between June and your failed assassins."

"Are you all right?" Leslie's worried face greeted him when he pushed his office door open. He'd called her to tell her he'd be late, explaining what had happened the previous night. She rounded her desk and embraced him, squeezing tight. "Did your shield runes work?"

"I got hit in the back and the arm," Alex said, stepping back when she finally released him. "But the runes held. I've got a few bruises, but I'm all right."

"What about the shooter? Did the police get him?"

Alex shook his head.

"I did," he said.

Leslie sighed and squeezed his arm and nodded. She'd been with him long enough to know that he didn't relish violence.

He didn't shy away when it was necessary either.

"I can live with that," she said, giving him one of her million-dollar smiles.

"I need you to dig up everything you can on William Ashford."

"The guy running for mayor?"

Alex nodded.

"He's only been a contender for the last few months, but no one seems to know anything about him before that."

Leslie raised an eyebrow.

"And you want to know—"

"Everything," Alex finished.

"That could take a while," she said.

"Make it top priority," Alex said, heading for his office.

"What about the psychic?" Leslie asked. "Madame Hortense."

Alex hadn't given any thought to the enigmatic Miss Knox. He was sure she was up to something but there just wasn't time to ferret out what that might be.

"Call her and set up an interview," he said.

Leslie gave him a look that said she thought he was crazy.

"She must be quite the looker."

"Don't worry," Alex said with a chuckle. "She's not in your league."

"Uh, huh," Leslie said, clearly unconvinced. "You're the boss."

———

Alex hung up his hat on the stand in his office before he sat down at his desk. Pulling his notebook from his shirt pocket, he flipped to the page where he'd listed the calls he needed to make. The first name on the list was Detective Zimmerman, so he picked up the phone and dialed the Central Office of Police.

"Zimmerman," the detective's voice came over the line once Alex had navigated past the police operator.

"What did you find out about Dexter Stevens, Detective?"

"Lockerby?" he said after a pause. "I figured you'd be in the basement of some government building with a light in your face by now."

"They let me out for good behavior. Now, what's the word on Stevens?"

There was a pause on the line while Zimmerman considered whether or not he should talk to a private detective.

"Paraffin test came back," he said. "You were right, Stevens was the gunman."

"Any idea why he shot up a diner?"

"Nope," Zimmerman said. "He lived with his parents in the west side mid-ring. I talked with them this morning and with his coworkers. By all accounts he was a good guy, usual habits, no vices." The line went quiet for a second then he continued. "You still saying you don't know him?"

"Never seen him before," Alex said.

"So he must have been gunning for that lady fed. Any idea why?"

Alex knew exactly why Dexter Stevens, clean cut kid from the west side, had shot through a diner window, but explaining it would take more time than he wanted to spend.

"No," was all he said. "You'd have to ask the feds."

"No thanks," Zimmerman replied. "I expect they'll send someone along to take this case off my desk before too long anyway. Then it will be their problem. Now, if there's nothing else, Lockerby, I've got work."

Alex thanked him and hung up. He gave a moment's thought to tracking down Stevens' parents and seeing if Zimmerman missed anything, but he didn't want to face them. Zimmerman had said that Dexter worked at Macy's though. That would be a much better place to dig into his life.

He picked up the phone again and dialed the number of *The Midnight Sun*.

"You finally going to give me a good lead?" Billy Tasker asked when Alex got him on the phone. There was no way Alex was going to tell a tabloid writer that he was on the trail of someone using magic to control people, so he dodged the question. "What about the Westlake poisoning in the inner-ring? I know you did some work for them."

"I think the police will be making an arrest in that case," Alex volunteered. "You might want to have someone stake out the *Northern Lights* club."

"Great," Billy said. "Now, what can I do for you?"

"Did you hear anything about a traffic death earlier this week?"

"Yeah," he said. "In fact..."

Alex could hear the rustling of papers over the line before Billy came back on.

"According to this, a guy named James Dawkins lost control of his car and almost hit a pedestrian before being killed...hey, this is only a few blocks from the *Northern Lights*, is it related?"

"No," Alex said. "I was the guy he almost hit, though. I wanted to give my condolences," he lied. "Do you know if he had any family?"

"Says here that he had a sister named Abigail, but I don't have an address," Billy said. "He did work for an ad agency called Wilson Brothers."

"That'll do," Alex said, scribbling notes. "I've heard of them."

"You're okay, aren't you?" Billy asked, once Alex finished writing.

"Yeah, he missed me."

"Well keep your eyes open from now on," Billy admonished him.

Alex thought of Dexter Stevens who was downtown at the morgue, and Agent Mendes, kept asleep in the hospital.

"I will," he promised, then bid Billy good day and hung up.

25

INK

The Wilson Brothers advertising agency was a modest office on the fifth floor of a mid-ring office building. Alex didn't know much about them, but he'd heard the name. If their lobby was anything to go on, they were doing well in these troubled times. Pictures of various products ranging from hair cream to fur coats lined the walls, illuminated by a long bank of windows along the back that filled the space with light.

Alex presented his business card to a stunningly attractive receptionist with pale skin, raven hair, and lipstick the color of a candied apple.

"Just a moment," she said in a smoldering, throaty contralto that flowed like honey and hinted at forbidden promises. She stood, revealing a high-waisted pencil skirt that was so snug around her knees that she walked in a series of short, sauntering steps. The effect made her hips sway in a mesmerizing motion and Alex had to force himself to look elsewhere.

A few minutes later the dark-haired vision returned with a dapper man in his forties in tow. He had a square build, with decent shoulders and a trim waist. His suit was the latest three-button fashion and of excellent quality with shoes polished to a perfect shine. Clearly the man was an important person in the office, but his face bore no trace of pride or position, only a thick mustache that bristled a lot like Iggy's.

"Mr. Lockerby?" he said, extending his hand. "I'm Andrew Wilson, but you can call me Andy."

"Alex," he said, shaking Andy's hand. As he did so, the receptionist passed by on her way back to her desk. Her brown eyes followed Alex as she moved by and when she saw him looking, the ghost of a smile crossed her sumptuous lips.

"I must confess, Alex," Andy went on, oblivious to his receptionist's flirtations, "we've never had a private detective as a client. What is it we can do for you?"

Alex pulled his wandering attention back to the conversation and explained about his reason for coming.

"Terrible tragedy about James," Andy said, shaking his head. "But I thought a policeman witnessed the crash. What's a private investigator doing looking into this?"

"His sister Abigail thinks there might have been something funny about it," Alex lied. "She asked me to look into it. Could I ask you a couple of questions?"

Andy looked torn. Clearly he was expecting Alex to be a customer, and this early in the day he probably had a desk full of calls to make. Still, he seemed sincere in his regret about James, so Alex hoped his desire to be helpful would outweigh his need to get back to work.

"Come back to my office," he said after a moment.

He led Alex through a door into a narrow hallway and through to a comfortable office. Like the lobby, the walls were lined with pictures of advertising. Thick books full of newspaper clippings were stacked on Andy's desk along with a sea of loose paperwork.

"Don't mind the mess," he said, motioning Alex to a

comfortable looking chair. "Everybody wants to change up their advertising with the new year."

Everything in the office was designed to convey the Wilson Brothers' expertise at their craft. Alex realized that the sexpot secretary had been part of that, literally advertising for the agency.

"I won't take up much of your time," Alex said, pulling his notebook from his pocket. "But if you could tell me what James Dawkins did here, that'd help."

Andy sighed and steepled his hands under his nose.

"James was one of our salesmen," he said. "He specialized in bars, restaurants, that sort of thing."

"Nightclubs?" Alex asked.

"Yes," Andy said, a bit hesitantly. "But not the ones in the core if that's what you're thinking. James was too new to be assigned to our high-end clients."

"Do you have any idea what he would be doing in that part of town after five?"

Andy shook his head.

"Nothing to do with his work."

Alex asked a few more questions, but Andy wasn't much help. James was a diligent worker and would have had a bright future at Wilson Brothers. He was well liked and if he had any enemies, his boss didn't know about it.

"Could I see his desk?"

Andy shrugged and led Alex down the hall to a medium-sized room with five desks in it. Two people were working, both on the phone, and all of the desks were piled with papers and books of newspaper clippings like the ones on Andy's desk.

James' desk looked exactly like the others. Alex didn't know what he might be looking for and Andy didn't seem to want to leave him alone to search. Most of the papers on the desk were proposals for various clients and notes about the kinds of things they wanted in newspaper ads. There was an appointment book, but all the entries were for businesses.

Not knowing what else to try, Alex began pulling open the desk drawers. Most were filled with blank forms, loose paper, and other office supplies. One held a box with a half dozen spare ties in it along with several small pasteboard books with yellow covers.

"What's this?" Alex asked, pulling one of the yellow backed books out and flipping to the first page. He didn't have to wait for Andy to answer, on the first page of the book was a minor purification rune.

"I get those for all my salesmen," Andy said. "This business is all about taking clients to lunch. You do that long enough, you're bound to get mustard on your tie."

Minor purification runes would certainly take care of a small food stain. Alex turned the book over and saw the smiling cartoon cat logo of Happy Jack.

"I used to get them from a local guy over on the east side," Andy continued, "but those are half the price. Too good a deal to pass up." When Alex didn't respond, he went on. "I tried to get their advertising, but they shut me down. I guess they don't advertise."

Alex thought about it and realized Andy was right — he hadn't seen a single sign, sandwich board, or bill for the cheap rune books.

That's probably why they're so cheap.

Alex dropped the books back in the drawer and stood up. As far as he could tell from his trip through James' appointment book, he had no contact with June Masterson, her husband Paul, or Dexter Stevens the Macy's employee. He thanked Andy and saw himself out. In the lobby, the receptionist gave him another sly smile that left him wondering if she was a better salesman than Andy.

Alex had never been to Macy's Department Store. When he arrived, he was amazed at just how big one store could be. After walking around for half an hour, he finally stopped someone and asked directions to the personnel office where they directed him to the sales manager, a fat, jovial man with a red face and a bulbous nose.

"It's quite the scandal," he said when Alex asked him about Dexter Stevens. "He was one of my best salesmen. Everyone loved him. I just can't believe he would shoot a stranger."

"Did he have any problems?" Alex asked. "Maybe with one of the customers?"

"Oh, no," the sales manager said. "He was so good with the customers that we had him working the courtesy counter."

"What's that?"

The man looked at Alex like he'd asked what color the sky was.

"It's where we send customers with questions or problems," he said. "We have some of our people there to help with all manner of things."

"Like what?"

"Mostly the staff there give directions to where certain items can be found in the store," he said. "But they can also sew replacement buttons on coats and fix handbag straps. That sort of thing."

"And how long did Dexter work there?"

"About four months."

Alex asked a few more questions of the sales manager but didn't gain any real insight into Dexter Stevens. So far as he could tell, the man had been friendly and genial with everyone. The only recourse left was to get Dexter's home address and go see his sister, something Alex really didn't want to do. Grieving relatives were hard to deal with in normal situations, but since he was the one that actually shot and killed Dexter, it would be a thousand times worse. With any luck, she wouldn't know who had shot her brother.

You're not that lucky, he reminded himself.

"I'll have to have someone from records pull his employment card," the sales manager said when Alex asked about the home address. "It will take a few minutes. Why don't you wait at the courtesy counter? That way you can see where Dexter worked. I'll have someone run the address out to you as soon as I get it."

Alex thanked the man, then asked directions to the courtesy counter. It turned out to be a long oak counter staffed by a helpful young woman in a floral print blouse. There were stands at either end of the counter that sold combs, nail clippers, pocketknives, change purses, and other small, useful items. As Alex watched, she took a leather tool case from under the counter and used a small screwdriver to reattach a wheel on a child's toy car. When she was done, the child's grateful mother thanked her profusely before leaving.

"You do that a lot?" Alex asked.

The girl nodded.

"Yes sir," she said. "You'd be surprised how many times customers break things while they're here."

"What do you do if you can't fix them?" he asked, a sneaking suspicion growing in his mind.

"I'm pretty handy," the girl said with a pleasant smile. "But if it's something big, I use one of these." She reached into her blouse and pulled out an all-too-familiar red-backed rune book. "These'll do most things."

"Very resourceful," Alex said, as a chill ran down his back. "Do you sell those as well?"

The girl nodded and rotated the display of pocketknives.

On the back side were vertical slots with several dozen of the red-backed books mixed with a few of the blue-backed and yellow-backed ones as well.

"I'll take two of each," Alex said, fishing out his wallet.

After he completed his purchase, Alex made for the two phone booths he'd seen by the front entrance.

"How did it go?" Iggy's voice greeted him once the operator completed the call.

"I found the connection between our killers," he said. "All of them used those Happy Jack rune books."

"Didn't you tell me they were showing up all over the city?"

"Yeah," Alex said. "As far as I can tell it's put a good chunk of Runewright Row out of business."

"So you're thinking that someone is using the runes in those books to influence people's minds?" Iggy asked. "That would explain William Ashford's sudden popularity, don't you think?"

The thought gave him goose bumps, and he looked through the glass door of the phone booth at the crowd of people in the store. The Happy Jack books had been in circulation for weeks; half the city might be under Ashford's sway.

"I think I'd better call Sorsha," Alex said as the enormity of the situation hit him.

"And tell her what?" Iggy said. "That one of the candidates for mayor is using rune books to win the election?"

He was right; it sounded insane.

"All right," he said, taking a breath to clear his head. "We need proof. Run down to that five and dime by the park and pick up a couple of those rune books."

"Why don't you just grab some on your way here," Iggy said. "We'll take them apart and figure out how Ashford is doing...whatever it is he's doing."

"You get started on that," Alex said. "I'm going to go by the offices of Happy Jack and see what I can learn."

"That's stupidly dangerous," Iggy chided him. "If you're right, Ashford has already tried to kill you on three occasions. Going down there would tip him off that you suspect him."

"I'm not going to nose around," Alex said. "Marnie asked me to check on a friend of ours, Benny Haines. He went to work for Happy Jack. I'll just go say hi to him and see what I can see."

"I don't like it," Iggy said.

"It's the middle of the day," Alex retorted. "I'll be fine."

"Have you redone the shield runes on your coat?"

He hadn't, which meant he only had three left.

"That's what I thought," Iggy said when Alex didn't answer. "Do you at least have your automatic?"

Alex tapped his left breast, feeling the hard edge of the 1911 beneath his coat. It was only a semi-automatic, but most people Iggy's age didn't differentiate.

"Yes," he said. He didn't mention that he hadn't reloaded it since last night.

"Well I suppose that could be useful," he said at last. "Be careful."

"Always," Alex said, putting a little swagger in his tone.

"I'll see if I can figure out what's going on with those rune books and we'll compare notes when you get home."

Alex hung up and, after looking both ways for anyone suspicious, headed out.

The offices of Happy Jack Rune Books turned out to be in a formerly-derelict factory building on the west side near the Navy Yard. The old carriage doors that had once allowed train cars to enter the factory had been replaced with new ones that had regular-sized doors built into them. There weren't any windows on the ground floor, so he couldn't see in. There was a front door at the end of the block, but Alex wanted to get a look inside, and he doubted whoever was in the office would allow that, especially if they knew who he was.

That thought gave him pause, and he looked up and down the sidewalk. In this industrial area, the streets were empty, so he was reasonably sure no one was following him. Deciding to take his chances with the factory door, Alex crossed the patch of open ground. The dirt outside the door was hard from the winter chill and worn bare from extensive foot traffic. The handle was cast iron, and the top left and the right side were worn smooth from many turnings. The paint on the doors looked fairly fresh, which meant the door hadn't been put in too long ago, and that meant Happy Jack had a lot of runewrights working for them.

Taking a deep breath, he took hold of the handle and turned it sturdily. The door opened easy and Alex stepped quickly inside. Closing the door against the cold, he found himself in a large open space at least two stories high. The machinery had been stripped long ago and now the factory was just a concrete slab with the belts that would deliver power to the machines hanging still and silent on a frame suspended from the ceiling. The space wasn't empty, though. Bright magelights had been mounted on the belt frame, bathing the factory floor in bright light. Rows and rows of angled writing desks dominated the space, each with a neat stack of fresh flash paper, a pot of ink and a bin for completed runes.

There had to be two hundred people in the room, each one hunched over their own desk, scribbling away. As Alex looked, he could see men and women of every race and age.

Clearly Happy Jack only cared about magical ability in their hiring.

No one seemed to have noticed him, so Alex started walking along the end of the rows. He recognized a few people but didn't see Benny. As he moved, something bothered him, but he couldn't put his finger on exactly what. When he reached the end of the line, Alex started to turn back when he suddenly saw a face he recognized.

"Marnie?" he said.

He was surprised to see her here, given how adamant she was that Happy Jack was up to something nefarious. Now that he thought about it, she seemed remarkably perceptive.

"Marnie," he said again, a bit more forcefully.

"A-Alex," she stuttered. She looked up from her work, blinking, and fixed him with a confused look.

"What are you doing here?" he asked, stepping over to her desk. She was the last person in her row with a half dozen empty desks beyond.

"You were right," she said, turning to face him. "I didn't want to come here, but I only sold a dozen runes this week. At least it's warm and they're paying me a bit more than I made on the row." She reached out and grabbed his arm. "Thank you, Alex."

Alex put a smile on his face and tried to think of something to say. He'd convinced her to come here against her better judgement and now he needed to get her to leave. Before he could think of anything, however, he noticed her hand. Taking it, he turned it over, palm up. Along the underside of the index finger, running over her palm and along her thumb, was a dark stain.

"Oh, that's just from the ink they have us use," she said, rubbing at the stain with her opposite thumb.

Alex hadn't thought of that. He'd seen the ink bottles on all the desks, but the kind of runes in the Happy Jack book could all be written with a basic pencil. In the old days runewrights used to use coal-gall ink, but since pencil lead was basically compressed graphite, it worked just fine.

That wasn't what bothered him, though. His mind flashed to the body of the Captain lying in the city morgue and the dark stain on his hand. He hadn't given it much thought, but he was thinking now. The Captain had been left-handed but the ink stain was on his right hand. Also, the man who came to hire workers at the Hooverville near the Brotherhood of Hope had rejected Lefty, who didn't have a right hand. Before Alex could follow that train of thought further, someone cleared his throat loudly behind him.

Alex turned to find a short, well-dressed man with a thick mustache and curly red hair standing behind him. He wore an irritated expression, his teeth clenched on the stub of a cigar. Behind him were two large men in shirtsleeves wearing equally sour expressions.

"Who exactly are you?" the red-haired man asked. "And what are you doing in my factory?"

26

FIRED

Alex regarded the little man for a moment. His clothes and his posture clearly communicated that he was someone important at the Happy Jack company. The two men who flanked him were so bland as to be interchangeable, but they were clearly present to make sure Alex wasn't a threat.

"Alex Lockerby," Alex said, sticking out his hand. He plastered a friendly smile on his face, but it wasn't returned.

"I'm sorry, Mr. Maple," Marnie said, moving up beside Alex. "He came looking for me. This is the man I told you about."

Maple's red eyebrow rose, and he seemed to see Alex for the first time.

"The private detective?" he asked.

"Guilty I'm afraid," Alex said. Maple finally took his hand and Alex shook it. The man's grip was firm but not overly so; he clearly felt he had nothing to prove.

"I've heard a lot about you, Mr. Lockerby," Maple said. "I'm Carlton Maple. I own the Happy Jack Rune Book Company. I understand you're a very talented runewright."

Maple's previous gruff manner had evaporated, and his voice was full of genial warmth.

"I get by," Alex said.

Maple laughed at that.

"Don't be so modest," he said. "Several of the runewrights who have come to work for me say you're the best runewright in the city."

Alex resisted the urge to blush. He wasn't used to so much praise. To cover, he looked around at the factory floor and its mass of scribbling runewrights.

"You seem to be doing well yourself," he said.

Maple grinned proudly and nodded, then his face turned serious again.

"I'd like to talk to you about coming to work for me," he said.

"I do well enough that I don't have to sell basic runes anymore," Alex said, trying to be diplomatic.

"I'm not saying you should," Maple said, waving his hand at the mass of workers. "This is just a start," he said. "Walk with me and I'll show you what I mean."

He put his hand on Alex's shoulder and steered him toward a row of offices on the far end of the space. Marnie excused herself and headed back to her desk. Alex wanted to stay and convince her to knock off early and go home, but Maple was giving him an opportunity to learn more about Happy Jack's operation. That was just too tempting, and he figured Marnie would be okay as long as he didn't make trouble.

"You see, Alex," Maple said as they walked. "The real problem with runes is that everyone's bought one from a bad runewright and had it fail. Then there's always a dozen different runewrights selling the same runes wherever you go, how's an average Joe or Betty supposed to know which one to choose?"

"You're saying too much choice is a bad thing?"

"Not usually," Maple admitted, "but in this case it is. Customers don't know who to trust and one runewright might call their mending rune a fixing rune or something else entirely. The customer doesn't know if it will actually do what they need it to do."

Alex was starting to see Maple's thought process.

"So you standardize," he said. "Hire competent runewrights, have them produce basic, useful runes, and then sell them under a recognizable brand."

"I knew I liked you," Maple said with a sly smile. "That's exactly it. The public gains trust in runes, they learn what they're called and what they do."

"And you sell them a whole book of them, so they find uses for them," Alex guessed.

"Exactly," Maple said.

Alex glanced behind where the two bodyguards were trailing along in their wake. They were several yards back wearing bored expressions, and didn't seem to be expecting trouble.

"That sounds like a good business," Alex went on. "But I don't see how I could be much help."

"Can you write standard mending runes?" Maple asked. When Alex nodded, he continued. "What about major mending runes?"

"I've got an example in my lore book," he said, "but I've never actually done one."

They reached the offices at the end of the large open space, but instead of going inside, Maple turned and led Alex down to where an aisle ran between the rows of scribbling runewrights.

"This is just a start," he said, gesturing to the workers. "Imagine every business in the city having an emergency rune book behind their counters. Runes to deal with wounds or burns or broken bones."

It was an interesting idea, and Alex realized Maple probably wouldn't stop there. High end rune books could be made for lots of industries, from mining to manufacturing to firefighting. There was, of course, one large problem.

"Where will you find enough runewrights to make all those books?"

Maple looked back and forth as they passed along the isle between the rows of runewrights. He leaned close as if he feared being overheard.

"That's the dirty little secret," he said in a low voice. "Most of these guys are talented enough to do standard runes. Some of them might even be able to do major runes; the problem is they don't know it. Think about it, Alex," he went on, his voice returning to normal. "We runewrights just scribble away in our own little spheres, hoarding our knowledge like a miser hoards gold. Imagine what could be done if every runewright had access to challenging runes."

Maple had a point, but Alex's thoughts were drawn to the Archimedean Monograph. Most of the runes in there were very powerful. In the wrong hands they could be dangerous, even deadly. There was a certain amount of wisdom to keeping them secret.

Alex was about to respond when that uneasy feeling he'd had when he first entered the factory washed over him again. When he'd been walking along the edge of the laboring runewrights, he hadn't been able to pin down what was bothering him. Now, however, in the middle of them, it became obvious. Large groups seemed to be moving in perfect unison, as if they were performing some kind of dance. As Alex looked around, he could see that they weren't alone; he spotted at least three separate groups moving in unison with each other. It was as if each group was taking their cues from a single person.

"I don't know if sharing information would improve a runewright's skill," Alex said. "But it doesn't really matter, does it?"

Maple turned and regarded Alex expectantly.

'That's not what you're doing," Alex went on. "Somehow you've joined these runewrights together like puppets on strings." He jerked his thumb over his shoulder at the offices in the front of the room. "Is that what's in there? Your most skilled runewrights?"

Maple chuckled and shook his head.

"Your friends told me you were smart," he said, wagging a finger at Alex. "But I have to admit, I didn't expect you to figure me out so quickly. It's too bad, too. I honestly believe we could have done amazing things together."

Alex tensed, ready to round on the bodyguards, but they were still standing back. Maple turned his back to Alex and threw his arms open wide.

"Everyone," he called in a loud voice. He waited until all eyes turned to him. It took longer than it should, probably because of the connection to the runewrights in the offices. "I have a job for you," Maple went on, turning to point at Alex. "This is Alex Lockerby. Kill him for me."

Alex had been ready for Maple or the bodyguards to rush him, or to pull weapons, but Maple just stood there, looking at him with an amused grin. The entire room was still for the space of several seconds, then every one of the runewrights stood up from their writing tables. As one, they turned toward Alex.

The sight sent shivers down his spine. It was otherworldly. The runewrights in the room, many of whom he knew, began to walk toward him at a determined pace. Alex started to reach for his pistol, but what did he intend to do, shoot his friends? Even those he didn't know were just innocent bystanders.

Maple saw Alex's hesitation and burst out laughing. Alex wished he had pulled his pistol, but it was too late now. The runewrights from the nearby desks were almost on him, converging in a silent mob.

Alex raised his left hand and triggered the plain brass ring he wore, covering his eyes with his right hand at the same time. One of the remaining flash runes on the ring ignited, bathing the factory floor in blinding white light. Maple and his thugs cried out, but the enthralled runewrights just grunted, trying far too late to cover their eyes.

The flash rune was specifically timed to burn for three seconds and Alex counted along. Once he knew the light had subsided, he looked up. All around him the runewrights were rubbing their eyes and blinking, trying to restore their vision. He didn't hesitate: pushing his way through the mob, he headed toward the door where he'd come in.

Grabbing the knob, he pushed it open, letting a gush of cold air wash over him. He started out, but hesitated. Marnie was standing on the edge of the crowd, groping blindly.

Cursing, Alex released the door and ran back to where she stood.

"Come on," he said, grabbing her by the arm.

On hearing his voice, she screamed and lashed out with the pen she still clutched in her hand. It struck Alex's shoulder and he felt one of his shield runes activate. The blow wouldn't have penetrated his coat, or even hurt him, but the shield rune didn't know that.

Around them, the other runewrights were starting to get their vision back. Turning toward the sound of Marnie's scream, they began to push forward with their arms out, groping for him.

Alex didn't hesitate. He balled up his fist and punched

Marnie right in the face. He felt bad about it, but he couldn't have her attacking him while he was trying to save her life. Stunned by the blow, Marnie collapsed and Alex caught her, hefting her up over his left shoulder like a sack of flour.

Hands grasped at his coat as the semi-blind runewrights reached him. Turning, Alex started back toward the exit, but the mob had spread out. They were now between him and the door.

Cursing, Alex turned toward the back of the open room. Several doors were there, closing off this workspace from the rest of the derelict factory. Alex didn't know what lay beyond them, but he was certain he'd last longer back there, especially once the runewrights could see clearly again.

Shifting Marnie on his shoulder, he moved as fast as he could away from the mass of murderous runewrights. When he reached the back wall, Alex kicked the first door he came to. It buckled but didn't give. Digging into his jacket pocket with his free hand, Alex slid his fingers into the holes of his knuckle duster. Drawing back, he hit the door with everything he had. The force runes on the end activated and the door buckled, breaking free and swinging open.

Rushing through the opening, Alex found himself in another large, open room that looked remarkably like the one he'd just left. Rows and rows of desks were set up in a straight line, each with someone sitting and working at them. These people, however, were clearly not runewrights. They were scruffy and gaunt, clothed in battered and stained garments.

These were the missing Forgotten.

Alex almost hesitated as his mind came to grips with what he was seeing. He didn't understand how Maple was controlling the runewrights, but it made sense that if he could, they would be able to write runes for him. These people weren't runewrights though. How was Maple using them?

"That was very clever Alex," Maple's voice boomed over

loudspeakers mounted in the ceiling. "I would never have thought of increasing the brightness of a light rune by decreasing its duration. What a team we could have made."

Alex didn't doubt Maple was right. Clearly the little man was a powerful and talented runewright himself. He shifted Marnie's dead weight on his shoulder again and quickened his pace across the second open space, heading for the far wall where several more doors waited.

"Listen up everyone," Maple said. "I have a job for you: run down Alex Lockerby and kill him."

He had to tell them to run.

Whatever control Maple had over his thralls, it dominated them. He'd told the runewrights to kill Alex, not to run. If he wanted them to do something different, he would have to give them more specific instructions.

The sound of running feet grew behind him, but that wasn't Alex's most pressing worry. As the echo of Maple's voice faded away, the Forgotten put down their pens and turned to look at him.

Alex swore again, scanning the wall ahead of him. Several of the doors had frosted glass panels in them. He had no idea where they led, but the Forgotten were already beginning to chase him.

His chest burned with every breath and his muscles were starting to quiver. He hit the first door he came to and it shattered under his assault. Stumbling through the bits of wood and glass, Alex found himself in a normal-sized room a bit smaller than Andrew Barton's cavernous lobby. Three hallways led out and he chose the left one as it seemed to run along the width of the building where he hoped he could find an exit.

Making the corner just ahead of the pursuing mob, he dashed down the hall, then turned at the next junction. Behind him the sound of running feet had subsided. Apparently the thralls were having trouble figuring out what to do.

Alex slowed to a walk. He didn't want the sound of his own running to give his pursuers anything to chase. The second hall ended in a large room that looked like some kind of lab or testing area. There were three doors that led out of the room and he tried one on the left. That turned out to be a closet. He started back, but stopped as Marnie's weight made him stagger.

He wasn't going to be able to carry her much farther.

"I have a job for you," Maple's voice boomed over the speaker again. "Spread out and search for Alex, then kill him when you find him."

"I'm getting real tired of that," Alex growled to Marnie's unconscious form.

Staggering back to the closet, he set Marnie down and pulled out his chalk. A few seconds later, he had his vault open and he dragged Marnie inside, leaving her on the small couch by his fake fireplace. He had a momentary thought of tying her hands, but he could hear the sounds of pursuit growing louder from outside the closet.

"Think," he admonished himself. Once he closed his vault, Marnie would be safe until he got somewhere else and reopened it, but what about Benny and the others? He needed to get out of the factory and call Danny. "You need to call Sorsha," he corrected himself.

Of course his ability to do any of that hinged on his ability to get out of the factory.

From outside he heard the closet door open. Alex had closed his inner vault door, so no light from his vault would spill out into the closet, but the big metal door was still sticking out of the wall. Whoever looked in didn't seem to notice the vault door in the darkness and a moment later the closet door shut.

"Well, you can't stay here," he muttered. He reached for his 1911 but hesitated again. There were at least three hundred people out there and his chances of getting by all of them weren't good. The 1911 was effective, but its magazine only held fifteen rounds.

Making up his mind, Alex moved to his gun cabinet, and took down the Thompson. Clipping one of the thirty round magazines into the receiver, he racked the slide, moving a bullet into the chamber. Taking the second magazine from its holder, he dropped it into his trouser pocket, which left it sticking out but secure.

"Okay," he said. "Let's try not to kill anyone."

With that happy thought, Alex slipped out of his vault, back into the closet. As silently as he could, he shut the vault door and pulled out the key. Marnie was safe for now, but if he managed to get himself killed, the vault would be her tomb.

"Try not to shoot anyone and don't get killed," he whispered.

Pushing the closet door open, Alex came face to face with one of the enthralled Forgotten. Without thinking, Alex hit him with the butt of the Thompson and he fell into an unconscious heap on the floor.

Stepping over his unconscious form, Alex moved to one of the other doors in the room. The first let to an empty, windowless office so Alex tried the second. This one led to a short hall with a set of stairs going up. That wasn't a direction he wanted to go, but he could hear someone moving behind him in the testing room. Maybe the Forgotten came to, or maybe it was someone else, but whoever they were, they made Alex's decision for him.

Up he went, the stairs creaking loudly under his feet. When he finally emerged back into the factory again, he found himself facing a long, metal catwalk that ran over the floor where the Forgotten had their desks. At the far end, a hole in the wall allowed the catwalk to go through into the main area.

"All right, everyone," Maple's voice blared from a speaker mounted right over where Alex stood. "I have a job for you. Return to your desks."

It took a minute for Alex's ears to stop ringing. Below him, the Forgotten were shuffling placidly back to their desks. They showed no sign of their former murderous intentions, looking for all the world like regular factory workers who heard the whistle to return to work.

"What's he up to now?" Alex whispered. It didn't make sense. The factory was big and Maple was only using part of it. A thorough search would take time, so why was he giving up?

The answer hit Alex's nose a few seconds later.

Smoke.

He swore again. Maple must believe that Alex had escaped and was headed straight for the authorities. That left him with no choice but to destroy the evidence of his operation. The runewrights would back his story that this was a perfectly ordinary business, but the missing Forgotten would be very difficult to explain.

Looking down, Alex saw the Forgotten men and women just sitting at their desks, waiting for whatever connection enabled them to write runes to begin again.

"They'll be burned alive."

The smell of smoke became more pronounced and below him, Alex could see one of Maple's goons dousing the wooden wall to the outside with gasoline from a can. Without hesitation, Alex shouldered the sub-machine gun and squeezed the trigger. The weapon spit fire and a dozen rounds tore through the wall. Alex hadn't had much time to practice with the

Thompson and the entire burst missed the gas-can wielding thug.

Dropping the can, the man turned and fired a snub-nosed pistol up toward the catwalk. Bullets hit the railing and the ceiling, but none came close. Alex lined up the Thompson again and shot.

This time the burst caught the man in the chest and hip. His gun fell from a nerveless hand and he slumped to the floor. Alex had managed to stop him from covering the wall with gasoline, but the hail of bullets from the Thompson struck a spark that sent cascades of flame rolling up the wall. A wave of heat rushed upward and Alex had to cover his face to keep from being singed.

Running blindly along the catwalk, Alex passed through the dividing wall and into the main part of the Happy Jack operation. The fire was already well established here, and the air was thick with heat and smoke. A gun fired from close range and a bullet hit him in the shoulder. He grunted as another shield rune activated.

Ahead of him on the catwalk stood Carlton Maple, pointing an enormous .357 magnum at him.

That explains why my shoulder is killing me.

Alex brought up the Thompson, leveling it at Maple.

"Tell them to leave," he yelled. "Tell them or I'll shoot you and leave you to burn."

"I'd love to know where you were hiding that," Maple yelled over the noise of the rapidly spreading fire. He fired twice more and another of Alex's shield runes absorbed a round that would have taken out his left kidney.

Alex pulled the trigger and the Thompson spat out two rounds and then stopped.

Empty.

Maple stumbled. One of Alex's rounds had clearly hit its mark.

"Tell them," Alex yelled as he dropped the empty magazine to the warehouse floor below. He jammed the new one in place and thumbed the lever that would release the bolt.

"Go to hell," Maple said, blood dripping from the corner of his mouth. He shot three more times, emptying the gun. Two of the rounds missed Alex, but one clipped his arm. All of his shield runes were expended, and pain erupted as the bullet tore through the fleshy part of his left tricep.

Alex shot back, holding the trigger down as the Thompson emptied itself. With his wounded arm, Alex's aim wasn't good but with thirty rounds it didn't have to be. Bullets tore through Maple's chest and abdomen and he slumped over the rail, falling to the factory floor below.

Gritting his teeth against the throbbing pain in his arm, Alex looked over the side of the catwalk. Maple lay in the ruin of a writing desk he'd fallen on, his lifeless eyes staring up, accusingly at Alex.

"Looks like you got there first."

27

GEORGE'S SECOND RUN

Alex sat on the frozen ground outside the factory of Wilford Textiles. It was a tall brick building that housed the machinery to make canvas and it was located across the street from the building that used to house the Happy Jack Rune Book Company. All that remained of that structure were chunks of the brick exterior walls and the cement floor.

A crowd of bystanders had gathered, but now that the fire was all but out, they were beginning to drift away, back to their lives. Alex didn't pay them any attention; he was cold, tired, and he just wanted to go home.

"You look like hell," Sorsha's voice drifted down to him, pulling him out of his thoughts.

Alex looked up to find her standing over him, wrapped in a white ermine coat that hung to her knees. He hated to admit it, but he was very glad to see her. A long succession of policemen had been questioning him since they arrived several hours ago. Alex had told them that he'd come to visit his friend, Marnie, saw the flames, and when he went in found everyone passed out. He'd hoped the cops would chalk everything up to an unfortunate gas leak, but it seemed like everyone wanted to hear his story over and over again. Finally he'd invoked Sorsha's name and her FBI connections, sending the policemen scurrying to contact her.

"Thanks for coming," Alex said, pushing himself wearily to his feet. He'd managed to forget the bullet wound in his arm and he winced as he lifted himself.

"What happened?" Sorsha said, eyeing his bloody sleeve.

"Long story," he said, looking around. There were still a few dozen policemen milling about the scene and the fire crew were packing up their hoses now that the fire was mostly out.

Sorsha saw him looking and raised an eyebrow, then made an offhanded gesture with her hand. Instantly the sounds of conversation and the noises of the crowd vanished, leaving Alex in a silence so profound he could hear his own heartbeat.

"There," she said, her voice sounding loud in the unnatural silence. "Now you can speak freely."

She looked at him expectantly, as if such magic was perfectly normal. Sorsha had an annoying habit of displaying powerful and often complicated magic as if it were the most ordinary thing in the world. It always reminded Alex in stark terms of the gulf that separated her mastery of arcane power from his meager abilities. Alex hadn't noticed it before, but even though Sorsha was wearing a coat, her breath wasn't steaming in the frigid air like everyone else's. He wondered how much power she was accustomed to using just for her own comfort.

It was probably more than he used in a week.

Alex looked around again, then took a deep breath and told the sorceress everything.

"I thought Maple's death would free the runewrights from whatever power he had over them, but..." He shook his head.

"Once I got off the catwalk, I dragged a dozen or so into my vault before the smoke got too thick. The rest...the rest are still in there." He nodded toward the burnt-out husk of the Happy Jack building.

Sorsha's eyes widened slightly but she kept her composure.

"How many?" she asked.

"A couple hundred at least," Alex said. "Including the missing Forgotten."

Sorsha swore, something Alex had never heard her do, then she sighed.

"What about the people in your vault?"

Alex shrugged.

"I pulled them back out over there," he jerked his thumb at the wall of the Wilford Textiles building where a white chalkline door was still visible. "When the cops got here, they took them to the hospital."

"All right," she said at last. "Your story of a gas leak is plausible. I'll make sure that's what the newspapers print."

Alex glared at her and she held his gaze with a stoic look on her perfect face.

"What about all the people who died in there?" he demanded. "Some of them were my friends."

"And I'm sorry about that," Sorsha said in a forceful voice. "But you did everything you could for them."

"What about Carlton Maple?" Alex asked.

"According to you, he's quite dead."

"Yes," Alex said, trying to get a grip on his growing anger. "Whatever mind control runes he was using might have been his design, but he wasn't working alone. I'd bet a C-note that June Masterson was under Maple's control when she murdered Hugo Ayers. Ayers didn't have any connection to Happy Jack, but he was part of the William Ashford campaign. If Ashford and Maple were in cahoots, Ayers might have found the money trail, which would explain why he was killed."

"That is worrying," she said. "But if your story is accurate, I suspect the death of Maple has put a stop to whatever plans William Ashford might have."

"How do you figure that?"

"Are you familiar with hypnosis?"

Alex knew that carnival performers claimed to be able to put people into some kind of trance where they became suggestible, but that was about it.

"I imagine whatever magic Maple was using is similar," Sorsha explained. "Every time he gave orders to the people under his control, he used the phrase, 'I have a job for you.'"

"You think it's some kind of code phrase," Alex guessed.

Sorsha nodded.

"One tied specifically to Maple himself — that way anyone wanting his services couldn't just cut him out once they learned how he controlled the people under his power."

That made a good deal of sense, but it did nothing to slake Alex's anger.

"Someone in the Ashford campaign still ordered Hugo's death," he pointed out. "They ordered June Masterson to kill herself, and when the string from her dress broke, they ordered someone else to bring her a thicker cord."

"And without Maple's help, Ashford will go back to being an obscure candidate," Sorsha said. "Once he loses the election, it will be much easier to investigate him quietly. Then we'll learn what happened, find the person or persons responsible, and see that they are punished."

Alex was about to argue, but something in her tone caught his attention. She wasn't unconcerned with the murders of Hugo and June, but she saw some bigger picture that was demanding her attention.

"What is it?" he asked.

"I'm surprised at you, Alex," she said in an admonishing tone. "You clearly haven't thought this through."

She gave him an enigmatic smile that was equal parts challenge and mockery. Alex's mind went racing down multiple possibilities. He and Iggy had been focused on the idea that this was a bid to become mayor of New York, an important and prestigious position to be sure, but what if it was bigger than that?

"The man-made plague," he said, the loose threads of his thoughts finally coalescing together. "Back then, you said that was a test; maybe this is a test, too."

Sorsha nodded grimly.

"Imagine what Hitler or Stalin could accomplish if they had access to this kind of magic," she said. "Whole nations could be conquered without firing a single shot."

The idea was chilling, terrifying even.

"I need to report this right away," Sorsha said. She snapped her fingers and the sounds of the outside world washed over them once again. "You should go home and have Dr. Bell look at that arm."

Alex took one more look at the burnt-out Happy Jack factory, then sighed and nodded.

"I'm sorry about your friends," Sorsha said, putting a hand on his forearm.

"You were right before," Alex said, shoving his own guilt aside. "I did what I could. The rest is Maple's fault."

Sorsha squeezed his hand, then turned and walked off toward the sleek, black floater that hovered at the side of the road near the end of the block.

Alex intended to head home and consult with Iggy on the whole mind rune business, but he knew Maple hadn't been working alone. William Ashford was involved somehow, and Alex wanted all the information he could get on the man. Leslie should be done with her research into Ashford's past, so Alex stopped by his office on the way home.

"What happened?" Leslie gasped when Alex trudged in twenty minutes before closing time.

He hadn't thought about it, but he must look terrible, covered in soot with his coat sleeve stained with dried blood. Alex was about to answer when he noticed the other person in the room. Seated on his waiting couch, wearing his expensive suit, was Arthur Hardwick, who rose to meet him.

"Is this a bad time, Mr. Lockerby?" he asked, running an appraising eye over Alex.

"Your clients have a nasty habit of contracting work and then not paying," Alex said, resisting the urge to just walk past the man. "That makes pretty much any time a bad time."

To his credit, Hardwick actually looked contrite at that.

"I wasn't told about that until recently," he said. "Part of the reason I came was to make sure your bill was settled."

"Why" Alex asked.

"You found that marriage license and secured a copy very efficiently, Mr. Lockerby," the lawyer said. "In my business I often have need of men with those skills and you proved yourself admirably. As I'm sure you can understand, I like to keep such assets happy."

It was a pretty good explanation and Alex bit back the sarcastic remark he had planned. His business was doing well, but that didn't mean he could afford to turn away a high-end client like Arthur Hardwick. If word got around that the firm of Finch, Hardwick, and Michaels used Alex's services, then other high-profile clients would seek him out as well.

Hardwick held out an envelope and Alex could see the dark outline of cash inside. Accepting the envelope, Alex tucked it into his jacket pocket without checking it.

"I appreciate that, Mr. Hardwick," Alex said as diplomatically as he could. "What was the other part?"

Hardwick looked confused, so Alex went on.

"You said that part of the reason you came was to cover my bill," he explained. "So what's the rest of it?"

"I'm here on behalf of George Sheridan."

Alex drew in a breath to tell Hardwick exactly what he could do with his client, but the lawyer held up a hand.

"Let me finish," he said. "I understand that you know George has been arrested for the murder of the Westlakes."

"If he's been arrested," Alex said, "that means the police found his fingerprints on a bottle of poisoned wine."

"I know it looks bad," Hardwick said. "But George didn't kill the Westlakes."

"He had plenty of reasons to," Alex said. "Since he's legally married to Vivian, he stands to inherit if they die."

"But they served George with divorce papers already," Hardwick pointed out. "That would give plenty of grounds for anyone to contest any will or probate settlement."

"Maybe George figured he'd take his chances," Alex said. "Or maybe he just didn't consult with his attorney before doing something rash. The fact is that his fingerprints are on the bottle. How are you going to explain that to a jury?"

Hardwick shook his head.

"I don't know how to explain it," he said. "What I do know is that George Sheridan didn't kill the Westlakes."

"What makes you think that?" Alex challenged.

"Because when George got those divorce papers yesterday, he called me," Hardwick explained. "He told me he wanted the whole thing with Vivian over and he signed the papers."

"If he signed them," Alex asked, "then where are they?"

Hardwick reached into his attorney's folio and pulled out a stack of papers that had been fastened together with a brass pin, and passed them to Alex.

"He would have sent them right back, but I wanted to look them over first," he said. "Make sure there wasn't anything funny about them."

Alex paged through the mass of typewritten legalese until he reached the final page where, sure enough, George Sheridan's signature appeared.

"Was there?" Alex asked. "Anything funny?"

Hardwick shook his head.

"They are perfectly ordinary divorce papers," he said.

Alex flipped the stack of papers closed and handed them back to Hardwick. He didn't want to bother with Sheridan, but Hardwick was right. George had no motive to kill the Westlakes, especially since he was bound to be a suspect even without his fingerprints on the poison wine bottle.

"If I take this, I want double my day rate," he said.

"Done," Hardwick said.

"And I want George paying it, not you."

"Done," Hardwick said again. He reached into his pocket and pulled out an alligator hide wallet. "Will a hundred dollars be enough of a retainer?" he asked, extracting a C note.

Alex hesitated. He already had a lot on his plate and Sheridan was a horse's ass. Still, it wasn't like Carlton Maple and his mind runes were still running around the city, so he could take his time looking into that.

"All right," he said accepting the money. "I'll go talk to the detective in charge tomorrow and see what I can learn."

Hardwick thanked him and bid him good day before withdrawing.

"I didn't think you'd take that case," Leslie said once the attorney had gone.

"Hardwick will bring us business" Alex said with a shrug. He pulled out the envelope of cash the lawyer had given him and dropped it on Leslie's desk. "Probably a good idea to keep him happy."

"You think his client is innocent?"

Alex shrugged again.

"Doesn't matter," he said. "I promised to look into it, and I will."

Leslie nodded, then raised an eyebrow at him.

"Are you going to tell me what happened to you?" she asked, nodding at his arm.

"Someone shot me."

"What happened to your shield runes?" she asked, concern washing over her perfect face.

"He shot me a lot," Alex said.

"What about him?"

"I shot back," Alex said, wanting to be out of this conversation. He'd have to tell Leslie the whole story at some point, but he just couldn't go through all of that again right now. "What did you find out about our pal William Ashford?"

Leslie regarded him coolly, probably judging whether or not to press for answers. After a long moment, she picked up her notepad and glanced at it.

"Ashford comes from money," she said. "His father is a former state senator, and his grandfather was a colonel in the Civil War. He tried to get into Harvard but they turned him down, so he ended up going to William and Mary."

"Hold it," Alex said, holding up his hand. "Daddy was rich, and a state senator, and he couldn't get his son into Harvard?"

Leslie checked her notes, then nodded.

With the kind of political influence a senator had, the fact that William's father couldn't get him into Harvard meant that William's academic record must have been terrible.

"What else?" Alex asked.

"William tried his hand at a few different things, but

ended up working in his father's bank. When he first got back from college, a few of the tabloids ran stories on him but there hasn't been anything for years. Not 'til he announced his run for governor."

"So he's a failure and probably about as interesting as a potted plant."

Leslie nodded and set down her note pad.

"That's my read on it," she said.

That was good but it was also bad. If Leslie's portrait of Ashford was correct, he was a man with unrequited ambition, exactly the kind of person to use magic to cheat his way into being Mayor. On the other hand, he didn't seem bright enough to cook up an elaborate scheme like this.

"Is Ashford's father still alive?" he asked.

Leslie shook her head.

"He died about ten years ago."

That meant that most likely someone else was urging Ashford along in his quest to be mayor. Someone pulling the strings from the shadows. It might have been Carlton Maple, but if it wasn't, then maybe the scheme to steal the election for Ashford was still on.

"I'm heading home," he said, turning back to the door. "Is there anything before tomorrow?"

"Tomorrow is Saturday," Leslie said in the voice she reserved for explaining simple concepts to idiots. "I'm going to be spending it with Randall."

"Right," Alex said.

"I got ahold of Sherry Knox like you wanted," she went on, her voice shifting to disapproval. "You have an appointment with her at ten on Monday."

Alex had forgotten about the enigmatic Miss Knox. He wondered if she might be mixed up in the Ashford scheme, but dismissed that idea as soon as it came. Ashford and whoever he was working with were using mind control, so they didn't need spies.

"All right," he said.

"Don't say I didn't warn you," Leslie called as he showed himself out.

"I couldn't if I wanted to," he said, heading for the door. "You'd never let me."

28

TRANSFERENCE

Alex found Iggy hard at work at the large walnut writing desk in his elegant vault. Ever since the old doctor heard about Moriarty's vault, he'd worked constantly to improve his own. He seemed to take an almost personal offense at the idea of a better vault than his. Now the front area was a well-appointed sitting room, complete with a crystal chandelier hanging from the vaulted ceiling.

Off to the right of this space was Iggy's surgery, and to the left was his workroom. Alex's vault had been outfitted with an angled drafting table he'd received in lieu of payment on a case. Iggy liked it so much that he'd purchased one of his own.

When Alex entered the workroom, Iggy was bent over his desk squinting through a large magnifying glass. On the drafting table were several square bits of flash paper and on the floor were the empty red covers of several Happy Jack rune books.

"It's about time you got here," Iggy said, still peering through the glass. "I know what these Happy Jack fellows are doing, I just can't figure out how they're doing it. Come here and take a look."

He turned to hand the magnifying glass to Alex but stopped short when he saw him.

"I take it you're not bleeding to death," he said, pointing at Alex's bloodstained coat sleeve.

Alex took off the coat and held out his arm for Iggy to examine. One of the first policemen who'd arrived at the scene of the Happy Jack fire had tied Alex's handkerchief around his forearm and it had long since stopped bleeding.

Moving carefully, Iggy peeled away the bloody cloth.

"Take your shirt off," he said. "I can't see under it."

Alex unbuttoned his shirt, but found he couldn't pull his left arm out of the sleeve because the dried blood had stuck it to his arm. When he pulled at the fabric, the wound throbbed and began to bleed again.

"Don't do that," Iggy admonished. He led Alex back through the sitting room to the surgery. Once he had Alex sitting on his examination table, he used a wet sponge to loosen the shirt sleeve. "It doesn't look too bad," he said, once Alex had the shirt off. "The bullet went straight through. Since you obviously ran out of shield runes, I'm going to assume you had an interesting afternoon."

"You could say that," he said. "I went by the Happy Jack factory."

"This needs stitches," Iggy declared. "So you can tell me all about it while I work."

Alex sighed and recounted the tale of his visit to Happy Jack and his subsequent encounter with Carlton Maple.

"So he had one runewright doing the actual writing but a bunch of other runewrights were copying the movements exactly? Iggy asked.

"As best as I can figure," Alex said. "I didn't actually see who was leading each group, they just all moved in unison."

"I suppose that's possible," Iggy said after a moment to think about it. "But I don't see how that would work with the Forgotten. They're not runewrights, so they wouldn't be able to channel the magic needed to make runes."

"I don't know." Alex shook his head. "What I do know is that they were at writing desks just like the runewrights, and the Captain had that coal-gall ink on his right hand despite being left-handed."

Iggy finished wrapping a bandage around Alex's arm, tying it expertly in place.

"Well, I suspect the Sorceress is right," he said as Alex got up from the table. "We'll have plenty of time to figure it out now."

"What about Ashford?" Alex asked. "Maple had to be working with someone else. What if they can still pull off their plan to get him elected? There have to be thousands of those rune books in shops all over the city."

Iggy considered that, then shook his head.

"Maple would never have let someone else in on the details of his mind control rune, and you know that," he said.

Alex did know that. Runewrights were a secretive lot who guarded their knowledge jealously. No one who was smart enough to develop a mind control rune would share that knowledge. Unless...

"He wouldn't have to," Alex said, grabbing Iggy by the arm as they headed back to the workroom. Iggy raised an eyebrow but waited for Alex to explain. "What if Maple didn't develop the mind control construct in the first place? What if he was controlled by whoever did?"

Iggy stroked his mustache for a minute.

"I don't think that's possible," he said. "You said the runewrights had to be given specific instructions when Maple sent them after you. That sounds like whatever control this rune offers, it's fairly rudimentary. If Maple were mind controlled as well, he wouldn't have been able to think on his feet. He wouldn't have been able to tell the runewrights how to hunt for you because he wouldn't know himself."

It was a good point and Alex had no rebuttal.

"Let's get your clothes patched up and I'll show you how Maple was using those rune books to get his hooks into people."

Iggy got a pair of mending runes from a file box in his workroom, passing them to Alex, and five minutes later Alex's shirt and coat were free of bullet holes. He'd have to use a cleaning rune to get the dried blood out, but that would make a mess in the vault, so he'd do that outside later.

"Okay," he said, slipping his shirt back on and buttoning it up. "What did you find out?"

Iggy held out the magnifying glass and Alex took it, leaning over the rune paper on the table. The rune was a minor mending rune, not as powerful as the ones he'd just used to repair his clothes, but built from the same basic construct. At first, he couldn't see what Iggy was looking at. Under the magnifying glass everything appeared as it should. He was about to ask what he was supposed to be seeing, when he noticed small, almost invisible creases in the paper. It reminded him of the indentations that pencils would leave on note paper. The writer would press down hard enough that the impression would be transferred to the page behind.

"What are these?" he asked.

"Get the lights," Iggy said, picking up his ornate multi-lamp from a side table. Alex walked to the door and turned the light switch, plunging the workshop into darkness. Iggy lit his lamp and the green glow of ghostlight shone out through the focusing lens.

"Put these on," he said, handing Alex a pair of pince-nez spectacles with green lenses.

Alex slipped the glasses onto the bridge of his nose, then

looked at the rune paper. The construct of the mending rune glowed brightly, as he'd expected, but there was nothing else to see.

"Watch closely," Iggy said, flicking his gold cigarette lighter to life. He touched the flame to the paper, and it vanished in a flash of light and a puff of smoke. The mending rune hung in the air for a moment, which was completely normal. Alex was about to say so, when, just as the rune began to fade, something else lit up behind it.

The new lines were a different construct, one much more complex than the basic mending rune. Alex could see dozens of delicate lines and symbols, but before he could even begin to recognize them, the entire construct just vanished.

"What was that?" he asked, turning to Iggy.

"That was your mind rune," he said. "Somehow it's on the paper, waiting for the mending rune to activate. When that happens, it draws power from the mending rune."

"How do you know that?"

"Because you can't see the rune with ghostlight," Iggy said. "If it had power, it would light up like Broadway."

Alex looked at the space where the rune had been, then back to Iggy.

"That could explain what Maple needed the Forgotten for," Alex said, rubbing his chin. "If that invisible rune has no power, then it's just a shape."

"And you wouldn't need a runewright to make it," Iggy said, nodding. "That could very well be it."

"Are we in danger of being affected by this mind rune?"

"No," the old man said. "Whatever that rune is, it's built on a suggestion rune, sometimes called a charm construct. It creates a weak connection between the runewright and whoever views the rune. The wards around the brownstone prevent any such links from being formed."

That was certainly true; with the notable exception of

Moriarty, nothing had been able to penetrate the brownstone's protections.

"Maybe we can see it with silverlight?"

Iggy shook his head.

"I don't know how your friend Maple managed it, but somehow there's an advanced, complex rune on these papers that no one can see."

Alex didn't have an answer for that. In order to really understand what Maple had done, they would have to be able to see the runic construct. Without that, they had no chance of unraveling it.

"Could we set up a camera?" he suggested. "Try to get the rune on film before it disappears."

"It's gone too fast," Iggy said. "Film needs more time to get a full exposure."

Alex sighed. So far Maple had been one step ahead of him from day one; now he was dead and still managing to taunt Alex. He could feel a headache coming on, and he pressed his fingers to his forehead.

"I could use a break," he said.

"Have you forgotten what today is?" Iggy asked.

"Friday?" He only knew that because Leslie had reminded him.

"Today's the big day," Iggy said, clapping him on his good shoulder. "I've arranged everything at the slaughterhouse."

Alex felt the hairs on his arms stand up. He and Iggy had been working on the life transference construct for a year. Moriarty proved it could be done, but working it out had taken months of research, attempt after attempt, and weeks of testing. Now it all came down to tonight. Either it would work, or Alex would explode like he'd been stuffed with dynamite.

"Relax," Iggy said, reading the look on Alex's face. "We've tested this construct. We know it works."

Alex forced his heartbeat back into a more normal rhythm and nodded.

"And it's not exactly like we've got time to wait," Iggy added with a lopsided grin.

"Thanks," Alex said, shooting him a dirty look. He knew Iggy was trying to put him off feeling anxious by ribbing him, and he appreciated the effort. Not that it helped. One way or another, the debt for his teleporting the entirety of Sorsha's castle three years ago would finally be resolved.

He'd known it had been coming, but he'd distracted himself with work, pushing the reality of it out of his mind. Now all the cases he solved, all the crooks and murderers he'd caught just faded into the background. In a few hours, his life would depend on how well he and Iggy knew their lore.

"Best get to it then," he said, turning to Iggy. "Let me grab a cleaning rune and take care of my clothes, then we'll go."

Iggy held his gaze for a long moment, then he nodded.

It was strange for Alex to be back in the attic of the slaughterhouse where Moriarty had taken him a year earlier. Just as before, he could smell the pigs down in the feed barn below and hear their grunts as they moved about. Iggy had made arrangements with the owner of the slaughterhouse to buy the pigs. If all went well, a crew would come in after midnight and load the carcasses onto the line where their blood would be drained. Since they were already dead, it would take longer, but the meat would still be usable.

"All right," Iggy said, climbing up the iron spiral stair that led down to the barn floor. "Everything's ready."

He'd been below setting up the rune papers around the pen. Alex waited as the old man paused to catch his breath on the top of the stairs.

"You know," Alex said, mostly to break up the oppressive silence. "If this works, we should be able to use it on you."

Iggy gave him a wry look.

"Just figuring that out, are you?" he said. "That's the first thing I thought of when you told me about Moriarty."

"I'm starting to think he was serious," Alex said. "When he talked about that Archimedes quote in the Monograph, about levers and moving the world," Alex said.

"Why?"

"Because just knowing that this is possible, that a runewright can take life energy from one creature and put it into another. For all intents and purposes, it's immortality. You and I, and anyone else we share this with could live forever."

Iggy chuckled at that.

"Well I might," he said with a wink. "You'll get yourself shot before you last a decade. It doesn't matter how much life energy you have if someone fills you full of holes."

Alex laughed and nodded.

"Maybe there's a better shield rune too."

"Tell you what," Iggy said, coming over to stand in front of him. "Let's get this bit worked out, then we'll work on that."

"Whatever you say. Let's just get this over with."

Iggy motioned Alex to a simple wooden chair they'd placed in the center of the room, just under the bare bulb that hung from the ceiling on a wire. The memories of his previous time in this place rushed back and Alex had to fight down a moment's panic before he walked to the chair and sat down.

"All right," Iggy said, handing him a rune paper. "Are you comfortable?"

"Does it matter?"

"Not in the slightest," Iggy replied. He pulled out his gold lighter and flicked it to life.

Before he could reach out toward the rune paper, Alex pulled it back, out of his reach.

"Iggy," he began, but hesitated. "Arthur," he went on. "If this doesn't work, I just want you to know that it's been an honor being your apprentice."

"Stop that," Iggy said, cuffing him on the shoulder. "It's going to work."

Alex moved the paper back into position and Iggy held the lighter near it.

"And I've had one hell of a time too," he said.

He touched the flame to the paper and it vanished with a whoosh of flame and air. Alex knew from experience that the three papers on the main floor were burning away as well, their runes activating and joining with the one before him. Unlike a normal rune, this one didn't hover upright but turned until it was horizontal. As it turned it grew, passing through Alex's body until it encircled him like Saturn's ring.

The rune glowed a color somewhere between blue and green with shifting patterns of darker reds and purples. Alex could feel the magic in it pulsating, getting faster and faster. It reminded him of an orchestra tuning up, each instrument coming in on different notes but as the seconds passed the tones slid toward a cohesive sound.

Alex's fingers and toes tingled and the hair on his arms stood on end. Magic power crackled like electricity and the construct ring began to slow as it aligned with its sister runes below. The discordant sound of the magic finally coerced into a harmonic chord that sent shivers through his body and the construct stopped rotating, turning a deep, cobalt blue.

Alex remembered that color; it was the same as when Moriarty's rune had activated. Just like before, a chorus of terrible cries rose up from the pigs below. Brilliant light flared from the rune and every muscle in Alex's body cramped and seized. The air was literally squeezed from his lungs as his body fought against the forces pushing on it.

He didn't know how long he hung, suspended by the magic and his cramping muscles, but his vision began to dwindle down to a tunnel of brightness surrounded by inky night. The crescendo of sound that marked the rune's final activation suddenly broke, ceasing as if some unseen conductor had waved his baton for silence.

Light exploded in Alex's vision, driving back the darkness and he gulped a great breath of air. He was vaguely aware of lying on the floor and shivering as if he'd been submerged in a tank of icy water.

"Take it easy, boy," Iggy said, grabbing his shoulders and trying to hold him still. "You're alive, just breathe."

The last time Alex had done this, he experienced a burst of unbelievable energy, followed by being so weak that all he could do was lie on the floor for an hour. This time he didn't experience the power, but neither did he have the weakness. It only took about five minutes before the shaking stopped and Alex could sit up.

As soon as he did, Iggy grabbed his head and tilted it up toward the light, looking him in each eye.

"How many fingers do you see? he asked, holding up the first to fingers and thumb of his right hand.

"Two," Alex said, pulling his head back out if Iggy's grip. "And a thumb."

Iggy snorted at him.

"You're not funny. How do you feel?"

"Not like exploding," he said.

Iggy grinned at that.

"That's definitely a good sign," he said. "Check your watch."

With hands that only shook a little, Alex pulled out his

pocket watch. Thumbing the crown, he released the cover and it popped open. He could feel the magic inside the watch spring to life as the cover moved. The glowing third hand that had been his companion for almost a year burst to life.

It was red and it pointed at about three minutes past twelve.

Alex looked up worriedly at Iggy, but the old man was still fixed on the watch.

"Give it a moment," he said, his voice barely a whisper.

Alex felt the magic change before he saw anything. As he looked on, the red hand began to move. It swept past one, then two, and when it passed three, it turned from red to blue. The hand continued until it had gone all the way around. When it passed twelve again, it changed from blue to green and it stopped on two o'clock.

"Is that a year and two months?" he asked.

"It might be," Iggy said, "but it could just as easily be ten years and two months. The life energy rune is only accurate to about a year. Green means you have more than a year, but it doesn't know how much more."

Alex threw back his head and whooped. He'd never regretted his decision to move Sorsha's castle, but neither was he excited about dying young. For the first time in three years, he felt like he had his life back.

It was a very good feeling.

29

MARKINGS

T he following morning Alex woke before his alarm and didn't even think about having a cup of coffee until he'd been up for almost an hour. He had a lot of work to get to, but Iggy insisted he give Alex a complete medical going-over first.

"All right," the old man said after he'd read Alex blood pressure, tested his reflexes, drawn a blood sample, and listened to his heartbeat. "You seem fine to me. How do you feel?"

"Like a million bucks," he said. "I feel like I could take on the world."

Iggy gave him an amused grin.

"Or move it?" he said.

Alex didn't take the bait, shrugging instead.

"If I have to," he said.

"Well I suggest you give some thought to a new escape rune," Iggy said. "While I don't approve of you moving buildings, it's always nice to have a last resort way to get out of trouble."

Alex had thought about that several times in the years

since he'd used his last one. He'd come up with several possible improvements, but he'd need to review them before he went back to have a new one tattooed on his arm.

"Right now I've got to go figure out who killed Fredrick and Isabel Westlake and tried to kill their daughter," he said, pushing the thought of tattooed runes out of his mind.

"I thought it was the nightclub owner," Iggy said, putting away his stethoscope.

"His lawyer came by the office last night and paid me handsomely to look for another suspect."

"Hmm," Iggy said, his mustache wrinkling up under his nose. "Do the Westlakes have any enemies?"

"Not that I know of," Alex admitted. "But I wasn't looking for any up to now." He pushed himself off the examination table and stood. "I'll let you know if I figure it out."

"What's your plan?"

"I'm going to call Danny and have him get me in to the Westlake's home so I can look around," he said.

"Why not just ask the butler?"

"He's not going to be thrilled about me working for George Sheridan," Alex said. "And he might be a suspect."

"Really?" Iggy said with mock disdain. "The butler did it?"

Alex laughed and shrugged.

"Stranger things have happened. Besides, I want to go by the hospital and check on Marnie. I can pick up Danny after that."

"Say hello for me," Iggy said.

Alex wasn't sure if he meant to Danny or Marnie, but he could easily do both.

When Alex reached the hospital, he found that the survivors of the Happy Jack fire had been treated and released during the night. That was good news, but he'd hoped the hospital would keep them for observation in case some vestige of Maple's control still remained.

Marnie had seemed fine when Alex helped her and the other survivors out of his vault. She hadn't even remembered that he'd hit her, which made Alex happy. Since there was nothing he could do about it, he resolved to go by Runewright Row and check on Marnie later. With Happy Jack out of business, she'd have to get back to her regular work to make rent.

His next stop was the Central Office of Police, where he found Danny slumped over his desk drinking coffee with both hands.

"Long night?" Alex asked.

Danny looked up at him with bloodshot eyes.

"I hate coming off night shift," he said. "It takes me days to get my body back on schedule. You look chipper."

"Thanks," Alex said, not bothering to suppress the grin that spread across his face. "Do you still have an officer keeping an eye on the Westlake place?"

Danny shook his head and downed the cup of coffee in his left hand.

"Don't need one," he said.

"Mind if I go by and have a look around?"

Danny's eyes opened at that and he sat up straight.

"You think we missed something?"

"No," he said without hesitation. "But George Sheridan's lawyer is willing to pay me to make sure."

"I don't like you working for my only suspect," Danny said. "So far this is looking like an open and shut case."

"And it probably still is," Alex said. "But if there are any problems, you'll want to know about it before the DA gets the case, right?"

"Uh-huh," Danny said in a voice that conveyed boundless

skepticism. "If you find something, you'd better bring me a viable suspect in return."

"Don't worry about that," Alex said. "At this point the only thing that would get dear old George off the hook is a better suspect."

Danny thought about that for a moment, then nodded.

"All right," he said at last. "I'll get my coat."

Alex raised an eyebrow at that.

"You're coming too?"

"There's no officer there to get you in, remember?" he said. "Besides, I want to get one of those coffees of yours. We can go by Runewright Row on the way."

"Deal."

There were more runewrights on the row than there had been earlier in the week, but it still looked pretty thin when Alex and Danny arrived. Alex was grateful that not everyone had gone to work for Happy Jack. As he climbed out of Danny's car, he spotted Marnie right where she should be.

"Alex," she called, catching sight of him. She left her cart and rushed over to grab him in a fierce hug. The left side of her face was covered in a dark bruise that made Alex flinch, but apparently Marnie still didn't remember where it came from.

She didn't say anything as she squeezed him, but she didn't let go either, so Alex returned the hug.

"Are you okay?" he asked, after an awkward silence.

"I'm alive," she said. "I don't know how I'm going to pay my rent, but I'm alive. Thank you. If you hadn't come by when you did..."

She trailed off and squeezed him again, then stepped back.

"Who's your friend?" she said, nodding at Danny.

"Danny needs some of your excellent coffee," Alex said after he'd made introductions.

Marnie smiled and nodded, but Alex could tell something was wrong.

"How far behind are you?" he asked as she poured a cup for Danny.

She shot him a dark look. Such questions simply weren't asked.

"Too far," she said when Alex held her gaze. "I'm pretty sure my landlady will give me enough time to make it up, though."

The tone of her voice told Alex that she didn't believe it. He waited until after Danny paid for the coffee, then pulled out his wallet.

"Here," he said, peeling off a fifty. "It's just a loan," he insisted when she started to protest.

"You know I won't be able to pay that back," she said, refusing to take the money.

Alex had been waiting for that, and he smiled.

"I'll tell you what," he said, reaching into his pocket for one of his business cards. He turned it over, then took out his pencil and wrote on the back. "I want you to fill up the thermos you've got with coffee right now. Then you get someone to watch your cart and we'll drop you at Empire Tower."

"What for?" she asked, peering over Alex's shoulder to see what he was writing.

Alex handed her the card and put his pencil back in his shirt pocket with his notebook.

"This is the coffee girl," Marnie read off the back of the card. She gave him a confused look.

"Go up to Empire Station," Alex went on. "There's a glass door on one wall with two security guards standing outside it.

Give them this card and tell them it's from Alex Lockerby
and it needs to get to Mr. Bickman right away. Tell them he's
expecting it and then wait for an answer. Got it?"

"Alex, I can't leave my cart," Marnie protested. "I need
every scrap of business I can find."

"That's just it," Alex said, putting a hand on her shoulder.
"I met with Andrew Barton earlier this week and he had
some of your coffee. He liked it so much that he wants you to
brew coffee for the whole of Empire Station."

"He's got a point," Danny said, holding up the cup Marnie
had given him. "This is the best coffee I've had in a long
time."

"T-the Lightning Lord?" she said in a voice that came out
in a squeak.

Alex often forgot how comfortable he'd become with
sorcerers. Most folks regarded them the same way ancient
Greeks thought of their gods, powerful, jealous, temperamental, and best kept at a distance.

He put a reassuring arm around her shoulders.

"Don't worry. Barton's just a guy who likes coffee and
wants to give you a really good job."

Marnie hesitated, then started to smile. Before she
finished, her eyes went wide.

"The king," she gasped. When Alex gave her a questioning look, she went on. "The King of Pentacles," she said.
"That woman who read your fortune said you would intervene between the king and someone in trouble. That must be
the Lightning Lord and me."

Alex wanted to scoff at the idea, but if there ever was a
king of magic, Andrew Barton was it. The other card was the
hanged man, who represented someone in trouble. He knew
the whole thing was smoke and mirrors, just Marnie reading
what she wanted into it, but Sherry's prediction was a little
too on the nose for Alex's liking.

"Sure," he said. "That must be it."

He smiled as Marnie hurried off to fill the thermos and get one of her compatriots to watch her cart, but Sherry's reading lingered in his mind. According to her, he still had to face two challenges, the Queen of Pentacles and the Wheel of Fortune, and if Barton was the King of Pentacles, he had a pretty good idea who the queen was.

———

"Can we go now?" Danny's voice droned from the foyer of the Westlake home.

They'd arrived around ten, after dropping Marnie off at Empire Tower. Now it was just after one.

"I need to get a sandwich or something," Danny went on.

Alex grit his teeth. He'd been over the Westlake house from top to bottom. He'd been through Fredrick's office and looked through his papers. He'd been to the wine cellar and examined the locks on the doors. All he had discovered was that Fredrick's business affairs and investments were handled by his broker, that Vivian was the sole heir in his will, and that Isabel had been a booster for the women's suffrage movement back in the teens. As far as he could tell, the Westlakes were quiet and well regarded by those who knew them. If there was someone more likely to poison them than George Sheridan, he was hiding his motive well.

He slammed the drawer shut on the file cabinet he'd been going through for the third time, and stalked back out into the foyer. Danny sat on an uncomfortable-looking couch by the door cradling his head in his hands with his hat on the seat beside him.

"What about the cook?" Alex demanded.

"We already found him," Danny said. "He ran because he thought the Westlakes had been killed by his cooking."

Alex was a bit surprised at that.

"How'd you find him so fast?"

Danny sat up and sighed.

"He's Cuban, so we just checked little Havana," he said. "The guy has a tattoo on the back of his hand, so he was pretty easy to find."

Alex bit his lip. He didn't really care about getting George Sheridan off a murder rap, but the lawyer Hardwick had a point — George had no motive other than pure bull-headed revenge. Alex knew men had killed for much less, but George wasn't stupid. He felt in his gut that something was off about the whole thing, but he had no idea what.

"What did you say?" he asked Danny, his mind suddenly snapping into focus.

"We found the cook."

"How, did you say?"

"By his tattoo," Danny explained again.

Something about the idea of a tattoo was picking at Alex's brain. Iggy had mentioned tattoos earlier, saying how Alex could get a new escape rune put on now that he had a decent amount of life energy. Escape runes were constructs that linked to a specific anchor that existed in, or pointed to, a specific place.

It's a kind of linking rune.

Alex's mind suddenly flashed back to the previous night, to the glowing, cobalt blue life transference rune. The one he could see from the chair was only a quarter of the entire construct, the rest had been set up below him, in the feed lot.

All of the runes were linked together.

"I know how he did it," Alex said as the puzzle pieces clicked into place.

"I thought you were supposed to prove that Sheridan didn't do it," Danny said.

"Not Sheridan," Alex said, quivering with excitement. "Maple."

Danny gave him a confused look and shook his head.

"You hungry?" Alex asked, knowing that his friend was. "There's a fantastic diner on the main floor of the Chrysler building," he went on before Danny could answer. "How about I buy you lunch?"

"Why at the Chrysler building?" Danny asked, picking up his hat.

"Because I need to talk to Sorsha right away," Alex said.

Danny gave him a hard look, then shrugged and put on his hat.

"As long as you buy me lunch," he said, heading for the door.

An hour later Alex breezed into the city morgue with Sorsha in tow. He had a hard time keeping a mischievous grin off his face as he marched down the hall and into Dr. Wagner's office.

"You do like living dangerously," Wagner said, looking up from his desk as Alex entered. He waited until Sorsha came in, but when no one official followed, Wagner smiled. "I'm really going to enjoy having you thrown out, Lockerby."

Alex put his hand on his chest with a wounded look.

"But doc, I thought we were friends now," he said with all the mock sincerity he could muster.

"Neither you, nor your girlfriend, are welcome in my morgue," Wagner said, picking up the phone on his desk. "Now, I'm going to make sure the police arrest you for trespassing."

Alex expected Sorsha to intervene well before this, but she just stood watching until Wagner picked up the phone.

"Where is Dr. Anderson?" she asked in a calm, cool voice.

"Oh, he retired," Alex said before Wagner could speak. "Where are my manners? This is Dr. Wagner, he's the coroner now. Dr. Wagner," he said, turning to the man, "meet Sorsha Kincaid."

The color drained from Wagner's face like water out of a basin, and he lowered the phone back to its cradle.

"Miss Kincaid is a special consultant for the FBI," Alex said, grinning from ear to ear as he rubbed copious amounts of salt in Wagner's wounds.

"Uh," Wagner said, leaping to his feet. "I'm sorry, Miss Kincaid," he said with an ingratiating tone. "No one informed me that you were coming."

Sorsha regarded him evenly, then raised a single eyebrow. It communicated volumes, and Wagner flinched.

"I understand two of the bodies from the Happy Jack fire were brought here," she said.

Wagner nodded and picked up a clipboard from his desk. After flipping a few pages, he looked up again.

"Yes, ma'am. They found two bodies with bullet holes. I took eight slugs out of them, small caliber."

"I'd like to see them, please."

"The bullets are in the evidence box," Wagner said, pointing to a large footlocker on the other side of the office.

"The bodies, Dr. Wagner," Sorsha said in a slightly exasperated voice. "I'd like to see the bodies."

"They're pretty badly burned," Wagner said. When Sorsha didn't answer, he just shrugged and pulled a ring of keys from his pocket. "The cooler is this way," he said, heading out into the hall.

The cooler was exactly as Alex remembered it, except now there were two charred bodies under sheets on one side. Wagner pulled down the sheets and Alex had to hold on to his gut. He never really got used to burn victims. For her part, Sorsha just looked the bodies up and down.

"Are you finished with these bodies, Dr. Wagner?" she asked.

When Wagner nodded, she thanked and dismissed him. Grateful for the excuse, he beat a hasty retreat. When he was gone, Sorsha turned her unamused gaze to Alex.

"Are you going to tell me why I'm here?" she said. "Beyond intimidating that doctor for you, I mean." Her tone communicated that she would not be amused if Alex's only reason for bringing her here was to bully Wagner.

Alex pulled out his red-backed rune book and took out two loose pages he'd tucked into the back. These were special runes he'd taken from his vault before getting Sorsha. Each one was a work of art, rendered in lines of red and gold and filled in with colors that made them look like stained glass windows. He placed one on each body, then pulled out his lighter.

"These look very complicated," Sorsha said, leaning close to one of the papers. She regarded him with her usual detached look but he could tell the wheels of her mind were turning quickly.

"They should be," Alex said. "They're temporal restoration runes. When I light them, they'll restore these bodies to the condition they were in when they died."

Sorsha looked as if she didn't believe that, but she nodded.

"I'd recommend not watching," he said as he squeezed the side of his lighter, snapping it open and igniting the wick.

"Go on," she said, folding her arms across her chest.

Shrugging, Alex touched the flame first to one paper, then the other. As the flash paper vanished, the complex runes sprang to life, burning brightly with red and gold light. Waves of magical energy pulsed through them, faster and faster until each rune exploded in a fountain of sparks that floated down slowly to the charred bodies below.

Alex wanted to look away. He hated this part, but with Sorsha looking eagerly on, he simply couldn't let her best him. When the sparks contacted the corpses, the bodies began to move, shimmering and roiling as if the skin had turned liquid. From the spots where the sparks fell, pink skin blossomed outward, replacing the burned and blackened flesh. In the larger cavities, muscle, fat, organs, and ligaments grew back, eventually covered by the rejuvenated skin. Milky liquid bloomed in the eye sockets, bubbling and steaming until it solidified into eyeballs and the restored skin finally crawled across the dead faces.

Alex's stomach churned at the horrific sight, and even Sorsha paled a bit, but her expression didn't change.

"Fascinating," she said once the process had finished. "You never told me you could do that." Her voice sounded impressed and Alex was a bit flattered. It wasn't every day that a runewright could impress a sorcerer.

"It's extremely complicated," Alex said. "And it only lasts about ten minutes, then the bodies are going to turn to dust."

Sorsha nodded at that.

"Backlash for reversing time, I expect," she said, reminding Alex that she was, in fact, a powerful and knowledgeable sorceress. "What are we looking for?"

The body closest to Alex was the thug he'd shot in the second room who had been trying to light the factory wall on fire. He looked the man over quickly, not expecting to find anything, but wanting to be thorough.

Satisfied, he moved around to the second table where the body of Carlton Maple lay. His body looked perfectly restored except for the five bullet holes that ran across his abdomen. There was a small tattoo of a Spanish doubloon on his left forearm, but Alex only gave that a cursory glance. What he sought was the large, colorful tattoo on Maple's chest.

"That looks like the escape rune you used to have," Sorsha observed.

"In a way, that's what it is," he said, quickly sketching the tattoo in his notebook. "An escape rune is just a construct that is anchored to a distant location. Maple's mind control rune linked him the same way, but not to a location." He indicated a series of runic text along the side of the tattoo. "This is what linked him to the people he was controlling."

Sorsha bent close to the tattoo, then pointed to another part of the construct.

"Isn't this more of the same text over here?"

Alex looked at it, then scribbled furiously in his book.

"No," he said, shaking his head. "It's close but not exact."

Sorsha looked up at him and waited expectantly.

"Well," she said when Alex didn't go on. "What does all this mean to you?"

Alex closed his notebook and met her gaze, holding up three fingers.

"One, it means that I know how Maple was controlling people," he said, ticking off one finger. "Two, it means that someone else is in on the scheme." He ticked off another finger. "And three, it means that, most likely, the plan to get William Ashford elected mayor is still on."

"Who is Maple's accomplice then?"

"I don't know," Alex admitted. "Most likely Ashford himself, but I'd have to get close to him to find out. Not that he's going to let me. By now he knows about the fire and that Maple is dead."

Sorsha smiled at that, not her cold, mocking smile, but one of dazzling radiance.

"Did I mention that my team and I are providing security

for the mayoral debate tonight? It's being broadcast on the radio."

Now that she said it, Alex remembered that she had told him about it days ago.

"Can you get me close to him?" he asked.

"Probably not at the debate," Sorsha admitted, though her smile never faltered. "But before the debate, Ashford is having a campaign rally at the Hotel Ritz. He's pretty much obligated to meet and greet the attendees."

"You wouldn't happen to be invited to that shindig, would you?"

Alex didn't know how, but Sorsha's smile got even more electric.

"As luck would have it, I am," she said. "And I haven't yet found a date for the evening. You wouldn't happen to own a tuxedo, would you Mr. Lockerby?"

Alex chuckled and offered Sorsha his arm.

"As a matter of fact, Miss Kincaid, I do."

She took his arm and together they walked out of the cooler as the bodies of Maple and his unfortunate henchman crumbled into dust.

30

THE RALLY

B ack before he used his escape rune to transport Sorsha's castle to the middle of the North Atlantic, Alex had needed a tuxedo to infiltrate a high-class nightclub. Those were the days when he didn't have two nickels to rub together, and cigarettes had been a luxury. On that occasion, Iggy had written an elaborate illusion construct to transform his ordinary suit. But illusion runes were expensive and temperamental, so Alex had made it a point to acquire an actual tuxedo as soon as he could afford one.

Ironically, he'd bought it almost two years ago, and hadn't actually worn it since.

"At least it still fits," he said to his reflection in the mirror of his tiny bathroom. He'd slicked back his hair and shaved, and felt he looked quite dapper in his silk shirt and black bow tie.

From below, he heard the doorbell ring and he consulted his watch. Ashford's political rally started at seven and it was only six-thirty. Sorsha was early to get him.

"She must want to make sure I wasn't kidding about

339

owning a tux," he said, slipping his watch back into the pocket of his vest.

He left the bathroom, grabbing the glossy black coat that hung across the back of his reading chair, and headed for the door. Below, he could hear the sound of Iggy opening the vestibule, then Sorsha's voice greeting him.

Alex's room was on the third floor of the brownstone so by the time he'd descended the stairs to the main level, Sorsha and Iggy were waiting for him in the library. He'd wanted to admonish her for being early, but could only stare when he reached the landing.

Sorsha wore a strapless red dress made of some shimmery material that glittered and moved while still managing to hug her every curve. The neckline plunged between her small breasts and the dress appeared to be gathered around her tiny waist. She wore an elaborate silver necklace that sparkled with diamonds, and deep red lipstick that seemed almost black in the low light. A long, thin stole of white fur was wrapped around her shoulders and over her arms with one end hanging down below her waist.

She was stunning.

"Why, Mr. Lockerby," she said, turning to look at him with her ice blue eyes. "You clean up nicely." Alex was about to respond in kind, but she went on. "Except for the gun."

Alex pushed at the butt of his 1911, forcing the shoulder holster further under his arm. His suits had all been cut with the holster in mind, but he hadn't thought to do that with the tux.

Sorsha looked from the bulge in his coat up to his face with a questioning look.

"These people killed almost everybody at the Happy Jack factory to cover up their schemes," he said. "I'm not taking any chances."

The sorceress looked as though she might object, but finally nodded.

"Just make sure you keep it hidden," she said. "I don't want to have to explain it."

Alex promised that he would, then took down his hat from the row of pegs by the vestibule door.

"That's the best hat you have?" Sorsha asked, with an arched eyebrow.

Alex looked at his hat, then back at the sorceress with a shrug. It was relatively new, and it was clean, so he wasn't really sure what she meant.

"Give it here," she said, holding out her hand.

Not wanting to argue, Alex handed it over. Sorsha held the hat up against Alex's tuxedo coat and he could see that while the coat was a deep, glossy black, the hat was grey. Her eyes flashed and the sorceress said something in her unnaturally low magic voice. The hat bristled and shivered, its color changing from grey to black while the nap grew finer and glossier.

"Here," she said, reaching up to put it on Alex's head. "Now you look complete."

It wasn't quite true. Alex had his trench coat for everyday wear, but he didn't have a greatcoat to match his tux. Still, he was a runewright. Taking one of his climate runes from the pocket of his coat, he stuck it to his hat before lighting it with his lighter. The magic expanded around him, sealing in the snug temperature of the brownstone.

"It's not raining," Sorsha observed, assuming Alex had used a basic barrier rune.

"Just a precaution," he said, offering her his arm. "Wouldn't want your handiwork on my hat to get wasted."

She seemed to accept that, and took his arm.

"Keep your wits about you," Iggy said as they headed for the door.

Alex promised that he would, then led Sorsha out into the frigid night air. Being a sorceress, and used to cold magic, Sorsha was perfectly fine in the weather, despite her thin attire. Her breath didn't even steam. As they made their way down the steps to Sorsha's waiting floater, Alex wondered if she simply lowered her body temperature to match the outside air.

The rally for mayoral hopeful William Ashford filled the grand ballroom of the Ritz hotel. Sorsha had the floater wait above the building until ten minutes past seven, then made a grand entrance with the sleek black flying car drifting down to the red carpet laid out in front of the building. When the uniformed bellman opened the door, Sorsha stepped out easily, as if she were simply going in to use the phone. A line of newspaper photographers were there to take her picture, and she paused as their flash bulbs went off.

Alex wanted to wait until they were done, but a line of cars had formed behind them, so he was obliged to exit quickly. Once he took Sorsha's arm, the newly replaced flash bulbs of the photographers exploded again, tracking them as they walked to the entrance of the hotel and through the doors. He had an uncomfortable feeling that he'd be the subject of several tabloid stories before Monday.

Once they were inside, another uniformed woman took Alex's hat and Sorsha's stole before they were directed to the ballroom. Alex had seen these formal affairs a few times before, but he'd never really gotten used to them. Inside the ballroom, several dozen people milled about, all dressed to the nines. The men wore gold rings with fancy watches and chains while the women had all manner of jewels dangling from necklaces, bracelets, earrings, and even the occasional anklet.

Sorsha reached out as if she were pulling something off an invisible shelf and when her hand came back, she held her long black cigarette holder. Alex had seen her do this many times, but it never ceased to amaze him, how casually she manipulated magic in ways he could only dream of.

"Do you have a cigarette?" she asked.

Realizing he should have offered her one the moment they arrived, Alex pulled out his silver case and popped it open. She selected one, moving slowly, almost delicately. Alex realized most of the women in this room were acting the same way, as if they were posing for a magazine picture.

"A certain air of breeding is expected," Sorsha said in a low voice as she inserted the cigarette into the holder. "It's tedious, but useful if one wants to mingle."

Alex took a cigarette for himself, then put the case away. He offered her a light from his humble brass lighter.

"Where is Ashford?" he said, once his lighter was safely back in his trouser pocket.

"He's not out on the floor yet," she said, leading Alex through the crowd.

"Isn't he supposed to be at a debate in an hour?"

"That's not until nine," Sorsha corrected him. "He's got plenty of time to schmooze these people for donations and support. Once that starts, however, it will be impossible to get a word in."

"So we need to talk to him now," Alex said. "How do we do that?"

"Luckily, I picked out his security," she said, nodding toward a door at the far end of the ballroom. A man in a suit stood there and as they got close, Alex could see that it was Agent Redhorn.

"What's he doing here?" Redhorn nodded at Alex once they arrived.

"Play nice," Sorsha said. "We need to have a word with Ashford."

Redhorn looked as though he might object, but stepped away from the door.

"He's in the kitchen practicing his speech for tonight."

Alex followed Sorsha out of the ballroom and into a large hallway at the back of the building. It was wider than Alex expected until he realized it was used by the hotel staff to bring in everything from tables and chairs to trays of food. At the far end of the hall was the hotel's kitchen, bustling with activity. It was not the place Alex would have picked to rehearse a speech, with all the noise of the cooks and clink of plates.

At the far end of the kitchen stood an older man with graying hair and a tuxedo surrounded by hard-looking men in normal suits. He had a gaunt face with hollow cheeks, beady eyes and a beak-like nose. The man definitely had a face for radio. He was reading from a stack of papers and pacing back and forth.

"I take it that's our boy," Alex whispered as Sorsha made for the back of the kitchen.

"William," Sorsha said in a radiant voice, ignoring Alex.

Ashford looked up and his face brightened as he saw the sorceress.

"Miss Kincaid," he said, taking her hand and kissing it. "You look as lovely as ever."

Seems polite enough.

"Are you ready for your big night?" Sorsha asked.

Ashford seemed confused for a moment, then smiled and held up the papers.

"Just going over my speech," he said. "For after the debate."

"Well, I came to make sure you were being taken care of," she said, indicating the FBI men. "This is my friend, Alexander Lockerby."

Ashford glanced at Alex and smiled pleasantly enough, but there was no sign that he recognized the name.

"Don't let us interrupt," Sorsha went on.

Ashford exchanged a few pleasantries with the sorceress, then went back to pacing and reading his speech. Sorsha led Alex a few yards away and leaned close.

"What do you think?" she asked.

"He didn't recognize my name," Alex said. "Carlton Maple knew who I was. I'm guessing if Ashford is his partner, he'd know too."

"Not necessarily."

"You've spent time with him," Alex pointed out. "What do you think?"

Sorsha looked back at Ashford, who droned on reading his speech in a grating voice.

"I don't think he has the mind for this plot," she admitted.

"So someone else is using him as a front man?"

Sorsha nodded.

"It's an obvious choice. He had the coin to mount his own campaign," she said. "Anyone else would have to raise money first."

Coin.

The word thundered in Alex's mind.

"Ashford wasn't even in the running until a few months ago," he said. "No one knew his name before that."

"So something changed then?"

Alex took Sorsha by the arm and led her away from Ashford, back toward the ballroom.

"A few months ago, Ashford hired a campaign manager," he said.

"Malcom Jones," Sorsha said. "You think he's involved?"

"Think about it. It was right after Jones came on that Ashford suddenly got popular."

Sorsha's nose wrinkled up, something she did when she was thinking, then she nodded.

"It makes sense."

"Where is Jones now?"

Sorsha shook her head.

"I don't know. I'm only in charge of guarding Ashford."

"We need to find him," Alex said, looking around.

"He might be here or at Radio City; that's where the debate is taking place. We should split up and search. I'll take my car over to Radio City and—"

"Not a chance," Alex cut her off. "These people are dangerous and we don't know who else they might have under their control." Sorsha opened her mouth to object, but Alex put a finger to her lips. "Remember what happened at the Happy Jack factory. We can't afford for that to happen in a hotel or a crowded auditorium. We stick together and we watch each other's backs."

"All right," Sorsha said. "What do we do first?"

"You ask Agent Redhorn to have the FBI find Jones, assuming he's here," Alex said. "Then meet me in the lobby."

"I thought we were sticking together," Sorsha said.

"We are," Alex said. "I just need to make a phone call first."

Two hours later, Alex and Sorsha had searched the hotel, then escorted Ashford to the debate. Finally they found one of Ashford's campaign workers, who told them that Malcom Jones had gone back to the Ritz to prepare for a private reception after the broadcast.

"This has been fun," Alex said as they entered the lobby of the Ritz for the second time. They'd waited so long for Sorsha's car to pick them up that he'd had to use his last climate rune just to keep from freezing.

"At least we know where he is this time," Sorsha said. Her voice had a hard, snippy edge to it, and she was carrying her fancy dress shoes. Clearly the search for Malcom Jones had taken a toll on her as well. "The reception is going to be on the roof."

The roof of the Ritz had an open area with a bandstand, a dance floor, and an adjacent space for two dozen tables, all under a greenhouse-style glass roof. There was even a fountain in the center of the space. Malcom Jones stood by the bandstand, moving the podium back and forth as he tried to find the best angle.

"It would be better over there," Alex said, pointing to the other side of the bandstand. "Less of the dance floor is in the way."

"Mr. Lockerby," Jones said in his cultured British accent. "What brings you here?"

"Same thing as before," he said. "Looking for Hugo Ayers' killer."

"I thought the police had his killer in custody."

"What happened, Malcom?" Alex asked. "Did Hugo find some payments to Carlton Maple that came from Ashford's campaign account?"

"I'm afraid I don't know anyone named after syrup," Jones said.

"Sure you do," Alex said. "I bet you've known him a long time. I bet he was real helpful with all those other campaigns you won. When did you start working together?"

"I really have no idea what you're talking about," Jones said, leaning on the podium. "Now I'm very busy, so if there's nothing else..."

"Was using mind control Maple's idea or yours?"

"I told you," Jones said, sounding irritated. "I don't know anyone named Maple. Now if you don't leave, I'm going to call security."

"I'm sorry," Alex said. "Where are my manners? This is Sorsha Kincaid; she's in charge of security. And I don't have to ask you if you've ever met Carlton Maple since you both have the same tattoo."

Alex was watching Jones very closely. When he mentioned the tattoo, Jones pulled his left hand back into the sleeve of his shirt.

Gotcha.

"You mean that linking thing Maple had on his chest?" Sorsha asked.

"No," Alex said. "The one of the coin, or more specifically an Ecuadorian eight escudos doubloon."

"Why does that matter?" Sorsha asked.

"Because that's the coin that Captain Ahab nailed to the mast of the Pequod in Moby Dick as a reward for whoever first sighted the white whale."

"So Mr. Jones and Mr. Maple are searching for the same white whale," Sorsha guessed. She turned to regard Jones. "I wonder what that might be?"

"The same one you're looking for, sorceress," Alex said, giving her a dramatic grin. "The Archimedean Monograph."

Sorsha looked stunned, but Malcom Jones just smiled and began to slowly applaud.

"Oh very good," he said. "How did you figure that out?"

"It wasn't easy," Alex said. "But a few years ago someone stole some pages that had once belonged to the Monograph and brought them to New York. Miss Kincaid here," he nodded at Sorsha, "thought I had something to do with it. To tell you the truth, I'd never heard of the Monograph before that. So I took it upon myself to look into its history — and you know what I found?"

"Do tell," Jones said, and excited smile on his face.

"There was a group of British runewrights who went hunting for the Monograph after the Great War. Three of them were arrested trying to waylay Arthur Conan Doyle."

"The author?" Sorsha asked, startled.

"The very same. I read the Scotland Yard report and they all had coins tattooed on their bodies. They claimed to be part of an organization called the Whalers, ex-military runewrights hunting for the Monograph."

"And they thought the creator of Sherlock Holmes had it?" Sorsha asked.

Alex shrugged.

"Apparently."

Jones clapped again.

"Oh, you are good," he said. "I knew you were going to be trouble the first time you showed up at Ashford's headquarters."

"To be fair, you did try to kill me on three separate occasions," Alex said.

"I should have tried harder."

"Too late now," Alex said. "I guess you and your puppet Ashford are out of luck."

Jones laughed and Alex felt the hair on his arm stand up. It wasn't the sort of laugh someone who'd been caught might use.

"Even if you had me, Ashford will still give his speech tonight," Jones said. "We've made sure a large percentage of the population will be listening."

"And Ashford will ask for their vote," Sorsha guessed.

"Tell them to vote for him," Alex corrected, checking his watch. "But the debate is still going on. Ashford won't give his speech for another quarter hour at least. I can stop that broadcast with a single phone call."

"You could," Jones said. "But you're going to be rather busy."

Alex wanted to reach for his gun but something in Jones voice made him stop.

"Sorsha," Jones said, turning to the sorceress. "I have a job for you. Be a dear and kill Alex for me."

31

COLD SHOULDER

Alex rolled his eyes at Malcom Jones. Sorsha Kincaid was a powerful sorceress who had no need for rune books, cheap or not, and the Happy Jack books were the key to his mind control.

"Get a load of this guy," he said to Sorsha.

The sorceress, however, did not respond. A blank look had come over her face and her eyes moved as if she was having trouble focusing. A chill ran up Alex's back as those ice blue eyes suddenly fixed on him.

Sorsha raised her hand and Alex could feel the magic gathering around it. Without even thinking, he pressed his left thumb against the flash ring, holding it up in the space between them. He exerted the will necessary to activate the rune.

But nothing happened.

Like his shield runes, the flash runes on the ring had all been expended.

Alex's eyes jumped from the ring to Sorsha in time to see her send a blast of arctic air at him. A fierce wind buffeted him, flowing over and around him, but although he could see snow forming at the edges of the wind, what reached him wasn't even cool.

The climate rune he'd used while they were waiting for Sorsha's car was still functioning. Without it, he'd have been dead. As Sorsha kept up the barrage of frigid air, Alex could feel the rune beginning to fail. It was designed to withstand normal temperatures, not whatever sub-arctic blast the sorceress was creating.

Sorsha gasped and pulled her hand back, causing the blast of air to vanish. She looked at her hand, then up at Alex, confusion on her porcelain features. Alex didn't hesitate. He was out of flash runes and the sorceress would have defenses against his 1911 so he did the only thing he could. Stepping forward, he closed the distance between them and punched Sorsha square in the jaw.

He felt something pushing back against his fist, probably whatever shield spell she used to repel bullets, but some of the blow got through. Sorsha cried out and stumbled backward.

Alex had a momentary thought of shooting Malcom Jones, but killing Maple hadn't stopped the people under his control. If he took the time to draw his 1911 and shoot Jones, Sorsha would turn him into an ice sculpture. Making up his mind, Alex did the only thing he could as Sorsha struggled to regain her balance. He turned and ran.

He'd only gone a few yards when he felt Sorsha drawing in more magic power. Dropping his hand into the pocket of his tuxedo jacket, he slipped his fingers into the rings of his knuckle duster. Sorsha cried out in anger as she released her magic. Alex jumped, sailing over the edge of the fountain in the middle of the room. As he passed over the water, Alex lashed out with his fist, hitting the tiled bottom of the fountain just as the first numbing blast of icy air hit him. The force runes on the knuckle duster went off, sending a curtain of water shooting up out of the fountain. Sorsha's arctic blast caught it and froze it instantly into a sold barrier behind Alex as he tumbled into the bottom of the fountain.

Sorsha let out a screech of anger, but Alex didn't stick around to congratulate himself on his cleverness. Keeping the frozen wall of water between them, he leapt up and ran for the stairs. He'd just reached the door when a ball of blue energy slammed into the wall beside him and exploded. Bone chilling vapor erupted out from the spot, washing over Alex and freezing the wet fabric of his tux as his climate rune failed entirely.

Momentum carried Alex through the door, and he hit the landing hard, sliding to the stairs and rolling down to the landing below. Pain tore through him from his numb limbs and the impact of the stairs, but at least the fall broke up the ice in his clothes, letting him move again.

Scrambling to his feet, Alex loped down to the next floor, then turned to keep going down. He looked up in time to see Sorsha throw another freezing sphere at him, and he jumped down to the next landing, hitting hard and slamming into the wall. Something in his shoulder popped but he didn't stop. Rolling along the wall until he was facing downward again, he pushed off and kept going.

Above him, Sorsha was descending the stairs, trying to keep him in view. As long as she could see him, she would be a threat. What Alex needed was to get out of the narrow stairwell to somewhere he could use his much longer legs to outpace the sorceress.

Running down to the next floor, he opened the door and found himself in a long, carpeted hallway. No one was in sight, but hotel room doors were visible on either side. If someone came out into the hall while Sorsha was trying to freeze him, it could go badly. He heard the sorceress hit the landing on the floor above. That made his decision for him.

Sprinting down the hall, Alex ignored the pain in his shoulder. He ran past the elevators, knowing they'd never arrive in time, and kept going for the stairs on the other side of the building. He'd just reached the door when a ball of ice slammed into his leg, sending a numbing cold through the entire limb.

Daring to look back over his shoulder, he found Sorsha walking down the hall toward him, conjuring another of the icy missiles in her upraised hand. Pushing through the stair-well door, Alex limped down the stairs as fast as his numb leg would allow. He passed the first landing, turning to the floor below, but at this pace Sorsha would catch him.

He was going have to do something risky if he wanted any chance to evade her, so when he reached the next landing, he pushed the door open and limped down the hall toward the opposite stair. This time, when he reached the elevator, he pushed the call button. Each of the room doors was set back from the hall by a few feet, so Alex stepped back into one of those little alcoves. If Sorsha looked down the hall, all she'd see would be the empty hall.

Alex waited, trying to slow his pounding heart, and listening for any sound. He heard the door at the end of the hall open, but then nothing. The sorceress was in her bare feet, so there wouldn't be any noise on the soft carpet, and he didn't dare take a look. After what seemed like an eternity, the door closed again. Alex couldn't be sure Sorsha had gone back into the stairwell, but if she hadn't, he was as good as dead anyway, so it made no difference.

The elevator car arrived with a chime that sounded far too loud for Alex's liking. Inside was an older man with a white mustache and an impeccable red jacket with gold braids.

"What...floor?" he asked, hesitating when he saw Alex's wet clothes and pronounced limp.

"Lobby," Alex said, then thought better of it. "Where do they keep the furniture for the ballroom?"

"Uh, that's in the storage area," the operator said. "It's on the third floor."

From the far end of the hallway came a high-pitched scream of rage and a ball of ice exploded against the wall just past the elevator opening.

"Time to go," Alex said, shouldering the man away from the control lever. "Take me to the third floor."

He'd said that last bit louder than necessary for Sorsha's benefit. He couldn't let her rampage through the hotel looking for him. In her state she might kill a bunch of people before the police could stop her, which would be when her shield spell finally failed and they gunned her down.

"What's going on?" the operator demanded as the car descended. "What was that thing?"

Alex didn't answer as he watched the arm above the door sweep downward through the floors. When it reached three, he pushed the operation lever up to the middle position and the car shuddered to a stop.

"Take this car down to the lobby and get off," Alex said, pulling the door open. "Stay there until the cops arrive."

That was all the time Alex could give the man and he hoped he'd make use of it. Limping away, Alex headed down the hall beyond the elevator until he reached a door marked *Storage*.

Pushing it open, he found himself in a large room filled with tables covered in dust cloths and stacks of chairs. Being careful to leave the hall door slightly ajar, Alex crossed the room to the far side. A space up against the back wall was bare, no doubt where the hotel staff had removed the tables that were being used for the reception on the roof. A door in the wall led to a room filled with shelves full of plates, silverware, glasses, and tablecloths, but without any other exits.

Working quickly, Alex went back into the main storage area and pulled the chalk from his trouser pocket. It was damp and a bit squishy, but it would do the job. He drew a door right next to the one leading to the dishware room, then tore a vault rune from his book, stuck it to the wall, and lit it. A moment later the solid steel door of his vault melted out of the wall.

Sorsha Kincaid hurried down the stairs, checking the number plaque on each floor as she passed. She had to hurry if she wanted to catch the bad man. He mustn't escape.

"Did he say the third floor?" she muttered as she reached the landing with the number three on its placard.

Yes. It was three.

Summoning a ball of ice to her hand, she pulled the door open, ready for any ambush, but all she found was an empty hallway. It looked like all the other hallways in this infernal building and she let out a growl of frustration.

He was here. He had to be.

Determination washed over her and she stalked forward. As she went, Sorsha noticed that this floor was, in fact, different from those above. There were fewer doors. As she passed, she checked each one, wondering what the bad man could have wanted on this particular floor.

She'd almost passed the one marked *Storage* when she realized that it wasn't fully closed. It looked like someone had gone through in a hurry and hadn't shut it behind them.

Clutching the ice ball in her right hand, she pushed the door open with her left. Nothing came at her from the semi-darkness beyond, so she stepped inside. A large bank of windows on the right side of the room let in dim light from the street below, illuminating the tables and chairs the hotel used for banquets and such. There was another light source in the room, a crack of brightness that seeped out from under a plain wooden door on the far wall.

Sorsha smiled as she saw it. The door was simple enough, but it was mounded inside a massive steel frame and a thick door, like the kind bank vaults had, stood open to the right of it.

It was a runewright's vault.

That's right, the bad man was a runewright. No doubt he'd retreated to his vault to find some weapon to use against her. As if such a lowly creature was any threat.

Something in the back of Sorsha's mind tried to warn her, something about breaking spells, but her mind was foggy for some reason. She briefly wondered why she couldn't remember what this potential danger might be, but the need to stop the bad man overwhelmed her curiosity.

With purposeful steps, she reached the wooden inner door to the vault. She took hold of the handle and turned it as quietly as she could. The door yielded to her, opening silently on well-oiled hinges. Sorsha had a moment's irritation at that. She had hoped it would be locked so she would have the pleasure of shattering it with her magic.

Later, she thought. *First find the bad man and stop him.*

The room beyond the door was large with a simple sitting area and library off to the left and a runewright's workshop to the right. Her quarry was nowhere to be seen, but a hallway ran off to the left and she could hear the sound of running water coming from that direction.

She flexed her fingers around the ball of ice, adding an enchantment that would cause it to burst into a freezing mist when it hit, then started forward.

DAN WILLIS

Alex didn't dare to breathe as he heard Sorsha approach. She was moving quietly, deliberately, and if she detected him, he wouldn't be able to stop her from killing him easily.

From his hiding place, he heard her open a door and look beyond it. She seemed to hesitate for a long minute, then she went inside, padding softly on bare feet. Reaching out, Alex put his hands flat on the smooth steel surface of his vault door, then with a surge of effort, he pushed. The door swung out from the wall, exposing the opening to the silverware room where Alex had hidden himself. A moment later the door swung around and slammed closed, trapping Sorsha inside.

Grabbing the key protruding from the lock in the center of the heavy door, Alex turned it quickly. Once it clicked in the locked position Alex heaved a sigh of relief. Before he could withdraw it from the lock, however, two shots rang out, booming in the quiet of the storage room.

At the same instant the sound washed over him, Alex felt bullets hit his back, one high and one low. Gasping, he dropped to the ground, turning to put his back to the door as he slid into a sitting position.

Gritting his teeth against the pain he pulled open his old trench coat and reached for his 1911.

"None of that," Malcom Jones said, looming out of the darkness with the snub nose of a .38 special pointed at him. Alex lowered his hands into his lap. "I must confess, Alex, you lasted a lot longer than I thought you would, and against a sorceress no less. Very impressive."

"How did you get her?" Alex asked, pretty sure he knew the answer.

Jones shrugged and laughed.

"I don't honestly know," he said. "I suspect someone told her that our rune books were being used to mind control

358

people and she thought that being a sorceress made her immune."

That's about the way Alex figured it, and he nodded.

"Sorcerers always think they're the smartest people in the room," he said. "It's their biggest weakness. Still, she must have gone through a bunch of your books for you to have that kind of control over her."

Jones started, a shocked look crossing his face.

"You know how our runes work," he said. It wasn't a question but rather a statement of fact.

"Linking runes," Alex said with a grin. "You didn't think you were the only bright boy in class, did you? Each time someone uses one of your runes, it activates an invisible suggestion rune. That rune was linked to Carlton Maple but not just to him. It was also linked to you and, I suspect, to William Ashford."

"Very good, Alex," Jones said. "What an ally you could have made."

Alex chuckled at that.

"What? No offer to let me join you?"

Jones shook his head.

"No," he said as he stepped forward and turned the key in the vault lock. "You're too smart and too moral for our purposes."

He took hold of the vault handle and pulled, forcing Alex to roll painfully away from the door.

"Now I suspect Sorsha is very cross with you," he went on. "And she has a job to do, don't you my dear?"

He stepped back and Sorsha stalked out into the storeroom. She turned to look down at him and her eyes were glowing with pale blue light. Before he could react, however, she smiled and turned back to Jones. Waving her hand at him, the gun in his hand froze solid. With a cry of alarm and pain, he dropped the weapon and started to turn before he simply stopped, held in place by Sorsha's magic.

"He can still breathe, right?" Alex asked, pushing himself to his feet.

"Of course," Sorsha said, her voice full of barely controlled fury.

"How?" Jones gasped as he tried to fight against Sorsha's invisible hold.

"Linking runes," Alex said, standing up. He walked around to stand where Jones could see him. "Every time someone uses one of your runes, it creates a link between them and you," he reiterated, largely for Sorsha's benefit. "That works great unless that link is forcibly broken, like if someone under your control was to be locked away in another dimension, say inside a runewright's vault."

Jones muttered a curse word, then seemed to regain his composure.

"Good luck getting anyone to believe you," he said. "You try to tell people that William Ashford, son of a beloved senator, is using an unknown magic to win the mayoral race and they'll have you locked up."

"I don't have to convince anyone," Sorsha growled, her hand flexing. Every time she squeezed, Jones let out a painful groan. "The FBI listens to me."

"You might convince them eventually, but by that time Ashford will already be mayor."

"You mean because during his speech tonight he'll tell everyone listening that he has a job for them and that's to vote for him?" Alex asked.

"Check the time," Jones growled. "He's already given his speech."

Sorsha shot Alex a worried look.

"Is he right?"

"Yes," Alex admitted, opening his watch. "It's ten-oh-five."

"So enjoy your victory while it lasts," Jones said.

"You're assuming the linking runes that connect Ashford to all those good people who used your books are still intact," Alex said.

Jones chuckled.

"You didn't have time to put Ashford into your vault, Lockerby. The die is cast and we won."

"Unless someone with an active nullification rune stood behind Ashford while he was on the radio," Alex said. "That would disrupt any runic links during the speech, and now that Ashford is off the radio, I'm sure I can arrange for someone to give him a tour of my vault."

"You're bluffing," Jones said, though his voice held a note of worry.

"I was in the kitchen when Ashford was practicing his speech," Alex said. "I heard him mutter that I have a job for you line half a dozen times. After that, I just called my mentor and had him get a very special cigarette lighter to my friend Detective Pak. He went to Radio City, posing as extra security, and stood behind Ashford the whole time."

"There's no such rune," Jones said, but he was grasping now.

"I guess you're really not the smartest boy in class after all," Alex said, enjoying rubbing Malcom Jones' smug superiority back in his face.

Alex looked at Sorsha, and she struggled to meet his gaze.

"I'm sorry," she mouthed at him.

He just shrugged, wincing at the pain in his back where Jones had shot him.

"Good thing you got your trench coat out of the vault," she said. "Did you know he was going to shoot you?"

"No," Alex admitted. "But it pays to be prepared. How do you know he shot me?"

"I can smell the gunpowder, and that's the coat you loaned Agent Redhorn last year, the one with shield runes on it."

Alex grinned. Every once in a while he forgot just how sharp the sorceress really was.

"Let's get Mr. Jones down to the Central Office and have him arrested," Sorsha continued. "You can tell me what happened after I blacked out on the way."

She started to turn, lifting Malcom Jones up into the air with a flick of her wrist, but Alex put a restraining hand on her shoulder. Holding someone like Sorsha was doing took a tremendous amount of effort and she was running on anger to fuel it.

"I think we should handcuff him to a chair in my vault," he said, looking meaningfully at the heavy door. "His connection to you might be broken, but who knows who else he's got access to?"

Sorsha looked slightly affronted by Alex's intervention, but angry as she was, she wasn't a woman to allow anger to cloud her judgement. She nodded and turned Jones back toward the vault.

"Wipe that insufferable grin off your face," she said to Alex, as she passed him.

Alex put his hand to his chest in a gesture of wounded ego.

"I'm sure I don't know what you mean," he said. "All I did was save the city and its most prominent sorceress from a nefarious plot to control them."

"I'm the city's only sorceress."

"Which makes you the most prominent by default."

She glared at him out of the side of her eye, but couldn't hold it, breaking out into a smile.

"Jones was right," she said. "You really are too smart for your own good."

32

POISON

I t was after midnight by the time Alex finally limped up to his room on the third floor of the brownstone. He'd gone with Sorsha to the Central Office to drop off Malcom Jones and get Iggy's lighter from Danny. After that, Sorsha's driver had taken him home.

He'd spent the next hour letting Iggy put a noxious salve on his leg to heal the case of frostbite Sorsha's freezing mist had given him. His shoulder turned out to be only a torn ligament, so a mending rune and a few days' rest would take care of that.

As he reached his room, he was tired, but it was a good kind of tired, the kind that came after a job well done. First thing Monday, he'd call Paul Masterson and tell him what really happened to his wife. She wasn't an adulteress or a murderer — she was just as much a victim as Hugo Ayers had been.

Alex hung his tux in the wardrobe in the corner, then flopped down on the bed. He tried to sleep, but he still had so many questions running around his mind. Clearly Maple and Jones had been working together, but were there more out there? Did anyone else have access to the linking runes besides William Ashford? If Jones really was a member of the Whalers, was he looking for the Monograph, or was he just plying his trade getting unworthy politicians elected?

Alex had no answers to these questions, and they kept him tossing and turning well into the wee hours. Finally he got up, opened his vault, and went to his reading chair. He opened the insulated box where he kept the boiler stone that heated his hearth and used a pair of tongs to set the stone in the steel grate. By the time he'd pulled a thin volume off his bookshelf, the hearth was beginning to warm up his vault.

Limping over to his reading chair, Alex switched on the lamp on the side table and settled down to read. The book was one of Iggy's, a small but very comprehensive monograph on poisons. When he was at the Central Office earlier, Danny told him that the police lab determined that the Westlakes' wine bottle had been tainted with arsenic. Alex hadn't dealt much with poisons in the past, so he decided to pass the time reading up on the subject until he got tired enough to sleep.

After fifteen minutes of reading, Alex knew he needed to go straight to bed. Tomorrow was shaping up to be a long day.

Despite getting to bed late, Alex was up early again, even before his alarm. Being Sunday, there wasn't much he could do until noon at the earliest, so he dressed and went to early Mass. After that he stopped by Bishop Cosgrove's office and filled him in on the missing Forgotten.

"That's horrible," the old man said when Alex finished. "I often see the dark nature of man, but this is the most insidious story I think I've ever been told."

Alex didn't blame him for not believing it. He'd been an

eyewitness to what happened at the Happy Jack factory and even he found it hard to believe.

"You're sure the people responsible will be punished?" Cosgrove went on.

"Yes," Alex said. "One is dead and the other is in police custody."

"Will the police believe your story?"

"Probably not," Alex admitted. "But the FBI is involved and one of their consultants was with me when we apprehended the second man. She'll convince them."

"Are you all right, Alex?"

The question caught him by surprise, and he looked up to find the old churchman leaning forward in his chair with a concerned look.

"I guess I am," he said after a moment to think about it.

"Well, if you ever need to talk about what happened in that factory, I'd be happy to listen."

Alex thanked him, then put on his hat and headed home.

By the time Alex got back to the brownstone it was only eleven, but he just couldn't wait any longer to call Danny.

"Can you arrange to have George Sheridan released into your custody?"

"Alex?" Danny said in a groggy voice after a long minute. "What time is it?"

"You still asleep? It's almost noon."

"I had a late night," Danny protested. "Your sorceress girlfriend kept me at the Central Office until I wrote out everything that happened at Radio City. She didn't believe that all I did was stand behind Ashford while holding Dr. Bell's lighter."

"She'll get over it," Alex said. "Now, can you get George Sheridan out of jail for a couple of hours?"

"What?" Danny replied, confusion thick in his voice. "Why?"

"I know who poisoned the Westlake family's wine."

Danny sighed so hard Alex could almost see him rubbing his eyes.

"Can't you just tell me, and we'll go arrest them at a decent hour?" he asked.

"That's the problem," Alex said. "I know who did it, but I can't prove it. That's why I need Sheridan."

Danny sighed again, this time in a head-shaking sounding way.

"But you know who did it?"

"I know," Alex said. "All I need is for you to have a couple of your boys get Sheridan over to the Westlake house by three o'clock."

"That's it?"

"Well," Alex hedged. "You'll also have to run down a drug store clerk."

"It's Sunday, Alex," Danny pointed out. "Stores are closed."

"You'll manage," Alex said. Since many store owners lived over their businesses, Danny could still find someone to talk to and there were only three or four stores he'd have to try.

"Fine," Danny said in a voice that communicated that he'd rather have dental work done. "What are you going to be doing while I'm running all over town?"

"I've got to call Sheridan's lawyer, then the Westlakes' butler, and finally I have to track down a wine steward," he said. "Now, do you have a pencil? Here's what I need you to do."

Alex arrived at the inner-ring home of the Westlakes just before three o'clock with Iggy in tow.

"You sure about this?" Iggy asked as they approached the bored-looking policeman standing outside the front door.

"No," Alex admitted. "But I think it's Sheridan's best chance to avoid a long, public trial."

"What about the wine steward?"

"He'll be here," Alex assured his mentor. "I just need to stall a bit."

The large foyer of the Westlake house looked just as it had when Alex and Danny had gone over the place yesterday with one notable exception. Arthur Hardwick sat in the far corner on the uncomfortable couch, dressed in a dark suit, with George Sheridan beside him looking irritated. A tall, broad-shouldered policeman stood beside George with his hands clasped behind his back.

"Well it's about time," Sheridan said, standing up. "You're supposed to be finding proof I didn't kill anyone, Lockerby, not dragging me all over town so you can put on a show."

Alex stifled a grin. He was pretty sure Hardwick hadn't filled George in on the proceedings, so he was just guessing, but it was a pretty accurate guess.

"Don't worry, George," Alex said. "I can prove you didn't do this." He turned to look at Hardwick. "Assuming you have my money."

Hardwick produced a check from his pocket and handed it over. Alex made a show of examining it, but he'd worked out the deal earlier by telephone. Hardwick had gone by the *Northern Lights* and gotten a check for Alex's fee from Sheridan's bookkeeper. With a smile of satisfaction, Alex tucked the check into the pocket of his coat while Sheridan made a sour face.

The door to the dining room opened and Danny emerged. He looked tired but had a smile on his face.

"Everything's ready," he said, walking over to the group.

Alex nodded, then conducted everyone into the dining room. Sheridan had a sneer on his face until he walked through the door. At the far end of the table sat Vivian West-lake, looking pale but as beautiful as ever. George's face grew red.

"What the hell is she doing here?" he demanded.

Before Alex could answer, Danny pushed Sheridan into a chair.

"Shut up," he growled.

George looked like he wanted to say something, but managed to control his tongue. Hardwick took a seat next to George at the far end of the table.

"Miss Westlake," Alex said, nodding at Vivian. "Thank you for joining us."

"It's not like you gave me much choice," she said, giving Danny a dirty look.

Ignoring her tone, Alex pointed to Iggy.

"This is Doctor Bell," he said. "He's here to make sure you're well enough to answer some questions."

Iggy looked Vivian over and asked her a few questions about her time in the hospital, then he turned to Alex.

"Arsenic goes through the body fairly quickly," he said. "Miss Westlake should drink lots of water to make sure the toxin is fully flushed from her system, but otherwise she should be fine."

Alex thanked Iggy, who then sat down next to Hardwick.

"Detective Pak," Alex said to Danny. "Would you ask the butler to bring some water for Miss Westlake?"

Danny nodded and moved around Alex, disappearing through the kitchen door.

"Just for the sake of transparency," Alex said, walking over to stand beside Vivian, "I'm here representing Mr. Sheridan. He asked me to look into this case."

"I thought you had better taste," Vivian said, anger in her voice. "He killed my family and he tried to kill me."

"No," Alex said as the butler appeared with a pitcher of water on a silver tray.

Alex took the tray and set it down in front of Vivian, then poured her a glass of water.

"In fact," he went on, handing Vivian the glass, "George didn't have a motive to kill anyone."

"My lawyer served him with divorce papers," Vivian said. "If I died before they went through, he would inherit my parent's wealth."

"The problem with that is that George," Alex pointed at Sheridan, who sneered, "signed those papers as soon as he got them, and then he sent them to his attorney." Alex pointed at Hardwick.

"That's true," Hardwick acknowledged.

"So?" Vivian said. "It can take weeks, even months for the courts to act. George knew that; he's been involved in lawsuits before."

"That's also true," Hardwick confirmed. "But the exis·tence of signed divorce papers would establish your wishes as well as his. It would give any other relation grounds to contest Mr. Sheridan being included as a relative in your parents' will."

Vivian rolled her eyes and looked back at Alex.

"If you think George didn't do this, then who did?"

"That's a very good question," Alex said. "Let's examine the facts that we know."

He turned to Danny, who produced a wine bottle from a leather bag he'd set on the floor.

"This," Alex said, taking the bottle from Danny, "is the bottle that contained the poison wine." He set the bottle in the middle of the table where everyone could see it. "At first I thought it must have come from Fredrick Westlake's wine cellar. He was a part owner of the Mist Valley Winery, after all." He turned to Danny. "When you examined this bottle, how many sets of fingerprints did you find on it?"

Danny pulled a notebook from his shirt pocket and flipped it open.

"There were only two sets of prints on the bottle," he said. "Mr. Westlake's, and Mr. Sheridan's."

"But didn't the butler give testimony that he poured the wine?" Alex asked, somewhat theatrically. "Why weren't his fingerprints on the bottle?"

"He wore gloves, of course," Vivian said before Danny could answer.

"Of course," Alex said. "He wouldn't want to get fingerprints on the glasses when he poured."

Vivian nodded and took a drink from her water glass. For a moment she made a face, but then finished the water.

"And the butler would have presented the bottle to your father to open, correct?" Alex went on.

Again Vivian nodded.

"Well, that explains how Mr. Westlake's fingerprints got on the bottle," Alex said. He picked up the water pitcher and poured another glass for Vivian. "So we're just left with how George's fingerprints got on the bottle."

"Simple," Vivian said. "He brought it here."

"No," Alex said, picking up the empty bottle. "I don't think so." He walked over to George and held the bottle so that the nightclub owner could see the label. "Mr. Sheridan, can you tell me what that number on the label is?"

George peered at the label then shrugged.

"It's a serial number," he said. "Rare wines usually have them to track the provenance of the individual bottles."

"And is this a rare wine?" Alex asked.

"It's a Mist Valley Cabernet from 1919," he said as if that

370

were obvious. "It was bottled just days before prohibition. There's only a handful of these that survived."

Alex looked up at Danny and nodded. Danny opened the door that led to the foyer and a policeman ushered a thin, brown-skinned man inside.

"Do you know this man, Mr. Sheridan?" Alex asked.

George looked at the newcomer, then got a sour look on his face.

"Yes," he said. "That's Marty Fairherst. He was my sommelier until I fired him."

Alex turned to Arthur Hardwick.

"Did you bring the book?" he asked.

Hardwick withdrew a large, leather-bound account book from his briefcase and handed it to Alex. A piece of paper stuck out of the book, marking a page, and Alex turned to it.

"Sit here, Mr. Fairherst," Alex said, setting the book down in front of the empty chair next to Iggy. "Would you be so kind as to tell us why Mr. Sheridan fired you?"

Fairherst looked nervous and shot a glance at Sheridan before focusing on Alex.

"He had a fancy dinner with his lawyer and some business-men," Fairherst said. "I was supposed to pick out the wine and make sure everything went smoothly."

"Is this the wine you picked?" Alex said, indicating a line in the ledger.

Fairherst squinted at the entry, then nodded.

"This is the log book for the *Northern Lights* wine cellar," Alex said, looking around at the table. "Every bottle is logged when it comes in and then again when it is sold, correct?" This last was addressed to Fairherst.

"Yes," he said. "It was my job to keep track of the wine."

Alex picked up the book and made a show of reading the entry.

"According to this, the wine you picked was a 1919 Mist

Valley Cabernet. That's quite the coincidence. Why did you choose this particular wine?"

"I didn't," Fairherst said. "I got a note saying that Mr. Sheridan wanted that wine at the dinner. I knew it was a special occasion, so it didn't seem out of place."

"What happened then?"

Fairherst looked nervously at George, then shrugged.

"Mr. Sheridan got angry when I handed it to him to inspect," he said. "Told me to put it back and bring something more appropriate."

"I keep those wines for my top customers," George interjected.

"So you took it back to the cellar?" Alex asked.

"No," Fairherst replied. "I set it aside and got one of the wines I had ready for another table to serve to Mr. Sheridan's party. By the time I got back, the 1919 Cab was gone, but I figured one of the staff had put it back in the cellar. I didn't find out it was missing until Mr. Sheridan called me into his office and fired me."

Alex pointed to the wine bottle in front of George.

"Would you read the number on that bottle, Mr. Sheridan?"

"Three hundred fifty-two."

Alex put the book down in front of Fairherst, pointing to the line where the missing wine was documented.

"Is that your missing bottle, Mr. Fairherst?"

The wine steward read the entry, then nodded.

"One more question, Mr. Fairherst," Alex said, shutting the book. "Do you wear gloves when you serve wine?"

"Of course," he said as if that were self-evident.

Alex thanked him, then turned to George and Hardwick.

"Now we know how Mr. Sheridan's fingerprints got on the bottle," he said. "When Mr. Fairherst got it from the wine cellar at the Northern Lights, he would have wiped the dust off the bottle, which would have removed any residual finger-prints. After that, the only person to handle the bottle without gloves on was George Sheridan."

"Or," Vivian said, as she sipped her water, "the finger-prints got there when George brought the bottle here."

"But George didn't bring the bottle here, Miss Westlake," he said. "If we're to believe that, then George would have had to steal his own bottle on the day you were married so he could kill your parents later."

"Not necessarily," she countered. "The bottle could have simply been misplaced. Then, when George found it some-time later, he decided to put it to good use."

"He could have," Alex admitted. "But he didn't."

"Then who did?" George demanded.

"She did," Alex said, pointing at Vivian. "She sent the message to Fairherst knowing that George wouldn't waste one of his most expensive wines on a business dinner. Then she waited for the bottle to be unattended, stuck it in her oversized handbag, and brought it back with her when Danny came to the club, presumably to rescue her."

Vivian scoffed as all eyes turned to her.

"Are you saying I put poison in wine that I was going to drink?" she asked. "That would be very stupid."

"You could have only pretended to drink it," George said.

"No," Danny interjected, consulting his notebook again. "The butler saw all three of the Westlakes drink the wine."

"There's no way she could have known how much to drink to just be a little poisoned," Iggy said. "It would be too easy for her to die as well."

Alex smiled and nodded as they spoke, waiting for all eyes to turn back to him.

"I wondered about that too," he said, "but then I remem-bered seeing this."

He knocked on the kitchen door and the butler came in carrying a framed picture which he handed to Alex.

"This was over the mantel in the drawing room," he said, holding the picture out so that everyone could see it. It was the photograph of Vivian as a teenager with her frizzy hair and bad skin. When he turned it so Vivian could see, she made a disgusted face and turned away.

"This picture is only five years old," Alex announced. "That's quite a transformation, wouldn't you say?"

When no one answered, Alex went on.

"I wondered how such an unfortunate girl could go from this," he held up the picture again, "to the vision we see before us."

Vivian rolled her eyes and shook her head.

"I grew up," she said, as if that were the most natural thing in the world.

"Most assuredly," Alex said. "But with regards to your skin and your hair, I think you had some help."

"If there was something girls could do to look like Viv," George said, "everyone would be doing it."

"That's just it," Alex said. "There is something, it's just very risky. You see, back in the late eighteen-hundreds, a beauty regimen came out of Austria. It became quite the fad in Europe and even found its way here to America. Women everywhere were taking small doses of arsenic."

"That's ridiculous," Vivian said.

"Not really," Iggy spoke up. "A side effect of taking arsenic is clear skin and a glossy texture to the hair."

All eyes turned to Vivian with her perfect face and lustrous hair.

"They were called arsenic eaters," Alex finished. "I'm guessing someone told you about it and you were desperate enough to escape from this," he held up the picture again, "that you were willing to try anything, even taking small doses of poison."

"That would explain how she had access to arsenic in the first place," Hardwick said. "But if she took too much, wouldn't she die?"

Alex nodded sagely.

"One of the other benefits of long-term exposure to arsenic, however, is that you build up an immunity to it. A dose large enough to kill an adult might just make you sick."

"That...that's an interesting theory," Vivian said, looking paler than before. "But I'd like to see you prove it."

Alex nodded to Danny and he opened the outer door again, ushering in an older gentleman with salt and pepper hair and a short, neatly trimmed beard.

"This is Dennis Brown," Alex said. "But I'm sure you know him, Miss Westlake. He's prepared to testify that you've been buying medicinal arsenic from his drug store for years."

"You still...still won't be able to...to," Vivian said, struggling to get the words out. She suddenly doubled over in pain. "You put arsenic in my water," she groaned, looking at Alex, then she slumped to the floor.

Iggy rushed to her side as the room erupted into chaos.

"What did you do?" Hardwick demanded while his client just laughed.

"Alex, did you poison her water?" Danny demanded. "To prove that she was immune?"

For his part, Alex watched the scene unfold calmly. It wasn't until Danny ordered the big policeman to arrest him that he held up his hands for quiet.

"I admit, I did put something in Miss Westlake's water," he said, picking up the pitcher and refilling Vivian's glass. "You see, arsenic has a metallic aftertaste." He picked up the cup and drank it down in one motion. "So I made sure to dump a small amount of powdered zinc into the pitcher before I poured the water. I tried to be obvious about it, but I wasn't sure if Vivian saw me. She obviously tasted the zinc, though, and knowing what arsenic tasted like, she assumed I had put some in her water."

"And since there's no poison in the water," Danny said, "there's no reason for Miss Westlake to be on the floor."

"At least not if she's innocent," Alex finished. "I mean if she'd never taken arsenic, she wouldn't know about the after-taste, now would she?"

Danny nodded to the policemen, and they marched around the table and hauled Vivian to her feet. She didn't resist, just glared at George and then Alex in turn until the policemen took her out.

"I don't get it," George said after she'd gone. "Why do all this? I mean if she stayed with me, she'd have been out of this house and she'd have gotten the money eventually."

"True," Alex said. "But this way she gets the money, you go to jail, and, since you're still married, she gets the *Northern Lights* as well."

George's mouth fell open as the full weight of Vivian's plan washed over him.

"That bitch," he said.

Alex nodded. He hated to agree with Sheridan, but in this case, the man was right.

33

THE INTERROGATION

Sorsha Kincaid looked through the one-way glass mounted in the wall of the FBI's interrogation room. Beyond the glass sat Malcom Jones, the so-called election consultant, looking more bored than afraid. That bothered Sorsha.

Jones had spent the previous night in the police lockup, then he'd been transferred to the New York Field Office of the FBI.

He should at least be a little worried.

Sorsha chewed her lip as she watched him. He had the air of a man with a contingency plan, one strong enough to get him out of FBI custody. Or so he believed.

As disturbing a thought as that was, she was more worried about where Jones had learned his rune lore. No runewright she'd ever met was more talented than Alex Lockerby, and he'd barely managed to unravel Jones' plot in time. To make matters worse, Jones had ensnared her in his plans, a fact that burned inside her in a cold little ball of fury.

She would make him suffer for that if the occasion arose.

The door to the observation room opened and Agent

Mendes came in. The doctors at the hospital had given her an alchemical ointment to speed up the regrowth of her hair, but it hadn't had enough time to work. Her usually thick, kinky locks were short, and it made her look like a tan Shirley Temple.

"You ready, boss?" she asked.

Sorsha nodded at her and moved to the door.

"You sure you don't want backup in there?" Mendes asked.

"No," Sorsha said with a half-smile. "Mr. Jones will be more talkative if it's just me."

Sorsha had found that people, especially men, tended to speak loosely to a lone woman. It was a fact she used to the utmost. She was wearing slacks with a white shirt and a set of suspenders. A dress might have suited her needs better, but there was no time to change so pants would have to do.

Taking a deep breath, she pushed the door open. Jones looked up at her and his bored expression brightened.

"Hello, my dear," he said in his cultured British accent. "I knew they'd send in someone to interrogate me, but I never expected you."

"Save it," Sorsha said, sitting down across the table from him. "You're in a lot of trouble, Mr. Jones."

"Oh, I rather doubt that," he said. "I doubt very much that there are any laws against using magic to persuade people to vote."

Sorsha gave him a tolerant smile.

"Election fraud will do just fine," she said.

Rather than looking chagrined, Jones leaned back in his chair and put his hands behind his head.

"That sounds great," he said with genuine enthusiasm. "When does my trial start? I can't wait for the press to hear the details." He leaned forward again, cradling his chin in his hand with his elbow on the table. "I expect they'll be particularly interested in your testimony."

Sorsha felt her cheeks turn pink at that and she bit her lip to stop it. Jones was right. No one was going to put him on public trial where people could learn that rune magic could manipulate people into voting, or worse, killing. It would cause a panic. Runewrights who couldn't use that kind of magic on their best day would be run out of town, maybe even killed. The city would descend into chaos.

Of course a public trial wasn't Sorsha's only option. She did work for the government, after all.

"You aren't a United States citizen," she said, leaning toward him with her arms on the table. "And you tried to interfere in an election. I'm pretty sure my government will consider you an agent of a foreign power. Which makes you a spy," she continued. "And, as a spy, I can have you locked up in the deepest, darkest hole I can find and throw away the key without the necessity of a trial," she paused for effect. "If you annoy me, I can even have you shot."

Sorsha wasn't bluffing, and she could see that Malcom Jones didn't think she was, but he showed no sign of concern.

"Well that sounds very serious," he said in a voice that conveyed no sincerity. "What can I do so you'll go easy on me?"

"Who are you working with?" Sorsha asked. "Who are the Whalers?"

She expected him to deny Alex's allegations about a secret group seeking the Archimedean Monograph but instead, he laughed.

"The Whalers?" he scoffed. "That's my father's obsession."

"It didn't stop you from getting that coin tattoo," Sorsha said. "The one that put Alex on to your scheme."

That hit a nerve, and Jones' face flashed into a scowl for a moment.

"Call it a misspent youth," he said. "I wanted to impress my father."

"Yet you don't share his cause?"

"There are bigger things in the world than a mouldering book of ancient rune magic," he said.

"Such as?"

Jones sat back and smiled at her, just staring for a long moment.

"I wouldn't want to spoil the surprise," he said.

Sorsha smiled right back at him. She'd been trying to get him talking and he'd finally given something away.

"So you are working with a group," she said. "Who might they be?"

If this hit a nerve, Jones gave no sign. He just kept his half-smile and relaxed posture.

"If you really want to know," he said, "you'll find that it's marked five, nine."

"What does that mean?" she asked, but he just shrugged and smiled. "You don't seem very concerned for someone in your position."

"I'm not," he said. "You see, I know something you don't, something you desperately want to know, and in five minutes you're going to let me walk out of here a free man."

Sorsha almost laughed at that, but Jones was deadly serious. He wasn't about to tell her who his friends were or what they wanted, so what could he possibly know that would induce her to let him go?

"Too many ears," he said when she asked him.

Sorsha looked back over her shoulder at the one-way glass. She knew Agent Mendes was back there, and perhaps other FBI agents as well.

"Fine," she said, turning back to Jones. Summoning a small amount of magic, she blew out a puff of air and the mirror behind her fogged up as the temperature dropped. Frost formed on the table, and Sorsha spoke ancient words of power. They weren't so much words, as sounds. Syllables of a long-forgotten language that turned her power, and her will, into magic. As the words echoed from her throat, she felt the air warm up while the frost on the table crystalized into a layer of ice. Similar crystals covered the walls, the ceiling, and the door.

"There," she said to Malcom, meeting his gaze. The magic was still resonating through her and her voice came out unnaturally low. "This room is sealed. No one outside can see or hear us. So what is it that you think you know that will buy your freedom?"

While she had worked her magic, Malcom Jones' smile had gotten wider and he looked around with a nod of approval.

"I have to admit," he said. "You sorcerers are an impressive lot."

"Enough games," Sorsha said, her voice returning to normal.

"All right, Sorceress," Jones said, leaning close and lowering his voice. "Here's what I have for you. I know where to find the thing that you want most in all the world."

Sorsha was not amused and she let her expression convey that emotion.

"I know who has the Archimedean Monograph."

Sorsha scoffed, but something in Malcom's face told her that he wasn't kidding. At least he believed he wasn't.

That makes no sense. If he knew where the Monograph was, he'd have gone after it himself.

Unless...

Unless he didn't know who had it until very recently.

Jones' voice flashed across Sorsha's memory.

There's no such rune, he'd said.

I guess you're really not the smartest boy in class after all, had come the reply.

381

"You think Mr. Lockerby has the Monograph?" she said with a chuckle. "Why?"

"That nullification rune he said he used against Ashford," Jones said, his voice sliding toward anger. "Nullification runes don't break links," he said. "They just stop nearby runes from activating. A construct strong enough to break existing runic links would be...I don't even know, some kind of blackout ward."

Sorsha favored him with a dry smile.

"So, because Mr. Lockerby knows something you don't, this blackout ward, you assume he is the one with the Monograph? That sounds like a bit of a reach."

Jones smiled back at her.

"Does it?" he asked. "Runewrights usually don't know very much about their craft," he said. "Each of us hoard our knowledge, keeping our secrets separate from our fellows. I don't have that particular handicap," he said. "I've seen hundreds of lore books, studied the brightest minds of our age, and I've never seen anything that even hints at the possibility of a blackout ward."

Sorsha felt something she was entirely unused to — a chill ran up her back. Her mind raced back to the city morgue, to a brightly colored rune that could temporarily turn back time. Sure it had a high cost, but that wasn't runewright power, that was sorcerer level magic, yet Alex had clearly used it before. He'd probably written the runes himself.

"See," Jones said, clearly reading Sorsha's face. "You know I'm right. How does it feel, knowing your little rune boy has been hiding the Monograph under your very nose all this time?"

Sorsha tried to ignore Jones' prodding, but her mind flashed even further back, to the moment she and Alex stood alone in the workshop of a dead runewright. She'd used a truth spell on him, asked him about the Monograph, and somehow he'd looked her right in the face — and lied to her.

White hot anger flowed through her, and she could feel magic being pulled into her body in response. Her fingers tingled with the energy and a white ring appeared around her vision. She knew from experience that her eyes were glowing, and she took a quick breath to quell the emotional response to her discovery.

"I see I'm not alone in finding Mr. Lockerby annoying," Jones said with a smirk.

"Alex is annoying, yes," Sorsha said, finally getting a handle on her emotions. "But if he had the Monograph, he wouldn't be eking out a living as a private detective, now would he?"

"It's the perfect cover, and you know it," Jones said.

"What I know, Mr. Jones, is that right now you should be worried about yourself. Whether I believe you or not, you've lost your bargaining chip."

"Have I?" Jones asked.

She looked up at him and found that cocky swagger back in his eyes.

"I guess I have at that," he said. "I guess you'll just have to put me in jail."

Sorsha raised an eyebrow. Jones didn't seem worried that he'd blown his advantage.

Unless he hasn't.

He'd offered to tell her that Alex had the Monograph but what if she hadn't guessed it? How would he leverage that information to get released? He must know that she would never let him go before he told her his suspicions. Once he told her, she could just as easily go back on her word and throw him in some military prison.

He never intended to escape, she realized. *But he wants me to know about the Monograph. Why?*

Sorsha sent her memory back, back to the times she'd been to Alex's home.

No. Dr. Bell's home. It was Bell who taught Alex everything he knows.

There were wards on the house, she knew that. She could feel them each time she approached the door, but they didn't seem overly powerful or dangerous.

You're thinking like a sorcerer, she chided herself. She had underestimated Alex in the past and he always managed to get the better of her on those occasions. The wards on Bell's brownstone might not feel powerful, but if he had the Monograph, and it would certainly be Bell, not Alex who possessed it, then the wards on that house would be formidable indeed.

So that's it. Jones is hoping that I'll get the Monograph out of Dr. Bell's house.

Whatever wards were on the house, she doubted they could withstand her power. Jones expected her to crack open that house and take the book.

But why?

If Sorsha found the Monograph, she'd be bound to turn it over to the government. She'd be a hero. Then the government would take the book to their rune research lab.

The answer struck Sorsha like a bolt of lightning. Jones wasn't bargaining for his release; he was caught and he knew it. He was trying to get the Monograph into the hands of the Government. Probably because his cohorts already had someone inside the rune research lab, ready to abscond with the Monograph the moment it arrived.

Sorsha's fear had always been that whoever found the Monograph would abuse the power inside it, but Alex and Dr. Bell had proven to be worthy stewards thus far. No matter how annoyed she was with Alex at the moment, she had to admit that the ancient rune book was safest right where it was.

"Yes," Sorsha said at last, answering the question of whether or not Jones had lost his leverage. "The fact that Alex is smart and annoying doesn't mean he has the Monograph. I can tell you with absolute certainty that he hadn't even heard of it until four years ago."

Jones' calm features shifted to anger and he didn't try to hide it.

"Oh come on," he said. "I know you're not just a pretty face. You're smart. You have to know I'm right."

Sorsha just looked back at him blankly.

Jones rolled his eyes and swore.

"I don't believe it," he said. "What is it? Did you fall for him? The legendary Ice Queen of Manhattan in love with a lowly scribbler? So, what are you going to do now? You think that if you turn me down the next government lackey to come through the door will too? What are they going to do to your boy when they find out? What will they do to you when they learn that you knew where the Monograph was, and you didn't tell them?"

"Don't you dare threaten me," she growled, standing up suddenly and leaning across the table to look him in the eye. Anger flowed through her again, but she was in control this time. For his part, Jones just leaned back in his chair, putting some distance between himself and the angry sorceress.

"I'm just pointing out the truth," Jones said with an easy, confident air.

Sorsha turned around so he wouldn't see her grinding her teeth. He didn't have a bargaining chip before, but if he outed Alex, the feds would raid his house. They might not find the Monograph, but if they did, he would be spirited away to a government facility, never to be heard from again.

That thought stung more than she thought it would. It wasn't the fact that it would be her fault that was bothering her, though, it was the idea of never seeing him again.

Get a hold of yourself.

"What's it going to be, Sorsha?" Jones said from behind her.

She sighed and rubbed her temple.

"You're betting that Alex has the Monograph," she said, talking to her own hazy reflection in the frosted mirror. "And that if he does, and if I take it from him, you or your friends will have a better chance of recovering it."

"It doesn't matter what my motives might be," Jones said, evading the question.

"I think you're wrong about Mr. Lockerby," Sorsha went on, "but you're right about one thing: it doesn't matter. If I don't do what you say, you'll spout your nonsense to anyone who will listen. The government will investigate. If they don't find what they're looking for, they'll ruin Alex's reputation and his business in order to force him to reveal whatever secrets they think he has. They might even come after me. It seems you have me neatly boxed in."

"Check and mate, Miss Kincaid," Jones said with a smirk. "I'll make you my final offer. Go get the Archimedean Monograph and bring it to me. You do that, and my people and I will have no reason to go after Lockerby or the good Doctor. Turn me down and my people will set your own government on Alex and all you'll be able to do is watch as they destroy him."

Sorsha took a deep breath, considering his words.

"There's only one flaw in your plan," she said at last. "You guessed that Alex had the Archimedean Monograph when he told you about the blackout ward. Which means that of all your friends, your confidants, and the people your friends control, you are the only one who knows about Alex. I'm sure you'll be able to pass that information along easily enough to some plant, possibly someone already here in the FBI. Right now, however, I think it's a significant liability. Don't you agree?"

She turned to find Jones slumped over the interview desk. His arms hung down over the edges of the table and his lifeless eyes stared off into space.

"That's what I thought," Sorsha said.

She walked to the door and touched the frost that sealed the room Instantly it vanished in a puff of fog that lingered a few seconds before it too evaporated. Taking hold of the handle, Sorsha composed herself, then she jerked it open.

"Mendes!" she yelled. "Anybody, I need a doctor in here! He's having some kind of fit."

34

LINKS

Alex arrived at his office early on Monday, having risen early for the third day in the row. He didn't know if Marnie had started working at Empire Station yet, but he found that the regular coffee Iggy made was fine. Having a huge chunk of his life energy back seemed to be paying dividends, and Alex felt sure he could get used to that.

Despite his early arrival, Leslie was there before him. When he pushed the door open, she was sitting at her desk writing. Alex checked his watch before closing the door.

"Do we have an early client I don't know about?" he asked.

Leslie looked up from her work and gave him a smile, but it wasn't her usual beauty-queen look. This time she seemed wistful and even sad.

"What's wrong?" he asked.

"Nothing," she said, picking up the notepad she'd been writing on and flipping back to the front page. She set it aside and stood. "I'm just making notes on...on how things run around here."

Alex understood. He and Leslie had been a team for almost a decade. Her leaving reminded Alex of how he felt when Babe Ruth left the Yankees. He went around the desk and hugged her. If he was honest with himself, Alex wasn't sure he could do this job without Leslie.

"All right," Leslie said, pushing him away. "Enough of that. I still think you're making a mistake with the palm reader."

Alex chuckled. He wasn't sure about Sherry either, but she had clearly gone out of her way to get the job as his secretary and he wanted to know why. It was a question she wasn't likely to answer directly, so he'd have to ferret it out of her little by little over time.

"Know your enemy as you know yourself," Alex said. "And you won't fear the battle."

Leslie cocked an eyebrow at that, and Alex laughed.

"It's something a famous Chinese general once said."

"Well I hope that general knew what he was talking about," Leslie said.

"Don't worry," Alex said as he hung up his hat. "I'll make sure to keep a close eye on Miss Knox."

"Is she pretty?"

"Not as pretty as you," Alex answered with a wink.

Leslie crossed her arms and gave him a hard look.

"I mean that maybe whoever sent her here wants you to find her pretty," Leslie said. "You know, so she can get to know you and they won't have to be afraid of fighting you."

It wasn't a bad idea. Sherry Knox was certainly attractive and young, but not really Alex's type. Still, if she had been sent here as part of some nefarious plan, whoever sent her wasn't likely to know what Alex looked for in a dame.

"I'll be on my guard," Alex assured her.

Leslie gave him another long, discontent look, then picked up her notepad.

"I've got a few potential clients on the list," she said. "How many do you want?"

"I'll take them all," he said.

"What about the Masterson case and George Sheridan?"

Alex sat down on the edge of Leslie's desk and offered her a cigarette. Once he had it lit, he recounted the weekend's festivities, and Leslie scribbled notes for the case file. When he finished, he put George Sheridan's check and the cash Hardwick had given him on the table.

"Call Paul Masterson and have him come in," he said as Leslie pulled out the cash box. "I want to speak to him in person."

Leslie nodded, but then gave him a shrewd look as she added the cash to the rubber-banded bundle in the box.

"Remind me," she said as she added up the new total. "What was it Miss Knox said in that card reading she did for you?"

Alex hadn't thought much about that, beyond Marnie's observation that the first bit might be her and Andrew Barton. It could just as easily have been anything else, of course, because that's how predicting the future for profit worked. He recounted the rest of Sherry's reading as Leslie finished with the cash box and returned it to her desk drawer.

"Let me see if I understand this," Leslie said, puffing on her cigarette. "Your coffee lady thinks that the Wizard King card—"

"The King of Pentacles," Alex corrected.

"That the King," Leslie went on after giving Alex a dirty look for interrupting, "was Andrew Barton, and the other card represented her."

"Right," Alex confirmed. "Facing the Tower card which was supposed to be some kind of disaster."

"Like her losing her job and being in danger of losing her apartment," Leslie said.

"Okay," Alex admitted. "It does seem to match pretty well."

"Oh, Kiddo," Leslie chuckled. "You really haven't thought this through, have you?"

"There's no such thing as precognition," he said. "What's to think about?"

"Well, maybe if you stopped for a moment and started thinking, you'd realize that if Barton is the King, then the Queen would be...?"

"Sorsha, I guess."

"And the Queen was facing an upside-down moon," Leslie recounted. "Which Sherry told you might represent an illusion."

The hair on the back of Alex's neck stood up a bit as he thought through that. Sorsha had been under an illusion of sorts when she was in Malcom Jones' control.

"And," Leslie went on, as Alex connected the dots, "the last bit was the Wheel of Fortune, some kind of momentous decision involving some lovers and a high priestess."

Alex saw where she was going with this.

"The Lovers are you and Randall," he guessed. "The decision is hiring a new secretary, and Sherry..."

"Sherry is your High Priestess," Leslie finished.

"That's where it falls apart," Alex said, feeling a bit relieved. "Everything else is so on the nose, but Sherry is a fortune teller at a side show museum. She's not a priestess of any kind. If everything else is specific, that would be too."

"Uh-huh," Leslie said, sounding thoroughly unconvinced.

"Falsification," Alex explained. "In science if any part of a theory is wrong, the whole thing is wrong. It's called falsification."

"I hope you're right," Leslie said, going back to her stack of pending phone calls. "Because if she really can see the future, she'll see you coming a mile away."

Alex just shook his head at that. He did have to admit, the idea that Sherry's reading had been accurate was unsettling. As far as he knew, there wasn't any magic that could do that, and he liked things that way.

He spent the next hour in his vault, putting new shield runes on his suit coat. He'd have to make a new flash ring as well, but that would require him to engrave the rune under a magnifying lens, so he'd do that in the evening when there was no chance of being interrupted.

When ten o'clock came around, Leslie buzzed him from the outer office, and he emerged to find Sherry Knox waiting. She wore a blue dress with a heavy jacket that didn't really match. Leslie wouldn't have been caught dead with such an oversight. Alex led Sherry into his office and asked her a few basic questions. Her answers were intelligent and correct, but he really didn't expect anything less. Whoever sent her would have prepared her for the role of an office secretary.

Once he was satisfied Sherry could do the job, he took her out to meet Leslie who walked Sherry through the day to day operation of the office.

"I'll have to teach you the ropes when it comes to doing research on clients," Leslie said at last. "But we'll have a few weeks for that."

"I'm sure I can have it down by Christmas Eve," Sherry said, an enormous smile on her face. She turned to Alex and shook his hand. "Thank you for giving me the job, Mr. Lockerby," she said. "You won't regret it."

"I don't doubt it," Alex said.

"Why don't you start by getting the mail from the lobby?" Leslie said. "Then I'll show you how to fill out a case report."

Sherry beamed and hurried out into the hall.

"Are you sure there's no such thing as precognition?" Leslie asked once Sherry headed down the stairs.

"Why do you ask?"

"Because Randall's oldest son couldn't make the twentieth, so we moved our wedding day to the 24th."

A wave of gooseflesh ran up Alex's arms and over his shoulders.

"Christmas Eve," he said. "She knew."

"I think maybe you'd better try to find out where she really came from," Leslie said. "I bet when you do, you'll discover that she's actually a High Priestess of something."

"Yeah," Alex agreed, somewhat absently. Now that he thought about it, he'd heard the term High Priestess somewhere before. Not recently, but he had heard it. He just couldn't remember where.

"What would your Chinese General say about this?" Leslie asked.

Alex looked at the door where Sherry had vanished.

"*All war is deception,*" he quoted. "I just need to figure out Sherry's."

"Is that you, lad?" Iggy asked when Alex came through the inner vestibule door that evening just after six. "How'd it go with the new secretary?"

Alex hung up his hat and entered the library. A small coal fire was burning in the grate and the room was snug with its warmth. Iggy sat in his usual chair by the window, puffing on a cigar. Normally he liked to be able to see out into the street, but the cold outside compelled him to draw the heavy drapes to keep in the heat.

Making his way to the liquor cabinet, Alex poured himself a scotch and grabbed a cigar from Iggy's humidor before sitting down.

"Sherry seems to be picking up the business in record time," Alex said, trimming the end of the cigar.

"That's hardly surprising," Iggy replied, sipping brandy from his glass. "She's been following you around, appearing at just the right moments to insert herself in your office. Whoever trained her and set up her false identity would have made sure she had the secretarial skills she'd need to do the job. Can't risk your firing her, after all."

"How did she know I'd need a secretary?" Alex wondered aloud. "Leslie hadn't told me she was leaving the first time I met Sherry. How did Sherry know?"

Iggy shrugged at that and puffed on his cigar.

"Doesn't matter," he said. "Maybe whoever's behind all this had someone keeping an eye on Leslie."

"I don't know," Alex said, dipping the end of his cigar in the scotch. "Seems like an awful lot of trouble."

"What's the alternative?" Iggy asked.

Alex looked at him for a long moment, then lit his cigar.

"Is it possible that she really can see the future?"

He expected Iggy to scoff or chide him, but the old man just sat there, sipping his brandy.

"Last week I would have said there was no such thing as a mind control rune," he said. "Two years ago I would have said that rune lore was only as old as the ancient Greeks." Iggy shrugged. "Now I'm not sure I know anything. Is it possible? Maybe, why?"

Alex told Iggy about Leslie's analysis of Sherry's card reading and about Sherry's knowing Leslie's wedding date.

"I think," Iggy said, then paused to refill his brandy. "I think you'd better find out what that High Priestess business is about."

Alex nodded in agreement.

"And," Iggy went on. "If Miss Knox tells you to avoid

certain streets at certain times of day..." His voice drifted off and Alex met his gaze. "Take her word for it."

Alex sat back in the chair and puffed his cigar while Iggy picked up one of his pulp novels and began reading. Closing his eyes, Alex let his mind drift back over the events of the past week. Between the life transference rune and the mind control rune it had been a week of firsts. Everything linked together.

Linked.

Alex's eyes snapped open and he sat up in his chair.

"Something bothering you, lad?" Iggy said, not looking up from his book.

"Linking runes," Alex said.

"What about them?"

"The life transference rune," Alex explained. "It's actually four runes, really four complete constructs."

Iggy put his book aside and made a non-committal noise.

"You use linking runes to tie them together; that's why you only have to light one of them, but they all burn. Then there's the mind rune. It uses linking runes to connect the victim to a specific person, or rather to a specific rune on that person's body."

"All very accurate," Iggy said. "What are you driving at?"

"Moriarty's vault," Alex said, turning to look at Iggy. He reached into his pocket and pulled out the ornate, old-fashioned key to his own vault. The back end of the key had a round, flat spot on it with a detailed engraving that matched the vault rune he used to summon the steel door.

"We like to think of the vault rune as the thing we burn," he explained. "But it's really just a fancy linking rune, isn't it? It connects the chalk door outline to the real rune, here." He held out his key so that Iggy could see the flat spot.

"Well, that's technically how it works, yes," Iggy said.

"The real vault rune is the one you make in the beginning. It imprints the magic on the key and enables it to summon the vault door."

"What if," Alex said, an excited grin spreading across his face, "when you created a vault, you didn't bind it to a key?"

"You can bind it to a block of wood if you want," Iggy said. "But once the magic takes hold, it will change into a key."

Alex thought back to when he created his own vault, remembering how the vault creation construct was put together.

"What if we separated out the vault creation from the key creation?" he said. "Right now they're all part of the same construct. But if we separated them, we should be able to put the vault rune on an object and then link as many keys as we want to it later."

"Multiple doors into the same vault," Iggy said, stroking his mustache. "I don't know, lad. The idea has merit, but—"

The doorbell sounded from the hall, interrupting him.

"You expecting anyone?" Alex asked, standing up.

Iggy shook his head and rose as well. Alex went through the vestibule to the front door. He could see his visitor as an indistinct shape through the stained-glass window in the door. Normally that wouldn't be enough for an identification, but this shape had platinum blonde hair.

"Sorceress," he said, pulling the door open. "What brings you here?"

Sorsha stood on the stoop and Alex could see her sleek, black floater parked by the curb below. She wore a pale blue dress that matched her eyes, and heels that brought her height up to Alex's chin.

"May I come in?" she asked in a strangely subdued voice.

Alex stepped back and allowed her to pass. She waited for him to close the outside door and open the vestibule before she went further. Alex wondered if she knew that she couldn't open the inner door, or if she was just allowing him to be a gentleman?

"Miss Kincaid," Iggy said as she stepped into the library. A smile of delight spread across his face and he moved to embrace her. "How are you these days? I heard you had quite the evening the other night."

He motioned for her to sit in Alex's chair while Alex went to the kitchen to retrieve one of the massive oak chairs from the kitchen table. When he returned, Iggy was pouring the sorceress a glass of his brandy.

"Thank you," she said when he handed it to her. She waited for Alex and Iggy to sit, then spoke. "I wanted to come by and thank you, Alex. I know you could have stopped me with those spell-breaker bullets of yours."

"I'm glad I didn't have to resort to anything that drastic," he said with a genuine smile. "What have you learned about Malcom's partners?"

She sighed and took a sip of the brandy.

"Nothing," she said. "He died in FBI custody."

"That doesn't sound good," Iggy said.

"Nothing like that," Sorsha said. "He had some kind of fit. The coroner is looking into the idea that he took poison to prevent being interrogated."

Alex ground his teeth. Malcom Jones was clearly part of some larger group and he desperately wanted to know who and what they were.

"Did he say anything about his partners?" Iggy asked, just as curious as Alex.

"Nothing that made any sense. All he would say was that his friends had been marked five and nine. Does that mean anything to you?"

"Marked fifty-nine?" Iggy said, stroking his mustache again.

Alex rose and went to the bookshelf, pulling down a large, leather-bound book. He sat back down and turned the pages until he located what he was looking for.

"Find something, lad?" Iggy asked.

"It's not something marked fifty-nine or anything else," he said. "It's a biblical reference. The Book of Mark, fifth chapter, ninth verse."

"Trust someone raised by a priest to know that," Sorsha said. "What does it say?"

Alex ran his finger down the page to the verse.

"And he asked him, What is thy name?" Alex read. *"And he answered, saying, My name is Legion: for we are many."*

THE END

A Quick Note

Thanks so much for reading my book, it really means a lot to me. This is the part where I ask you to please leave this book a review over on Amazon. It really helps me out since Amazon favors books with lots of reviews. That means I can share these books with more people, and that keeps me writing more books.

So leave a review on Amazon for me. It doesn't have to be anything fancy, just a quick note saying whether or not you liked the book.

. . .

Thanks so much. You Rock!

I love talking to my readers, so please drop me a line at
dan@danwillisauthor.com — I read every one. Or join the
discussion on the Arcane Casebook Facebook Group.

And Look for Limelight: Arcane Casebook #5. Coming Soon.

ALSO BY DAN WILLIS

Arcane Casebook Series:

Dead Letter - Prequel

Private Detective Alex Lockerby needs a break and it materializes in the form of an ambitious, up-and-coming beat cop, Danny Pack. Alex and Danny team up to unravel a tale murder, jealousy, and revenge stretching back over 30 years. It's a tale that powerful forces don't want to come to light. Now the cop and the private detective must work fast and watch each other's backs if they hope to catch a killer and live to tell about it.

Dead Letter is the prequel novella to the Arcane Casebook series.

Get Dead Letter at danwillisauthor.com

In Plain Sight - Book 1

In 1933, an unwitting thief steals a vial of deadly plague, accidentally releasing it in at a soup kitchen in Manhattan. The police, the FBI, and New York's 'council of Sorcerers' fear the incident is a trial run for something much deadlier. Detective Alex Lockerby, himself under suspicion because of ties to the priest who ran the kitchen, has a book of spells, a pack of matches, and four days to find out where the plague came from, or the authorities will hang the crime squarely on him.

Get In Plain Sight on Amazon

Ghost of a Chance - Book 2

When a bizarre string of locked-room murders terrorize New York, the police have no leads, no suspects, and only one place to turn. Now private detective Alex Lockerby will need every magical trick in his book to catch a killer who can walk through walls and leaves no trace. With the Ghost killer seemingly able to murder at will and the tabloids, the public, and Alex's clients demanding results, Alex will need a miracle to keep himself, his clients, and his reputation alive.

Get Ghost of a Chance on Amazon

The Long Chain - Book 3

In a city the size of New York, things go missing all the time. When New York is blanketed in an unnatural fog, Alex finds himself on the trail of a missing scientist, a stolen military secret, and a merciless killer leaving a trail of bodies in their wake. Now Alex must unravel a tangled web of science, murder, and missing memories before the clues vanish into the ever-present fog.

Get The Long Chain on Amazon

Dragons of the Confederacy Series:

A steampunk Civil War story with NYT Bestseller, Tracy Hickman

Lincoln's Wizard

Washington has fallen! Legions of 'grays' -- dead soldiers reanimated on the battlefield and pressed back into service of the Southern Cause -- have pushed the lines as far north as the Ohio River. Lincoln has moved the government of the United States to New York City. He needs to stop the juggernaut of the Southern undead 'abominations' or the North will ultimately fall. But Allan Pinkerton, his head of security, has a plan...

Get Lincoln's Wizard on Amazon

The Georgia Alchemist

With Air Marshall Sherman's fleet on the run and the Union lines failing, Pinkerton's agents, Hattie Lawton and Braxton Wright make their way into the heart of the south. Pursued by the Confederacy's best agents, time is running out for Hattie and Braxton to locate the man whose twisted genius brings dead soldiers back to fight and find a way to stop the inexorable tide that threatens to engulf the Union.

Forthcoming: 2020

Other books:

The Flux Engine

In a Steampunk Wild West, fifteen-year-old John Porter wants nothing more than to find his missing family. Unfortunately a legendary lawman, a talented thief, and a homicidal madman have other plans, and now John will need his wits, his pistol, and a lot of luck if he's going to survive.

Get The Flux Engine on Amazon

ABOUT THE AUTHOR

Dan Willis wrote for the long-running DragonLance series. He is the author of the Arcane Casebook series and the Dragons of the Confederacy series.

For more information:
www.danwillisauthor.com
dan@danwillisauthor.com

facebook.com/danwillisauthor
twitter.com/WDanWillis

Made in the USA
Middletown, DE
09 February 2020